Matthew Byrne

HEAVEN LOOKED UPWARDS

MACMILLAN

First published 1996 by Macmillan

an imprint of Macmillan Publishers Ltd
25 Eccleston Place, London SW1W 9NF
and Basingstoke

Associated companies throughout the world

ISBN 0 333 66118 4

Copyright © Matthew Byrne 1996

The right of Matthew Byrne to be identified as the
author of this work has been asserted by him in accordance
with the Copyright, Designs and Patents Act 1988.

1 3 5 7 9 8 6 4 2

A CIP catalogue record for this book is available from
the British Library

Typeset by CentraCet Limited, Cambridge
Printed by Mackays of Chatham plc, Chatham, Kent

For Weena
who's read it already
and whose love, support
and encouragement
made writing it
an even greater pleasure

'Earth and sky changed places for a space,
And Heaven looked upwards in a human face.'

– G. K. Chesterton

CHAPTER ONE

It was a sultry day in Nazareth. The white city on the hills struggled half-heartedly with its listlessness, wishing the weather would change.

Squat houses, built of limestone quarried from the surrounding hills, gleamed, dazzling, in the sun, and hemmed-in streets sloped up and down with the rise and fall of the hill.

Here and there, where the slope became too steep, were stairways of limestone steps, well worn and gouged by years of tramping people and animals and of trundling carts.

On the flat roofs of houses, children lolled against balustrade walls, no longer eager to play, or slept under lean-to awnings, oblivious of the noise that clamoured from the streets below. And sparrows swooped and pecked around them, searching for lost crumbs of bread.

By walls that offered shaded shelter from the heat of the sun, their mothers ground corn. There was a kind of rhythm in the work that kept the grinding-stone turning, turning. Mop the brow, dry the hands in the lap, pour in corn – grinding, grinding. And they wondered, every now and then, to passing neighbours, if the breeze whispering in the mulberry trees meant there was a storm brewing. Please God, it would come soon and clear the air a bit.

They'd have been glad of anything to clear the air in the merchants' street, where booths and animals, stalls, shops and people battled for space and room to move. And smells – good, bad and putrid – hung, stagnant, everywhere.

At the end of the street, the road forked. To the left, it turned quickly into the market square – as busy and noisy as the merchants' street, but brighter and a bit more airy. To the right, sets of steps descended the long slope down to the square where the synagogue stood. And the well.

It was a cool spot, by the well, with water from the spring gently washing out over the surrounding flagstones. The women there were glad of it, and lifted the hems of their long, blue dresses to paddle their feet while they filled the waterpots or doused the clothes. Meanwhile, they caught up with the scandals and worries and tittle-tattle of the day.

Out from the market square, out from the town, a road ran as if into broad daylight. The cramped, dark, narrow streets were gone, as were the squalor, the smell and noise, the houses and buildings that blocked out any view.

Now it was the cool, bright air of the mountain, with birds swooping and soaring, and silent-gliding butterflies.

Beyond rose more mountains, stretching away, away. And below extended the plains with cactus hedges dividing the fields daubed with great splodges of colour. Yellows and reds and whites, crimson, purple, gold – the hues of marigolds and cyclamen, tulips, geraniums, anemones.

Here and there, flowers grew by the road that ran, by twists and turns, along the hill to where Joachim had his house.

This was a busy day for Joachim. A great day for himself and his wife Anna. Their older daughter, Miriam, was getting betrothed to Yosef of Bethlehem.

Joachim tried his best not to fuss, and told himself often

that he was completely relaxed, and not the slightest bit worried. But just as often he checked to make sure that Miriam and Yosef were comfortable, sitting beneath their ceremonial canopy in the garden of his house. Or checking the dignity of the four young men holding the rods that bore the canopy aloft.

The garden was already filling with friends and neighbours, manoeuvring their way to vantage points around the canopy.

Rachel eased herself through the group and settled herself by one of the four young men holding the canopy aloft.

'It looks like a storm,' she said.

He tried to ignore her.

'You'll have a job holding that thing up.'

He said nothing. But his companions, supporting the other three corners, eyed him. He blushed, trying not to catch their gaze.

Rachel winked at them. She could see everything from here, and she'd miss nothing of the betrothal ceremony. She sensed the four young men at their posts staring at her, measuring her, willing her to look. But she deliberately avoided them. Instead, she looked over the small family group, tucked tidily at the far edge of the canopy, Joachim, his wife Anna, and their younger daughter Salome.

She liked Joachim. He was a gentleman, she reckoned. He wore his richness quietly. And he certainly was rich. He made his money from his huge stock of cattle, sheep and goats pastured in the plains. But he was a generous man, by all accounts. They said he divided his income into three parts, giving one part to the Temple, one part to the poor, and living on the rest himself. If the rumour were only half true, Rachel decided, then all she could say was that he was very rich indeed. He lived well, his family lived well, and they were short of nothing.

But they'd had their own troubles, God help them, Anna

and Joachim. Childless for years, and ostracized because of it. A punishment from God, the pious said, for some hidden sin they had committed. Till they'd had Miriam. And then, as though God were making it up to them, they'd had Salome.

But Rachel's eyes kept coming back to Miriam, seated beside Yosef, cool and shaded from the sun, waiting for the Rabbi, and the Seven Good Men of the Town, to begin the ceremony.

How beautiful Miriam looked, Rachel thought. The dark hair framing the almond-shaped face, the sharp-cut features, the clear, soft, lovely skin. And lucky, Rachel decided. But was she wise in becoming betrothed to a southerner? There was no love lost between north and south. And down there they took a poor view of Nazarenes especially. She only hoped it would work out for the couple.

'Yosef is some man,' a female voice said behind her.

She recognized that voice and, without looking round, knew it was Deborah. She stood her ground as Deborah's generously bosomed body tried to oust her from her vantage point.

Yosef was some man, Rachel agreed, taking in the sturdy figure sitting beside Miriam. Springy, red-brown hair round a weather-worn face, and the eyes dark, deep set. Compassionate eyes that said the man could feel the pain of hurt.

He was quite a man. But she wasn't going to say that to Deborah. Not gossipy Deborah. She'd be back to Isaac with her own interpretation. By tomorrow, everyone who bought bread in their bakery would hear the well-embroidered tale of how Rachel was trying to seduce Yosef even at his betrothal ceremony.

Rachel smiled to herself as she relished what she was going to say to Deborah. *Did Isaac know his wife was out eyeing other men?* That would shut her up. She turned her head to look full into Deborah's fat face.

'Does Isaac know—?'

But the rest was lost in the hubbub as Joachim stepped out to meet the new arrivals, the Rabbi, Ezekiel and the Good Men of the Town. They walked solemnly, like the corporation they were, aware of the weight of their responsibility for the welfare and good order of Nazareth.

They stopped as Joachim came up to them.

'Rabbi, shalom,' he said, 'and welcome. And may God bless you in your presiding at my daughter's betrothal.'

They kissed in greeting, almost in passing, as Joachim moved to greet the Seven Good Men, standing formally, waiting.

He greeted Ezekiel first, the eldest and the leader of the group. 'Ezekiel, you are welcome, as ever, old friend, to my home. And today especially, to the betrothal of my daughter Miriam. And I greet you and your colleagues whose care is the welfare of our town.'

They kissed. The other six bowed back, acknowledging Joachim's greeting, as he gestured to them to take their places around the canopy.

Ezekiel led the way, walking with Joachim and the Rabbi.

'I think there's a storm brewing,' he said. 'It'd be no harm to get things started.'

'You're right,' agreed Joachim. 'Yosef's go-betweens are already here.' He pointed through a gap between the guests towards the two men standing not far from Yosef.

'I recognize Barzillai,' the Rabbi said, 'but who's the slight man with him?'

'Shebna,' advised Joachim. 'A southerner, from Jerusalem, like myself.'

'Yosef might have chosen somebody different as a go-between,' Ezekiel offered. 'He looks a hard man to me.'

The Rabbi nodded agreement. 'Let's hope the pair behave themselves. Shebna won't show much sympathy.'

'You need have no fears, Rabbi,' Joachim assured him.

And they guffawed as Ezekiel muttered, 'The ways of a man with a maid.' They settled themselves behind the family, making a semicircle round Miriam and Yosef.

Ezekiel saw the wind ruffle the canopy. He fidgeted, uneasy, for a moment, and tugged nervously at his beard. But as quickly he regained his composure and gave Anna a secret smile of reassurance.

Anna smiled back. She had guessed his meaning. And she hoped he was right. The last thing she wanted was a storm in the middle of everything. She cast a glance at Joachim, but he was not looking her way. His attention was riveted by Miriam, her hands playing nervously in her lap, her head inclined to hear some word of encouragement from Yosef.

Joachim decided it was time to begin, and beckoned to the Rabbi and his entourage, who nodded their approval.

Joachim raised his hand, and even the chattering women were silent, for all that some of them had lost their places when making way for the Rabbi and the Seven Good Men.

He bade them all welcome, and began a speech that would tell them he was delighted that, a year from now, Yosef of Bethlehem would be his son-in-law. But Joachim was too overcome. Yesterday, in his mind, it had been a grand speech, and he'd made it umpteen times. He had been word perfect. But today it was different. In the emotion of the moment, he could remember nothing.

He talked, stumbling through it, hoping it all made sense. Then he threw up his hands. The murmur of sympathy told him they understood.

He sat down, motioning to Yosef that it was his turn to speak. But the gesture indicated that he would understand if Yosef, like himself, couldn't manage to remember.

Yosef stood up. He was stocky, well built.

Rachel was definitely impressed. Deborah dug her in the back. Rachel would have turned to tell anyone else just what

a man she thought Yosef was. As it was, she did not move.
She just enjoyed looking at him.

Yosef bowed his acknowledgement to Joachim. And saw
the old man's affection crinkle his bearded face. He glanced
shyly at Miriam, and then began his brief declaration. They
noticed his accent. It hadn't the northern burr to it, and
there was a crispness in the way he spoke.

'Receive this pledge as a token that you shall be my
spouse.'

As he spoke, he was drawing his arms out of his cloak,
toying with the piece of silver in his hands. He bent towards
Miriam. They smiled awkwardly, conscious of being the
centre of attention.

Miriam reached out her hands, nestling them in Yosef's
palm. And he, as though it were a fragile thing, solemnly
placed the coin in her hands, and folded them with a
gentleness that belied his strength about the token of his
promise that she would treasure all her life.

The Rabbi waited long enough for everybody to savour
the moment. But there was still work to be done. He held
the parchment roll aloft, brandishing it till everybody noticed
it.

He then stepped out from his place beside Ezekiel and
the Good Men of the Town, unrolling the parchment as he
settled himself to read.

'It is my duty,' he told them, 'my pleasant duty, to read
the betrothal declaration which Yosef and Miriam have
signed, and which Barzillai and Shebna have signed as
witnesses.'

Barzillai and Shebna nodded their heads to show things
were as the Rabbi said.

And then he read. And they listened, though they could
guess what he'd say, for betrothal contracts were much the
same anywhere, no matter who the family was. It sounded

as though the Rabbi himself appreciated the fact, for he read at some speed, though without robbing the occasion of its proper and necessary solemnity.

'On this day in the month of Nisan, Yosef son of Heli, said to Miriam daughter of Joachim, Be thou my spouse according to the Law of Moses and the Israelites; and I will give thee for the portion of thy virginity the sum of two hundred zuzims, as it is ordained by the Law. And the said Miriam has consented to become his spouse on these conditions, which the said Yosef has promised to perform on the day of the marriage. To this the said Yosef obliges himself; and for this he has engaged all his goods, even as far as the cloak he wears upon his shoulders. Moreover, he promises to perform all that is intended in the contracts of marriage in favour of the Israelitish woman. It is signed by Yosef and Miriam, with the names of Barzillai and Shebna as witnesses.'

Miriam hardly heard a word. Everything came to her in a haze. The silver burrowed in her hands. Excitement blurred her ears, and the words came to her like the sound of falling wool. Faces crowded all around her, bright, beaming, like a thousand lamps in darkness that dance in unmolested pleasure. The Rabbi's hands raised high in blessing. Clapping hands. Pounding feet. And the never-ending cymbal sound of joy.

They ate and drank and wished her well. They joked with Yosef and, with mock severity, gave her good advice.

And then they were gone, leaving the house with no one but the family there. And herself, with bedlam-crowding memories, as she settled down to sleep, clutching the coin she'd not been parted from since Yosef put it in her hands.

Outside, the night grew cold. But there was no rain. And though the clouds hung full in the darkness, the storm that had so long threatened, did not come.

*

In Jerusalem, Herod the Tetrarch coughed. With each spasm, his lungs felt as though they were grit-filled bags being squeezed by calloused hands. His body burned through every pore, and in his skull the pain clawed from far, far back, gnawing its way till even the hairs of his head suffered individual hurt.

There was no sense in trying to shift to ease the agony. He knew that. Long years of endurance had taught him it was best to stay as he was, propped up by cushions on his couch, and wait for the torment to wreak its havoc.

Bagoas, his Chamberlain, stood waiting. He knew the course the attack would take almost as well as Herod himself. He had witnessed it too often over the years. And he knew, too, that Herod would rant and rave at him, cursing him for being useless and, whenever he made a move to help, roaring at him to get away.

The physicians stood crowded round the couch. Helpless. They could not tell the cause of the King's disease, nor, for all their years of trying potions and remedies, could they find a cure. But they had to be there. And they waited, knowing the abuse the King would heap upon them in his ravings.

Bagoas looked at the pitiful sight. But he could feel no pity. This King who had slunk, sly, like a fox to the throne, who had reigned for almost thirty years like a roaring lion, was now dying like a dog. And all Bagoas could feel towards the man was hate.

Could he be as callous as his King, he reckoned, he would relish Herod's agonies, and wish him worse. Herod's sufferings, he decided, were but poor retribution for the pain and death and degradation he had meted out as the tyrant Tetrarch of Judaea.

No list was long enough to name and number Herod's victims, no book thick enough to contain the debauches of this half-Jew who usurped the throne of David . . . But what retribution was there, Bagoas wondered, sufficient for a man, king or not, who could order the death of his own sons?

Aristobulus and Alexander were dead. Strangled not a month ago, in a back street in Samaria, on their father Herod's directions. And at the same time, three hundred soldiers stoned to death in Caesarea, at his instigation. With Tero and Tero's son. And Trypho, Herod's own barber, who had daily shaved the King, and served the vanity of this ageing tyrant who dyed his hair black . . .

Bagoas noticed the King's limp hand scratch the hair from his forehead. Pained eyes searched the company round the couch for comfort.

The physicians huddled in consultation, avoiding a move, knowing the King would fly into a temper and make his convulsions worse.

Carus, fragile, fair-headed, and looking more beautiful than a woman, and who sometimes shared the King's bed, eased forward to stroke the King's brow. But Herod motioned him away. And Bagoas could have sworn he saw Carus pout like a maiden scorned.

'Mariamne,' roared the King. With the voice of a man in full health.

Bagoas knew what to expect. He had experienced it all before.

'Mariamne!' bellowed Herod, repeating the word till the room echoed with the sound, and the name rang through the ornate corridors of the palace.

Till the Queen appeared.

She, too, knew what to expect, for she had suffered the humiliation often enough. She was Mariamne and his wife. But she was neither the Mariamne nor the wife Herod called out for. And she cowered, resigned, by the couch, as he cursed and abused her for what he decided in his own mind was her trickery.

Her husband was haunted by the memories of a dead

woman. By the Mariamne who had been his wife seven
wives back, and whom he had murdered more than twenty
years ago because he suspected she had been unfaithful while
he was visiting Antony in Laodicea.

The Queen stood, speechless, waiting for the routine to
end. Hating while her husband roared and raved as the
guilty memories rampaged through his mind, and his body
convulsed, swollen, misshapen, grotesque.

The convulsions stopped.

The Queen, as quietly as she'd come and stood and
endured, left.

Bagoas signalled to the others to go. The physicians left,
trying not to look as though they made haste to be gone.
Carus minced after them.

The King's head slumped on his chest. His easier breathing showed the attack was past. And the King rested. The
bodyguards by the door relaxed.

And Bagoas took the opportunity to take a rest himself.
On a cushion by the couch. He was no sooner down,
though, than the King stirred. Bagoas jumped up.

'Chamberlain, you were in my presence.'

'Majesty.'

'You were tired, Chamberlain?' And the sarcasm told
Bagoas that the King was recovering.

'Majesty,' said Bagoas civilly. He dared not do otherwise.

'Of course, Chamberlain. We are all tired. The King is
tired, waiting to die. And you are tired . . . waiting for the
King to die. But not yet, Chamberlain, not yet.'

'May the King live for ever,' put in Bagoas. It was an
expected comment. It was required, if Bagoas were not
automatically to be suspected of treachery. He tried to make
it sound as though he meant what he said. But he noticed
the smirk on the pain-pinched face, and wondered if Herod
might already be aware of his involvement with the anti-
Herod faction in Jerusalem.

'But the king *cannot* live for ever, Chamberlain,' said Herod. 'The King is an old man and, by God's will, has ruled over this ungrateful nation for more than thirty years.'

They have little to be grateful for, thought Bagoas. But he nodded dutifully, acknowledging what he heard, amazed that Herod, after a reign of such tyranny, could speak of himself being king by God's will.

He dared not speak what was in his mind, yet he could think of nothing else to say in reply. Bagoas waited for the flow of venom. But none came. Instead, Herod went on as if he had expected no comment from his chamberlain.

'If Menahem was right, Chamberlain, then your King is near his end.'

Bagoas was taken aback. Menahem he didn't know. Was he part of another group working against the King? Jerusalem was riddled with societies and groups that planned and plotted and prayed for the downfall of Herod. And each kept its plans exclusively to itself, partly in the hope of making a sudden swoop, but basically to protect itself from Herod's spies. Menahem was certainly not part of the faction Bagoas supported.

Or was Herod trying something on? Had he heard rumours, had his spies fed him something, and was he now fishing for information in his usual devious way?

'Menahem, Majesty?' questioned Bagoas innocently.

'A good man, Menahem,' explained Herod. And there was an affection in his voice that Bagoas had never heard before. 'I met him when I was a boy.'

Bagoas felt relieved by the information, and settled to listen.

'On my way to school one day, Menahem, who until then was a total stranger, met me in the street. 'Hail, King of the Jews,' says he. I told him he was mistaken, for I was just an ordinary boy. What did he do, Bagoas? He smiled at me.'

Herod paused to give his next statement full effect.

'And then, Bagoas, he bent down and slapped my backside.' The King guffawed, enjoying the recollection.

Bagoas quickly joined in, relieved that his master seemed to know nothing of the moves against him.

'But there's more, Chamberlain,' explained Herod when the laughter stopped. 'This same Menahem told me straight that while, indeed, I was a lad on my way to school, there would come a day when I would be King. God, he told me, thought me worthy of it.'

Bagoas coughed, smothering a cry of anger, and only half hearing as Herod explained how, when he had become King, he sent for Menahem and asked how long the reign would be. But Menahem made no reply. Would it be ten years, Herod had wondered. Not ten, Menahem had said, but twenty, nay thirty years.

Bagoas also felt sorry that Menahem had not been more precise, so that he might know how much longer the nation must suffer.

'Good years,' remarked the King.

How much blood, how many murders, Bagoas wondered, made up good years, how much tyranny and oppression? Once in thirty years, the King had cared for his people. And the nation still remembered. In the thirteenth year of his reign it was, when famine seared the land. Herod sold everything he had to import food for his people. And they loved him in gratitude, and were prepared to forget his earlier misrule. Till the famine had ended, and it looked as though he had kept them alive only for the pleasure of persecuting them again when the famine was past.

Bagoas remembered the days of his youth, when people wished they had died in the famine rather than suffer as they did when Herod treated them as slaves. They were not allowed to meet together, or walk or eat together. Spies watched everywhere they went, and everything they did. And those who transgressed were punished bitterly or put to death. And he had heard his father often say that Herod disguised himself, and went at night to mix with the ordinary people, to spy, and snare any unfortunate citizen who might express a bad opinion of the King . . .

'Good years—' Herod was repeating. 'With God's assistance, I have advanced the nation of the Jews to a degree of happiness which they never had before.'

The Chamberlain stooped to hide his face, and gave the impression of listening intently, as the King went on about the benefits his reign had brought to his people. The cities he had built – Caesarea, Samaria, Jericho . . . The fortresses that secured the nation's peace . . .

'And look,' commanded Herod, 'look at the most glorious of all my creations. Go, Chamberlain, look through the window at the memorial of my thanks to God for the blessing I have received from him.'

There was no ignoring the King's command. Bagoas turned, crossed the room, and looked through the window, across the city, to the Temple. Had it not been Herod's handiwork, Bagoas would have been glad to admire it. It was magnificent.

'A thousand wagons brought the stones,' Herod assured him, as he stood and stared blankly out. 'The skill of ten thousand men, iron workers, lead workers, carpenters, did the work. And Bethlehemites taught them the art of stone-cutting——'

Bagoas became aware of the King's voice trailing away. Then he was silent. Bagoas waited a while. Then he turned from the window. The King was asleep and, by the looks of things, would sleep for an hour or two.

He felt tired himself, and would be glad to rest. He bowed deeply towards the King, lest Herod was feigning sleep, and would upbraid him for his lack of proper respect.

The chamberlain left the room, his footsteps soft on the carpet. The bodyguards saluted him as he passed.

Joachim was pleased with the way things had gone. It was a good party, even on reflection a week afterwards. And now Shebna had called especially to tell him how much he had enjoyed himself.

The two men stood in the courtyard, in what shadow the wall cast in the high sun. It was as far as Shebna would go. Joachim would understand he was not spurning hospitality, but he was in a hurry, because he had business in Jerusalem.

If the betrothal party was anything to go by, Shebna was assuring him, then he'd wish the year to go by quickly to be back for the wedding celebrations.

'And frankincense I'll give your daughter for a wedding present.'

Joachim raised his brows in surprise. 'But that's far too expensive.'

'Not at all,' declared Shebna expansively. 'It's my business.'

The little man's offer, Joachim felt, was to establish his wealth rather more than his open-handed generosity. And for a moment Joachim was amused.

'A rich man,' he observed. And Shebna was pleased, raising himself up and down on his toes as though to give himself height. 'And widely travelled,' Joachim added, chuckling to himself as Shebna seemed to revel in his admiration.

'I make a living,' said Shebna. 'But it's hard work. There's no place for fools.'

And Shebna's nobody's fool, Joachim decided. Pompous, maybe, but hard-nosed.

Anna appeared through one of the cloister arches, shielding her eyes from the brightness to see who was the man with her husband. Seeing the two men together, she realized how short Shebna was.

She made him welcome, and wondered if he would stay and eat with them.

Shebna greeted her, kissed her, but declined the invitation. It was no more than a thank-you call, he was sorry to say. He could not stay, because he was on his way to Jerusalem.

It was no time of the day to start a journey to Jerusalem, Anna advised him. It was far too hot, and would get hotter.

'Shebna's in the frankincense business,' offered Joachim, as though it explained everything.

'You sell frankincense!' exclaimed Anna. She'd used frankincense. It scented rooms. It killed bad odours. It perfumed the body, and gave fragrance to clothes. It flavoured wine. On festive occasions in the house, they burnt it in lamps in place of oil. But never before had she come face to face with someone who actually traded in it for a living.

'I import it,' corrected Shebna, careful to disabuse Anna of any thought she might have of his being a mere back-street trader. 'From Arabia and Persia. I've been to Arabia, to Hadramaut,' Shebna told her, 'and have seen the very trees that supply the frankincense I sell.'

Anna was all ears, but Joachim slipped away to fetch some wine. It was obvious Shebna was warming to his subject. And it would take time.

'It's a simple process, really,' he explained, not noticing that Joachim was gone. 'They make a deep incision in the tree. Beneath this incision, they cut away part of the bark. The sap then oozes from the cut, and is collected. It's left then for three months, by which time it's ready for use.'

'Dear, dear,' said Anna at the end of the lesson. 'And have you been to Persia, too?'

Shebna was sorry she'd asked. He had never been to Persia, but he was looking forward to impressing Anna with his travels in Arabia, his perils in the Red Sea, the hazards he had faced in the cities, and the people he'd met . . .

A call from the shadows of the cloisters, however, stopped the conversation. Joachim and a servant appeared. And Shebna realized he had not noticed Joachim going off.

The servant stood, holding the wine jar and a tray with fruit and wine cups on it.

Joachim walked over. It would be cooler inside, he suggested. And they all needed a cool drink.

Shebna was easily persuaded. He would enjoy a drink. It was too late, now, to start out for Jerusalem. And, besides, he felt he was beginning to like Anna and her husband. They were good people.

The house was cool, the wine good. Shebna settled himself deep into the cushions and, for a while, at any rate, setting off for Jerusalem didn't seem all that important. There was a quietness about the place, Shebna thought. He admired the fittings and the furniture. It was the home of a man who lived well. And he liked it. As he looked at Joachim and Anna, sitting now that they had made him welcome, he thought how much the house itself reflected the couple's own serenity.

'You enjoy Jerusalem, Shebna?' wondered Anna.

'I enjoy my friends there,' Shebna replied. 'The city itself, though, is not a happy place.'

'Certainly, from the rumours we hear,' said Joachim, 'it sounds like the world's most unhappy city.'

'There's too much going on there,' said Shebna. 'And I don't mean just business and commerce. It's a dangerous place. Worse, I think, now than at any time since Herod became King.'

Joachim nodded, but said nothing, waiting for Shebna to go on.

'The whole city is seething over the murder of Alexander and Aristobulus. Not that anybody was surprised at it. The awful thing is people expect such things from Herod. They're sickened at the length of time he took to do it.'

'You'd have thought', put in Joachim, 'that having killed Mariamne, their mother, and been haunted by her ghost for all those years, he might have spared his sons.'

'What are sons to a man who can kill their mother?' gesticulated Shebna. 'I was in Caesarea the other week. Do you know what they're saying there? They say that when Augustus Caesar heard the news in Rome, he is supposed to have quipped, 'Better Herod's pig than Herod's son—'

'But what's to come of all this killing and butchery?' asked Anna.

'Somebody'll murder Herod,' said Shebna.

'Well, they tried it before,' observed Joachim.

'I don't know,' mused Shebna. 'It's a madhouse, anyway. And I've got to go there. So I'd better be on my way.' He got up as he spoke.

They walked him to the entrance arch, and wished him God's blessing for his journey.

'If Herod's spies don't catch me,' whispered Shebna, leaning towards them like a conspirator, 'I'll bring you the latest news as soon as I come again.'

He was well on the road when he turned and shouted back, 'And I'll bring some frankincense for Miriam. She can use it to scent her bottom drawer.'

Anna and Joachim laughed.

CHAPTER TWO

Miriam was happy. She enjoyed being engaged. But she looked forward to being married, conjuring in her mind the sights and sounds of her wedding day – the garden filled with happy people. Herself adorned in jewels, and lovely in the wedding dress her mother made. The joyous roar of the guests, 'blessed is he that cometh', as Yosef appeared. And the strong, loving voice of her father pronouncing his benedictions before she paraded, on Yosef's arm, through the streets of Nazareth. And neighbours and well-wishers strewing her walk from the wedding to her new home with money, sweetmeats and flowers . . .

The months till the wedding could not go fast enough. Yet the days were full, and she enjoyed them.

She liked meeting the women at the well in the town square, where they drew water, washed clothes, and filled up the gaps in the day's gossip. They quipped with her, and ragged her. But she relished it. They no longer lowered their voices when she appeared, and they were talking womanly things. Their banter told her she was a woman, now, and she was one of them.

'You've a good man there,' they told her. And Miriam felt proud.

'Even though he's a southerner.' And they all laughed with her.

'But he's a man—' a voice warned her from the far side of the group. 'And never you forget that, my girl.'

And they all agreed in the mumble that was lost in the sound of squeezed water showering from a fist of clothes.

They joked about the ways of a man with a maid. 'There be three things that are past finding out,' quoted Rachel. 'And that's one of them,' she added, giving Miriam a knowing look.

Everybody giggled, till aged Martha, secure in her long widowhood, sobered them all, and rehearsed Miriam in the acrostic from the Book of Proverbs about the virtuous woman.

There were Sabbaths when she went to synagogue with her parents and her sister Salome. And her mother would nudge her in the prayers for staring too long at Yosef.

Or the rare days when she climbed the hills that wrapped around Nazareth. As she did now. Free. Her hair streaming in the mountain air. The freshness on her face. Dangling her sandals in her hand, the long skirt billowing as she danced along the hilltop.

And when she sat to rest, the mountain flowers speckled her green-grass couch with crimson and yellow and blue and white. And all around her, the world spread out on view.

Off to the north was Lebanon where, Barzillai said, the iron he worked came from. And snow-capped Hermon.

She tried to visualize what snow was like. Hard, her father had told her, in the cold of night. But in the noonday sun it softened and you could hold it in your hand. And if you held it long enough, it would turn to water. And she heard in her head the voice of her father quoting the words of the Prophet, 'Hast thou entered into the treasures of the snow?'

To her left, Mount Carmel. And out beyond the glistening vastness of the Great Sea, sheltering another world behind it.

If she looked round behind her, she could see the Plain of Esdraelon . . . but she didn't feel like turning round, for her mind was already on other things.

She was looking off to the valley of her lovely Jordan. Her mind's eye ran with the length of the river that now raced, now dawdled, its long way south to near Jerusalem. She tried to shape her own picture of the city from what Yosef and her father had told her about it. In imagination, she travelled the journey further on to Bethlehem, to Yosef's home town. She could hardly be sure even where Bethlehem was. But she felt she knew it from all Yosef had said about it. And she wondered if she'd ever go there. Maybe one day . . .

And suddenly she shivered a little in the fading sun. And decided it was time to head for home.

Barzillai felt the roughness of the stone dust as he rubbed his hand across his face to wipe away the sweat. It was a long time since he had worked so hard. Even after all this time in the quarry with Yosef, he would never get used to it.

Whatever admiration he had for Yosef, he had no great liking for the work that earned Yosef his living. With every lump of stone he manhandled, his liking grew less. It was certainly different from working in a forge.

But for all that, he had a sneaking kind of pleasure in the thought that he was helping Yosef build the house in which Miriam and he would start their married life.

And he could not help admiring Yosef's skill. He made everything look so easy, and there was a pride in the way he

did things. He was so obviously proud of being a Bethlehemite stonemason. Everything had to be right. Only the best
was good enough, as though the reputation of all his fellow
stone-cutters were at stake.

Barzillai eased the boulder from the quarry face. It had
taken him hours of hammering, picking, probing, to get so
far.

He leaned on it to rest and get his breath. A gulp of water
and a handful splashed on his face, and he was ready to start
again.

He held the chisel on what looked like the edge of a seam
in the boulder. The hammer hit, heavy, strong. And the rock
split. Clean.

'Clean,' murmured Barzillai to himself. 'The thing has
broken clean.' He was delighted with himself. The past few
weeks had not been wasted, after all. He was beginning to
learn. 'It broke clean,' he shouted across to Yosef. The
sound reverberated off the quarry walls.

'Good man,' came back the word from Yosef.

But there was no pause in the work. And now that he had
tasted success, Barzillai himself was not too keen to stop.

Until Yosef called over, 'It's time to rest, Barzillai.'

'Yes, boss,' Barzillai mocked, holding his back as he
straightened up, and walked towards Yosef who was sitting
under the canvas awning rigged up between two piles of
stone. 'You're getting through them,' he said, looking at the
pile of dressed stone, now larger than the rough heap
opposite.

'They're coming on,' Yosef replied.

'It means we'll be back quarrying more.'

'Aye. But not much more, you'll be glad to hear. At least
we can make a serious start on the house with this lot.'

'Come on. Let's eat,' said Barzillai, easing himself down
on to the stone Yosef had been working on.

Yosef reached back into the awning, and pulled out the

bag of food, and a leather bottle of wine. 'You'll feel better with some of that inside you,' he said, putting the bottle on Barzillai's lap.

Barzillai drank. Deep.

Yosef handed him a hunk of bread, some fish, and lettuce.

'You'll have to learn neater ways than that when you're married,' Barzillai joked as Yosef swapped the food for the bottle.

Yosef laughed. And the bottle at his lips spluttered wine into his face. 'Aye,' he said.

And there was silence while they ate.

'You're a good man, Barzillai, to help me. I'm grateful,' said Yosef between gulps.

'I hope I survive till the house is finished,' Barzillai quipped. 'It's a long time since I worked so hard. I'm not used to it, you know.'

'Never mind surviving,' retorted Yosef, feeding lettuce into his mouth as he spoke. 'By the time this house is finished, you'll be good enough to call yourself an apprentice stonemason.'

'You're on,' roared Barzillai, slapping his thigh. 'And after that I'll make you a master iron-worker.'

'Ah no,' said Yosef. 'Never give a fool a good teacher. I'd never learn, Barzillai. I haven't the art to twist and turn and shape that you have.'

'Come on,' reprimanded Barzillai.

'No,' pleaded Yosef. 'Leave me to my chisel, my mallet and my bits of stone.'

'Come on, then, let's get back to your bits of stone.'

'Aye,' said Yosef.

And they both shared the remains of the bottle before they settled down to work again.

Shebna made his way along the bridge that spanned Jerusalem's deep valley. He hurried, angry with himself. He had slept late, and broken the habit of a lifetime's visiting Jerusalem.

The first day of every visit, he went to the Temple in time to witness the Dawn Ceremony from beginning to end. This morning, he would miss the beginning. He might be in time to see the priests return from the Pinnacle of the Temple for the trumpet that sounded the time for the day's first sacrifice. He might. If he hadn't to cope with pilgrims all over the place. Did nobody ever sleep in this city? Thousands of them. Thronging everywhere. And it'd be worse around the Temple.

Being late, though, wasn't entirely his own fault, he told himself. The caravan from Jericho was slow. He'd have been quicker on his own. But he wouldn't take chances on the road from Jericho to Jerusalem.

He side-stepped gossiping groups gazing in wonder over the parapet at the depth of the valley below. He was bumped into by people who seemed to think Jerusalem belonged to them. And they weren't even Jerusalemites! They were foreigners.

It was hard going through the merchants' streets towards the Temple. A rabbit warren of shops already open for business. And doing business.

Another morning he might have dawdled. He might even have talked to Abishai in his tailor's shop. And Hezekiah who dealt in balm and perfume. But not this morning. This morning he battled on, weaving and pushing his way through till he reached the Temple.

Here it was a bit easier. There were still crowds. But at least everybody was moving in the same direction. And he arrived just as the trumpet was sounding the time for the day's first sacrifice.

As the silver tones faded on the air of the brightening dawn, Shebna stood for a moment and felt the wonder of it all. He shut out the bedlam, noise and clamour all around

him. And stood. Lost, rapt. Proud to be Jewish. Blessed to
be allowed to stand on Mount Zion.

'I was glad when they said unto me, let us go into the
house of the Lord—' he murmured to himself.

He moved with the crowds into the long shadow of the
Temple in the morning sun. It towered over all, its white
stone gleaming, still new-looking, for all its having been
built twenty years ago.

They could say what they liked about Herod, Shebna
decided. They could damn the King as the most reprobate
of all men. But there was one thing good about him. Herod
knew about building, about grandeur, and beauty. Maybe
he had built the Temple as an atonement for having
murdered Mariamne and the High Priest, her brother. But
he had built the pride of Jewry. It was the most glorious of
all his works.

Shebna was through the Gate of Huldah and in the
Temple Court while he was still musing.

Inside, unfortunately, was not greatly different from the
city streets on the other side of the wall. The noise was
almost unbearable. Shebna tried to shut it out as he made
his way across the Court to the steps into the Temple. But it
was inescapable.

All round him the milling crowds. Even at this hour of
the morning. Excited people. Animals . . . calves, lambs,
birds . . . demented by the din, waiting to be bought and
sold for sacrifice. Pilgrims, worshippers and sightseers. All
caught in the suffocating bedlam that made mockery of
everything Shebna imagined the Temple stood for. And
traders and money-changers taking advantage of people who
had travelled far to make their lifetime's pilgrimage to the
Holy Place.

A golden dinar for a pair of doves that on the other side
of the wall would have cost a quarter of a silver dinar. But
these doves, the trader would explain, had already been

examined and declared ceremonially clean by the priest. The pilgrim had to agree it was a great convenience. But for that convenience, the pilgrim, who bought the doves because he could afford nothing else, paid one hundred times the price that even the most crooked trader in the market place beyond these holy walls would charge.

Shebna felt dirty even passing such men who grew rich by robbing the poorest of the poor. And in the name of God.

The money-changers he passed, ensconced at their tables, were no better. They made their money easily, and used the Ten Commandments of the Law of Moses to justify their robbery.

Every Jewish pilgrim, no matter where he came from in the world, was expected to pay his Temple dues while in Jerusalem. There were twelve great trumpet-like containers inside the Temple to receive them.

But no pilgrim dared pay in the coinage of his own country, for that would almost certainly have the image, the graven image, of his country's king or god or emperor. And because he dared not bring a graven image into the Holy Temple, the pilgrim, instead, must change his coinage for a Temple shekel. And pay the money-changer expensively for the service.

Shebna was angry at it all. But, today, he told himself, he would not torment his way to prayer by inveighing in his mind against the way the hierarchy organized the accoutrements of his religion. And allowed the Holy Place to become a den of thieves.

Two men and a young woman walking up the steps in front of him suddenly stopped. He knew why as he passed, and heard them read aloud the inscription on the Stone of Forbidding in front of them. And there was a tremble of incredulity in their voices. 'Let no one of the Gentiles enter within the screen around this Holy Place. Whosoever transgresses shall himself bear the blame for his ensuing death.'

They were still standing where they had stopped as Shebna passed through the screen, and took his place in the crowded Court of Worshippers.

Here was quietness at last. No sound. Till the intoning of the priest filtered from the Holy Place where the sacrifice was being offered. And silence, then, waiting for the murmur of the priest making the incense offering.

Shebna knelt. Waiting. All round him, kneeling people waited. Some looked up from prayer, shifting, rustling. Wondering.

An old priest, maybe, whose age made slow movement through the ritual.

But the waiting grew too long. And Shebna felt the tension all around him, unsure whether to leave or stay.

And then the mumbling began. Up near the front. And Shebna strained to look. And saw the priest. An aged priest, indeed. Standing in the Nicanor Gate that separated the worshippers from the altar.

The congregation stood. And Shebna stood. On tiptoe. Straining to see over the heads of those in front of him. It was difficult, though, and he had to depend on his neighbours to tell him what was going on.

The old priest had appeared and signalled to a Temple servant. 'Not speaking, mark you,' said Shebna's informant. 'The servant's gone away . . . now he's coming back. And the priest is writing on the slate he's brought.'

The crowd was hushed. Shebna's neighbours watched intently, listening. 'It's all over,' the informant advised him. 'The priest has gone back through the gate. We can all go home.'

They left the Temple as quickly as decency allowed. And the whole congregation surrounded those who had been near the front. Shebna listened. But it was hard to believe what he heard. The priest, they said, declared the Angel Gabriel had appeared to him at the altar. And the priest was now deaf and dumb.

Shebna was intrigued. Did things like that still happen in Israel? But he'd get to the bottom of it. His cousin was a priest who took his turn in the Temple. He'd get the full story from him.

Shebna had to wait two days till his cousin had finished his tour of duty. But it was worth the wait. For while there were as many rumours as people to spread them about what had happened to the old priest, Shebna believed in hearing things from as near the source as possible.

His cousin had the details. And Shebna liked the succinct way he told them. No frills, no surmisings. Just the facts.

The priest, the cousin explained, was Zecharias. An old man now. Married for years to Elisheba, herself the daughter of a priest. But for all their piety, prayers and longings, they were childless.

On the day in question, it was Zecharias's privilege to make the incense offering. This, the cousin interrupted the story to explain, was a privilege that came to a priest only rarely. Since Zecharias was so old, he was unlikely ever to have the opportunity again.

Why the events occurred, nobody could be sure. Among themselves, the priests reckoned that, during his own private devotions, Zecharias had brought the problem of their childlessness before the Lord.

Anyway, the cousin informed him, what had happened was that, on the right side of the altar, where no mortal man is allowed to stand, there appeared an angel.

It was the Angel Gabriel, who stands in the presence of God, the cousin confided. And the angel announced that Elisheba would give birth to a son whom Zecharias was to name John.

Zecharias, it appeared, could not believe what he saw and

heard. And was struck dumb for his unbelief. 'And will be dumb until the time his son is born,' said the cousin, ending his tale.

There was no need for the rest. Shebna knew that. He had seen for himself, the speechless, bewildered priest come from the Holy Place to face the congregation.

Miriam wished the days would pass more quickly. She saw little of Yosef. Custom ordained it so. But custom or no, it could not be otherwise. Yosef was busy. And what leisure he had was taken up, with Barzillai manfully helping, building the house that would be their home.

When Yosef was allowed to visit her in her home, her father, hardly knowing what he did, monopolized him. And the two of them talked and talked about the house. Joachim longed to see it. Yosef wanted everybody to wait until it was finished. The old man was agreeable, and for long enough allowed himself to be satisfied with Yosef's chalk sketches of the progress of the house.

But now things were nearing the finish. However the others might have felt, Miriam herself was too excited to wait much longer. Yosef relented, though he did not need much persuasion. And off they trooped. Joachim stepped out in front. Miriam, with her mother and sister Salome, followed, chattering, behind.

The house was not too far away. On a tiny patch a little further up the hill.

To get to it, they had to pass Azariah's house. Azariah was tethering a goat under the shade of a tree, and shooing away the hens that searched for invisible morsels in the ground around him. Naomi his wife sat in the shadow of the house, grinding corn with a millstone her old hands could hardly manage.

The old man saw them. He left the goat, and made towards them.

'Anna and the family are here, Naomi,' he called out as he shuffled, stooped with age.

Naomi got up. 'Anna, you are welcome. You must all come and drink,' she called, wiping her hands on her apron as she walked.

'God bless you, but no,' said Anna as they all met and greeted each other. 'We're on our way to see the house.'

'The house,' beamed Naomi. 'I'm delighted.'

Azariah was delighted, too, but he let his wife do the talking. He was content to nod. Naomi wondered, was it nearly finished?

'Come with us, and see,' offered Miriam.

But they both declined. And for all Joachim's encouragement, they would not be persuaded.

The path was now no more than a track, roughed and rutted in the earth by the carts that had transported the stone from the quarry in Nazareth's hills.

They picked their way, avoiding the jagged edges, stopping every now and then to pull out pebbles lodging in their sandals.

They came upon the house suddenly, as they skirted the far corner of Azariah's olive grove.

Miriam stood still.

There, squat and strong, was the house, its white limestone glistening against the green and gentle-rising hill behind.

Her house. Could she believe!

She hugged Salome, and nearly knocked her father over as she embraced him. Anna did not wait to be hugged. As Miriam turned, Anna enfolded her in warm, tender, loving arms. 'I'm happy for you, daughter.' And they both cried, blubbering over each other.

'Women—' muttered Joachim, grabbing Salome by the hand and stalking off towards the house.

Miriam walked with her mother, trying to take in every

detail, as she moved towards its open, welcoming door sitting between two windows like a nose between its eyes. On the other side, the deep stone steps ran up to where the parapet round the roof was still unfinished.

Yosef waved to her from the roof where he was standing with her father.

'From here, you can see right along the valley,' he shouted to her. 'Come on up and see.'

Miriam waved back. She really wanted to see what the inside looked like, but since Yosef seemed so keen, she did not want to disappoint him. But by the time she had reached the steps, he was already down, waiting to greet her.

Yosef was like a boy. And he could not contain his excitement. Houses he had built before. But this one was different. This house was theirs. And Yosef was proud.

'Look inside,' he offered. And he led her in.

Her mother and Salome were already there. 'There's even stone on the floor,' Salome told her. 'Trust a mason to make his own house comfortable.'

Miriam looked. Instead of the familiar hardened earth, covered with mats, to make a floor, Yosef had laid stones, smoothed and shaped and levelled.

'You can thank Barzillai for the floor,' he assured her. 'It was his idea. He reckoned he wanted practice at dressing stone.'

'And what will the masons' guild say about that?' quipped Salome. 'A retired iron-worker getting in the back door.'

They laughed.

Miriam was still taking it all in. It was clean and rich and cool. The windows threw their light into the corners, making everything bright. Across the floor, and rising about knee high, was a wall supporting an upper floor. The sleeping place. At one end of the wall, a set of steps from one floor to the next. And halfway along the wall, a manger fixed.

'Bezaleel made me the manger,' he told her, 'as a gift.'

Miriam squeezed his arm and whispered in his ear. And Yosef smiled. And then she was off, looking, touching. The jars, the pots and mats and lamps, the rich rug coverings on the walls.

Yet she saw nothing. Only Yosef hovering, excited. Boyish, proud, gabbling.

'When I've finished the wall round the roof,' he was saying, 'I'll build a guest chamber of stone there. Better than setting up an awning every time somebody comes to stay. And we'll put a table in it, and a bed and a candlestick.'

'That'll be nice,' she said, broadening her face into a smile. The idea of Yosef trying to manage in an overcrowded house amused her.

Jerusalemites had something new to talk and gossip about. And they were relieved.

For a month or more now, in any company where they were sure Herod had no spies, they'd been venting their feelings about the King's murder of his sons. And they'd had enough of his excesses. Not that they were surprised at the murders; experience had taught them to expect nothing better from the King. What sickened them was his trying to make the stranglings look like justice. And his adding insult to injury by bringing the bodies from Samaria to Jerusalem to be buried alongside their mother.

But now the city buzzed with a new rumour, and Jerusalemites latched on to it with relish.

From the maze of market stalls and shops and alleyways beyond David's Wall to the more sedate grandeur of the south-west corner of the city, they clustered and wagged their heads in discussion. Even in the squares that fronted Herod's own palace, Jerusalemites huddled and nodded, gesticulating, squinting, whispering and muttering their gossip and speculation about the assault, it was said, that the Pharisees were now plotting against Herod.

There was nothing secret about them. They were an Association who made their objectives clear – to oppose, by all means, Roman power in Judaea, and to remove Herod from the Jewish throne. All Jerusalem knew about the Pharisee Association.

It was their openness, perhaps, that saved them. Had they intrigued and plotted, Herod might have been concerned. They did not. So Herod could not take them seriously. At the same time, he could not let them continue unchecked.

It was an easy matter to arrest some of the leaders. Herod's instructions to them were simple. They would recant and forswear their allegiance to the Pharisee Association, and they would swear unswerving allegiance to Caesar and the King.

The men refused.

Herod was taken aback. The men were mad. They must be. Didn't they know they could die for their obstinacy?

They did. And they were prepared to die rather than commit an act that they considered the worst form of ungodliness.

Herod smiled, wondering that men coud be so stupid. They made no defence, asked for no leniency, offered no reason for their stubborn unwillingness to obey. They stood like men who were already condemned in their own minds. They had no interest in what was going on.

But as he watched them, Herod became aware of their derision. The atmosphere of their contempt towards him became more and more oppressive. Herod felt it. It was worse than if each one of them in turn had physically attacked him.

They would die. He had decided. But he wouldn't tell them yet. Wait long enough, and one of them would break. Then another. And they'd beg to be allowed to live.

Herod measured the men in front of him. Slowly. All along the line, searching each of them, one man at a time. But there was nothing in the stares that came blankly back.

Something clicked in his mind. There was no cause so good that it could command such self-sacrifice. There was far more to them than met the eye. Of that Herod was now convinced. The brazen openness of their Association hid more than it revealed. The *naïveté* of their blatant honesty was a cover for something more sinister. These were subtle men. With an approach to intrigue Herod had not come across before. And he almost laughed out loud, for he was looking forward to the new game his prisoners had devised.

He changed the decision he was just about to announce.

They would not die. Not yet, anyway. This time they would pay a fine. A fine, he decided, that would cripple them, and drain whatever money the Association had.

He announced his decision quietly, matter-of-factly, revealing nothing of his thoughts. He would be lenient with them, he explained. They would pay a fine, and would be given time to see the error of their ways.

Herod thought he caught a look of disappointment in their faces. So his surmisings were right. These were a new breed of conspirator.

The fine, he told them, was due in three days.

The men listened, unmoved.

He dismissed them, smiling to himself as they were marched out. He was looking forward to the game that was obviously just beginning.

Or about to stop dead, perhaps. If there was no money forthcoming, he calculated, it meant the Pharisee Association was no more than a coterie of cranks. They had no real support, for all the noise they made. And a few judicious executions would bring the whole nonsense to an end.

Long experience, however, had taught the King that nothing was as simple as that. There was always the alternative.

Money paid must mean the Pharisee plot had strong support from a large following. To be able to meet the crippling fine he had laid on them would indicate patronage from someone outside the ordinary run of things. And that kind of patronage could come only from his own court circles.

Herod jolted at how naturally he had reached his conclusion. And felt sickened.

His godforsaken family. Would they ever stop? Anything they had, they had because of him. He'd made them rich, he'd given them power. For thirty years he'd protected and sustained them. And all the thanks he'd ever got was jealousy, bickering and jockeying for position.

They even hated each other. And the only time they bothered to meet together and pretend to be civil to each other was when they laid plots against him.

And, if he were guessing correctly now, they were at it again.

Herod was right. Old man as he was, and broken as he was physically, he had lost none of the guile that had kept him always one step ahead of his enemies for thirty years. And kept him on the throne.

The Pharisee Association began with a few in Jerusalem who had grown sickened and frightened by the King's excesses. It began slowly, quietly, insinuating its influence into important places. Aware of the animosities that existed in Herod's own househould, it set itself to weave its way in there.

Success at the lower level of power was an encouraging start. But soon it attracted men close to the King himself. Bagoas was drawn in, and Carus.

It was only a matter of time before the tentacles reached into Herod's own family.

They were not motivated by any great conviction about the Pharisees' principles. It was enough that the Association's aims to remove Herod from the throne coincided with theirs. They were content to use them as a means of gaining their own ends.

Doris, who had been Herod's first wife, joined. Long since divorced, she still lived in the palace, had the privileges of a queen, and managed the royal household. Doris had waited long enough for revenge. She also wanted the throne for Antipater, the son she had borne to Herod.

Antipater himself was being groomed for the succession, and even now had charge of the affairs of state during the worst bouts of his father's sickness. The taste of power was sweet to him, and made him lust for kingship. Anything that would end his father's reign had his support.

Despite its infiltration so deep into Herod's household, the Association managed to evade detection by either Herod himself or his spies. With its prestige enhanced by the royal connection, it built up a membership of about six thousand in Jerusalem.

Its influence spread beyond the city walls, across the Kedron Valley and through the hills to Bethany, the sleepy village two miles from the capital, and on the road to Jericho.

The King's brother, Pheroras, lived in Bethany, with his wife Jochebed. Bethany was near enough to the city to keep them in touch, and far enough away to keep them out of Herod's close company. The arrangement suited both sides.

Jochebed hated Herod with as much venom as he hated her. And each reckoned the hate was well founded. Herod considered her no more than a slut who had beguiled Pheroras into marrying her. She hated Herod because he made his view clear whenever she appeared in royal circles, and tried all means to break up the marriage.

Jochebed needed no persuasion to join the Pharisee Association. She was absolute in her commitment. Pheroras her husband joined, with no great feeling either way, just to please his wife.

Herod's conclusions about the patronage were confirmed when his treasurer advised him that the Pharisees had paid their fine in full.

The task of discovering who the patron was he gave to his sister Salome.

In a family torn apart by feuds and personal hates and animosities, Salome was the one person who seemed to be able to mix with them all.

Some of them pitied her, because Herod had prevented her from marrying Sylleus whom she dearly loved, and forced her to marry Alexas because it suited the King's political ends. Others cultivated her friendship because of the influence they imagined she had with the King.

Salome already had her own suspicions, and went about her task like a cat stalking a bird. And found it easier than she expected.

Pheroras caused her no alarms, and she could scent nothing that made her suspicious of him. He was harmless enough. He withstood Herod, indeed, but was not maliciously opposed to him. And coveted nothing Herod had, least of all his throne. She admired his determination, and only wished she could have been so adamant with Herod when he had so obstinately refused to allow her marriage with Sylleus.

Pheroras was content enough, she reckoned. Content with his wife, and his little power as Tetrarch of Perea. And now he was overjoyed that Jochebed was expecting his child, and wanted everybody to rejoice with him.

Salome might readily have joined the general merriment, had not Antipater and his mother, who were normally at daggers drawn with Pheroras, appeared so eager to join in.

The cat was scenting her real quarry now.

Doris was dangerous.

Antipater himself, with something of his father's cunning, saw the value of the position his father afforded him. He used it to carve himself a niche, bestowing favours where he calculated advantageous harvests might later be reaped.

There would come a day, Salome decided, when Antipater would over-reach himself. Herod's subtlety he might have, but he lacked his father's patience. He moved too quickly. And in the wrong direction altogether, Salome thought, when he began to work on Pheroras. And with the wrong people. Herod would never use women in this kind of enterprise. But Antipater did. And the worst women, when he made an accomplice of Doris and Jochebed's mother and sister.

Salome waited, and kept their company. And watched. And when she was sure of what she saw, reported to the King.

But Herod found it hard to believe.

So Salome explained it all again. Antipater and his mother were now suspiciously close friends with Pheroras and his family.

'But they squabble here in front of me,' laughed Herod, 'and tittle-tattle behind each other's back.'

'When they are in public,' Salome reassured him, 'they make it look as though they are at variance. And even speak about each other as though they intended each other mischief.'

'But, in private, you say, it is not so?'

'In private, they act in concert. And swear they will never leave off their friendship, but will fight against those from whom they conceal their designs.' Salome said she was not sure. She calculated, though, that their secrecy argued it could only be against the King.

Herod was amused. Salome's imagination was working

overtime. Two parts of the family wanted to forget a bitter past, and his sister reckoned it was calumny.

He smiled. And Salome was angry.

'If they are not plotting against the King,' she flounced back, 'they would not be ashamed to have their meetings in public, and would not pretend to be at enmity.'

Perhaps she had a point, Herod conceded. But who could be the plotter?

He waited for Salome to offer a view. She had her own ideas, but felt that, at this stage in the conversation, it was better to let Herod express his own opinion.

'It's beyond Jochebed's capabilities,' he decided. 'And she's not plotting while she's with child. Pheroras has no ambitions . . . and certainly not for the throne. And as for Doris, so long as I allow her to play queen over the servants, she'll cause no problems . . .

Salome raised her eyebrows. Involuntarily. But Herod noticed.

'You don't agree?'

Salome did not answer immediately, to give the impression that she was being forced to think new thoughts about Herod's one-time bedfellow. Her answer was slow. Grudgingly spoken. 'I think Doris is dangerous,' she offered.

Herod laughed.

'She's ambitious for her son—'

'Nonsense,' roared the King, mocking the very idea. 'Antipater is being groomed for the kingship. And Doris knows it.'

'Doris is impatient. She once sat near the throne, and wants to taste the power again.'

'Antipater will control her,' Herod interrupted.

'Antipater does control her,' scorned Salome back. 'It is Antipater, I believe, who has set this new intrigue afoot.'

'Jealousy, Salome,' chided Herod.

'It is not jealousy,' Salome remonstrated. 'It is concern for the King. The authority you have given Antipater in your affairs has made him hungry for more power.'

'You are jealous, my sister. Would you have the power for yourself?'

Salome would not rise to the bait. 'Know it or not, King and brother, Antipater your son is already using his power by bestowing favours—'

But Herod would not listen. 'It's hatred, then,' he roared, rising uncomfortably from his couch, signalling the interview was at an end. 'You think too much, woman,' wondering to himself if Salome's information were really a cover for her own calumny. She was not, after all, he decided, incapable of plotting herself. And there was enough in their relationship to give her reason to hate him.

'We'll leave it so,' he remarked as he dismissed her, 'and wait to see what happens.'

The night was gentle over Nazareth. Only the chatter of cicadas and the night insects disturbed the quiet darkness. And it was cold. The new-built, empty house stood lonely in the night. In Joachim's house the family slept where the fretting embers of a dying fire etched shadows on the smoke-blackened walls.

On a straw palliasse, wedged in the low alcove, Miriam slept, tossing and turning, uncomfortable.

Sound blurred in the far-off dark. And a light, shapeless, shifting, glared with an awful presence that enthralled her and wrapped her round in fear till she could not tell whether she slept or yet was wide awake, while the sound grew and grew, whispering, lisping in rivulets along the channels of her mind, to become a stream, torrenting, tumbling, ocean-sounding in her head, and the very room she slept in seemed a sea of words.

'Hail to thee on whom God's favour is conferred. Blessed art thou among women.'

Fear-stricken in the flood, her mind plummeted and plunged, searching to fathom what the greeting meant. But the billowing speaking gave her no time to think. 'Miriam . . . have no fear. Thou hast found favour with God. And, behold, thou art conceiving in thy womb.'

A dream, she comforted herself. A dream it was. Conjured by her mind, revelling in harmony with her body that longed to be wed to Yosef and bear his child . . .

'And thou shalt bring forth a son—'

Dear God, what did it mean?

'He shall be great. And Son of the Highest shall he be called. To him his father David's throne shall be given. Over Jacob's house for ever shall he reign. And of his kingdom there shall be no end.'

Stop . . . The voice must stop . . . The never-ending sound must cease. And she must speak . . . Was she to bring shame on Yosef? Did her body long so much that she could not bide the hour of God's commanded time? Had demons taken the Almighty's place, that a maiden might be mocked upon a bed of chastity . . .

Her voice was fever-pitched. And she heard herself cry out, 'No . . . No . . . This cannot be. For I have slept with no man—'

But yet all round her the ocean swelled. Its great sound drowning her words as though she had never spoken. 'The Holy Ghost shall cover thee like a cloud. The power of the Highest overshadow thee. Therefore, that holy thing which shall be born of thee shall be called the Son of God.'

Sanity told her she was mad. This could never be. The married were barren whom God did not bless with child. And would God mock himself by giving child to a maiden who had not even known a man?

'But consider thy cousin Elisheba. She also, in old age, hath conceived a son. And this is now the sixth month with her who once was thought incapable of bearing a child.'

But Elisheba was married. And faithfulness God would reward. But was her own chastity to have no reward . . .? was her virtue so unprotected . . .? Had God himself turned nature against the very laws that he himself had made . . .?

Calm now the sea of sound, its swirling ceased. All noise and clamour gone. And a soft wind sighed the answer to her thoughts, 'Nothing shall be impossible for God.'

Miriam wept. There was nothing more to say, nothing to do. The ways of God were past finding out, she could not search his understanding.

She murmured softly in her sorrow. The sound was lonely, broken, submissive. 'Behold, the handmaid of the Lord. Be it unto me according to thy word.'

The dream was ended. The phantom gone.

The night closed dark again.

Miriam slumped on the rough hard bed, tossing, turning, tormented.

The embers in the fire were black. And no light shone.

CHAPTER THREE

Nazareth heated and cooled in the rising and setting sun. But the passing weeks brought Miriam no relief. She had dreamed the dream, and nothing could stop its unended recollection. It clung like a cancer. Growing. Gnawing.

Time brought her no healing. Her body knew the dream was a reality. And realizing it made tragedy close consort with terrorizing fear.

Miriam was tired. The bloom had wilted in her face, no joy lit her eyes. Fear sculpted aching hollows in her cheeks. Her step had no more pride. And sorrow slouched in young shoulders suddenly grown old.

Now the neighbours knew. They couldn't help it. The women who once joked with her when drawing water at the well knew all about these things. And they had the instinctive knack of spying pregnancy in a girl who was not wed. They revelled in the bit of scandal. They took longer at the well, clustering, nodding their heads, as she came and went. She could feel them relishing what they decided was her immorality.

Miriam was sorry for them. They didn't understand. She

didn't understand herself. Only Rachel, among them all, was kind. She made no comment. But there was pity in her look.

The family gave no hint that they suspected anything. Salome looked and watched. And wondered silently. But said nothing.

Her father was incapable of suspicion. The thought that the daughter he so dearly loved might be with child would never cross his mind.

He was worried about the way she looked, but decided it was the strain and nervousness of being so near to marriage. In an awkward way, he tried to jolly her along. And when he took her in his arms to comfort her, she tried to tell him all. But the words she wanted would not come. And he nestled her head, and cuddled her like a baby when she cried.

Her mother wept when Miriam told her. Dumbfounded, mesmerized, she heard the torrent swirl of words. She tried to catch them here and there to shape them into sense. But the cascade, tearing, tangling, overwhelmed her. Great God, she wondered, was there any meaning to it all . . .? Could it really be that her daughter was a trollop? Could she so cheaply give her body to a man, and then compound her sin by blaspheming God . . .?

Was her poor daughter mad . . .? The new thought jolted Anna. She looked at Miriam, the poor head burrowing for comfort into her lap, the shoulders heaving with heartbreaking sobbing that sounded as though it would never stop. Poor, poor Miriam.

Anna herself could not understand. And could she expect her child to comprehend? Her hands involuntarily trembled towards her weeping child, and rested on her head, patting, patting . . . immeasurably loving.

And Yosef knew.

Somehow, Miriam felt a sense of relief. For long enough she'd lived in agony, her imagination conjuring every kind of way in which she might break the news to Yosef. She'd endured the tensions when they'd met, sidling away from all talk of marriage, angling for an opportunity to blurt out the speech she had rehearsed and rehearsed again. And Yosef, with the intuition of a man towards the maid he loved, sensing there was something wrong, yet never daring to conclude the obvious.

But now he knew. The gossiping women had done their work well. And their workmen husbands taunted Yosef, and joked about the ways of a man with a maid.

Yosef faced her now. In her father's house.

'I have been shamed, Miriam.'

He spoke softly, but there was quiet anger in his voice. The sound of disbelief.

'I have been made to look a reprobate, though I have done no wrong.'

Miriam pitied him as she watched him, observing hurt sorrow in his face and the dejected way he stood.

'The other men make sport of me, for their wives tell them you are with child.'

She lowered her head, frightened, lost. Searching in her mind; struggling to summon the words she needed to explain her predicament.

'It cannot be true. You are a chaste woman, Miriam. I am an honourable man who would not bed you till you became my wedded wife—'

'I am with child, Yosef.' The words were out now, but not the words she wanted. 'But let me try to explain—'

Yosef stopped her. 'You cannot be. It's impossible. Before God, Miriam, I am no child's father. And you know yourself I have fathered no child on you.'

'I know, I know, Yosef. But I am with child.'

Was it anger she heard as he spoke? Or pity, sympathy in his soft tones as he measured every word.

'Who is the man?'

'There is no man,' she stumbled. But even as she said it, she realized how ludicrous it sounded. Now she heard anger.

'There *has* to be a man, woman. You must not treat me as a fool. There is no way a woman can bear a child—'

She knew, she knew . . . and heard the anger and the hurt, the disappointment, the heartbreak . . . and she wished and prayed that there was something she could say or do to soften his pain. But she herself knew so little, she understood too little to be able to explain and make him understand.

Miriam wept. Deep, gulping sobs, till Yosef feared her heart would break. He longed to reach out and touch her, take her in his arms and comfort her, this poor, dear Miriam whom he loved. But he could not, would not, dare not, for now she belonged to another man.

The realization stabbed deep, with choking, heart-scalding wounds. Who was the man, his mind kept probing. What kind of man could have taken advantage of his frail, innocent, gracious Miriam?

'One night three months ago, I slept, Yosef,' Miriam was whispering, sobbing the words through her tears. 'And in my sleep, I dreamed. And in my dream the Angel Gabriel appeared, a messenger sent from God.'

The weeping stopped. She looked full into Yosef's face, speaking as though she were now reliving all she spoke about.

'"Fear not", the angel told me, "for you have found favour with God. You are conceiving in your womb. And shall bring forth a son—"'

Yosef had been patient, but now he had heard enough. 'Stop, Miriam. Stop. Don't talk of dreams. No woman yet in Israel has conceived a baby through a dream. Nor angels either—'

Miriam hardly heard him. She saw him mouth the words, but she was looking past him, not aware of what he spoke.

Her head rang with the voice of that night months ago, and she continued echoing the word of the heavenly messenger. 'Thou shalt call his name Jesus. He shall be great—'

Yosef would hear no more. 'Enough, Miriam. I said, enough. God does not break his own laws. I'll have no more blasphemy.'

Miriam fell silent, and bowed her head.

'Do not presume to teach me nonsense, woman, as though I were a fool.'

'I speak only of things as they are, Yosef, and I speak the truth. Believe me, I would not lie to you.'

'You speak like a fallen woman. You have done wrong, Miriam. And would you now compound your sin with blasphemy?'

She listened for the familiar kindness and patience in his speech. Instead she heard anger: the anger of a man betrayed, belittled. And she pitied him. But could he not understand how she felt? Could he not feel sorry for her? Where was the concern and affection and love he had once lavished on her?

'There is but one way a woman can be with child,' he was saying. 'You know that, and I know that. And all the stories in the world about angels and their messages cannot change that.'

His voice was raw, measured, emotional – kind and cruel all at once.

'You refuse to tell me who this man is, Miriam. But whoever he is, *he* knows. And you know what this all means.'

'Dear God,' Miriam breathed from her heart, 'is there no way I can convince this poor, broken man that what I say is true?'

'Because we are promised in marriage, Miriam, the Law looks on us as though we were already man and wife. So your unfaithfulness to me is as though you had been unfaithful as a wife—'

'Is heaven itself closed against me?' Miriam was murmuring to herself. 'I need words, O God, a sign . . . a proof . . . anything that will help this man to see how wrongly he judges me.'

'I am not the father of your child, Miriam.' He continued softly. He paused before he spoke again, and his speech could hardly be heard, as though his heart was not in what he said. 'You have committed adultery.'

But Miriam was only half listening. It seemed as though she had heard it all before. She had lived these moments many times in her mind in the weeks gone by. Then, she had countered all the arguments. But now, try all she might, the words she moulded from the once convincing thoughts sounded naïve and arch.

And Yosef's voice grew soft and hushed, talking in a distant quietness, as if fearful of the counsel he gave himself. How could he be one flesh with a woman who had shared herself with someone else? The Law forbade it. And the Law was cruel. Adultery meant death . . .

Miriam heard no more. She wasn't listening any more. The brutal helplessness she had felt that night came back again. There was nothing she could do. She dared not plead. It was a man's world. She was the victim of men and angels . . . be it unto me according to thy word.

Shebna was back in Nazareth. With a tale to tell. And a small stock of incense for Miriam.

He'd rest a while after his journey, he decided. Then he'd call on Joachim, deliver the gift for Miriam's bottom drawer, and have a long chat with her parents.

He was looking forward to that as he sauntered, astride his mule, through the narrow streets. Joachim was a good listener, and Anna asked the kind of questions that gave him plenty of scope. And she'd have plenty of questions tonight,

Shebna reckoned. This time it wouldn't be just about Herod's goings-on in Jerusalem, though that could keep them going. It wouldn't even be about his trip to the coast, and the ships that came and went in Caesarea, or who'd just sailed out or who'd arrived from Rome.

Tonight he was coming with news that not many people knew about. And he was already picturing their faces as he told them about Zecharias, the old priest who was struck dumb by the Angel Gabriel at the Altar of Incense.

He was outside Isaac's bakery now. The mule stopped. Almost out of habit. It was a regular call whenever he arrived in Nazareth. Isaac's bread was good. And it wasn't out of his way to collect a loaf as he passed.

He was a bit early, he reckoned. Isaac was probably finishing off his siesta. But he'd not mind being disturbed. Anyway, his wife Deborah would be delighted with the gossip.

Deborah was the first to appear when he shouted from the door. She was still rubbing sleep from her eyes, welcoming him, and calling out to rouse Isaac, all at the same time.

Isaac pulled back the curtain dividing the shop from the living room. He had a bottle of wine in his hand.

'Come in, Shebna,' he said. And, as he spoke, he turned back and had the wine poured even before Shebna sat down.

Deborah fussed and fixed the cushions behind their guest.

'Welcome,' said Isaac, raising his glass.

The men drank. Deborah did not. She was busy, behind Shebna, waving her glass, nodding her head, shaping her mouth in silent speech, 'Tell him. Tell him, now.'

Isaac drained his glass, tipping his head back to take the last drop.

'I'll get your bread while I think of it, Shebna,' said Deborah. With a frowning urgency in her look towards Isaac, and a silent, 'Tell him,' she was gone.

Isaac refilled the glasses, slowly.

'It's good wine,' complimented Shebna. 'And doubly good after a long journey—'

'You've got a problem,' blurted Isaac, fearing that once his guest got started, he might take a long time to stop.

'You've got a problem,' Isaac repeated, 'with Yosef.'

Shebna looked anxious. 'What kind of problem, Isaac?'

'Well, more a problem with Miriam rather than Yosef . . . if you take my meaning.'

Shebna thought he understood. But he wanted to be sure. 'You're going to tell me, of course.'

Deborah came back with the loaf as he spoke. She was annoyed that Isaac obviously hadn't told Shebna the story.

'Haven't you told him yet?' she snapped at her husband. And then, with a kind of relish, to Shebna, 'Miriam is with child.'

The room was quiet.

Now that they had told him, Shebna tried to dismiss the whole idea of it from his mind. He couldn't take it in. This was not the Yosef whose honour Barzillai and himself had vouched for. What would Joachim think of them . . .

'Are you sure?' reacted Shebna, knowing, even as he asked, that it was a stupid question.

'Sure?' exclaimed Deborah. 'You'd need to be blind not to notice.'

'Does Barzillai know?'

'If he doesn't,' commented Isaac sadly, 'he's the only one in the town who doesn't.'

Shebna knew what he meant. 'I didn't expect anything like this,' he said. 'Yosef has always been an honourable man. And Miriam comes of decent people.'

'You can be sure of nobody,' Deborah advised, placing the loaf on the table, and folding her arms across her bosom, ready to pontificate for as long as the men were prepared to listen.

Shebna ignored her. He thought it was a pity she seemed to take such pleasure in it. 'It's bad news, Isaac,' he said, taking the loaf from the table. 'Barzillai will feel hurt too.'

He departed.

Royal patronage seemed to be good for the Pharisee Association. It boosted membership, so that now there were about 6000 supporters in Jerusalem. And when Jochebed herself paid the fine Herod had imposed on the four leaders, she not only rescued the four themselves, but saved the whole membership from financial ruin.

The same royal patronage seemed to breed a new audacity. The Pharisees, though, claimed it was divine inspiration that constrained them to proclaim their new prophecy. Not only would God put an end to the House of Herod, they announced, but now the Messiah would be born.

And word had it that Jochebed would be the mother of the Messiah.

Jochebed asked no questions. It did not concern her that people said the Association acted as they did simply to reciprocate her own generosity in paying the fine. The men who prophesied, she believed, were godly men. They knew the Law, and it was said they were inspired by God. They had prophesied. And she believed the child she was carrying would be the Messiah of Israel.

Her family clamouring round her, though, made it hard for her to be calm.

Bagoas came all the way from Jerusalem to Perea to congratulate her. The promised King, he assured her, meant a new era for Israel, a new life for all its people. God was, indeed, visiting his people.

He waxed eloquent about the vision he had of Israel's future with Jochebed as the mother of the nation. He said nothing of the thoughts that rampaged through his mind as he contemplated what the prophecy and the Pharisees had suggested about himself. And he, who had been made a eunuch in boyhood, would be a eunuch no longer. The new King would have all things in his power. The King would enable him to marry, and beget children of his own body. It sounded too good to be true. But Bagoas wanted it to be true.

Pheroras was pleased for his wife. The new prophecy raised her high above the ranks of all the women of Israel.

But, pleased as he was, he wondered how Herod his brother would react. A prophecy about the Messiah, coming so close on the heels of the promised doom on his reign, must surely mean danger for all whenever Herod heard the news.

Pheroras was right.

In Jerusalem, Herod heard. And Herod had had enough. The Pharisee Association, he decided, had gone too far. And for a moment the King's dementing sickness eased. A new strength possessed him.

He heaved himself from his couch, his scabbed body swollen to twice its size with water sacs round the pit of his belly and his legs. His physicians tried to restrain him. He pushed them away, cursing their clumsy incompetence and their failure to find a cure.

He stood, balancing his unwieldy form, grasping great gulps of air to feed his smothered lungs, shouting between gasps that he would spite them all and live ... live long enough to know the sweet pleasure of making those people regret their presumption.

His sister Salome entered, choosing her moment. She knew the intrigues and their instigators. She had watched it all fester. And now that the boil was ripe for lancing, she was preparing Herod to perform the surgery.

The King scanned the list of names she gave him. He manoeuvred himself on to the couch, and crouched, poring, now over the names and the misdeeds Salome alleged them guilty of.

Now and then he muttered to himself, with a malevolent satisfaction, as he devised the manner of their death. The principal offenders in the Association would be burned alive.

'Burned alive,' he repeated, as though he relished the prospect. Herod belonged to the Sadducee sect, which believed there was no life after death. He despised the Pharisees' teaching of a resurrection. Now he saw their belief as a means to a more destructive revenge.

'If they have no body to be buried,' he gloated, 'they'll have nothing to be resurrected.' He tittered to himself, gleeful at his originality. And noted with pleasure that there were nine to be burned.

There were nineteen other men on the list who had minor roles in the intrigue. They would be beheaded.

'And Carus—' boomed Herod, straightening out of his couch, and looking at Salome for the first time. 'Carus will be strangled.'

Salome winced.

'He lived for men's embraces,' wheezed the King. 'Let him die in a man's embrace.'

Salome sensed the hate in every syllable her brother spat. She hadn't expected this reaction. It wasn't for treachery, she reckoned, that Carus was being killed. Her brother felt betrayed by a lover, as a man might feel towards an unfaithful wife. Carus the lover was being strangled for his unfaithfulness.

Four women on the list who had played small parts in the plot were to be strangled. Along with Carus.

Next in the list of names came Doris, her brother's former Queen. And Jochebed. Salome waited for her careful strategy to work. Herod's wrath, she had calculated, unleashed against Carus, would increase in venom against these two women who, Salome reckoned, had escaped for too long. This time they would not go free.

Herod paused as he read through the names again.

Salome felt the taut atmosphere all around her, physicians and attendants and bodyguards resenting – and sickened by – the butchery Herod was planning to perpetrate in the guise of justice.

Herod looked over the top of the roll shaking in his hands, and smiled at his sister. Salome waited for his pronouncement.

'I need advice,' said Herod, beckoning to his chief physician.

The physician bowed acknowledgement.

'Is it possible', enquired the King, 'for a man who has been a eunuch from his youth to father a child?'

A faint smile showed round the eyes of the physician.

Salome was disappointed. Angry. It looked as though her strategem was failing. Herod was passing over the two women, and was having a bit of fun before deciding Bagoas' fate.

'I am not joking, physician,' barked the King.

The smile disappeared. 'It is impossible, Majesty.'

'Impossible?' retorted Herod. 'But could a King not make it possible?'

The physician frowned. Herod frivolous was Herod dangerous. A careless answer could sour the King's humour.

'Majesty,' he began carefully, 'we can recollect no record . . . of even the most mighty King . . . not even Solomon, whom even Your Majesty would consider the wisest of them all—'

'And yet,' Herod interrupted, 'herein is a strange and wonderful thing.' He waved his arms to include the whole company in his exposition. 'Bagoas our chamberlain, it seems, will be made fit to marry and father children of his own when the Pharisees' new King and Messiah ascends the throne.'

The company waited. Nobody spoke.

'And Bagoas, I assure you, was made a eunuch in his youth. To serve the King, you understand. Nor could he be our chamberlain were he not a eunuch,' Herod explained, glancing round them all. Till his gaze settled on the chief physician.

It was obvious the King expected a comment from him, but the physician was silent.

'You have a view, physician?' questioned Herod when he judged the silence long enough.

'A view, Majesty,' the physician blustered. 'Our view, with respect, is that it is still impossible. Bagoas has been puffed up.'

'Lost his head, would you say, physician?' And Herod paused to give his audience time to prepare for what he considered was a shaft of wit. 'He'll not miss it, then, when we take it from him altogether.'

The company chuckled. For safety's sake.

'And the world will not miss its greatest fool.'

Herod would have been glad if that had ended the session. And he might have dismissed them all, but for Salome. She had the look of a woman who considered the agenda had not been completed. And he felt her condemning him for not dealing with Jochebed and Doris.

He half agreed with her. But, for all her silent arguing, it wasn't easy. However he might wish it himself, he could not easily rid himself of these two women. The nation still remembered the execution of Alexander and Aristobulus. He would invite even deeper hatred if he were to execute two women of the family. He could survive that, of course. What frightened him was the thought of their ghosts joining the ghost of the long dead Mariamne to haunt him even in his waking hours.

But Salome still stood and stared, willing him to act, her face set, her dark eyes burning, her whole body defiant.

Herod beckoned to the bodyguard standing nearest to him.

'Call the chief executioner,' he instructed, 'and invite Doris, the former Queen, to attend here.'

Salome felt the shock run through the company. She was surprised herself. And, for a minute, she regretted that she had defied her brother, and pushed him so far. Punishment she wanted and expected for Jochebed and Doris. But never this. Never murder.

She made to speak.

The King impatiently waved her to be silent. He was tired of his sister. Grateful, yes. She had done a fine job tracing and incriminating those who plotted against him. But she was robbing him of too much. He would miss Carus. And Bagoas, for all his stupidity, was the nearest thing he had to a friend. His sister was overstepping the mark.

The executioner arrived. Brusque, neat, efficient. Salome thought he looked almost jovial, a man with nothing more serious on his mind than his next social engagement.

He bowed his way into the King's presence.

The bodyguard paced more slowly behind him, followed by the former Queen.

Dignity in every step she took. An old lady. But old with age that had only matured her beauty. And she knew that every eye in the room measured her.

Even Herod. He tried to stand when she entered, but could not. But as well as he could manage, he sat like a King who knew he was receiving royalty.

He watched her. Tall, regal. Mascara and rouge discreetly enhancing the features of her lovely face. She was plumper, now, perhaps, than she had been all those years ago. But still beautiful. And, as he admired her, Herod knew why she had once enthralled him. But she was shrewd, too, and calculating. And that showed, now.

The company bowed and made way for her.

She saw none of them, her eyes fixed only on Herod as she made her royal way towards him. When she stopped, she realized she was standing beside the chief executioner. And suddenly she was afraid. For the first time in her life, she felt fear in the presence of the man by whom she had once been besotted. There he was sitting in front of her, feasting his senses in admiration of her, and yet she was afraid of him.

She curtsied in respect for the King's majesty.

Herod raised a hand in recognition, and then turned to address the executioner on her left. He eased forward as he spoke, reaching Salome's roll towards the executioner.

'I have marked those who are to die,' he said, 'and the manner of their death.'

The executioner took the roll, but did not read it. He toyed with it in his hands, not daring to raise his head, avoiding Doris's look.

Doris knew, now, the reason for her fear. She would go the way of Mariamne, her successor in Herod's heart and affection. Israel had a madman for a King. And this only proved it. It proved, too, that all her intrigues and calumnies against the King were right. If only she had succeeded . . .

The sound of Herod's voice cut into her thoughts. 'I will speak, now, of the former Queen,' he was saying. He was addressing the chief executioner, and he spoke as if she were not even there.

Doris shrugged to herself. So much for the courtesy of kings.

'I will speak of her intrigue, misdeeds and calumnies,' he went on. 'And of the penalty I have prescribed.'

Doris shut out the sound. She knew what the end of it all would be. She would not listen. She wouldn't give this man the pleasure of thinking that she even heard.

Deafening herself, she stared, flint-faced, her eyes burning into the King, willing him to look at her.

But his gaze was settled on the executioner. He could have looked anywhere else, and he'd have avoided the blinding beam of sunlight shafting through the window arch. But in case he might see her, he was fixed on the executioner.

Puffed eyes squinted. A swollen arm, red, blotched and scabby from endless scratching, lifted a podgy, ulcerated hand to block off the light, and it flopped, heavy, hurting. And he fought for breath after every exertion, heaving to gulp the air.

It was pitiful to watch.

And Doris felt pity for him, seeing this deformity of the man she once loved and was wife to. The eyes lost in the face pocked, scarred. The mouth parched, scabbed, struggling to shape words that came on stinking breath whose stench reached her even where she stood.

She didn't know what he was saying. But whatever it was, he stopped speaking. Slowly he turned his head and looked straight at her.

Doris jerked. Startled, frightened, apprehensive. Wondering how she would react when the blow fell.

'I have devised for you, madam,' he began, speaking slowly, deliberately, as though every word came from a chasm of pain, 'the only punishment you deserve and your misdeeds warrant.'

Doris waited as each word dragged out. No pity, now. Only hate for this man who seemed to revel in the torture he was inflicting.

'You will go from this palace . . . banished . . . a pauper, deprived of all rights, titles and properties and pensions. And I will look on your face no more.'

She saw the lips stop, the head turn away. But she heard nothing. Stunned, mesmerized. All she knew and understood was that she was not to die.

'Go,' moaned the King.

She felt the arm round her shoulders, turning her and leading her through the sculpted pillars of the doorway, into the long corridor.

In the shadow, as they walked, she looked to see her companion. It was Salome. And she smiled. She could always depend on Salome.

Yosef's problem was easier to see than to solve. And that he had a choice of courses he might take only aggravated his predicament.

He needed sound advice. Or rather, as he admitted to himself, he needed someone to confirm the plan already forming in his mind.

Whoever else he might consult, he was duty bound to see Shebna and Barzillai. They were, after all, his *pronubae*, his go-betweens with Joachim, who had arranged his promised marriage, and whose task it was to protect his interests till the wedding day.

It was more than time to thrash out the problem with them. But even as he made his way to meet the two men at Barzillai's house, Yosef still had no idea how he could tell them the complete story without appearing totally insane.

Barzillai, perhaps, would try to understand. He was that kind of man. With a human warmth about him. Secured against the snags and hardships that affect ordinary men, Barzillai took unending pains for his friends who were in trouble. He offered his opinions easily, and advice that sometimes sounded glib, as though it cost him nothing, and lacked judgement. But those who knew him well knew differently, and knew that he was usually right.

Shebna was different. A good man, indeed, but he had an inclination to be harsh. A man who sometimes allowed his judgement to be clouded by his prejudices. And, in the present atmosphere, this worried Yosef. For Shebna had no great regard for Galileans. And neither Nazareth nor its people held any real charms for him. It was a rotten town, in Shebna's view, and he agreed with whoever it was who first asked, 'Can any good thing come out of Nazareth?'

It would be difficult, Yosef decided, with Shebna.

The two men greeted him. Coldly, he thought, for friends.

Barzillai beckoned to his servant to offer his visitor the basin and towel.

Yosef accepted. But the atmosphere upset him. Their greeting had an angry face. Barzillai was courteous, but too formal, Yosef thought, for Barzillai. His heart was not in his welcome. And he looked strained, uneasy. Shebna was aloof, with a see-nothing look. Something rankled in his mind.

Yosef swilled his hands and face and feet. It was refreshing after the heat of travelling. He was drying his feet when it dawned on him . . . no wonder their welcoming was cool. He had made an unforgivable mistake. His friends already knew the state of his affairs. He must be a fool . . . for anybody who knew of the betrothal knew, as well, that Miriam was with child. Could he imagine that his two friends would be different . . .

'We know already, Yosef,' said Barzillai, breaking the silence as he ushered Yosef from the servant to a room whose grandeur, for an instant, overwhelmed him. He felt it was like a courtroom. And, inexplicably, he felt condemned.

'What's to be done?' asked Shebna.

Yosef noticed that the two men were already seated, while he was left standing. He felt a little like a prisoner before his judges. And he couldn't resist a smile as he looked around, but could find no cushion on which he could sit.

'I asked what is to be done,' Shebna said again. This time there was an edge to his voice, as he arranged himself haughtily, imperiously, on his seat.

Shebna was playing at judges, Yosef decided, and was

prepared to laugh. Until he realized that the man was in earnest. This was serious. And it was too much for Yosef.

'Ludicrous,' he shouted. 'Ludicrous and monstrous. You shall not be judge over me. I have offended you, but unwittingly. I left you to hear from gossipmongers—'

Shebna tensed, the anger rising, showing in the slitted eyes and reddening cheeks.

Barzillai sensed the brewing row. He sidled off his cushion and offered Yosef a seat. 'We are sorry for your trouble,' he said. 'We are sorry, too, that you did not tell us earlier. But now that you are here, we must remember we are friends, and try to help.'

While he was talking, Barzillai filled three generous cups of wine. The tension eased. He mumbled a consolation to Shebna as he offered him a drink. Shebna relaxed, and shifted his posture as judge.

'You'll marry the girl, of course,' Barzillai suggested, handing Yosef the wine.

Now Yosef understood their anger. If that's what they believed, their anger was justified. They believed he had disgraced them.

'I am not the father of the child,' he told them.

'Not the father of the child,' echoed Barzillai.

Shebna placed his cup on the table, walked across the room and put his hand on Yosef's shoulder. There was remorse in the touch.

'My brother Yosef,' he began, and his speech was slow. 'I am sorry I was angry with you without a cause.'

Yosef stood up, expecting Shebna to continue. But Barzillai interrupted.

'Who is the father, then?'

'Does it matter who the father is?' put in Shebna, annoyed at the irrelevant question.

Barzillai ignored him. 'Are you still prepared to go on with the marriage, Yosef?'

'He that retaineth an adulteress is a fool,' interjected Shebna. 'How can he marry the woman if she is already guilty of adultery?'

'You quote the Law too quickly, Shebna,' advised Barzillai, impatiently. 'The man, don't forget, is betrothed. Is he expected just to shrug the woman off? The Law says he need not marry her. It does not say he shall not.'

Shebna tried to make a point, but Barzillai was in full flight.

'Use the rules, Shebna, to help the couple, not like a mason's mallet to batter them. For when you've fixed the annulment of the contract, you're left with the problem still unsolved. The girl will still have her baby. She'll still be scorned, and her child cursed—'

Barzillai wasn't finished yet. But Yosef signalled him to stop. So he wound slowly to a halt, reminding Shebna that, in the end, there was Joachim to consider, and Anna whose heart was broken enough already.

Yosef began. The two men listened. They worried as the tale unfolded, alarmed that a young woman could concoct so blasphemous an excuse for her profligacy, frightened for Yosef's sanity, if he could believe half of what he told them now.

He finished. There was a tautness in the room. Nobody spoke, nothing stirred. Only the crackling of the cicadas reached in, daring to breach the stillness.

Joachim had long stopped trying to get information from his daughter, either by coaxing or by bullying. There was no moving her from the tale she first told. She stuck obstinately to her story of the angel's visit, and steadfastly refused to name the father of the child.

He could forgive her, but forgiveness brought him no nearer to understanding. And he was weary, now, of struggling to find a clue.

He despised himself for the chasm that had grown between himself and his daughter, but there was nothing, any more, that he could think of to span it. He waited, dreading the inevitable day when Yosef would put an end to his contract to marry Miriam. His heart was heavy when he thought of what would become of Miriam then. His mind reeled with terror when he thought of what would happen if they found her guilty of adultery. Had they a mind to, they could stone her to death outside his own front door.

Anna tried to console her husband. She worried for her daughter's health, and the child she carried. Having a child in ordinary circumstances was hard enough, but this strain and tension could not but take their toll.

Anna herself was oppressed by the atmosphere in the house, saying Amen to family prayers that had a hollow ring, flailing at the painful silences with talk and chatter that, sometimes, sounded nonsense, protecting Miriam from the neighbours that came, prying, to the door, or stood within earshot of the house, and with the mocking sympathy of gossips, sorrowed loudly at the degradation that had befallen Joachim's household.

She tried to comfort Miriam. But it was a bitter kind of comfort, now, with no love in it. She sometimes found it hard to be warm towards her daughter whose explanation of her condition had her hovering between terror at what would be the outcome of her daughter's flying in the face of God, and pity for her sad, lost girl, stricken with madness.

The days were far too long for Miriam. Her once carefree hours now were worlds away. She no longer ran in the wild hills. No flowers blossomed there. And the grass that once had made a carpet for her feet was burned, brown, and withered in the sun.

Yosef came no more.

She felt old and worn and weary. And she fretted in a

mind too tired, now, to seek solutions, or wonder what the end would be.

It was hot, the sun high. The parched ground shimmering back the heat.

Miriam balanced the water pot on her shoulder, wiped the teeming perspiration from her brow, and dried her hands on the hem of her skirt. Even the jutting stones she trod were hot, and the burning dust showered her sandals, caking her sweating feet.

It was the wrong time to be out. But for her, it was the best time. Nazareth slept its siesta, there would be nobody about. She could collect the water for the household, and still avoid the scornful women at the well. If they didn't see her, they couldn't mutter about her, and brand her *maggi-dala*, harlot.

She walked carefully for fear of being heard, glancing right and left for fear of being spied on. She passed a beggar asleep beneath a stunted palm tree. Miriam crept quietly by. The old man stirred but didn't wake. A mangy dog, stretched out beside him, eyed her, and moved a listless tail. Miriam smiled at the touch of friendliness and felt the tears fill up her eyes.

In the bright sunshine, the water glistened in rivulets down the steps from the black, gaping cavern of the well, seeping itself into the dryness in the ground around.

Miriam kicked off her sandals as she drew near, and mounted the uneven steps, swishing her feet in the fresh-water coolness. At the top, she put down her water pot, stooped and dowsed her face, and sat to rest, relaxed in the cool air of the deep cave that sheltered the spring.

Her hands idled in the water. And she buried her face in the swimming ripples.

There was peace in the murmuring stillness.

It was good to be here, she thought. And she remembered

the noisy days, not long ago, when the cave echoed with the nonsense talk and laughter of them all, and the way they joked when they heard she was betrothed. They were good days then. If only she could start at the beginning again . . . The baby swelling in her womb told her there was no going back . . .

'Miriam,' a voice sounded through her reverie.

Startled, Miriam looked up to see a figure move in the half-dark on the far side of the cave. She snatched her water pot, filled it quickly, and made to go.

'Miriam . . . don't go. It's me. Rachel.'

Rachel was running towards her, her arms outstretched, her veil and shawl billowing behind.

'So it's true,' she said as she came closer to Miriam. 'You are with child.'

Miriam nodded.

'Imagine . . . you of all people. They said you were. But I didn't believe them. Then you stopped coming when we're all here—'

Miriam began an explanation.

'Oh, I know exactly how you feel,' assured Rachel, not allowing Miriam to get properly started. 'It's happened to me. But after a while you grow accustomed to it.'

Miriam listened, seeing the lovely face, etched with the wear of life and scarred with the lines of sickness. She watched the mouth shaping the words that kindly tried to make light of the burden she could hardly bear.

'Rachel, Rachel—' The words were whisper soft, almost unsounded. Tears welled in the eyes that searched for comfort in the face of a friend.

'Dear Miriam.' And Rachel comforted her like an infant in her bosom, smoothing a gentle hand on the sobbing head that confided the strangest story she had ever heard from a girl in trouble. But Rachel listened. In dumbfounded silence.

When Miriam stopped, Rachel laughed. There was no

mockery in the laughter, though. It dismissed a problem that, Rachel reckoned, did not exist.

'Angels are not good enough, dear,' she advised her. 'You'll have to find a man.'

'But there was no man—'

'There's nobody will believe that,' Rachel explained, her hand rising and falling on the veiled head in time with each syllable, patting her opinion, as it were, into the head too confused to take it.

They were both silent.

Rachel struggled hard to find how best to offer her advice. But there was no neat way, she at last decided. The only thing was to blurt it out, and hope for the best. 'Blame it on Yosef, and your problems are solved.'

Miriam jerked her head up. Gazing, unbelieving.

Right or wrong, Rachel couldn't tell. But she'd started, so she'd go on. 'It stands to reason,' she declared, with a feeling of pride that her experience of the world of men could be useful to somebody. 'Yosef can't prove he isn't the father. It's your word against his. After all, he is betrothed to you. You're made, girl. And he'll have to marry you—'

'But it wasn't Yosef,' came the disarming reply.

Rachel felt stymied. The girl meant it. And she searched Miriam's incredulous face to prove it was a lie. But there was no guile, no cunning. This unfortunate girl knew nothing about real life.

And Rachel pitied her.

But if she hoped to get out of this mess, what she didn't know, she'd have to learn very quickly, Rachel decided. And she launched herself into the task of giving her innocent lamb some vixen cunning.

'Let me explain, Miriam,' she began, taking her pupil's hands in hers. 'You're in the family way, and you're not married. So. At the moment you're a bit of gossip. But don't let that worry you. You're not the first. And tomorrow there'll be somebody else. And the scandal won't kill you.'

Rachel was motherly. Her voice was tender. And as she spoke, she gazed at Miriam's hands, stroking them absent-mindedly.

'But start telling them it was an angel, Miriam, and they'll have you. They'll hate you. They'll say you're possessed of the devil . . . You'll be lucky if they don't kill you. They'll stone you to death for blasphemy.'

She paused to let her message sink in. Miriam sat stock still.

'So,' Rachel resumed, 'like it or not, you'll have to have a man. And Yosef of Bethlehem, I reckon, is as good as any.'

Miriam started back, pulling her hands away. 'I tell you, it wasn't Yosef.' Miriam was angry.

'So it wasn't Yosef. All right.' And there was a hint of exasperation. 'I don't really care who it was. And they don't care either. So long as it's a man . . . don't you understand, Miriam. I'm trying to get you out of a mess. Let it be any man. A merchant on business in the city. A soldier on leave from Caesarea who took you in a cornfield . . . it happens a thousand times a day in Nazareth—'

'Stop! Stop!'

Miriam's anger filled the cave. 'You'd have me no better than a whore.'

'Whores are women,' breathed Rachel.

Miriam heard the faraway sorrow in the voice.

'Rachel, forgive me,' she begged, holding her friend's face in her hands.

Rachel threw the episode away with a weary shaking of her head.

'You could say it was rape,' she said. 'They'd pity you for that.' But it was half-hearted. There was no spirit in her tongue.

They sat, neither of them knowing how to restart the conversation. Miriam rubbed the droplets of water off the water pot. Rachel ploughed her hand backwards and forwards in the pool, slapping the surface every now and then, as though retaliating for all the hurts she'd endured in life, yet glad to know that her vengeance could not harm the water.

They both heard the commotion at the same time. They looked, startled, at each other.

Siesta time was ended, and the women, some of them with their boisterous children, were out in the streets again, and heading towards the well.

Miriam grabbed her water pot, splashing it in her face as she raised it to balance it on her shoulder, and dashed away.

Rachel raced after her, and caught her at the bottom of the steps. 'Don't run away, Miriam,' she pleaded. 'Stop and face them. Do it now, and it's done with. I'll stay with you.'

But Miriam couldn't stop. She was too afraid. She could hear them coming nearer and nearer. It seemed as though all Nazareth were advancing on her. And she could hear the cloud of conversation getting louder.

She tugged her shawl from Rachel's grip, and raced away.

Joachim stood among the vine leaves on the terraced patch above the house, and scanned what roads he could see, down towards the town, for Miriam. She was a long time gone, he reckoned. She was usually back before siesta time ended. And he was concerned.

He mocked himself for imagining he could see so far with faded eyes. He shook his head disconsolately, and told himself he was getting old.

A little way to his left, he made out two men walking. They walked officiously, urgently. He felt he recognized them. Not from their appearances, for he couldn't see their features, so much as from the sense of foreboding that overwhelmed him as soon as he'd caught sight of them.

It was Barzillai and Shebna.

The old man made his way carefully from one terrace to the next, avoiding the stones that had fallen from the drystone walls, till he reached the level ground.

'Anna,' he called as he came into the house, 'get out the cups and the wine. Two guests are coming.'

The visit would be as painful for them as it would be for himself, he judged. There was no reason why he should not make them welcome. It was a relief that they'd come. What the outcome would be, he didn't even want to guess. But at least it was an end to the waiting and the apprehension.

The greetings on both sides were formal. The warmth and glow of friendship he had known in the days when they'd come seeking Miriam for Yosef were gone. In those days, Joachim remembered, Shebna executed his task efficiently. But reluctantly. As though he never quite approved of Yosef's choice.

Joachim measured Shebna now, but couldn't make up his mind whether it was satisfaction or sorrow that brought the frown to the man's face.

Anna brought the wine. And quickly went again, flouncing her skirt, shooing away some pecking hens, as though they might overhear the conversation.

Joachim filled and distributed the cups. He sat his visitors beneath the trees whose cooling shade stretched along the dry ground, to touch the house, and rest along the wall.

'My brothers,' Joachim began, and he spoke softly, lifelessly. 'What can I say? For my daughter's grievous fault I am sorry. For any wrong she has done against Yosef, I am in your hands—'

The two visitors watched, the wine cups in their hands still untouched. Barzillai made to speak, but Joachim had not finished.

'Those words do not say what my mind wants to say. I am grieved by my daughter's state but, understand, my daughter is, too. And tortured by the scorn and ridicule they heap on her in the town . . . as though she had committed the wrong all by herself . . . with no Yosef there—' He hardly paused. And there was anger, now, frustration, hurt. 'My wife, my family, my whole household are the laughing-stock of Nazareth . . . Treat *me*, my brothers, how you like. But do not stand in judgement on my daughter, my wife, or any of my household.'

He stopped, looking vacantly towards the trees, not noticing that Barzillai was preparing to speak again.

'My daughter is no trollop, as you both well know,' Joachim murmured defiantly. He turned his head, ignoring Shebna, and looked directly at Barzillai. 'The child she carries belongs to no other man but Yosef—' He paused, and when he spoke again there was the sound of sadness, of dereliction.

Barzillai heard the emptiness, and was sorry for the man. He put his cup on the ground and stood up, Shebna following his example.

'We have come,' he offered, 'to speak on Yosef's behalf.'

'Can the man not speak for himself? Or has he gone to Bethlehem to spread the news that they might taunt his father—?'

'We were his appointed go-betweens, after all,' Barzillai advised gently, with sympathy. 'And it is a delicate matter.'

Joachim nodded.

Barzillai continued, 'Yosef wishes me to say that he will not sue to break his contract to marry your daughter.'

'And Yosef is a fool,' hissed Shebna through his beard.

Joachim ignored him, trying to concentrate on Barzillai's news. Had he really nothing more to worry about? Could it be that Miriam had been shielding Yosef all along, and now at last the truth was coming out? Yet there was no admission

in Barzillai's curt message. Was Yosef the father of his
daughter's child or was he not? But what matter now? His
daughter would be married.

And he reached in gratitude to touch Barzillai's hand. But
the younger man gestured that he was not quite finished.
Joachim drew back. It was not going to be easy, after all.

'Yosef declares, by God, that he is not the father of your
daughter's child,' Barzillai was saying. 'He is an honourable,
law-abiding man, and we believe him.'

'And if he were not an altogether stupid man,' cut in
Shebna, 'in the circumstances he'd do what he's told, and
save his reputation by being rid of her.'

Joachim heard the words, and felt the hurt – for himself,
and for his daughter.

'Barzillai,' he pleaded, 'what does this mean? You would
not play with my daughter. If she has wronged Yosef, then
Yosef knows the course he must take. He must end the
contract.'

'My opinion exactly,' observed Shebna.

'And nobody wants your opinion,' Barzillai rounded on
him. 'Nor did Yosef send you here with permission to
express it.'

Shebna drew himself up to retaliate, disdaining the man
who was to receive his onslaught, flexing his lips while he
measured his words.

Barzillai waited, but nothing further came from Shebna.
He merely stood there, pouting his contempt. Barzillai
turned back to Joachim.

'I began badly,' he said. 'I wanted to be kind, to bring
you gently to understand what Yosef had in mind to do, and
why. But I have upset you. And, worse, I gave you false
hopes.'

'I am grateful that you intended to be kind,' replied
Joachim. 'Yet, even if it hurts, I would rather know quickly
and plainly what is to happen. My daughter will soon return,

and I would rather you were not here when she comes. It were easier for her to hear whatever news it is from me alone.'

Barzillai nodded; he understood. And he felt for the old man in his predicament. He spoke quietly. 'Yosef is not the father of your daughter's child.'

Joachim winced at the insistence.

'We all know the Law, Joachim. Because they are betrothed, the Law treats them as though they are man and wife. Your daughter is now . . . as though she were a wife who has committed adultery.'

Joachim tried to speak, but no words came.

'For this, Yosef is entitled to bring her to court – to prosecute her in court and have their contract of marriage set aside.'

'And have my daughter publicly damned as an adulteress?' interrupted Joachim. 'He would surely not do that.'

'Could you believe how dearly Yosef loves your daughter, you would know he would never make a public example of her.'

Joachim wanted to believe.

'And what I am to tell you, today, is that Yosef has decided he will not sue. There will be no public court case, no public disgrace.'

'But *has* my daughter committed adultery?' searched Joachim. 'Who is the other man?'

Barzillai slowly raised his shoulders and stretched out his arms, his hands wide open.

'Miriam, as you know yourself, tells her own story to explain the conception of the child she carries. But Yosef cannot believe that story. He cannot understand it, any more than I can . . . Can *you* believe it?'

Joachim spread out his own hands. He had no answer for Barzillai, who bowed his head in acknowledgement.

'Yet your daughter is no liar,' Barzillai continued. 'And

Yosef will not call her an adulteress. But Miriam will not let him dismiss her tale. Were he to present such a tale in court, she would be branded a blasphemer.'

Barzillai paused, but Joachim knew what else was in his mind, and spoke it for him. 'Then Miriam would be stoned to death.'

For all the warmth of the day, Joachim suddenly felt cold – chilled by the fear that overtook him as the tragic truth of this conclusion ate into his thoughts.

It was Barzillai who finally broke the silence.

'Your daughter's story may be no more than the fancy of a demented young woman . . . possessed of devils. Who can say? If she is in fact mad, please God it is a passing madness. Yosef would rather she be pitied than punished.'

Joachim was listening, head bowed, shoulders drooping, hearing spoken the thoughts that had pulsed without ceasing in his mind for almost three months now. Whatever the outcome of it all, he told himself, he would never doubt that Yosef was a good man. He was sorry for him.

'But there will be no marriage,' Barzillai was saying, struggling to be kind, trying to pour salve on the wound he knew he was inflicting, yet urgent to speak plain the message Yosef had sent him to deliver. 'No marriage,' he repeated, as though Joachim had not heard.

Joachim did hear. The wedding day they'd settled on just a year ago would soon be here. But now it would come and . . . and go . . . and his poor daughter . . . poor, wretched, afflicted Miriam . . . O thou afflicted, tossed with tempest, and not comforted . . . And his wife . . .

Barzillai was still explaining. 'To save shaming Miriam in public, to ease some of the hurt you yourself and your wife must feel, Yosef would rather breach the contract quietly and privately. He will not prosecute Miriam, but neither will he – and you will understand yourself the hurt and sorrow he himself feels – neither will he marry her.'

Joachim raised his head and searched the faces of his two visitors. For a while nobody spoke.

'Does Yosef realize what he's doing?' asked Joachim, at last, trying to make sense of Yosef's plan.

'I think he does,' Barzillai reassured him. 'We have discussed it over and over again. And Shebna here has tried to dissuade him from this course. He has tried to make Yosef understand the invidious position in which he'll place himself.'

Shebna nodded, pleased to be drawn back into the conversation.

'But if he does neither one thing nor the other,' advised Joachim, if he neither takes her in marriage nor sues to breach the contract, it will look as though he's reneging on his promise. He will be bringing the scandal on his own head. They'll hate him, and the loathing they now feel towards Miriam will be turned on him – only with even more venom.'

'We've told him all that,' said Shebna, and now there was humanity, pity in his tone. 'He seems to understand everything his actions will entail. But it was he who first decided on this course, and he is adamant that this is how it all should be.'

'But why?' asked Joachim.

Nobody answered.

Then Shebna pointed down the hill. The others turned and saw Miriam hastening towards them, her water pot on her shoulder.

The two visitors took their leave. And Joachim waited.

CHAPTER FOUR

Yosef's decision brought him no ease. There was
something about it that he felt was not right. He
knew no peace. The problem chiselled at him in the
burning brightness of the day, and stalked, relentless, in the sleeping darkness of the night.

By day he argued the rightness, the kindness and justice
of his act. By night, the juries that held court at the far
corners of his mind judged it was really no solution at all.
In the long run, the scandalmongers would ferret out the
truth, they'd realize they had been duped. And then
they'd set themselves to make life a hell for the woman he
declared he loved, and whose welfare his decision sought to
serve.

Each night it was the same. Faceless voices. Pummelling,
pounding speech, questing, probing. Leaving him racked in
the early watches of the day, their repeated mockery clinging
to the tatters of his brain. All the time sifting, sifting, 'And
what if her story be true—'

He worked at the house that was to have been their home,
and finished it. But he had no relish for the task. He felt
forced to do it. It had to be done. He was a proud craftsman,

and it was against his nature to leave a job uncompleted. But there was no satisfaction now; the joy had died.

Not even the guest-room on the roof, when he'd finished it, gave him any pleasure. It hurt, in fact. It recalled his promise, and the first day he'd brought Miriam to see their home.

All the while her voice was in the house. And all the noise he could make would not still the sound. She moved where he moved, stopped where he stopped.

He recalled the days when this delighted him, when he enjoyed sensing her presence, and revelled in imagining the comments she would make on each piece of work. But now it was a torture.

Yet he felt he must struggle to keep going till everything about the place was done as well as he could do it. The house he built must not be a standing mockery of his craftsmanship.

Bezaleel's manger wasn't right, he reckoned. He saw the wrought-iron basket on the platform wall was askew. Hardly noticeable. But it offended his professional eye. And he reprimanded himself for his lack of care in the first instance.

Now, carefully, he prised the manger from the stone, chipped out the holes for the new nails, and secured the basket in its new position. This time it was right. It looked right. Now it looked a craftsman's job.

Unconsciously, he stood back to admire his handiwork. And Miriam's whisper to him on their first day in the house came, haunting, back to him. 'When our firstborn comes,' her voice said, 'we'll sleep him in it for safety and for warmth—'

'Dear God,' he cried out in pain, 'must everything be agony—'

But there was no answer in the well-built, lonely house,

where his own voice gave no echo back, and all the sounds had died.

Nazareth was about its business on market day. The city was bustling. Wares spilled off stalls into the streets. Beggars plied their trade, preying on the emotions of passers-by for an extra pittance. Scavenger dogs had a field day in the junk and dirt that strewed the streets. Drovers shouted and cursed their way through with sheep and cattle. And frightened groups of the pious squeezed themselves tight against the walls, letting them pass, to avoid contamination. Soldiers marched, some with the conqueror's abandon, some with the lonely march of men sad in the land they occupied in Caesar's name, homesick for their families.

Two lads played hide-and-seek, dodging in and out of the measured steps of a priest mincing his way to his religion.

Rachel picked her way along. She still felt tired: worn from days of battling with another bout of her old sickness. Was there no cure for it, she wondered. Would she ever be free of it? She was observing the two soldiers swaggering towards her in the mêlée. They'd noticed her. And she smiled to herself, watching them suddenly adopt their men-of-the-world air as soon as they spotted her.

Out of the corner of her eye, she caught sight of the women. They had clustered round the baker's shop. And they had her under view, agog to see just what would happen, their curiosity willing her, their disgust judging her.

And the soldiers measuring her.

But what a disappointment they were all going to get. The soldiers included. Though it would be difficult, she reckoned, to imagine they'd believe she'd come out for no other purpose than buying bread – just like the poor silly women craning their heads to miss nothing of the harlot's progress.

But she couldn't avoid the soldiers. To dodge out of their path meant landing in a pile of fish guts on one side or finishing up on the other in great heaps of putrifying fruit. To turn back in the opposite direction would be an open invitation to Caesar's fighting men. It might please the soldiers. It would certainly excite the gawping women.

But she was in the mood for neither. She was too sick to be interested. All she wanted was bread from Isaac's shop – and to struggle home again.

The soldiers slowed slightly as they drew nearer. Rachel's practised eye took them in quickly. They were hardly more than lads, with no more experience than they mustered from the tales they'd heard in the barrack room.

She walked by as though the soldiers weren't even there. She was aware of their surprise that she hadn't so much as looked in their direction. But she was past. The soldiers were gone. And she felt relieved.

There was an awkward silence among the women when she reached the baker's shop. Things had so obviously not gone the way they'd expected. And they were disappointed. They were angry.

Rachel wasn't sure whether to hate or pity them. Did they despise her because they were jealous of her, or because she disgusted them? But how little they knew, married as they were, protected at least, if they were not loved. And safe and clean. They could never know how much she longed to change places with any one of them.

She took her place on the fringe of the group, waiting for the atmosphere to ease. The soft, comforting smell of baking bread made her feel hungry. And she realized she'd not eaten since yesterday's breakfast.

She knew all the women: five of them. She'd never call them her friends – not that they ever showed any great friendship towards her. Indeed, sometimes, she felt that, if they didn't exactly despise her, they certainly resented her.

Some of them she knew only from meeting them at the well or in the market, in the shops or at the stalls. Like Leah, soft-eyed and beautiful. She could have any man she liked, Rachel reckoned. And Rebecca, the only widow among them. The others – Hannah, Sarah and Abigail – she knew better. They were near neighbours.

Hannah was tiny and skinny, with a sharp tongue and a voice to match it. How any man could live with her, Rachel couldn't understand. But, nevertheless, she had a husband: a wisp of a thing who'd given her five children.

Sarah was fat, flabby and slovenly, but soft-natured with it. Rachel supposed her husband would call her comfortable. And she envied Sarah her gentleman of a husband, even her seven fat, slovenly but happy children.

She saw Abigail skulking, waiting to intrude herself into this group who had no great love for her. They'd have been happier had she not been there at all.

So would Rachel. Abigail lived three houses away from her. With seven children and a miserable, browbeaten husband, in a hovel not much better than her own. Yet this same woman had not spoken to her for years, and would look through her if they passed in the street.

Abigail turned her sour, brittle face to stare at her. And from the corner of an ugly mouth, lisped some sarcasm about 'not talking to the soldiers today' that was meant to hurt.

Rachel winced a bit, but was glad it had happened. Abigail, whatever her intentions, had broken the silence.

And everybody seemed glad. Now the banter began. Desultory at first, with no interest in it, but slowly gathering. From Leah here, Rebecca there. And Hannah chirping in now and again, with her well-known inconsequentialities which everybody, from long experience, ignored. Sarcasm. Insult. Raucous, crude, but building, quickening, warming with humour, till the air was cleared of the first awkwardness.

And they wanted to know what gossip Rachel had.

She had none.

But they couldn't believe that. 'You couldn't be missing for four or five days without hearing something we've not heard,' Hannah assured her.

'Would you ever ask me have I been sick, dying, for four or five days?' retorted Rachel.

Sarah folded her flabby arms over her bosom, and hoisted herself together. 'Any news of Miriam, then?' she asked.

It was an innocent-sounding question, but suddenly everybody was all ears. Even Isaac, in the process of pulling the bread from the oven, stopped. His buxom wife Deborah, red-faced and perspiring from kneading another batch of bread, eased her chubby hands on to the baker's long handle, and prodded it into Isaac's ribs, reminding him there was work to do, if the bread was not to be burned.

'I've not seen Miriam for weeks,' said Rachel.

They were crestfallen.

'Well, is the wedding on or off?' queried Rebecca, not sure whom she was addressing, so long as she got an answer.

But nobody knew.

'If the baby's his, he'll have to marry her,' chimed Leah, fluttering her eyelashes.

'But Joachim's foolish daughter says it's not,' Rebecca offered. 'She's still sticking to her story about the angel.'

And Hannah chirped, 'I'll have my next by an angel.'

But Rebecca was serious. 'I believe Yosef of Bethlehem declares he's not the father of her child. So what's going to happen?'

Nobody offered an opinion.

All heads turned towards Isaac who, by now, had laid the batches on the slab, and was prepared to serve his customers. He kept them waiting for an answer till they'd each bought their bread.

Then he spoke. 'I don't know what's going to happen.'

He spoke slowly, deliberately, like a man who considered he was expected to be wise. 'But I say that something better happen soon. And if they both agree that Yosef the Bethlehemite is not the father of the child, then Yosef better get moving quick, and annul the contract.'

'If he's from Bethlehem, he's a southerner,' proclaimed Sarah. 'You can't trust these Southerners.'

'I don't know,' said Isaac, trying to be impartial, and remembering his grandfather came from Hebron, in the south. 'I must say I like the man. He struck me as an honest, godfearing man.'

'And where does that leave the girl, then?' Sarah wanted to know. 'Are you going to tell us she's an adulteress?'

'Well now,' breathed Isaac, warming to his task of enlightening his customers on the frailties of human nature, 'I look on Joachim's wretched daughter—'

But he stopped. And stared.

They all turned towards the door, to see what he was staring at.

There, stooped, haggard, holding the doorpost for strength, was Joachim. The fading light of the dulling day fretted around him, silhouetting his lonely shape between the doorposts, filtering his wan shadow into the well-worn darkness of the shop floor. His face was lost in shadow, and he made no move to speak.

Embarrassed, they filed out one by one. Leah, Rebecca, Abigail, Sarah, Hannah. Not looking, trying not to see Joachim as they squeezed past him into the darkening sun that heralded the coming wind. Hoping their broken neighbour would not notice them.

They left Rachel waiting.

Isaac, who had spoken so much, could find no more to say. He worried. And wondered how much Joachim had heard. He toyed with a loaf on the counter. His wife busied her flour-dusted hands in tidying the dough-pocked basins.

Joachim shuffled in, took the bread he'd come for, and paid. He spoke no word.

Rachel watched. And bit her lip in sorrow for the woebegone man.

Joachim faltered as he passed her, the uneven ground catching his unsure steps.

Rachel caught him as he stumbled. He looked at her, but there was no liveliness in his face, and the light had died in his eyes.

She linked the trembling arm in hers. And through the gathering storm, she led the old man gently towards his home.

The storm raged at the house, the wind whining, seething its fury through crevices in the walls. Gusting, angry rain beat on the door, seeping through where the two halves joined, trickling like tears down the parched wood to the floor.

The shutters, hastily placed to block up the windows, could no longer stand the pounding. The violence outside had found the weak spots in the old skins on their warped frames, and now shamelessly, remorselessly, shredded them, adding the whipping of their flitters to the clamour that already filled the house.

Everybody moved noisily, clumsily, coping as quickly and as well as they could in the sudden darkness where only the sneaking glow of the fire gave any hint of light.

Miriam lit a lamp, shielding its flaring brightness till the flame took hold. The dancing light startled the hens, perched, frightened, among the pots and jars on the shelf near a tormented window. A cockerel, roosting on the manger, shook his comb and tried to look brave. Miriam couldn't help smiling to herself at his pomposity.

Joachim, not long home, and still wet from the sudden downpour, nursed life into the fire. And it went through his mind that the commotion caused by the storm wasn't such a bad thing, after all. At least it distracted them, even for a little while, from the obsession that had afflicted them all for too long. It would do his wife good, too, though he knew she'd be annoyed at everything being so topsy-turvy when the start of Sabbath could not be all that far away.

From the corner of his eye, he watched her, on the opposite side of the brightening fire, nursing the lamb he'd rescued from the deluge. There was a calmness in her face, and in her eyes a peace he'd not seen there for many a day.

The storm was dying now. And above the slight fluttering from the torn skins in the windows, he heard Anna's soft voice keening, her gentle crooning soothing the fear and pain from the lamb in her lap. And he watched her motherly hands caressing the woolly frailty, easing tenderness and healing into its injured limb.

Anna looked at him, and caught him peeping at her. She blushed a little. And she smiled. How long was it since he'd seen her smile? And his heart lifted.

'Come now, Joachim,' she said, feigning annoyance, 'it'll soon be Sabbath call, and just look at the state of this place.'

Anna cherished the lamb, and made across the room. 'Off bird,' she shouted at the cockerel, shooing him off his perch.

The bird launched himself angrily towards the hens' shelf, disturbing them all, till he got himself comfortably ensconced. And then turned, watching Anna, chuntering while he watched.

'He's a noisy bird,' Anna explained to the lamb as she puckered the hay in the manger. 'But you just lie there, and have no fear.' And she laid the lamb, like a baby, in the hay.

Snuggled in, the lamb made no stir, even when the trumpet in Nazareth sounded its clarion over the booths, shops, fields, houses and busy people.

In Joachim's house they heard the sound, and knew that in half an hour the sun would set, and Sabbath would begin.

Joachim took his woollen cloak from the peg near the door. It never crossed his mind to explain what he was doing. He did it automatically, naturally. He'd done it every week since he was married. It was routine, as much for the family as for himself.

And, as she always did, Anna gathered the cloak about him. Even her advice was a refrain, a catchword of the long years of being Joachim's wife. 'It'll be cold when you're coming back from synagogue,' she said.

Joachim pulled open the heavy door.

The storm was ended, the wind and the rain gone. The ground, revived and refreshed for a little while, oozed its delight into the quiet air, drugging the slowly coming night with heady scents.

Devoutly Joachim touched the Shema scroll on the doorpost, kissed his fingers, and was on his way, the head of the house, to join the heads of other houses in the synagogue to prepare for Sabbath.

Anna was sorry there was so much to do, for there was so little time. But they buckled to, bustling for the next half-hour, cleaning, clearing, sweeping, tidying, storing, so that everything would be right and ready for the Sabbath. She set the low table in the upper part of the house for supper. Miriam gave the floor a last quick sweep, and stored the broom away till the Sabbath was gone. Anna prepared the cup of wine, and the water that Joachim would need for hallowing the Sabbath, and placed them on the stand near the door.

The woman of the house gave a last look round. She was satisfied. Everything was ready. And they stood at the door to greet her husband on his return.

Anna watched her husband separate himself from the cluster of men coming up the hill. As he drew near, she wondered to herself if tonight he would bring a blessing with him.

But there was no fervour in his voice that prayed at the threshold.

Joachim hung his cloak on the peg. His family formed a semi-circle near the stand that held the wine cup and the jug, ready for the hallowing.

Anna watched him hold the cup in his hands, as he asked that God would bless them on the Sabbath Day. 'God for it, and God over it,' he said. But it was a formal prayer, Anna thought, as she received the cup from her husband. There was no spirit in his words.

They each drank from the cup, and Joachim returned it to the stand, and took the jug.

Anna held out her hands, and Joachim poured some water over them. And it splashed brightly on the floor. Salome, his younger daughter, next. Then Miriam stretched her hands. Joachim poured. Nervously. And the water trickled uncertainly.

They went to supper.

Salome tried to start a conversation when the formalities of their religion were over, but it was a desultory thing that had not strength enough to last.

They finished their meal in silence and went to bed.

The cockerel got his own back. The new day had hardly touched the sky, and his raucous screeching through the house had the family out of bed.

Joachim opened the top half of the door, and leaned out to greet the morning.

The cockerel and his brood needed no urging to be out. Their beating wings made a din as they flew through the opening. They scampered about the muddy ground, scratching, pecking, searching.

Anna looked at her lamb. Its eyes beamed back at her, the

body wriggled, and the tail twitched nervously, rustling the hay. Anna lifted him from the manger, and ran her hand along last night's injured leg. It seemed all right. She stood him gently on the ground. He steadied himself, and then began to frisk around, the tail flailing backwards and forwards.

He was better, Anna decided. She poured him a dish of milk, and led him out by the wall to drink. The goats in the far corner looked on. Anna couldn't be sure whether they approved or not.

Herod disliked Jerusalem on the Sabbath Day. Not that he was greatly enamoured of the city on any day. Indeed, he was never sure why he stayed in the place at all.

Sometimes he beguiled himself with the notion that he stayed to please his people. They thought that Jerusalem was where the king ought to be. So he stayed, but in comfort: in the splendid magnificence of the palace he built for himself on the west side of the city.

Three towering castles of white marble protected the palace, set in its parklands of trees and fountains, groves, pools, walks and artificial rivers. Gold, silver and precious stones gleamed on every side in the palace itself. Ceilings and walls elaborately carved in rooms so large they could hold hundreds of guests at a time.

And he'd have been delighted had the people of Jerusalem used the parklands for their enjoyment. Some did. But most didn't. The carvings and statues that decorated the park, they complained, desecrated Jerusalem. It was stupidity like that which made him wonder why he bothered to live in the city.

But he wondered, sometimes, if he stayed, in fact, to honour the memory of Antipater his father, and to remind himself of how it all began. But they were rare times. Private moments, when he thought of how different things might have been. Frightening moments, when he remembered that the King of Palestine was the offspring of at least two generations of slaves

He did not dare search back beyond his grandfather who had been a slave in the shrine of Apollo-Melkart in Askelon.

His father Antipater had been a temple slave in Jerusalem. And might have continued so had Pompey not captured the city.

Antipater, the temple cleaner, betrayed a friend to the conquerors, and began his career of bettering himself. He married well when he married Cypros, the daughter of an eminent Arabian family. He wheedled his way into Caesar's favour. And Caesar, as a reward for services rendered, appointed him procurator of Jerusalem.

It was the beginning.

Twenty years after he'd begun his social climb from destitution to power, Antipater was poisoned. His assassination made way for the appointment of his son Herod as Tetrarch.

Herod owed his father so much. Yet, for all his sense of gratitude, he sometimes felt he was ashamed of his father's past, and would rather those around him did not know of it. For all the deep, indelible, oft-recurring memories, he put up no prominent memorials to his father. And he could find no explanation that would satisfy him. He called his palace in Jericho 'Cypros' in memory of his mother. He could not bring himself to have so solid a reminder of his father and his past.

Given the choice, he'd have moved out of Jerusalem altogether, and lived in his palace in Jericho.

Jericho had all he liked, the way he liked it: style, dignity. And up-to-date architecture that could hold its own with the best in Greece and Rome. It was a city to be proud of.

He chuckled, and told himself he was right to be proud. He'd built it. And given half a chance, he could do the same for Jerusalem. If the place had anything at all today, it had only him to thank. A forum, a theatre. Even Rome was impressed by the Antonia Palace he had built on the northeast corner of the city. And, however the nation might despise him for not being a full-blooded Jew, they still stood in awe and admiration of the Temple he had restored for them. Restored ... He had demolished what they called Solomon's glory brick by brick. What they now had surpassed anything Solomon could have built. And flocking pilgrims from the world over said so.

But the Jerusalemites complained. He had erected an eagle of gleaming gold over the portico. They called it an idol and a desecration, and were constantly threatening to pull it down.

And one of these days they would, he reckoned. But not today. Today was the Sabbath. And but for the services in the Temple, nothing happened, nothing was allowed to happen in Jerusalem on the Sabbath Day.

And that, he decided, was why he disliked the Sabbath Day in Jerusalem. The Jerusalemites seemed to relish making a sadness of their religion. They made the city drab – and he disliked drabness.

Especially today. Today he felt good. He had wakened with the dawn. Fitter than he'd been for weeks, and well enough to struggle, unaided, out of bed, and make his way – slowly, arduously maybe, but by himself – across the room, to stand by the window.

His house was full of his family and their guests, waiting to be entertained. The city was full enough with people searching for diversion. He could see the crowds from where he stood, thronging the tree-lined avenue in front of the palace, milling in Xystos Square. Down the hill, beyond the park, crowding across the Tyropoeon Bridge. Arabs, Greeks, Egyptians, Babylonians, Syrians, Phoenicians ... who were not so overwhelmed by their religion as the Jersualemites were. Men and women, rich and poor. Filling their time in the city, visiting the Temple where the bulk of them would not be permitted beyond the outer courts.

And there, all the while, in the city centre, was the Amphitheatre. Empty and silent, when today, the one day in the week when nobody worked in Jerusalem, it could be ringing and echoing with pleasure, excitement and cheering people.

It grieved him as he looked out over the city, for he had at his command all that was needed to provide the pleasure, excitement and recreation. Music, and the musicians to play it. Dancers and wrestlers. Runners who would race naked. Chariots and charioteers with teams of two, three and four pairs of horses. Man-eating lions. And prisoners, already condemned to death, who would fight with them.

But not today. Jerusalem's religion would not allow it. They deplored it at any time; they wouldn't countenance it today.

From his great height, he watched them all down there. Spread through the squares and streets and alleyways of his city, scuttering like ants, with here a lonely one lost, there a group stopping, nodding and changing direction. A stranger searching a way. A lonely man trying to make conversation with a city girl . . . But let them be miserable, if that's what they thought their religion decreed.

Here in his palace, with his family and their friends, he had his feast to look forward to. And even Jerusalemites could not gainsay his right to that. Even they believed in eating well on the Sabbath Day, and had a long-established tradition about it. They dressed in their best, and paraded their finery to and from their religion. And then they'd go home, bringing their guests with them, and eat sumptuously.

Herod waited for his feast.

In the meantime, his priests came and attended to his religious observance. They thanked God noisily that the King looked so well, and seemed to be recovering.

Behind closed eyes, the King smiled at their well-meaning stupidity, for he knew better. Though, he had to admit that some of his awful pain had gone, the shaking in his hands had eased, his legs felt stronger. And if the swelling round his belly had not got any less, at least it didn't prevent him moving around.

Fresh air, he decided, would do him good.

Two servants arranged him on his couch, and four Nubian slaves manhandled it into the garden.

They sat him by a pool, shaded by almond trees, where he could hear the cooing of the doves in the dovecotes.

And he played latruncula with the soldiers, from the general, through the ranks, to the common soldiers. The general and his officers behaved like gentlemen, and let him win. So he had no need to cheat. The stakes meant nothing to them.

The soldiers, though, were different. When they got over their awe of playing with gold draughtsmen on an ivory board. He enjoyed their gutsiness and the tussle to cheat. With a week's wages at stake in every game, the soldiers watched him like hawks. And rousted him when they caught him. And he bawled back, matching their rowdiness, revelling in their mateyness.

And when he was tired, and the servants came to bring him indoors again, he scattered his winnings among the soldiers. And gave the board and the draughtsmen to the gutsiest of them all.

He was well rested by the time the feast began.

He ate well. Though he never found eating difficult. It seemed to be part of his disease that he always had a ravenous appetite. But so had many of his guests, he noticed as he looked around. And they didn't suffer from his sickness.

It was a good party. And he felt pleased that the assembled company was so obviously enjoying his lavish hospitality.

Till his eye lit on Jochebed. She was sitting opposite Pheroras, and surrounded by admirers. There was no denying that she looked beautiful. And pregnant . . .

Herod paused. And he felt the thought dredging into consciousness from the lost depths of his mind, 'pregnant with the expected Messiah, the King who was to bring the House of Herod to an end'.

He had not dealt with Jochebed for her treachery. And as he watched her, it angered him that she behaved as though there were no punishment the King could inflict on her.

Jochebed was mistaken. She was about to be so degraded that none would consider her fit to be the mother of a great king. And, by the time he had finished with her, she would be such a dereliction that her child would be born in filthy obscurity.

Herod feigned a collapse. The physicians were around him immediately, easing him back in his cushions, but taking care not to lie him down for fear he might have an attack of his convulsions.

He waited till the talk and noise all around him had ebbed into silence. 'Jochebed,' he whispered, as though he hardly had voice to speak, but loudly enough to change the tone of the whole company.

He felt the hold of the physicians tauten. Through half-closed eyes he watched Jochebed, surrounded now by admirers who had turned away from her, pretending she wasn't there. A brazen woman, Herod reckoned, but she looked frightened now, as her eyes searched over to her husband Pheroras.

From where he sat, Herod could not see Pheroras who

was placed three or four people to his right. In his 'faint' state, he dared not quickly turn his head. But he guessed his brother would be glancing courage to his wife on whom he so clearly doted. But even the doting, Herod comforted himself, would be finished by the time the party was ended.

He was aware of Salome staring at him. The expression on her face said she wasn't at all taken in by his collapse. Her cold eyes judged him for having taken so long in dealing with her dangerous sister-in-law. Soft fingers with well-manicured nails fondled the gold brooch clasping the robe at her shoulder. But there was a secret impatience in the tender touch. He would miss the moment, it said, if he waited much longer.

She was right, of course. And Herod took the signalled advice.

He spoke quietly. His listeners were all attention as he explained the aggravation Jochebed was. A cancer, he told them, that ate slowly at the heart of the family, a leprosy wasting away the nation.

He named her offences which, he declared, all knew, and none would deny. She had abused the King's virgin daughters Roxana and Salome, his children by two of his former wives. Over the years, she had studiously introduced a quarrel between his brother and himself, and both by her words as well as her action, she had brought them into a state of war.

The same woman, he told them quietly, had protected those who plotted against the kingdom and the welfare of the people. And those conspirators who had been tried and sentenced to be punished, she had enabled to escape.

The list of her crimes and misdemeanours was endless, and he might have gone on. But Herod considered he had said enough.

The silence and the nodding heads about him gave him the feeling he was winning.

'Nothing,' he told them, bringing his prosecution to an end, 'nothing which of late has been done against this kingdom has been done without her.'

The courtiers waited. All eyes turned on Jochebed, expecting the King to pass sentence on her, convinced that she would go the way of the fateful Mariamne.

Salome was pleased at the way things were going. Had she been able to catch the King's eye, she was ready to smile her satisfaction.

Antipater, the King's son, watched. Apprehensive. Fearful lest Jochebed, when she had heard her sentence passed, might save herself by divulging the intrigues he had plotted with her against his father.

But Herod ignored Jochebed, not so much as glancing in her direction. He knew what they all expected. He knew that were he now to say that Jochebed must die, they all would call it justice. And he saw Pheroras fretting, the pallor draining the colour from his face, already feeling his bereavement.

The King shifted his position on the couch for comfort, pushing his physicians away.

The whole room fidgeted. And tensed again when Herod called 'Pheroras', beckoning his brother to come and stand nearer.

Pheroras stood. Blank, mindless, resigned. Staring, sightless, beyond his brother.

'Pheroras,' the King was saying, 'you have heard the indictments I have brought against this woman, your wife, and how she destroys the kingdom and ourselves.'

The voice Pheroras heard was soft, compassionate, concerned.

'You have heard these things, my brother?'

Pheroras tried, but could not speak. He bowed his head, acknowledging that he had heard.

'What then, think you, should the sentence be?'

Pheroras made no move to answer. His brother was making sport of him before the company. He might have respected the King had he announced plainly and quickly that Jochebed and himself must die. But, instead, Herod dallied, toying with him for his own malicious gratification.

The brothers stared blindly at each other. In a long silence.

Till the King spoke. 'Be this my advice to you, my brother,' he said. 'You would do well if, by your own accord, your own command, and not by my entreaty or as following my opinion, you put your wife away as one that will still be the occasion of war between you and me. And Pheroras . . . if you value your relation to me, put this wife of yours away, for by this means only will you continue to be a brother to me and will abide in your love to me.'

Pheroras was dumbfounded. He could not have heard aright. But the buzz that murmured through the assembly slowly brought it home to him that what he heard was not a delusion. Jochebed would not die. There was no death sentence on anybody. And Herod's advice seemed a generous alternative.

In a moment of exhilaration and relief, he almost agreed. 'I will put away my wife . . .' shaped in his mind, forming itself on his tongue.

As he began to speak, he saw the smile smudge into his brother's cheeks.

And then the truth shocked him into awareness. He saw Jochebed. Head bowed she sat, forlorn, hands folded, the wife of his body and his heart, and who now carried the offspring of their love. He could not live without Jochebed. Here he had stood, expecting and prepared to die. And Herod had spared him. But with kindness that was more cruel than death.

He heard himself addressing Herod. 'My Lord, I will not put away my wife.'

'Think upon what you say.'

But Pheroras had thought. 'As I would not do so unjust a thing as to renounce my brotherly relation to you, my King, so I will not leave off my affection for my wife. I expected to die today. And I would rather choose to die than to be allowed to live deprived of my wife who is so dear to me.'

Herod was taken aback. It was not what he expected. Yet, wasn't it . . . when he remembered how dearly he had loved his Mariamne, and had verged on madness when she'd gone, calling her and expecting an answer though she had been so long dead . . . And Herod felt gentle towards his brother. And dismissed him from his presence.

But punishment of some kind there must be. If Pheroras must continue with his wife, then they would both be ostracized by the King's command.

And Herod directed it so, addressing himself loudly to his son Antipater. 'Have you, my son, no more dealings with Pheroras and his wife. I forbid you, from this day, any conversation with them. And warn well your mother that she take care to avoid the assemblies where Jochebed and her family are. I have been lenient here, today, but let all men know that I will not show mercy if I have cause to call you again.'

The King had lost. Things had not gone the way he had planned, and he was angry. But patient.

Joachim led his family into the synagogue. They were the last to arrive. Deliberately. For, nowadays, they could not always be sure of the reception they'd get. And they had grown sensitive to the coldness, the unseeing stares, the forced greetings, the muttered conversations as they waited for the service to start.

It was no different this morning.

Not far from the door by which they entered, Joachim

sat. He watched Anna and his daughters make their way to the women's section behind the screen.

Once there, Anna, Miriam and Salome sat. On the mats spread on the ground. They enjoyed the sweet scent of the herbs scattered on the floor.

All round them the talk was of the damage the storm had done, and the losses the people had suffered. Each family had its own tale to tell.

'Rain on Wednesday is well timed,' observed Hannah, with nobody paying much attention. 'Rain on Fridays is a curse,' she muttered on, unaware that she was being ignored, and chuntered away till she had finished the proverb, 'But rain is a blessing on the Sabbath.'

But nobody was listening. Blessing or no blessing, the last thing they wanted on this Sabbath was rain. Everybody agreed they'd had enough.

Sympathy washed down the walls of the building. Those expressing it doled it out in lavish abundance; those receiving it wallowed in it.

Nobody, though, wondered how Anna and her family had fared. And it was clear that they didn't want her to join in the criss-crossing chit-chat.

Miriam looked all round to find Rachel's friendly face. But she was nowhere to be seen. And Miriam wondered if she wasn't well again.

The hubbub stopped as the elders filed in to take their seats arranged in front of the Reader's platform. The Parnas – the Ruler of the Synagogue – took the centre seat. Flanking him on his left, sat the Shamas, the Synagogue Steward. On the Parnas's right, the Hazan who would lead the service just as soon as the other elders, and those who had been given the seats of honour, were sitting down.

'Holy, holy, holy, Lord God of Sabaoth,' the tenor voice of the Hazan rang out, subduing all other sounds, calling the congregation to worship.

All waited.

Near Joachim, a man broke the hush, clearing his throat, preparing himself for his part in the service.

The Hazan sang again. 'O give thanks unto the Lord, for He is good.'

'For his mercy endureth for ever,' came the chanting response of men and boys, their sound swelling, filling the whole building with bursting praise.

Dignified, austere, aware of his responsibility, the Parnas rose from his seat of honour. His action was a signal to the whole congregation.

Shifting, heaving, scraping, young men and old women, rich, poor, old men and maidens, the whole congregation got to its feet. And its lifting, lilting 'Shema Yisrael, adonai elohenu adonai echod,' sounded out in one great rumbling voice.

A nod from the Parnas, and the member chosen by him for the day stepped out, read the prayers, and then stepped back to his place.

The Hazan moved the curtain that hid the cupboard in which the Scrolls were stored. He drew back the curtains, and began to open the doors. There was a rustling in the assembly as those near the front got themselves ready to surge forward when the Scroll of the Law was taken out.

The Hazan selected the chosen Scroll. He unwrapped the linen cloth, revealing the ornately decorated case, from which, with painstaking reverence, he slid the Scroll.

Everything waited as the worshippers nearest to him pressed forward and kissed the Scroll. And then, one by one, from the congregation, came the seven men to read a portion from the Law, returning again to lose themselves among the worshippers.

Reverently, the Hazan returned the Scroll to its place. Now he selected the appointed Scroll of the Prophets, and delivered it to the chosen reader.

Miriam found it difficult to see from where she was standing. A pillar blocked her view of what was happening at the front of the synagogue. But she was aware of the hush that had fallen over the assembly.

And then she heard the voice. Yosef's voice.

It was no good her trying to see. For even were there no pillar in the way, she still could not see. Fear misted her vision. Sorrow blinded her. The words she heard rampaged in her head, and they frightened her. They were the words of Isaiah's prophecy, but it was Yosef's voice that shaped them, spoke them, gave them life. And there was strange meaning in them.

'More are the children of the desolate than the children of the married wife, saith the Lord,' Yosef's voice declared.

Was everything to mock her? Was there no solace even when she came to worship? She would not listen. But nothing could staunch the words.

'Fear not, for thou shalt not be ashamed . . .' They echoed a sound that seemed to come from long ago. 'For the Lord hath called thee as a wife forsaken, and grieved in spirit . . .' Yosef's voice was clear, and each word moulded to carry its proper weight. He had rehearsed the passage well, Miriam thought. He read it as though he knew every word by heart. And Miriam felt proud of the man she loved.

'For a small moment I have forsaken thee, but with great compassion I will gather thee. In a little wrath I hid my face from thee for a moment . . .'

Miriam listened, reckoning she heard the hidden nervousness in Yosef's voice. It were as though what he was reading gave him pause also. She gripped her sister Salome's hand, strengthened a little by the comfort that flowed back.

'O thou afflicted, tossed with tempest, and not comforted . . .' Miriam was afraid. Afraid of the silences that suffocated the building. Afraid of what she knew they must be thinking. And suddenly she wished she could run out, away, far away. From Yosef. From her family. From the tension-laden piousness of the synagogue that seemed to sit in scornful judgement on her. 'And every tongue that shall rise against thee in judgement thou shalt condemn. This is the heritage of the servants of the Lord, and their due reward from me, saith the Lord.'

Then Yosef stopped. The reading was ended. Miriam felt the unspoken relief among the rest of those who had listened with her, the buzz that rippled from one member to the next, giving vent to their sense of consternation that Yosef had been invited to read at all.

Yosef left the reader's desk, kissed the Scroll, and handed it back to the Hazan to be stored away.

Miriam knew, from the noise of shuffling in the front, that the Rabbi had replaced Yosef at the desk. She heard the old man rattle a nervous cough, conscious of the awesome task of trying to expound what had just been read. She smiled at Salome as they sat down again, and Salome eased her hand from Miriam's grasp. Miriam kissed the hand when she saw how her fingernails had cut into it. Salome puckered her face.

Settled in his seat on the Reader's platform, the Rabbi began his exposition of the passage from Isaiah's prophecy.

Miriam paid little attention. For her the word from the Prophet, now, was too individual, too personal, too intimate. And all the Rabbi's eloquence about Zion's forthcoming greatness could not push out the thoughts that possessed her. The Rabbi used the Prophet's phrases, but it was Yosef's voice she heard. And somewhere from the hidden depths of the well of words, there reached up an uncanny, inexplicable, inexpressive hopefulness. 'For a small moment have I forsaken thee. But with great compassion will I gather thee . . .'

She walked with her mother as they left the synagogue, and they linked arms as they went.

Anna beamed reassurance, but her touch said that her daughter's hopes were straws in the wind.

Azariah held his wife's arm and helped her through the synagogue portico, and down the long flight of steps.

It was a difficult manoeuvre, more difficult today than usual. Normally, by the time Azariah and Naomi had started their descent, everybody else was well on the way to lunch, either as a guest or as host to someone from the congregation. But today, they were slow to go. Today, nobody seemed to want to go home. They were loitering on the steps, spread everywhere, in clusters of twos and threes, in big bundles. All in deep conversation. And Azariah had to work his way round and through them, guiding his wife as carefully as he could.

'I wonder which of them is being scandalized,' Naomi commented to her husband. 'Yosef for not being guilty, or the ruler of the synagogue for treating him as an honourable man?'

Azariah sniggered back. He enjoyed his wife's estimate of the worshippers' piety that could leave its godliness on the other side of the synagogue door. 'Everybody's a ruler now, my dear,' he said.

Barzillai saluted them, and went back to making a point to his group. Shebna was waiting, eager to contradict whatever it was Barzillai was saying.

They watched Isaac the baker gathering round him a gang of cronies.

'It'll not be much of a Sabbath rest for Isaac's wife,' suggested Azariah, 'if he's bringing all that lot back to eat.'

'And the Sabbath will be gone,' began Naomi. And then she paused, leaning to rest on Azariah before he helped her ease herself down the last of the steps, 'if we don't get some kind of move on.'

They took the road gently. Unhurrying. They found the sun too hot, even at this pace.

A little way along, they sat on a boulder that was partly shaded by a lonely clump of olive trees. And they watched the self-appointed rulers of the synagogue go by, still offering their opinions, still trying to convince each other on the issue of Yosef's having read the lesson.

'The poor Rabbi needn't have bothered,' Naomi observed.

'What hope have his words of wisdom this morning,' wondered Azariah in reply, 'when there's the chance of a juicy bit of gossip?'

They were on their way again, when Shebna came rushing past them. He hardly returned their greeting.

'It looks as though he lost his argument, Azariah.'

'Aye.'

'Well, at least he'll not have to eat with the riffraff of Nazareth today.'

'Poor Shebna. He must be a kind man underneath it all.'

'He'd be a better man if he were married,' concluded Naomi.

Shebna was well out of earshot by now, following the road that forked right, thinking his own thoughts. With things as they were in Nazareth, he reckoned he'd be happier out of it. He was due to go to Rome in a couple of weeks. And he was looking forward to that. The months away from Nazareth would give him a chance to get over all this nonsense. *But why wait?* he asked himself. There was nothing to stop him going any time he liked. His mind was made up: he'd leave in a few days' time.

Azariah and his wife walked in silence for a while. They took the road that forked left to their house. From here on, it was a quiet journey. They were not likely to meet anybody, for at the end of the road were only two houses. Their own, and the new one Yosef had built for himself and Miriam.

'What will Yosef do with the house, if he doesn't marry Miriam?' wondered Naomi to her husband. It was an inconsequential question. She didn't really expect an answer.

'I don't know,' commented Azariah, equally lethargically, helping his wife, now that the road was becoming steeper.

They could see their house now, nestling white on the fringe of the olive grove.

A few goats grazed fitfully on the ground, concerned less with food than with the enjoyment they derived from aggravating the hens in their unending search for morsels. The donkey that, by now, was more ornamental than useful, let out a long, wailing braying, in a forlorn attempt at restoring peace and order in the domain where, compared with himself, all the rest were upstart newcomers.

'D'you think Yosef will marry Miriam?' Naomi asked.

'That's a hard question,' observed Azariah, not keen to become involved. 'And Yosef is the only man who can answer it.'

'If you were Yosef, would you marry the girl?'

Azariah didn't like the question. It was awkward. It meant Naomi really wanted an answer. She had a trick of judging what a man ought to do by finding out what her husband would do were he faced with the same kind of situation. But Azariah wasn't sure of the answer. To say 'yes' might shock Naomi. And saying 'no' might hurt her, for consciously or unconsciously, she would measure his reply against the background of the long years of their life together.

But Naomi was pressing. 'Supposing it was me instead of Miriam. Would you still marry me?'

That was the very problem he was trying to solve in his own mind. But he was an old man now, being asked a young man's question. And it was hard to decide how he might have reacted as a young man.

Azariah hesitated.

'Well, would you still have married me?' insisted Naomi.

'I want to say "yes", Naomi. But only because we've been man and wife so long. Yet part of me wants to say "no". Really, it's not a fair question. It makes us different people. It makes you a different woman from the wife I married. You see, you didn't get yourself with child during the betrothal . . . and if you had, would you have wanted me to marry you?'

Naomi didn't know.

'And if I were not the father of the child, you certainly would not have put round the strange stories Miriam is spreading abroad.'

Naomi agreed. 'Poor Miriam,' she whispered.

'Poor Yosef,' retorted Azariah. 'I don't envy him. No matter what he does, now, it won't be right in everybody's eyes.'

They had reached the house.

He pushed open the door for Naomi, and followed her in.

They rested in the coolness for a while before they ate.

The sun was high and far away. The sky scorching, empty, bereft of any tinge of softness. And no bird flew. The ground burned underfoot, all yesterday's dampness gone. And only the sniffing of a mangy dog, scavenging far off his familiar tracks, disturbed the parched quietness.

Yosef stood looking at the lonely house. How long he'd been there, he couldn't guess. He'd come from the synagogue, not properly aware of the road he'd travelled along. He'd come quickly, he remembered, despite the heat. And all the way along, he'd kept telling himself he was coming to the house to see what damage the storm had caused.

But standing there, now, he knew it was only an excuse. It was a sturdy house. He had built it well. He was still proud of his workmanship. He didn't really expect any damage. And he found none.

It was an escape. Coming here, he was away from the condemning faces, the probing questions of his friends. From the never-ending, never-pitying advice. And from those words he'd read this morning to the congregation from the prophet Isaiah.

But there was no relief. He was a fool to imagine there would be. The synagogue scene painted itself again on the tormented canvas of his mind. The questioning looks of the assembly, unable to mask their anger at his being asked to read. Barzillai concerned. Shebna offended. The women wagging their heads. And generous, kindly Joachim, unsure, frightened at the face value of the words reaching out to him through the choking resentment, afraid of the strange meaning the situation afforded them.

He'd not seen Miriam in the synagogue. But he knew she'd been there. He could sense her presence. And aware of her there, his mind had shaped new meaning for the message as he'd mouthed the words: 'a wife forsaken, and grieved in spirit . . .' Poor, dear Miriam. 'O thou afflicted, tossed with tempest, and not comforted.'

Yosef tried to shake the picture from his head. But the dye was too deep, the lines too indelibly drawn. The sounds haunted him. And he heard his own voice whispering back to him on the dryness of the lonely air. 'For a small moment I have forsaken thee, but with great compassion will I gather thee . . .'

The mangy dog, unsuccessful in his search, shoved himself against Yosef's legs, rubbing himself there for comfort.

Yosef was grateful for the disturbance. He moved in response. The dog, suddenly frightened, started away. Yosef called him, but he would not come. It was a stupid thing, he knew, but he opened his basket, pulled out the dried fish he carried in it, and threw it on the ground.

Now he became aware of the sun that had played too strongly on his neck. He moved towards the house. And as he walked, he noticed that the dog moved cautiously towards the fish.

The house was cool.

In the corner, his eye caught the glint of the pool of water where yesterday's rain had blown in. And he found himself wondering what Miriam would have said about it were she here.

And then there dawned on him the real reason for his coming to the house today. Here, he was, somehow, near to Miriam. He heard the echo of her voice. He could touch the things that she had touched. He walked about the house, looking, touching. He strained the silent air to hear sounds of Miriam's speech from days gone by. But there was no laughter in the sound he heard, no lilt, no joy. And he was muttering to himself, 'O thou afflicted, tossed with tempest, and not comforted.'

He climbed the few steps on the platform wall. He felt tired, drowsy. The sun had been too much. He'd been longer in it than he'd imagined. A sleep would do him good.

He unrolled the mat that leaned against the wall, spread it out, and lay down.

It wasnt' long before he was sound asleep.

Outside, its stomach full, the dog curled itself into the shadow of the wall, to sleep, to wait on the whims of his new-found, generous master.

Rachel tried again to shift her body on the hard bed, to ease the endless, crucifying pain. But it was no use. It made no difference.

She lay back. Hopeless. The pain pounding, punishing.

The footfalls of the worshippers on their way to the synagogue had wakened her from the fretful sleep she'd snatched from the bitter hours of suffering. Their sounds were long gone now. How long, she couldn't measure, but in the sullen silence they'd left behind, she hated them. And yet, she waited, wishing they'd return. For in waiting there was hope. There might be someone who would hear her cry, and come, comforting, to dull the terror of her agony.

She dragged herself from the rags around her, and struggled on her knees to reach the table near her bed.

A loaf lay on it, part nibbled by the mice that kept her company in the night. Her stretching, unsteady hand knocked it, and its fall made a dry, hard crack on the floor.

She remembered Joachim and Isaac's shop. And realized how long she'd lain in bed.

Her hand, at last, grasped the handle of the little jar. Still crouched, afraid to move again for pain, she put the jar to her lips. It tasted like poison. But she swallowed the concoction, gluttonously sucking out the last dregs. But it had no effect. The pain still tore at her stomach, gorging venomously in every tender part.

She fell where she knelt, the jar crashing with her, smashing in her hand.

Dear God . . . that she might die. Ah, there would be release . . . for even in Gehenna, they said there was Sabbath rest from pain . . . She saw the fishing net hanging on the wall, and the brightening sunshine cudgelled in it pictures of a friendly face, beckoning to her from her childhood on the shores of Galilee . . . and the boats . . . the hills that hemmed the lake, and the smell of fish in the Pickleries at Capernaum. And the shouts and guffaws of fishermen.

Her ears strained, and caught the sound as the pictures faded in her eyes. And the sounds, the footstep sounds and voices grew nearer and louder in her ears.

They were on their way back from the synagogue.

Rachel cried out to them as they passed the door. But even as she cried, she knew they couldn't hear her. There was too much life outside for them to hear, and her call too faint.

She lay where she'd fallen, and listened as the silence slowly came again.

Antipater was not impressed by his father's leniency towards Pheroras and Jochebed. He knew his father too well; it was all too ostentatious. The King hated Jochebed too bitterly to let slip so choice an opportunity to be rid of her. That he had not executed her, and indeed her husband with her, could mean only that he had other plans and other people in mind.

How much his father might or might not know already about himself was what caused Antipater concern. He guessed his aunt Salome had provided the names of those who had so lately occupied the executioner. He could not be sure, though, how much it was Salome's advice and counsel that had influenced Herod's action towards Pheroras. Was it she, he wondered, who had recommended Herod's scrap of mercy in order to bait the bigger fish which she reckoned were using the small fry symbolized by Pheroras and his wife.

And the more he reflected on his father's strong advice to him to avoid having dealings with Pheroras, the more sure he was that Herod had unwittingly sounded the alarm. The King, Antipater felt, knew more than he pretended. And Salome was paying too close attention now to all his actions and the company he kept. However he might beguile his father, his aunt knew him too well, and was too clever a woman to be deluded.

There was danger lurking in the atmosphere. His half-brother, Archelaus, was the wise and lucky one, Antipater told himself, for Archelaus steered clear of everybody and everything connected with Herod, and lived like a king in Samaria where his mother had originated – and he let the court in Jerusalem fester in its hates and jealousies and intrigues. Antipater wished he himself could be so lucky: far away from it all . . . a thousand miles away . . . in Rome, perhaps . . . where else? The Rome he knew so well and loved so much that he considered himself as much a Roman as a Jew.

It was easy to be nostalgic about Rome. And reminiscing at least blurred out for a while the unhappiness and uneasiness that shadowed him now.

They'd been sent there as young boys, Archelaus and himself, to be educated. To learn Latin and Greek, arithmetic, literature and rhetoric.

And they had learnt. Lucinius their magister, who was handsomely paid by their father, saw to that. Though without the corporal punishment in the classroom that seemed an essential ingredient in the education of their friends. Not that they escaped discipline entirely. They had lived with Lucinius and his wife, who was as slim as Lucinius was fat, and their two children, in a well-appointed villa set in a splendid garden. Lucinius considered himself *in loco parentis*, and punished their misdemeanours as harshly as he dealt with those of his own children, Publius and Domitilla.

He could see Publius now in his mind's eye: fat, red face, piercing eyes, podgy like his father but as generous and kind. And Domitilla . . . lovely Domitilla who became even more beautiful as she grew towards womanhood, and whom he had idolized for most of his teenage years.

He laughed out loud, recollecting the mischief they got up to: pinching melons from the market stalls, stalking the wine-vendor through the streets till he left his cart to make a delivery – then they'd sneak up, undo the stopper in an amphora, topple it on its side, then hide again to watch him return to see his wine gurgling into the roadway.

He could still recall the noise and excitement at the Games on the Emperor's birthday, where men raced naked – it could never happen here at home – and the chariot races when Marcellus advised them all which chariot to bet on. Shrewd, knowing Marcellus – his father was a senator. Antipater admired Marcellus; they'd grown together into manhood, and were still firm friends, if only now by letter.

Antipater quickly put an end to this bout of nostalgia. For now, it dawned on him, he had someone who would willingly provide a way of escape from his present situation. Shrewd, knowing, practical, well-connected Marcellus.

It did not take long to write the letter: some news, a bit of gossip, the usual enquiries about mutual friends. And then the request. Would Marcellus write to Herod, urging him to allow Antipater to come again to Rome to spend a little while with his old friends?

The letter written and sealed, Antipater entrusted it to Bathyllus, his manservant, to take to Caesarea, and there to bribe the centurion in charge of the fastest troop-ship to deliver it to Rome.

It would be about two months before a reply would arrive, but Antipater could depend on it. And he could profitably use the waiting time to shape the plans already forming in his mind.

He could arrange to have his father murdered while he was far away from all suspicion, safely ensconced in Rome.

The new day dawned. They were early up in Joachim's house. There was enough to be done after the Sabbath rest.

Joachim himself was out and about even before the sun had begun to warm. The hens had given a good yield of eggs. And when he'd gathered them, he picked out the hen that would make the dinner for today.

He'd looked at the few sheep in the far field, and he was able to report to Anna that her little lamb was back in the flock again. The goats had been recalcitrant, and he'd had to give Salome a helping hand with the milking.

Now, he was settled in, repairing the breaches in the

terrace walls where the rain and the wind had loosened or dislodged the stones. The damage wasn't too bad. But it was never wise to leave it too long unattended.

He worked steadily, measuring while he worked what still needed to be done. And, so far as he could judge, there was little hope of finishing the job before the sun got too hot for working.

Not far away from him was Miriam. She was tending the plot preserved as a herb garden. Straightening what the rain had bent, pulling out what was broken by the wind. Tidying and cleaning. And, every now and then, plucking a leaf, rubbing it in her hands and smothering her face in the aroma. Or chewing a lettuce leaf.

Joachim was pleased to see his daughter so contented. And he enjoyed listening to her crooning to herself as she worked.

Miriam stood up for a breather. She had tugged off a lettuce leaf, and was cleaning it, ready to eat, when something made her look down the hill.

Her crooning stopped. And Joachim looked up.

'Something wrong, Miriam?'

'Nothing, Father. I saw a man coming towards the house just now, and I could have sworn it was Yosef. But I must have been mistaken.'

'We shall know soon enough, my dear,' Joachim assured her. 'Your mother will call out and tell us.'

They went back to work, careful not to waste too much time in the cooler hours of the morning.

Joachim put the episode from his mind, though he reflected that this was the first time Miriam had mentioned Yosef's name since the day Shebna and Barzillai had come to explain that there'd be no wedding. It was a healthy sign, Joachim thought, and felt a sense of relief.

Miriam wondered how she could have made such a mistake. To confuse someone you knew well with somebody else ... It was a whole conglomeration of things, she decided. The reading yesterday in the synagogue, the recollections in her fitful sleep again last night. And the burning, bodily longing that daily became more urgent as the child grew within her.

It was a natural enough mistake in the circumstances, she advised herself, and pushed the whole affair from her thoughts. It couldn't possibly have been Yosef. In any case, Yosef wouldn't have a dog near him. And she certainly hadn't mistaken the scraggy thing that followed obsequiously behind the caller to her home.

'Joachim, Joachim,' Anna's voice broke in on Miriam's reverie.

There was new lightness, an easiness in the sound, Miriam thought. She looked down towards the house, to see her mother standing, waving her arms. And it struck her that her mother was like her old self again. 'Joachim!' Anna repeated her call.

But Joachim was already on his way, stuffing his mouth with the chicory stem Miriam had given him as he passed her.

Miriam watched her father picking his way carefully down the terraces. She watched till she saw him join her mother at the house, and go inside. From where she was, it looked to Miriam as though the two of them had something to be excited about. She went back to work, but somewhat half-heartedly, wondering what it was that had brought such sudden pleasure to her parents. In her spasmodic attacks on the herb plot, she cast glances at the house, as though glancing would reveal to her what was going on inside.

She glanced again. Her sister Salome was signalling her to come.

Miriam wasted no time. Not knowing what to expect, she paused at the door and tidied her appearance before she entered.

There was gaiety in the house. The air was filled with laughter that was suddenly stifled as she came in. And everybody feigned ordinariness. The table creaked with bread and meats and sweets. The best cups were filled to the brim with dancing wine. Her mother pretended to be serene, working her hardest to suppress her effervescent excitement. Her father beamed. And Salome fussed as though the new-come guest was a prince from a far country.

'Yosef . . .' Miriam wanted to shout when she saw him. But the sound came only in a lisping, faltering whisper. And she wept.

And then noise. Gay, raucous, merry shouting. About weddings and wedding feasts, and happy days and dreams. She felt Yosef's strong arms about her. And through the subsiding bedlam came the comfort of his voice, speaking of things she could not understand.

He wanted to marry her.

Miriam could not believe it. A little while ago, it was all ended. Now he wanted to marry. She wanted to laugh . . . And Yosef who, not long ago, could not understand her explanation of her vision, was now explaining what had made him change his mind.

A dream, he kept telling her. A dream in which a messenger from God had spoken to him. 'Yosef,' the messenger had said, 'Yosef, thou son of David, fear not to take unto thee Miriam thy wife. For that which is conceived in her is of the Holy Spirit. And she shall bring forth a son. And thou shalt call his name Jesus, for he shall save his people . . .'

Miriam could hear no more. She was afraid to listen, afraid to believe what was happening.

Anna nodded to Yosef, and took her daughter in her arms. 'Give her time, Yosef,' she said. 'Give her time.'

*

It was late in the afternoon when Yosef left the house, Yosef and the dog. A happier house than when he'd arrived. And Miriam and her parents were still waving goodbye as he turned the bend in the road to make for his own house . . . *our house*, he corrected himself.

He walked brightly. Even the dog had a lighter air about it, and bustled along beside him, wagging its tail.

Till Yosef stopped abruptly. 'We've made a terrible mistake, dog.'

The dog looked up.

'We've gone and changed the plans without even telling Barzillai and Shebna. Worse than that, dog, I've broken the rules by going to Miriam's family myself to tell them the news. It's Shebna and Barzillai who should do that. They're my *pronubae*, my go-betweens . . .'

The dog stood staring up at Yosef.

'They arranged the marriage with Joachim for me. Then they cancelled it. And I should have told them *first* that it's on again; and then they go and tell Miriam's father.'

He stared down at the dog, as though expecting it to understand.

'We'd better go and make our peace with them.'

He turned back along the road he'd come, and made for Barzillai's house. Barzillai first, he decided, because he would be more sympathetic.

And he was. Though he smiled a little as Yosef retailed the dream that had made him change his mind and his plans.

'I'm sorry for smiling, Yosef,' he interrupted. 'I'm not mocking. But it's a bit beyond me. It's dreams everywhere.'

'I know,' nodded Yosef.

'It's a bit ironic, you'll admit yourself. A while ago none of us – not even yourself – could credit Miriam's story about her dream. And, now, here you are . . .'

'Aye,' Yosef agreed, searching awkwardly, as he realized

how Miriam must have searched, for a way to explain things. 'That's what they've just been saying in Miriam's home.'

'Joachim knows already?' questioned Barzillai, trying to hide his surprise – to say nothing of his disappointment.

'I'm sorry, Barzillai. I know it's really your job to tell him.'

'Forget it, Yosef. We can't be always standing on ceremony. You're marrying Miriam. That's the important thing.'

'Thank you for your understanding, Barzillai. You're a good friend.'

Barzillai bowed his head. 'I understand, Yosef.' He spoke softly, deliberately. 'And one or two others will understand. But the rest . . .' He stretched out his arms slowly, like a man drowning. 'The marriage, in fact, could make things far worse than they are now. No matter what you do now will be judged as wrong. Neither of you can win. They'll despise Miriam for wrongdoing, or for trapping an innocent man. They'll hate you, either as a fool for walking into the trap with his eyes open, or as a reprobate who finally admitted his responsibility.'

'I'm only too well aware of that—' Yosef began. But Barzillai interrupted him.

'The awful thing is that they will hate your child also . . . your son, as you think the child will be. He'll become a grown man, Yosef, and they'll still remind him, when it suits them, that he was born of fornication.'

Both men were silent.

'We'll have some wine,' said Barzillai eventually, pouring some as he spoke. 'Have you any plans for after the wedding?'

'We have,' Yosef assured him, as he took the proffered cup. 'Miriam has been through a lot in the past few months. And her family, too.'

Barzillai was nodding agreement. 'And there's a lot more to come.'

'We think it would be good for Miriam to leave Nazareth for a while.'

'Aye,' agreed Barzillai. 'Where will she go?'

'She'll go to the south, to Juttah. To her cousin Elisheba – the woman in Miriam's dream. She'll be safe there. Elisheba's an older woman, and will be a comfort to Miriam.'

'To say nothing of giving some meaning to the dream,' Barzillai offered.

Yosef said nothing. He drank deep, and drained the cup. 'I'd better go now. I've still to tell Shebna.'

'Well, when you're telling him, Yosef, remember he's a good friend, too. He can't help it if he sees everything in black and white.'

Yosef smiled wanly as he took his leave. The dog greeted him as he came out.

'That's the easy hurdle,' he told the animal as they set off to Shebna's house, with a noticeably slower pace than had earlier brought them to Barzillai.

Shebna's welcome was formal. Stiff and correct, but not chilly, and Yosef was grateful for that.

A servant offered him a basin to bathe his face and feet and hands. Shebna signalled another servant to prepare some wine.

'We'll take our drink on the veranda,' he advised the servant when he returned, then ushered Yosef out.

Yosef admired the veranda, floored with the best marble. Beautiful and best – that spoke of Shebna's good taste, and the craftsmanship of the mason who had laid it.

The veranda gave a clear view of the plains below. And then hill on hill that stretched to faraway Mount Hermon whose snow-capped peak shaped shadows in the fading sun of the day's last light. Were he on a different mission, Yosef would be happy to sit and wallow in the loveliness of it all.

Shebna hovered till his visitor was comfortably seated, then sat himself and beckoned the servant to offer wine.

Yosef acknowledged his host's generosity. The wine, too, was a mark of Shebna's discerning taste. Both men drank.

'Well?' enquired Shebna. 'It's a pleasure to welcome you, Yosef. But I imagine you've come for a particular reason.'

'I must talk to you of my plan now to marry Miriam.'

'Indeed,' was Shebna's reply.

It wasn't the response Yosef was expecting. He couldn't decide what exactly it implied. Was it surprise? Anger? Sarcasm? Was the man even interested?

'I have decided, Shebna, to honour my promise to marry Miriam.'

'Have you, now?' grunted Shebna, rising from his seat and moving to stand in front of Yosef. He eased himself up and down on his toes as he spoke. 'It's hardly a breathing space ago, Yosef, since you decided that you would annul the marriage contract with the woman. And you gave Barzillai and myself the sorry and unenviable task of inform-ing her father.'

He paused to let the point sink in while he supped twice and heartily from his wine cup.

Yosef watched. It was obvious that Shebna had still more to say, so Yosef waited. And it struck him what a tiny man Shebna was. It was an inconsequential thought, in the circumstances, and he chided himself for thinking it. But Shebna really was so short and slight, and seemed to accentuate his lack of height by his odd habit of raising and lowering himself on his toes when he was making a point. As though, by adding inches to his stature, he gave weight to his argument.

Shebna wrapped both hands round his cup.

'But no matter,' he started again. 'May one ask the reason for the present change of mind?'

'A dream,' blurted Yosef. And felt it sounded even more ludicrous here in front of Shebna than ever it had with sympathetic Barzillai.

'Ah,' retorted Shebna, 'a dream.'

This time the sarcasm was clear, and Yosef felt the cut. He tried to counter the rebuff. 'It was a dream, Shebna,' he offered, 'in which the angel of the Lord appeared to me—'

'Be careful of dreams, Yosef,' Shebna whispered softly. 'God speaks in dreams, indeed – we know that – but not to every man. And God certainly does not speak in every dream a man has.'

'This dream was clear, Shebna. There was no mistaking it was God's intervention.'

'Go on, Yosef, tell me the dream.'

'The angel of the Lord appeared to me and said, "Yosef, thou son of David, fear not to take unto thee Miriam thy wife. For that which is conceived in her is of the Holy Spirit—"'

'Yosef, Yosef,' was Shebna's almost inaudible interruption. Poor Yosef, he was dwelling too much on the story Miriam must have recited over and over again to try to explain her condition.

But Yosef didn't hear the interruption. '"—and she shall bring forth a son—"'

Shebna stretched out a hand. 'Wait, Yosef,' he called out. 'I'll finish the dream for you. I'll tell you what the angel's message was.'

Yosef stopped.

Shebna was on tiptoes almost, his voice sonorous, each word deliberately announced. 'And thou shalt call his name Jesus.'

Yosef was silent, shocked.

And Shebna waited, feeling he might have done the wrong thing.

It was a different sound when he spoke again. There was gentleness, concern, comfort.

'I am your go-between, Yosef. And honoured to be. And it is my duty to be concerned for your well-being, to try to guide you. And certainly to protect you from any act that would bring you harm or disgrace.'

Yosef sat silent, turning his wine cup round and round in his hands.

And Shebna spoke again. 'Your dream, my brother, is Miriam's dream. Your angel's message are the words you heard first from Miriam's lips.'

'But the dream was clear,' cut in Yosef.

'Of course the dream was clear. Even the words were clear,' Shebna soothed. 'But don't you see, Miriam's very words have now become embedded in your mind, and follow you into your sleep? And shape themselves on the lips of an angel in your dreams. Yosef, Yosef, would you for once stop and realize the state you're in?'

'Shebna, you are a wise man, a good friend. And I know that everything you say is meant for my good. But don't you think that I have argued with myself, as you have argued with me now? The dream was real, Shebna. And God's direction in it clear. I cannot, I will not gainsay it.'

'Then you beguile yourself, my poor friend. I beg you not to follow this course. For if you do, you will heap sorrow and trouble on your head. And on the woman's head. For marriage will not save either of you from the harsh and cruel judgement of your neighbours.'

'We both are only too aware of that, Shebna.'

'Yet you persist.'

Yosef made no reply.

'There's no point, then, is there, in us talking any more?'

'None, Shebna. I'm sorry.' And Yosef rose to leave.

'It could be that I am wrong, brother Yosef. And time will be the judge of that. I wish you blessing in your marriage . . . if that doesn't sound hypocritical, but you know what I mean.'

'Shebna,' muttered Yosef, and reached out to shake his host's hand.

Shebna shook it warmly. 'You'll understand if I don't attend the ceremony.'

Yosef nodded, understanding.

'I'm setting off for Rome tomorrow. That will take some of the bad look off my not being there.'

Yosef handed his cup to Shebna. And took his leave.

CHAPTER FIVE

It was still early when Shebna joined the caravan gathering itself for the journey to Caesarea, where he'd board the ship that would take him to Rome. In the light of the rising sun, distant snow-capped Hermon still slumbered dark and shadowed. Nazareth was not properly awake yet, but already all around him camels and mules, braying asses and busily chattering travellers made the place noisy enough to sound like noonday.

He reined his fidgeting mule as he waited for the signal to move, acknowledging now and then the greetings from people he knew.

He was glad he'd already settled on going off to Rome that much earlier. It would save Yosef and himself from embarrassment at the wedding. No doubt Yosef would explain things to his bride. And Joachim and Anna would not lose face with their guests. The guests would understand a merchant having to go to Rome. Business in Jerusalem or Damascus or even in Arabia could be postponed for a wedding, but business in Rome was a different matter. That meant sailing the Great Sea, and reaching places in time to make connections with ships.

But he couldn't help feeling disappointed about the whole thing, though, even now, he was not sure in his mind whether Yosef was courageous or stupid to get married at all in the circumstances. Maybe it was out of kindness, for the Yosef he knew could hardly be described as stupid or hasty. But kindness, courage or stupidity hardly mattered, for Shebna didn't like it. Though he hoped now that his disagreement and disapproval hadn't appeared too obvious. Bad enough marrying, but to feel that your marriage had lost you friends would be *too* much. And Shebna reckoned that, one of these days, Yosef would be in need of a friend.

The mule was in a stubborn mood, and that annoyed Shebna. Not least because he wanted to get away from the group of boys, excited at the prospect of their journey, who were making more noise than he could endure. He stopped his musing and concentrated his mind, his hands and his heels on getting the mule to do his bidding.

As the mule responded, Shebna manoeuvred himself into a more congenial place in the caravan – alongside a merchant making his way to Tyre to take ship for Cilicia, where he traded for goat-hair to make cloaks and sailcloth. They'd be companions now till they reached Sepphoris.

Shebna began to enjoy the journey. The mule settled into its stride, and he rode comfortably. After the first mile or so, even the excited boys became more likeable. They had quietened down, and every now and then came and walked alongside Shebna and the merchant, listening enraptured as the two men swapped travellers' tales.

The journey passed pleasantly enough: tiring, but not arduous, for all it was a hilly ride most of the way. The lads took themselves off once they caught sight of the walls of Sepphoris in the distance, and left Shebna and his companion to themselves for the remainder of the road.

Everybody now relaxed, and excitement tingled through the travellers as they got nearer to the city. Even the camels and mules and asses joined in the general clamour as the caravan moved through the magnificent gate of Galilee's sophisticated capital city.

Here the caravan would rest for a while, not that the four miles from Nazareth had worn them out. But this was the capital, and the shopping centre of the province. And even the poorest of the travellers, who had foot-slogged it every step of the way, had money to spend before the main caravan split up – with some heading for Tyre and the rest for an overnight stop at the caravanserai at Mount Carmel.

Shebna was glad of the break. He had no shopping to do, but he had cronies in the city he wanted to see. So he declined his companion's invitation to go drinking with him.

It took him no time to find Shealtiel's house. Grand, airy, ornate; so obviously Greek – in keeping with the Greek style that influenced the whole of this beautiful city. The house was a reflection of Shealtiel himself: expansive, cultured, generous. And grandly hospitable, as Shebna quickly learned, after he'd been ushered through the colonnaded porch and across the garden, where fountains made music among the profusion of scented flowers and shrubbery.

No sooner had he greeted Shebna than Shealtiel summoned a servant and dispatched him to invite other residents of the city to come and meet their old friend. He was still adding names as the servant hastily disappeared, and Shebna reckoned that if all were to come who had been invited, he'd have no time to talk to any of them properly before he'd have to be on his way again.

Shealtiel clapped his hands and a flurry of servants appeared with basins and towels to wash his face and hands and feet, cleansing away the dust and sweat of travel. They worked quietly and calmly, with well-practised expertise.

The garden had quickly told him that, despite all the foreign influence, Shealtiel was still a Jew, for there wasn't a single statue in sight. His chattering bonhomie, as his servants made Shebna feel cool and fresh, affirmed that he had lost none of his Jewish instinct for welcoming a guest.

'We'll sit on the terrace,' Shealtiel said when the ablutions were finished and the servants had left. 'The others should be there by now. And it'll be nice and cool for you before you're on the road again.'

The others were indeed already there: Amaziah and Jonah, Yakob, Simon and Boaz. It was a noisy meeting as they greeted each other. They were all old cronies. Boaz and Amaziah he'd grown up with in Jerusalem. Jonah and Simon were merchants who traded with him, and had become dependable friends over the years. Yakob he hadn't expected to see; he normally lived in Alexandrium, but happened to be staying with Shealtiel for a while.

They had started their drinks when a servant appeared, ushering in another guest.

Shebna didn't recognize him, but it was obvious that the others knew him well, and showed great respect for him. Shebna himself was impressed by the cut of the man, the set of his face, the steely eyes, and the sense of presence about him.

'You don't know Judas,' said Shealtiel, introducing the newcomer. 'But you will have heard of his father, Hezekiah.'

The two men greeted each other.

'Hezekiah was murdered by Herod, a good many years back,' Shealtiel went on, 'while Judas was no more than a lad. Indeed, when all of us were no more than boys.'

And then Shebna knew why Judas impressed him. His father was the Hezekiah who had led a revolt against Herod and Herod's taxes many years back. The rebellion had failed, and Herod executed Hezekiah as a robber. Judas, Shebna thought, had all the makings of a man who could lead a revolution, and possessed the charisma that could attract others to follow him.

Shebna wasn't sure how the conversation got round to it.

Perhaps he'd got carried away in reflecting on Hezekiah and Herod and revolutions. However, by the time he became aware of it, the others were already discussing the news of Caesar Augustus's decree that there should be a census throughout the land. Shebna was now all ears. This was news he'd not heard before, and he told them so.

'We've only just heard it ourselves,' Boaz assured him, 'but Sepphoris is a city of rumours.'

'Not rumours like this,' mused Amaziah. 'I reckon this one is serious.'

'It had better not be,' burst in Judas. 'It'll mean trouble.'

'Give him room,' joked Boaz, spreading his arms out in front of him to make space in the air. 'He's off on his high horse again.'

Judas smiled at his antics. 'But this is serious, Boaz,' he said quietly. 'A census is only the prelude to crippling taxation.'

They waited, realizing that he was in earnest.

'The people of this land have already suffered more taxation than they can bear. That madman Herod thinks God made us just to pay taxes simply to satisfy his grandiose notions. This very city, for instance . . . we're still paying Herod's bill for building it. We're still buying back Jericho from Cleopatra—'

'A census needn't mean taxation, Judas,' interrupted Yakob. 'The Roman Emperor wants to know the number of his subjects in the kingdom, so he's counting them. There's nothing sinister in that.'

'Counting the people is a sin,' opined Amaziah.

Judas had been about to speak, but now looked, instead, at Amaziah for an explanation.

'Read the prophet Samuel,' Amaziah advised them. 'Remember when King David counted the people of Israel? God punished him and the nation with a plague.'

They listened, waiting for more.

'It is against God's will,' Amaziah reaffirmed.

'We must *still* be being punished,' offered Yakob, 'for have we not been plagued these long years by that tyrant Herod?'

Judas was grateful to Amaziah for reminding them of history. 'A census now . . .' he assured them, measuring each word; 'a census now would mean an even worse plague inflicted by an even more powerful tyrant. And a tyrant, at that, who calls himself a god.'

He paused to let the thought settle in their minds. 'The Jews have no God but Jehovah,' he told them. 'And we've paid enough tax already, and have made too many tax gatherers too rich for too long. The Jews should pay no tax but the Temple tax.'

Shebna wasn't sure whether he was enjoying this conversation. It wasn't what he had expected. A quiet drink and a bit of gossip with a few friends was what he'd come for. But this was politics. Indeed, it began to feel to him what he always imagined sedition to be.

Quiet-spoken Judas, whether he knew it or not, was sowing the seeds of rebellion. There was a battle-cry sound in the words he used, no matter how softly he said them.

'No God but Jehovah,' Judas was repeating. 'No tax but the Temple tax.' And five heads nodded approval.

It was safe here, Shebna felt, in the morning air, on the terrace of a rich man's home, where friends talked and drank. But Judas was clearly rehearsing, preparing the slogans that, beyond these garden walls, would rouse men by their thousands throughout Galilee.

'The mantle of Hezekiah has surely fallen upon his son Judas,' Shebna found himself saying aloud.

They roundly clapped and cheered his observation.

'But this is sedition,' he said, staring at Judas, noting the determined face and the eyes burning with fanaticism. 'It's rebellion.'

Judas raised his eyebrows in reply, but said nothing.

Shebna felt fear – or was it exhilaration? It was time for him to go, but he couldn't resist one comment to Judas as they bade farewell. 'Rich men plotting Israel's uprising?'

'Give us time,' encouraged Judas.

As he rejoined the caravan, Shebna wondered just how much time Judas would need.

He found two new travelling companions as they left Sepphoris: a wealthy sheep farmer and his son.

Sheep and the high price of salt were the topics of conversation now – and the problems of hireling shepherds. A far cry from the discussion back in Sepphoris that still criss-crossed his mind. But Shebna was grateful: it took his mind off revolution and weddings. And off Yosef, whom he still could not understand or explain to himself. How any man could allow himself to be so easily beguiled was beyond him.

However, his new companions gave him little time to brood. They wanted to talk – or, rather, the father did. The son said little or nothing, and Shebna paid him scant attention, anyway. Too foppish, too effeminate, he reckoned. A young man with too much money and for whom a good day's toil would work wonders.

'Out there,' the father was explaining, 'out there is where my money is,' pointing leftwards, waving his arm to take in the vast expanse of the Valley of Esdraelon. And he detailed the problems involved and how he might be even richer and more successful were it not for hired shepherds who seemed to have no interest in the job beyond the money they earned.

Shebna listened, and hummed and hawed and nodded and shook his head at appropriate times. Not that he was all that interested, but the conversation passed the time and took some of the monotony and discomfort out of travelling.

The caravan halted just before noon. Sheltered from the sun, everybody ate, and then slept.

An hour later, the sheep farmer had him on the move again before the rest were properly organized. A veteran traveller, Shebna decided, as the man explained his reason. 'Travel where you like for the first part of the journey but later, if you want a comfortable place for the night, be up at the front of the caravan. That way you make sure of a good spot at the caravanserai.'

Some of the harshness of the heat had faded, and it was an easier road. Mount Carmel commanded the view in front of them, its long ridge changing colour as the sun moved with them towards the west. And, out beyond, the Great Sea gleaming, speckled with the little ships of busy fishermen.

Shebna was enjoying the journey now, and he was prepared to forget the worries of the world, and revolutionaries, and weddings, and the cut-and-thrust of business, and be carried away by the sight of it all. And he might have succeeded had it not been for the sheep farmer, who insisted on chattering.

They rested briefly when they crossed the ford at the River Kishon. Talking farmer and all, Shebna could not help feeling moved and overcome. Maybe it wasn't altogether holy ground beneath him, but at least he was walking on the ancient history of his nation – in the footsteps of the great prophet Elijah. Up there on the ridge of Mount Carmel, the stories of his religion had told him, Elijah had won his contest with the prophets of Baal. The prophet of Israel had called down fire from heaven to save Israel from tyrant rulers and foreign ways. The plotters back in Sepphoris would relish that, he mused, and then was back with reality again. And was making his way, with the rest of them, towards the coast, till they reached the caravenserai under the bluff of the mountain, with sunset already darkening the sea.

The sheep farmer's wise experience paid off, and Shebna was grateful to him for the comfortable place he found to bed down in for the night. They had already finished the hard and slow part of the journey. Tomorrow should be easier.

And it was. A straight road, almost. No hills to climb. No awkward spots to negotiate. And always, never far away on the right, the sea.

It was fresh and clear, with a clean smell all of its own. And Shebna wondered to himself why people chose to live in towns and cities when they might live here and enjoy the cleanliness of it all.

The mule needed no further attention. It had settled to the pace of the caravan, and the road was easy for it. So Shebna was able to ride in comfort and allow himself to become distracted, gazing about and storing the sights and sounds in his memory. The broad, illimitable sea, changing its dawn colours under the brightening, brightening sun till it glistened like silver that a man had spent a lifetime polishing. And hardly moving, except on the shore, where it soughed and sighed on the sands, coming and going in white, foamy reaches. Children played in it, jumping and dancing as it sneaked into the beach, catching them unawares before easing out again.

Shebna revelled in the sight of it, feeling tempted to call back encouragement whenever their cries of pleasure and excitement reached his ears.

Here and there, the fishermen sat in groups on the shore. After the night's fishing, their boats were pulled up on the beach, the nets spread out drying in the sun. The tired men just sat there, their fires glowing and the smell of cooking fish that would make their breakfast tanging the air.

The aroma was too much for Shebna to resist, and the sheep farmer and his son readily agreed when he suggested they might stop to buy some cooked fish from one of the groups.

Others in the caravan had the same idea, so Shebna felt no embarrassment in offering to buy, and the fishermen were only too willing to sell. They waited patiently till it was cooked.

Then they ate. And Shebna noticed that even his foppish young travelling companion gorged himself, licking the grease that ran over his fingers. That wasn't surprising, for this was *real* fish: fresh and sweet, straight from the water. And beyond comparison with the fish that came already pickled from Bethsaida, which he was long accustomed to.

The fishermen were friendly enough, but they talked little. They themselves ate when the travellers had been served – and then wasted no time before they settled in to repair the damage of the night's work, the nets torn and ripped. And while they worked, some lads were already off, waist deep in the surf, casting their throw-nets to reap the daytime harvest from the sea.

Shebna took pleasure in it all: the artistry of the fishers in the surf. He watched, fascinated, the ease with which one man could throw the net away from him – the sweep of it through the air, like a patch of grey mist. And its gentle fall, as though net and sea caressed each other, and the sea spuming momentarily white. Till the net itself sank and was gone. And the fisherman waited.

Shebna held it all in his mind, like a dream, travelling the road oblivious almost of everything else around him, of the sheep farmer and his son, of the noisy, chattering, journeying caravan. Even of the mule he rode as it paced its rhythmic way, knocking up little dust clouds as it avoided the ruts and holes and loose stones, flicking its ears to clear away flies.

It was a good mood to be in, and lasted the long, hot miles till the flat skyline was at last broken by the shapes of shadows of Caesarea.

Off to the left of the city stretched the long, snaking

aqueduct. It started three miles back at Crocodilopolis and reached across the plain and over the swamps, bringing the fresh waters of the Zerka River to the coastal city.

Caesarea was a new city. Herod's city. A forgotten fishing village once, where a handful of people struggled to make a living, now it was different. Herod's enterprise, slave labour and Egyptian architects had built and rebuilt till they had made a city that – Shebna had to admit – outshone even Jerusalem.

Herod had named it Caesarea after Augustus Caesar. The marble temple that dominated the city he had built in honour of the Emperor.

A man would have no feeling who could fail to be moved by the splendour of Caesarea. And Shebna *was* moved. He despised the King. He hated him for the crippling taxes he levied to pay for such building enterprises. Like every other Jew, he wished him dead for the degradation he brought on the religion of Israel. But there was no denying the King's genius as a builder: Caesarea was magnificent. Everything Shebna's religious upbringing condemned was there, but he couldn't help admiring it all: the hippodrome for Herod's chariot races, the marble theatre and, rearing majestic and powerful from the rock in the centre of the bay, the palace-fortress, a gesture of defiance to the King's detractors. And a challenge to the elements that for months in the year wreaked havoc on the coast and made shipping in the Great Sea impossible except for the foolhardy and for soldiers in transit to and from Rome, who must travel whether they liked it or not.

Fresh breezes from the sea blew in the broad, wide streets and parks, and kept the city clean and fresh. Herod's aqueduct brought water. The carefully planned drainage system carried its sewage far out to sea.

Jews avoided this city if they could, as they did with the other cities Herod had built. But the Romans made good use of it, which Shebna quickly realized as they made their way towards the harbour. Everywhere he turned, he met Roman soldiers, for they had made it a garrison town, housing the Imperial Army in a huge military barracks. It provided a good port where Rome's Army could come and go safely. The breakwater built by Herod guaranteed that. For almost a mile, this crescent mole stretched out to sea, broader than the width of three Roman roads, and guarded by defence towers that looked impregnable and capable of withstanding any force man could devise.

It made a good military headquarters for the region, and its strategic importance was enhanced by the new military road that ran straight from Caesarea, through the Megiddo Gap, to Tiberias on the shores of the Sea of Galilee.

The caravan had dispersed by now, and the travellers gone their separate ways. After a short stop at a street stall for bread and soup, the sheep farmer and his son took their leave of Shebna. They were off to the depot to meet the Tesserarius, or Quartermaster, with whom the farmer was expecting to clinch his annual deal to supply sheep for the Army.

Shebna wished him well, and then made his own way to the harbour and booked his passage. He felt pleased with himself. He'd been expecting to have to spend the night in the city, but now he'd managed to get a place on a grain ship that had called from Alexandria, and was sailing on to Rome once it had loaded its cargo of salt mined and transported from the cliffs of the Dead Sea.

His business now was to find a horse dealer who would buy his mule. That meant a search along the docks.

Cargo and merchandise lay in heaps waiting for ships. Merchants haggled and bartered in noisy groups. A few travellers caroused on the pavement outside a wine shop. Soldiers and sailors balanced on stools round three-legged tables, swilling wine to wash down their bread and fish-relish.

Innkeepers and stall proprietors accosted him as he tried to make his way along. He could eat cheaply, one of them urged him: meat and bread and a pint of wine, all for next to nothing. 'And entertainment for a little extra,' he added, pushing one of his girls almost under the mule's hoofs.

He found a horse dealer ready to pay the price he asked without too much haggling. It was a good deal, Shebna reckoned, but then the dealer would have no difficulty selling it on for twice the price. And, by the looks of things he'd sell it pretty soon, for a pilgrim ship was already discharging in the port. There'd be any number of pilgrims, so intent on getting to the Temple in Jerusalem, that they'd pay whatever price the dealer asked.

Shebna wasted no time getting back to the ship and going aboard. The Egyptian and Phoenician crewmen were humping the last great sacks of salt aboard. Two sets of planks joined vessel to shore. The sailors delivered across one set, pacing their movements to the rhythmic rise and fall of the ship. The planks sagged and bounced beneath each man and his burden. Meanwhile, deep in the bowels of the ship, men cursed and shouted as they worked at stowing the cargo safely. Then the loaders came back on shore by the second set of planks to fetch another load, wiping away the sweat that coursed all over their bodies, shielding their eyes from the sun after the darkness inside, shouting comments and obscenities back and forth to each other.

A great cry went up when the job was completed. The men below called out that all was well and safe, and they made their way up on deck to join their mates. And drank long and deep from the cask the captain provided.

They were finished drinking by the time two rowing boats came alongside. A couple of men in each boat seized the ropes hurled over the bow. And while they held them fast, the others rowed, manoeuvring the ship to the end of the mole. By the time they'd reached the open sea, the huge sail was already broken and taking the wind on the great mast amidships.

Shebna stood in the bow, deep-breathing the sea air.

The house was so crammed in preparation for the wedding that Anna hardly found a comfortable space to sit to sew. It seemed more a storehouse than a home, and what could not be stored inside was heaped in its own pyramids outside. A week of almost non-stop rush, she reflected, and it all seemed to have achieved so little.

It wasn't long enough. And what was left would not be nearly long enough if everything were to be properly ready for the day. It was the first wedding in the family, and she wanted it to go well. She'd have been glad of more time, for there seemed no end to the work. The storing, salting, preserving: fruits, wine, fish, vegetables, cheese. And the buying, from merchants whose coolness upset her. They seemed unable to share her joy, and made no effort to enter into her excitement. They took her money but were no more forthcoming than they needed to be.

Yet she was grateful that things had turned out as they had. It could all have been so very different. A little while ago, she reflected, there was to have been no wedding at all. But now, thank God, her daughter was not to be degraded, nor Joachim's good name too disgraced.

Anna spread out the skirt of the wedding dress to be sure that the seam she was sewing was straight. And it dawned on her that, never once, in all her torments of the past months, had she given a moment's thought to what might happen to Miriam and the child she carried if Miriam were not married. She shuddered, frightened a little by the reminder. The thought played in her mind and distracted her from her work. Her sewing hand strayed and she pricked her finger, and could not sew again till the blood congealed.

It was all so strange, though. There was so much she did

not understand. She was murmuring to herself as she waited to start work again, thinking her confusion aloud, putting order, as it were, into the faraway thoughts that sauntered in haphazard review in the distant limits of her mind. So much, in the beginning, had looked so promising. And the enthusiasm and delight of it all came tumbling back to mind: the childishness that overtook them all as they planned and arranged, and ran backwards and forwards to see the new house taking shape.

Her eyes glowed, reflecting the once felt happiness. Her hands sewed deftly, gaily, neatly.

But so much had happened since. O God, so much . . . Her mind cut off the avalanche of memories that threatened her. But nothing could staunch the ache that overwhelmed her heart. And there was nobody in the house to whom she could turn to unburden herself. Miriam was in the city. Salome was grinding corn in the shelter of the back wall of the house. And the *sock – sock* of wood on wood sounding from the patch across the way told her Joachim and the men were still busy erecting the wedding tent.

Anna spread the dress over her lap. And rested her arms. And thought about Miriam. How hard it was to understand her poor daughter's explanation of her child's conception. Arch, the neighbours thought it was. Blasphemous. Or, when they would show kindness to her, they called her mad. Yet with what ease a man might change his mind. And say that God had spoken to him in a dream . . .

She picked up the dress again, and sewed the last stitches. They were mixed threads, Anna thought, that seamed her daughter's wedding gown. And, as she folded the dress to pack it safely away, she wondered what marriage and the child she carried would bring for Miriam.

In an alleyway in the warren of streets behind the synagogue, Miriam stood, trying to decide in which of the hovels Rachel lived. The street had been hard to find but now, having arrived, after the weary searching, she had the feeling – from what she could recall of Rachel's description of it – that *this* was the place. Walls that leaned towards each other from opposite sides of the street in their unremitting conspiracy to block out the sun. Mean, dirty doorways, and windows agape. The endlessly running gutter, urging its putrifying progress along the middle of the narrow road, round the crowding feet of desolate folk milling their distracted way through this unceasing bedlam. Children ran and played, bawled and shouted and fought. Dogs barked and snarled, fighting each other for each stinking morsel, oblivious to the feast provided by the rich harvest of filth that was their battleground.

Miriam stood by the shop. 'Asa. Silversmith,' she read. And the name brought it all back. Rachel's rings. She remembered Rachel's rings, seeing in her mind's eye the festooned fingers glinting in the shafts of sunshine at the well. Every other week brought a new one, and each time there was the ritual of admiration as Rachel revealed the new gaudy finery, explaining how Asa had made it, breathing his name with a respect that hinted he was silversmith to kings. And this, then, was where she bought them, where a few drachmas could be turned into the tinsel of temporary majesty. This was Rachel's gate of heaven.

Miriam hesitated, debating whether or not to go in and ask Asa where Rachel lived. But she was inside before the debate was properly ended.

The shop was empty. Miriam coughed to make her presence known, looking round while she waited for a response.

The flame on the bench shivered in the draught her entrance had created. And, gleaming in the light, the tools of the silversmith's trade were spread out in neat array. Miriam liked the place. There was gentility in the atmosphere, an air of quietness that seemed impervious to the noises of the street outside.

Asa appeared through a curtain that divided the shop: a little man, lost in his beard. A cap sat carefully on his head and, as he came nearer to her, he tidied the shawl around his slight shoulders, tightening his eyes, squinting, trying to see, warring against the constantly threatening blindness.

He bowed to Miriam, and enquired how he could help her. And Miriam noticed the tapering hands shaping the question his voice sounded.

She had not come to buy anything, Miriam explained, but simply to find out where a friend lived.

He would be only too pleased to help, if he could.

Miriam liked the man. There was a kindness about him, a sympathy that seemed to flow out from him.

'I'm trying to find where Rachel lives,' she said.

The eyebrows lifted. Faintly. Imperceptibly. 'You are a friend of Rachel?'

She nodded. 'My name is Miriam.'

'Ah, yes, Miriam. Rachel talks of you.' He spoke slowly, as though remembering. And his eyes, as he spoke, searching her from head to toe, told Miriam what he knew about her.

'Rachel is sick,' he told her. 'She's recovering now. She had the fever for nearly a week. But now the fever is gone, and she is on the mend again.'

Miriam was sorry at the news, and wanted to know about this fever.

'Her life,' Asa said hurriedly, hoping that Miriam would understand, and not ask him to explain further. 'I was getting ready to go visit her, when you arrived. And now I will be glad to take you to her.'

'Thank you.'

'But first let me finish the broth.'

Miriam apologised for having interrupted him while eating.

The little man laughed, embarrassed, as though he had been caught doing something wrong. 'Not at all. I was not eating. Publish it not in Gath, tell it not in the streets of Askelon . . . I was cooking. She would have nothing to eat if I did not bring her food. So I've made some broth. But come, let me finish the preparations.'

He moved towards the partition, beckoning to Miriam to follow. He pulled back the curtain, securing it with a well-worn rope in a fold against the wall. He gestured for Miriam to wait in the opening.

The living quarters were every bit as neat as the shop. Miriam was impressed and reckoned her mother would be surprised to see this, for Anna considered that men who lived alone were slovenly people. But here everything was in its proper place. Asa had a craftsman's tidiness about him. And, as she caught the aroma of simmering chicken soup, Miriam decided he wasn't too bad a cook either.

She watched him ladle the broth into a jar, and place it carefully in a basket. Then some bread beside it. He wrapped some lettuce leaves in a damp cloth, paused and, as an afterthought, threw in some chicory. The cloth was neatly wrapped again, and the parcel found its place in the basket with the rest.

'If you would like to carry that,' he said, turning to Miriam, and presenting the basket. Miriam accepted, and, Asa stooped and struggled to manhandle the water pot.

She was intrigued by this man who seemed to think of everything, and wondered why he should go to so much bother for a girl like Rachel. He did not seem like a man who would involve himself in a dishonourable relationship. Yet his actions, Miriam couldn't help feeling, sprang from more than mere friendship. These were quick, vague impressions that sprang to her mind, and she gave no further heed to them.

'Rachel lives just a few doors down,' he told her, ushering her through the shop door, and manoeuvring the water pot on to his head. His cap was knocked askew in the operation.

Miriam could hardly believe it: a man carrying a water pot. But nobody else in the street seemed to think it odd. They greeted Asa as an old friend. They made way for him through the crowds. And the children called out to him in tones of affection and respect.

Miriam's once inconsequential wonderings came hurrying back, this time staying as questions needing answers.

'Have you known Rachel long?' she probed.

'Since the day she was born,' replied Asa, looking straight ahead. Sharp and crisp, as an answer it hid a lot more than it said. Miriam wanted to ask a good deal more, but the tone of Asa's reply made it clear there must be no more questions. He lifted his arm, ostensibly to support the jar on his head, thus hiding his face from her till they reached their destination.

'It's Asa,' he called out, pushing at the door. 'And I've brought a friend to see you.'

Rachel eased herself up and rested on an elbow, her tired eyes searching the new shadow in the doorway.

'Miriam,' she whimpered, 'you've come to see me.'

'Rachel.' She moved towards the bed, but was intercepted by Asa, who took the basket from her.

'You talk, and I'll fix the food,' he said.

The two women were silent, Miriam kneeling beside the bed, holding Rachel's hand, studying the worn, wan face.

Miriam realized she was seeing Rachel's real face for the first time. There was no paint now to disguise the outcrop blotches of disease, no paste to fill up the lines gouged by too much living in too few years. Her skin was dry and drained, with no resilience. And yet there was beauty, Miriam reckoned. The nose was proud, and even sickness with its pallid hand could not deprive the lips of their luscious fullness. And there was kindness in the lonely eyes set black and deep.

Asa fetched a little water in a basin. Miriam took the hint and coaxed cool freshness into the face of her friend.

'Asa . . . he's good to me,' breathed Rachel. 'He brings me food and drink, cleans this hovel of a house—' She rose slightly and waved a limp arm.

Miriam followed the erratic arc, and recognized around her the neat hallmark of Asa's handiwork.

After this effort, Rachel rested for a while. 'He's good to me,' she said eventually. 'And he pays the physician.' She looked over towards where Asa was dishing out the soup. Turning back to Miriam, Rachel smiled. 'He's a good man,' she confided.

Asa delivered two bowls of soup, gave Miriam time to raise Rachel and bolster her comfortably. Then he brought his own, squatting comfortably beside them.

'Well, now,' he beamed, 'you have not come here and brought no news, Miriam?'

Rachel paused with the spoon at her mouth. 'I'm sorry, Miriam, I've done nothing but talk about myself since you came in.'

'I'm getting married,' Miriam blurted out.

'I'll be there,' said Rachel, suddenly coming alive. 'When is it to be?'

'Four days from now.'

'Who is it? How did you manage it? Did you do what I said? Is it Yosef?'

'It's Yosef.'

'So he is the father, after all.'

Asa realized he was no longer part of this conversation, so he concentrated on his soup, pretending not to be interested. He kept an eye on Rachel, however, happy for her, grateful that Miriam had brought such liveliness to her, though he hoped she wouldn't get too excited.

'Eat up your soup, Rachel,' he interrupted.

'I can eat my broth when Miriam's gone, Asa. Come on, tell me about Yosef.'

'Yosef is not the father. I told you that long ago.'

'Why's he marrying you, then?'

Miriam told her, and Rachel listened.

Asa raised his eyebrows as he bent his head over the plate. Women were beyond his comprehension. And some were harder to understand than others. He felt glad he'd not been quick to join in their conversation.

Rachel chuckled when Miriam had finished. 'It goes from bad to worse, Miriam, with you it's angels, with Yosef it's dreams, but no matter, anyway, you're getting married. And I'm delighted for you.' She put down the bowl of broth which she'd hardly touched, leaned out of the bed, and hugged her visitor.

'Do my hair,' she said to Miriam. 'Get out the warpaint, and we'll have a drink to celebrate.'

Asa disappeared without a word.

Miriam brushed and combed and ribboned, bringing life to the long jet locks.

Rachel watched this operation, holding the mirror shakily in one hand, offering advice every now and then about where a ribbon or the combs should go. Then Miriam watched her apply her make-up, enthralled at Rachel's expertise, amazed at the change it made in her appearance.

By the time she was finished, Asa was back again, with his arms full. He beamed all over his face when he saw Rachel looking so radiant, fixing on her fingers the last of the glinting rings.

'I got some wine.' And he fixed the cups, and filled them.

Rachel wasted no time in proposing the toast. Holding her cup aloft, her hand trembling a little, she called out, 'To

you, Miriam, to Yosef . . . and,' with a laugh that could give
no offence, 'to the baby, whoever owns him.'

Miriam blushed. And they all drank.

Poison, Antipater decided, was the surest and safest way of
killing his father. A sick man dying was a natural thing. And
in a man so sick as Herod a totally expected thing. It would
arouse no suspicion, nor cause any questioning. His father
would be buried; the real cause of his death would go
unnoticed. The poisoner would remain unknown, and safe.
Not even his aunt, Salome, the King's sister and self-
appointed protector, would suspect.

He needed the poison. He needed also a man he could
trust, and on whom he could depend to administer the lethal
dose at the most appropriate time.

It took no great thinking for him to decide both who
would supply the stuff and who the executioner would be.

Theudion would provide the poison; there was no doubt
about that. He could certainly depend on Theudion – the
man, after all, was his uncle; brother to Doris, his mother.
And if there was any man in Jerusalem who loathed and
hated and despised the King, Theudion was that man. He
boasted with pleasure among his close friends that he looked
forward to the day when he could dance with exultation on
Herod's grave. Theudion's love of intrigue, his ambition for
his nephew, and his urging passion to see him King, were
sure guarantees of his utmost discretion, Antipater convinced
himself.

He congratulated himself on his choice. And there was no
need to beat about the bush when presenting his request.

Indeed, Theudion found it hard to suppress his delight.
'A solemn duty . . . I consider it a solemn duty. An opportunity to avenge my sister who has been for so long disgraced
and degraded by that tyrant.'

But could Theudion supply the poison?

Of course he could supply the poison. No problem. No problem at all.

Was he sure?

'Sure?' he roared. 'My nephew, would you insult your uncle? My good and close friend Antiphilus – you know him – has a brother who is an apothecary in Egypt ... in Alexandria, to be exact. I will ask him.'

'But are we sure we can trust him, uncle?'

'Antiphilus will ask no questions,' Antipater was assured. 'So far as Antiphilus is concerned, if Theudion wants poison, Theudion gets poison. That's it. Believe me.'

Antipater believed him.

'Have no fear, nephew, because I will be careful to ask him. Antiphilus will himself go to Alexandria and fetch the poison. He will bring it to me, and I personally will deliver it to the person who is to administer it.' Theudion paused, and then, with what seemed an afterthought, he asked, 'Have you decided yet who that will be?'

Antipater hesitated. But what was the point in keeping it secret? Theudion was already involved, and Antipater had committed himself.

'Pheroras,' he told his uncle.

'The King's brother!' exclaimed Theudion. 'You choose the best.'

'Who would suspect Pheroras?' replied Antipater. 'The whole kingdom will tell you how dearly Pheroras loves the King—'

'But you and I know differently. Have you asked him yet?'

'Not yet. He won't poision him just for the sake of poisoning. He'll need a reason, and I've not yet decided on the most convincing one. Is it because my father is a sick man so far beyond recovery that he'd be better dead?'

'Kill him out of kindness, you mean,' croaked Theudion.

'Or because he's a tyrant destroying the kingdom?' went on Antipater.

'Pheroras doesn't care a fig for the kingdom. You know that yourself. The whole place could fall apart, and Pheroras wouldn't turn a hair. He'd hive off somewhere with his precious Jochebed and wait for her child to be born – her Messiah, as the Pharisee Association would have her believe.'

'He'd kill for Jochebed – ' mused Antipater aloud.

'Pheroras would kill, nephew. It's as simple as that.'

Antipater raised his brow, staring at Theudion, trying to work out what exactly he meant.

'Who d'you think murdered the King's sons Aristobulus and Alexander? Pheroras, their uncle – your uncle. And you're worrying about how to entice him. I know the man.'

Antipater was silent, taking it all in. Shaping a new view of Pheroras.

'Don't make too big a business of choosing what ploy you use to involve your uncle.' Theudion advised. 'Just ask him, as bluntly as you've asked me.'

Theudion paused and stroked his beard, as though he had finished. But then he put his hand on Antipater's arm.

'But don't ask him just yet,' he said. 'The timing is important. He mustn't have too long to dwell on it. A day or two before you actually sail for Rome will be time enough. In the meantime, I'll go ahead and organize the where-withal—'

It seemed shrewd counsel to Antipater. And he took it.

The widow Rebecca piled into Isaac's bread shop with a bunch of her cronies. 'Well, the wedding is on, Isaac,' she announced, spitting it out as though it soiled her lips. 'What d'you think of that?'

Isaac tried to smother his surprise. The women waited for his comments.

Isaac was embarrassed. He felt that somehow Yosef had

let him down, his authority had been undermined. From now on he'd not be able to hold forth so dogmatically on questions that puzzled his customers and to which *he* knew the answers.

The women watched the shock pale his cheeks, and Isaac's eyes raked their bitter faces. Their cold, demanding silence frightened him. They were angry. Their gossipy tongues had been robbed of a victim, and they were searching for someone on whom to vent their spleen.

He prayed that skinny Hannah, with her rasping tones, might burst out with some bit of stupidity and rescue him. But Hannah stood there, her mouth twitching, trying to appear as venomous as the rest of them.

Behind the heavy curtain that hid her from the rest of the shop, his wife Deborah poured some wheat between the millstones, and got on with her grinding. She'd heard Rebecca's grating voice and now, over the comforting rumble of the stones, she sensed the tension engulfing the shop. And Isaac's unusual quietness could mean only that he was put in an awkward spot.

Deborah got up and walked to the corner of the room. There she manhandled a split millstone away from the wall and, with all her strength, hurled it to the floor.

'Isaac!' she called, 'Isaac!' injecting into her summons as much terror as she could muster.

The shop erupted with sound, and Isaac, fear-stricken, rushed to join his wife.

Deborah put a finger to her lips as he appeared through the curtain, then stretched out her arm to signal that everything was all right.

He paused beside her, nonplussed, confused.

Deborah began groaning dramatically, but in between she whispered to him the reason for her accident. Isaac was grateful for the contrived interruption.

'D'you need any help in there?' Abigail called.

'I think everything's all right, now,' Isaac called back. 'It was just a millstone falling.' He tidied the pieces away noisily, and loudly comforted his wife who was already sitting down again, ready to get on with her work. Isaac sat down beside her, and idly poured in more wheat.

Beyond the curtain, they could hear the droning voices of the women. They tried to catch snatches of the conversation but only a buzz came through.

Deborah nodded with satisfaction. 'Give them a bit longer to wait, and they'll go home,' she assured her husband.

She had hardly finished whispering before Rebecca called in to them. 'We'll come back later, Isaac.' There was no grating in her tone now. 'I hope you'll feel better soon, Deborah.' And they all grunted, echoing her sentiments.

Isaac nearly laughed out loud as he heard them shuffling from his shop, but his wife's hand covered his mouth and she smiled at him.

'Thank you,' said Isaac, relieved.

But Deborah was back to grinding flour.

The sun was glaring and hot. All round, the burning brightness of the still-young day had drained life and colour from the sky, and bleached the trees and plants and houses, fields, rocks and rolling hills of all that gave them character, tingeing everywhere and everything with a blinding, feature-less greyness.

Joachim stood by the door and looked, unseeing, into the shimmering distance. He had stepped out to give the women inside some privacy as they dressed Miriam for her wedding. He shielded his eyes from the penetrating glare, and wished for a good day. But even as he wished, it seemed for a glancing speck of time that the earth stood still, and a pall of sadness fell over the day. It was an odd feeling.

Long months ago he had announced this day's cel-ebrations, and had invited his guests. And everybody, then, was keen to come. Nothing, they'd told him, bar death itself, would stand in their way. His daughter's wedding feast, they'd promised, would be well furnished with guests.

But how different it was now. The rollicking delight of their acceptances had now become mealy mouthed mutterings that proffered excuses for their absence. Like Laban who had just bought two yoke of oxen, and this wedding day was the only time he could find to test them – as if any man worth this salt would buy oxen without first having run his hand over them. Mordecai had just got married, so he reckoned he couldn't come either. Was he ashamed of his wife or something? Others claimed they had no suitable garments for the feast, and they refused to expect Joachim to provide them, on top of all his other expenses.

Joachim felt wounded; he knew what they were at. But Shebna was worst of all, going off to Rome to look at merchandise he had already paid for.

Yet Shebna's action didn't surprise Joachim. It was the kind of cussedness that characterized a man who lived his life like a vinegar bottle: rosy and palatable to the eye, but sour and bitter when the seal was broken. It was clear that Shebna had taken a dislike to Miriam. Come to that, he didn't seem to think much of the whole family nowadays . . . Well, there was no sense in upsetting himself over Shebna.

Joachim brushed his hand across his brow, trying to rub away these thoughts. It was going to be a long day and, with such a beginning, Joachim felt he would not be sorry to see it ended. In the meantime, for Miriam's sake, he must make the best of it.

He walked to the wedding tent which Barzillai had lent them, and he himself had helped to pitch. And he busied himself, checking everything, making sure that all was ready, or as ready as it could be.

*

Miriam stood speechless with joy, beaming delight at her mother.

Her sister, Salome, raved about the dress, and hugged her close. 'God be with you, Miriam,' she whispered.

Anna was pleased. The dress was certainly worth all the work. And she was proud of Miriam, the tender-eyed, sharp-cut, slender face framed in hair weaving its jet-black way down to rest on shoulders smooth as the driven snow. She was a gentle girl, and looking at her now, Anna realized how much she loved her.

'The veil, now, Mother,' Salome said.

Anna was grateful, for she was on the verge of tears. 'Be careful how you lift it, Salome.'

But already Salome had taken it from its box, and was arranging it to go over Miriam's head.

Anna took over, tying it here, fixing it there, till Miriam stood dressed as a bride.

Anna could be composed no longer. She cupped the head in loving hands, and kissed the quiet face. 'God bless you, Miriam—' she wanted to add much more to her blessing, but could not speak for sobbing.

Miriam gathered her mother in her arms, comforting her.

Salome, trying to be practical, waited a little, then hustled her mother to finish getting dressed herself. 'And cry too loudly, Mother,' she scolded, 'and we'll not hear them when they make the call.'

'It's only me,' said the voice through the door.

The three women looked round.

'Rachel,' Miriam cried, as the figure added body to the sound.

'You look lovely, Miriam. Everybody's waiting in the tent, but I just had to come over to see you. You look beautiful, just beautiful.'

'But, Rachel,' stammered Miriam, still amazed that the

woman who was clearly dying when she made her promise a few days ago was now actually standing in front of her.

'But, Rachel, nothing. I said I'd come. I wanted to come. And I'm here. Asa brought me, I hope you don't mind, and he'll take me home again. He's like a hen with a chick.'

'I'm glad to see you, Rachel, but are you well enough?'

'It's surprising the wonders a bit of paint will work,' quipped Rachel, putting her hand under her chin and pushing her face forward for Miriam to glance at the robust health painted there. 'And, in any case, I wouldn't have missed your wedding even if they'd had to carry me here in my bed.'

Anna, listening with a mother's ear, heard the weakness in Rachel's voice, and saw in her face the illness that all her powder and handiwork could not disguise from a mother's eye.

'Rachel,' she said carefully, 'if you'd like something to eat before the ceremony, I'll set you up some broth and some wine.'

'I'd like that,' returned Rachel, 'but I'll have the wine first, if I may.'

There was a tinkle of laughter in Anna's voice when she replied. 'You can have the wine at both ends of the broth, if you like,' and she was away.

Rachel worked gratefully through her broth, sifting in her mind the many questions she wanted to ask the bride. Had Miriam's mother and sister not been present, she might have blurted out what she wanted to say, knowing that Miriam would understand she meant no unkindness. But now she felt she must be careful, for they did not know her quite so well, and might easily think her nosy and impudent.

The questions racing round her head, however, refused to shape themselves with the elegance and propriety she reckoned would avoid giving offence to Anna and Salome. Yet she *must* ask, for she was concerned for this strange, lovely girl who had become her friend.

'Will you be living in the new house after your wedding?' she whispered over a spoonful of soup.

It was more a probe to test the atmosphere than a serious question, but she was relieved that it had caused no ruffle among her audience.

'My father and Yosef have talked it over,' said Miriam, 'and Yosef says it would be better if I didn't live there for a while, at any rate.'

She saw Rachel raise her eyebrows.

'He thinks,' Miriam continued, 'he thinks it will give the hatred time to die down, and the gossipmongers a chance to forget.'

'Never mind the gossipmongers,' Rachel interrupted, no longer greatly concerned about Anna and Salome, or their reaction. 'Think of yourself. If you're away from them, it'll give you a chance to build up your strength, and allow you a bit of peace and quiet for bringing this child to birth,' she advised, approving Yosef's plan. 'But where else will you go?'

'To Juttah,' Miriam answered. 'To my cousin Elisheba.'

'She's the old woman—' suggested Rachel, feeling her way to the next question. 'She's the cousin your . . . your angel talked about.' And Rachel felt alarmed that such an outlandish collection of words should fall seriously from her lips.

Miriam nodded.

'You'll be able to check up on a few things there,' commented Rachel, not really understanding what she meant.

Miriam agreed.

'When are you going?'

'Tomorrow.'

'Tomorrow. So soon? I'll miss you, Miriam, while you're away.'

Joachim came in then, trying to look as though he were

in control. 'Is everything ready, Anna? The Rabbi and everybody's here now.' And then he noticed Rachel, and said how glad he was to see her. 'They tell me Yosef is on his way, and it'll not be long before he's here,' he gabbled out of nervousness.

Anna now took charge. She checked that the young men were stationed outside with the canopy. She positioned Miriam ready to walk out, with Salome immediately behind her. Joachim and Anna herself would follow.

'Have you everything you need, Talitha?' asked Joachim of Miriam, as though he would keep his daughter a little longer to himself.

'You're fussing the child, Joachim,' reprimanded Anna. 'What more do you think she could need?'

'Oh, my piece of silver,' said Miriam. 'The silver Yosef gave me. It's in the niche there by the window.'

Joachim felt pleased he'd asked. Salome was gone, and back with the piece in a trice.

'Now, at last, we're all ready,' announced Anna, pretending to sound pompous, but there was a touch of sorrow in her voice.

Rachel held the door open.

Outside, in the sunshine, the canopy cast a cool shadow, and the four bearers beamed as Miriam stepped towards them. Rachel kissed her as she passed, and pressed something into her hand.

As she proceeded sedately, demurely, sheltered from the sun, Miriam opened her hand to look at Rachel's gift. 'What else could it be?' she whispered to herself. 'A ring.' And she put it on her finger.

They surged forward from the tent to greet her: a little group. Fewer than she had imagined there would be.

The procession stopped, and Miriam stopped too.

A cry went up from the company: 'Blessed is he that cometh.' And they cheered with an embarrassed, self-conscious kind of cheer, cleaving at the same time a passage through the company for Yosef to enter.

Miriam searched down this human tunnel, with its frisking, clashing colours of their robes, seeking for Yosef her bridegroom.

Yosef approached steadily, and there was a manliness in his stride that gave her strength. She recognized Barzillai stepping out beside him, talking with him, perhaps making some witty asides about the company. She liked Barzillai; he was a good friend to Yosef. But where was Shebna? Her mind asked the question but, in her building excitement, it found no enthusiasm to work out the answer.

The Rabbi stepped out, and partly blocked her view. The gap closed, a sea of faces turned, a rioting turbulence of colour washed in front of her and all around.

Yosef stood beside her under the canopy, but his face and shape were blurred by the tears that filled her eyes.

The chatter died; her surroundings fell away. And only the sound of interchanging formal voices crept into her ears. She spoke occasionally herself, but not completely conscious of the words she said. Her mind was not her own and played a multitude of games with her, racing her through days gone by . . . the women at the well, the dream, and Rachel's loving kindness, and rings, and Asa's shop, and Yosef's face of sorrow, her mother comforting, and Barzillai, the new house built upon the hill, and her father in the herb garden . . . Everything jumbled, fleeting, soundless . . .

Yosef caressed her hand, and the pressure of his gentle strength rubbed her palm hard against the piece of silver seated in her grip.

She heard her father's faltering voice, joined with her mother's tender tones in benediction. And the loud 'Amen' from the company told her the ceremony was ended. And she was Yosef's wife.

CHAPTER SIX

Yosef stood watching the night sky gently lightening. A soft wind was rising. And he could just discern the dying echoes of sheep bells from a distant, fidgeting flock. The coming dawn reminded him it would be soon time for Miriam to be on her way to her cousin Elisheba in Juttah.

The realization saddened him. A few short hours ago, they'd been pronounced man and wife. The words still sounded in his head, though, in the lonely, timeless space between the night and day, it seemed that they were said so very long ago. And now, in even fewer hours, Miriam would be gone.

The expectation of her departure sat like a bird of death, brooding in his mind. He chided himself for his heartlessness in letting Miriam go. But he was right. He knew it in his heart and soul. It was the only way, if Miriam were to escape nagging, perverting, soul-destroying persecution in Nazareth.

It may have needed a clarion call from heaven to convince him that the marriage was a proper thing, but nothing and nobody, he told himself again, had any need to advise him that encouraging Miriam to get away from Nazareth was wisest for them both.

He turned abruptly towards the house, fighting the sorrow that snared him. Miriam was standing in the doorway.

'It's right, Yosef,' she said, as though she knew what was troubling his mind. 'It's right. Try not to let sorrow fill your heart.'

It was a wan smile in reply. He touched her hand gratefully, shyly as he came through the door. And Miriam turned and went in with him.

The dimness of the house was made darker by their coming from the glare of the early sun. The fire had burned out, neglected in the sleeping hours. But on the upper floor, protected from the draughts, the saucer-shaped lamp, kept constantly alight, glowed defiantly.

Their eyes became accustomed to the dimness, and they set about getting ready for the journey.

Miriam prepared some food, though she felt in no mood for eating. And while the meal cooked, she packed provisions for the road – nuts and figs and dates, hard biscuits made of flour and water, and some dried fish.

Yosef worked quickly, packing clothes and a bed roll, but worried lest he pack too much for her to carry.

Nothing was said, and only their feet shuffling on the stone floor and the occasional clatter of dish on dish made any sound to break the silence.

The house was lonely. Inhabited, indeed, but there was no life in it. It had everything a house might need. And Yosef looked round, seeing what his sweat and handiwork had wrought. But there was no presence in it, no life: only a kind of melancholy, a feeling of disappointment. It was a place where people met, paused briefly, nor ever spoke nor touched, nor looked each other in the face, but sorrowed silently, died a little, waved farewell, and went their separating ways.

The house that was to have been his home was now no more than a staging post in a pilgrimage of sorrow. His marriage, which seemed once to have had heaven as its sponsor, had brought him nothing, and had conferred no greater privilege on his young bride than the right reserved to a married woman of travelling unchaperoned on so long a journey.

It was mockery. And Yosef wanted to be angry. But he could not be sure how or where or on what to vent his anger.

He tugged the strap too tightly on the bed roll. It snapped, and Yosef groaned.

Azariah wakened with the dawn, and lay wide awake, worried. Wondering about Miriam. Today, he reflected, the young woman would be setting out on the long journey south to Juttah. At any time it was a long road for a woman, but being pregnant made things more difficult.

His mind filled with what he remembered of the road. Suffocating heat and thirst. And fears – of vagabonds who travelled in the caravan, of highway robbers who swooped suddenly, plundered and were gone again to the safety of their hide-outs in the hills. He'd not like Naomi to have to travel that road alone.

He thought of Miriam measuring every mile, step by faltering step. And it worried him all the more because he liked her, and could not help himself respecting Yosef for risking his good reputation and marrying her, not knowing whose child it was she was carrying.

Naomi was still sound asleep, and he smiled as she let out one great throaty snore.

He eased his old body from his bed roll, stood up and settled his chiton around him, stretching it to the calves of his legs to press out the creases of the night. He did it mechanically, as he did every morning. And, out of the same habit, he slipped on his shirt, and tied his girdle round his waist.

By the time he'd dressed, he knew what he must do. The question that had been hovering and hankering in his head had an answer. He had thought of giving Yosef two sheep as a wedding present. But he wouldn't now; instead he'd give the donkey.

He had his cloak on, and was on his way before he realized he had not discussed this change of plan with Naomi. But it'd be all right, he reckoned. Naomi would agree it was a good thing in the circumstances.

He was turning the donkey to head towards Yosef's house when he caught sight of Miriam and Yosef already near the joining of the roads.

'Yosef,' he called, and gave his surprised mount an unfamiliar jerk in the new direction.

Miriam turned in response. Yosef dumped the heap of baggage on the ground, turned and waited, wondering what the old man could want so early in the day.

Azariah noticed the baggage, and felt glad he'd planned to give the donkey. It would be much easier for Miriam. And he congratulated himself for having thought of strapping the panniers on the animal, though, as he tried to coax a bit of haste out of the beast, he noticed they made riding uncomfortable.

'Is anything wrong?' enquired Yosef as the old man drew close.

'Nothing,' puffed Azariah. 'Just help me off this animal. It's for Miriam for her journey.'

Yosef was stunned, and tried to stammer some kind of thanks.

'There's nothing to be said,' ordered Azariah. 'Let's not delay, now. Pack all that stuff in the panniers, and get the young woman on her way.'

Yosef did as he was told, while the old man held the

donkey's head, murmuring softly to it, patting it every now and then: slow, tender farewell strokes on the shaggy neck.

Everything was ready now, and they were on the move again. They didn't mind Azariah leading the donkey all the way to the square.

And the old man was grateful.

Joachim and Anna and Salome were already in the square to meet them. It was Yosef who spotted them standing forlorn on the fringe of the shouting and bustling crowd already gathered, and everybody telling everybody else that any minute now the caravan would be on the move.

Her father looked as if the world had come to an end, though he tried to smile as he signalled back to Yosef's call. He hugged his daughter as they met, and her mother hid her sadness by reminding Joachim that he was in public. 'Even fathers are not allowed to greet their daughters like that in public,' she advised in mock reprimand. But her humour eased things a bit for everybody.

Salome kissed her. 'That's permitted, even in public,' she joked, looking over at her mother. She thrust a bag at Miriam, carefully wrapped and tied. 'Some food,' she said. And Miriam almost laughed out loud. Food she needed! With enough to see her through a famine already stored in the panniers on the donkey.

Salome sensed the reaction. 'I know, but I couldn't let you go empty-handed. Someone else will eat it on the journey if you can't.'

Barzillai arrived as the sisters were talking. However he felt like greeting Miriam, he obeyed the formalities, and did no more than bow and wish her 'Shalom'.

A blanket,' he said to her as he offered the gift. And a leather bottle.

'Wine, Barzillai?' Yosef exclaimed.

'Just water,' returned Barzillai, and added by way of

explanation. 'I know there are rivers and streams along the way. . . . But there's a day's march through Samaritan country . . .'

'And the Jews have no dealings with the Samaritans,' quipped Salome.

'Exactly,' agreed Barzillai. 'And it's a long way, believe me, from Engennin to Jacob's Springs.'

Even Joachim nodded. And almost smiled.

Azariah had barely time to pack Salome's food and the blanket in one pannier and tie on the water bag before the call went up that it was time to move.

Salome said a quick goodbye. Her mother hugged Miriam as though she would comfort her for ever, but kept back the tears. Tomorrow she could cry, she told herself, and kissed her daughter tenderly.

Joachim broke the rules again, his fatherly arms embracing her. And then he held her head in his hands, searching her face. 'The Lord bless you and keep you—' he whispered. And turned suddenly away, and stood beside Azariah.

Azariah took him by the arm. 'There's something I must tell you, Joachim.'

Yosef helped her mount the donkey, sitting her side-saddle. 'Wife,' he whispered, folding her hands into her lap, and patting them as the donkey moved to join the caravan starting its journey out of Nazareth.

They stood and watched and said nothing till the caravan had turned the far corner of the square.

'Naomi said you're to come and eat in our house,' Azariah announced. 'You, too, Barzillai, now that you're here.'

He didn't wait for an answer, but turned and began to make towards home.

And they all followed.

Miriam was shy with the other women as the journey started. They were just as shy with her and with one another. But by the time they had made their way through the valley from Nazareth and had reached Nain, they were talking away as if they had known each other for years.

And there was time to talk. There were only three other women besides Miriam herself. She couldn't be sure how many men there were. Twelve, or maybe more.

Her companions were all married. Their husbands were with the other men, travelling, as custom ordained, separately from the women. They'd all come from various places further north, but the place names meant nothing to Miriam.

Two of the women were going to Jerusalem, one of them with an infant. 'Our firstborn,' she told them. 'We're going to show him to my husband's parents.' The second, Miriam felt, was somewhat boastful. She seemed to want to show off how wealthy she was. Her son, she told them, pointing towards the men, was twelve years old. She and her husband were taking him to Jerusalem, to the Temple, for his Bar-Mitzvah, when he'd become 'a son of the Law', and be considered, in his religion, an adult and no longer a boy. She talked as if those she addressed knew nothing about their Jewish religion.

For long enough, Miriam couldn't decide whether it was sadness or shyness that made her third companion seem so quiet and withdrawn. Yes, she was married, she told them, when the rich woman asked her.

'No sign of any children yet?' Richness enquired.

'Not yet.'

Miriam thought she detected the sound of sadness.

'How long are you married?' asked the nursing mother. 'I was expecting almost as soon as we married.'

The reply was slow in coming. And Miriam thought she could guess the answer – and the reason for the girl's sadness.

'Three years,' she said softly. Almost apologizing.

And there was quietness. Till the nursing mother offered her assurance. 'You've plenty of time.'

But after that there wasn't much chatter as they went through Nain and joined the main thoroughfare that ran south to Jezreel.

The road was now a busy place: a highway of caravans of people coming and going. Pilgrims to and from Jerusalem, some of them, Miriam reckoned. Travellers, merchants, and even ordinary people like herself on business that only they themselves knew about.

And she admired the mass of colours they presented as they passed. Reds and greens and blues and yellows on the women. The grand merchants in their white robes and yellow headscarves, the burning scarlet saddles on their grey horses. Homely dull-brown camels graced their way, dwarfing the donkeys of the camel-drivers who rode in front of them, leading the train. And herds of black goats; bulky red oxen labouring along. Shepherds in their short cloaks, yellow or red kerchiefs folded over their heads and falling down the neck and shoulders. And sheep, slowly nibbling as they went, their shepherd watching, keeping them within whistling distance.

It was like a moving market day. And at another time Miriam might have revelled in it all.

Village after village. Always the children greeted them. Tousle-haired, barefooted, bodies gleaming brown in the sun. Running alongside, almost the length of the village street, shouting, waving – being pushed aside now and again by the bigger, stronger ones eager to sell their wares: trinkets, sweetmeats, grapes, fruit, vegetables.

Sometimes they stopped in a village. Without dismounting they'd buy a cup of dibs – grape syrup – that was refreshing and left a lingering taste in the mouth. And they'd buy grapes and cucumbers to eat along the way.

Oh, that things might be different, Miriam wished. That Yosef could be here and they could enjoy it all together. She gazed, lonely, blankly at the lovely countryside. The beautiful plains of Esdraelon, stretching away, away. Fields of wheat and corn. The hill slopes crowded with orchards and vineyards and olive groves.

The donkey, as though it had caught her mood, plodded almost aimlessly, making little dust clouds on the road.

They rested in Jezreel. And Miriam was glad of it. The sun was burning hot, and it was good to get out of it for a while. The women round the well made space for the travellers. The husbands now took charge of the animals. The Bar-Mitzvah boy asked politely if he might look after Miriam's donkey. Miriam was grateful, and told him so. And congratulated him on his courtesy.

She took a food bag out of the pannier before the lad led away the donkey. And then she was off herself to the well, slaking her thirst, splashing her face, glad to wash away the dust and heat of travelling.

There was deep, shadowed coolness beneath a nearby clump of palms. Miriam made towards them, where she noticed her sad companion sitting by herself. 'May I sit beside you?' she asked, already putting down her bag of food – Salome's food bag.

The woman patted the ground, making a space for Miriam, as it were. Making her welcome.

Miriam shared out the food, and her companion gladly accepted. And Salome's quip about somebody else being glad of it flashed through Miriam's mind. She smiled to herself.

'You're off to Jerusalem?' offered the girl.

'To Juttah, just beyond Hebron.' Miriam told her. 'To a cousin.'

'Your husband not with you?'

'He's at home.'

'He believes in keeping the old customs, then?'

Miriam was taken aback. Old customs? And then it dawned. It was a custom, she recollected, once upon a time, for a woman to go away from home in the early months of pregnancy. To be cosseted, to have her diet regulated. To be sure she'd eat no grapes and drink no wine, and not take food that would upset her. But not too many practised that custom nowadays. She'd never heard of anybody observing it. Not in Nazareth, anyway.

'You're lucky,' her companion told her before she had any time to reply. 'We're going to Shiloh,' she said as Miriam took a bite of Salome's dried fish. 'To my husband's home.' And then she paused, as if wondering whether or not to say more.

She eased forward her hand to touch Miriam. 'I wouldn't tell the others this, but I feel I can tell you, and you won't laugh at me. We want children,' the girl confided. 'Three years is a long time to wait, and you know what they say about a man and wife who produce no children.'

She searched Miriam's face to see there was no judgement there.

'My husband is a good man. We have committed no wrong that would deserve such a cruel punishment from God.'

Miriam stroked the hand that rested on her arm.

'We're visiting my husband's parents in Shiloh. But really, we're going to Shiloh to pray that God will bless us with a child.'

She seemed relieved that she'd said it.

'Please God,' said Miriam. What more could she say?

'I'm sure it will happen,' the girl announced with confidence. 'It will happen if we pray in Shiloh.'

Miriam wasn't sure what to answer. Even as she was thinking, the angel's words of months ago came whispering back, '*Consider your cousin Elisheba who was called barren.*'

The ways of God were past finding out. And it could be that they'd be every bit as strange in Shiloh for this girl as they were in Nazareth for herself.

The girl was talking again – or was she thinking aloud, trying to transform her flimsy hopes into certainty?

'It happened in the ancient history of our people,' she was murmuring, in her tenseness tightening her grip on Miriam's arm. 'It was in Shiloh, the Scriptures say, that Hannah prayed for a son. Barren she was, and broken-hearted, sad, for all Elkanah her husband loved her, and never chided her for being childless, and was better to her than ten sons—'

Miriam listened. And was sorry for this poor, young, longing woman who trawled the far-back history of the nation for a crumb of comfort and some faint gleam of hope.

'And Hannah prayed in Shiloh,' she was saying. 'She prayed to God to look on her affliction and not forget her . . . You remember the story . . . how often we heard it in synagogue at Sabbath worship.'

'Yes,' answered Miriam, 'I remember. And Hannah, indeed, had her prayer answered.'

'And conceived,' rushed in her companion. 'And bore a son, and called his name Samuel.'

'Yes,' said Miriam, sounding tired.

Her companion noticed. 'I've talked too much,' she told Miriam. 'In your condition you should be lying back, resting. Lie back now,' and she got up to settle Miriam comfortably. 'You'll not tell the other two women what we've talked about, will you?'

Miriam assured her she wouldn't, then closed her eyes and lay back to rest.

And enjoyed a good sleep before Richness's husband, who seemed to have appointed himself leader of the group, came to advise them both that it was time to move on.

'If we continue now,' he advised them, 'we can make Engennin before the sun is set. We can get a good rest, and then start before daybreak for our journey through Samaritan country.'

His Bar-Mitzvah son was already waiting with the donkey to help Miriam mount. And they were on their way again. This time with music, since one of the men was playing a jaunty tune on his pipes.

'That's my husband,' the sad companion announced to all. And she sounded happy. Proud.

And Miriam was pleased.

Engennin was a welcome sight in the setting sun. Miriam and her three companions ate well and gladly when they reached the khan – the caravanserai – while the men watered and fed and bedded the animals. The nursing mother suckled her baby, and then, together, the four women found a place to sleep.

It was a whole new experience for Miriam. She had never been so far away from home, and this could have been the far side of the world. Never in her life before had she slept in a roadside lodging. Never had she been on the borderland of Samaria.

There was little time, though, for her to think about it. She was asleep almost as soon as she tucked Barzillai's blanket around her. And slept a good night's sleep.

It was still dark when their leader had them up again. It was hill country now, he explained to them all, though some of them didn't need to be told. It was easier travelling in the cool of the night before dawn, he said. And, anyway, there'd be no welcome from the Samaritans in any of the villages along the way.

And there was no welcome, even when the sun was up. The day shining warm and bright. They passed through villages where, if they weren't exactly contemned, they were certainly ignored. Not even the local children ran out to greet them.

Surely their parents didn't teach them to hate us, Miriam

asked herself. *The Jews have no dealings with the Samaritans*, she recollected, but the Samaritans themselves were not too forthcoming either. It was sad, she thought, that a quirk of history long dead and gone should leave people hating each other so deeply. As though they were entirely different races entitled by nature to hate each other.

They are different people from ourselves, the blended sounds of her father's and the Rabbi's voices murmured through her thinking. *When Nebuchadnezzar conquered our land and carried off almost the whole nation into slavery and captivity in Babylon, some were left behind, in Samaria*. The voices were teaching her. Not history, though it sounded like it, but – as the Rabbi had said so often – religion. The religion of Jewry. *Those who were left behind befriended and intermarried with the conquerors. They mixed their blood with the blood of the heathen. They were no longer Jews. They are a different race.*

'But that was over five hundred years ago,' she said aloud, and shook the thoughts away. It was a pity, she told herself, a tragedy that a nation could still be tearing itself apart because of things that happened once that people now could neither remember nor imagine.

The little group rested near Dothan, while the midday sun burned hot. The rich, fertile fields were crowded white with sheep. And memories of Joseph and his brothers who threw him into the pit . . . Even then, reflected Miriam, when her nation was still only in its infancy – even then Jews couldn't agree, and brother fought against brother as though they were born to be enemies.

There was music again today as they journeyed. From her sad companion's husband again. He played some of the lively tunes he had played yesterday: marching music, almost. And Miriam thought maybe he felt as she did, that they were marching the byways of their nation's history.

Every now and then the Bar-Mitzvah boy would ride

alongside her, to enquire if she was all right, and was there anything she needed. His mother smiled at him for his kindness. And Miriam agreed with her: he was a good lad, and a credit to his parents.

Miriam's travelling friends, men and women and the Bar-Mitzvah boy, might have been glad to rest the night at Sychar, the main city of Samaria.

'But we'll be given no welcome there,' the leader assured them. And some of the men who were used to travelling agreed with him. 'And we dare not eat their food,' he added.

'He who tastes the bread of a Samaritan is as one who eats the flesh of swine,' intoned one man, making it sound like Holy Writ.

So they skirted round Sychar, and made for Jacob's Springs, set in a beautiful valley and named after the Patriarch Jacob himself.

The khan here was more elaborate than their sleeping place the previous night. Large rooms to sleep in, all built round a square. And an area specially set aside where the animals too could sleep comfortably. It was built and owned by a Jew, who also played host to the travellers who, certainly tonight, crowded the place.

'It's been like this every time I've been here,' one of the men remarked as they sat around the glowing fire, drinking soup and eating the bread and meat provided by their host, and brought to them by a young serving girl. And good strong wine.

'The poor fellow must be worn out,' said another.

'Worn out counting his money,' quipped the seasoned traveller. 'You can work out what he's taking tonight alone.'

Miriam didn't wait to hear what that amount was. She herself and her companions had found a good space in one of the women's rooms, and there bedded down for the night. One more night like this, she reflected, and two full days' travelling, and I'm in Juttah.

As she fell asleep, she smiled sadly to herself, wondering to which nation Jacob the Patriarch belonged. To the Jews of Judah whose border was only a short distance away, and that she'd be crossing tomorrow? Or to the Samaritans, in whose land the cool, rich springs gave enough sweet water to refresh a whole city and slake the thirst of travellers?

On the road through Judah next day, Miriam couldn't help feeling delighted. Bleak, bare hills they were, maybe, but she still tingled with strange, warming pleasure. Among her own . . . She was every bit as bad as the rest of them, she scolded herself. Whether she liked it or not, history and religion had shaped her as it had shaped them.

They made no stop till they reached Shiloh, for all the sun burned hot. Nobody disagreed with the decision, for they knew the sad companion and her husband were keen to get there. And they all owed him a kindness for his music that had brightened their journey.

The two made no delay once the caravan arrived in Shiloh. They bade farewell to their companions, but the young woman kissed Miriam as she was leaving. 'Pray that God will answer my prayer,' she whispered.

'God bless you,' said Miriam, hoping the girl's prayer would be heard and answered.

There was a tingle of excitement in the remaining group. Jerusalem was not all that far away, and nobody wanted to delay getting there.

'I know, I know,' the leader explained. 'We all want to be in Jerusalem. But we also need to rest, and so do the animals. An hour . . . some sleep . . . and then we'll be on our way.'

So they rested. And some of them slept. In the shade of huge palm trees that blocked out the sun so completely that it might have been night-time in their shadow.

Miriam felt the better for her short rest. And the donkey, too, she thought, for it carried her with extra care, and comfortably.

Where should she look, in this countryside all round her? A land that up to now she'd only ever dreamed about. Names were places now. Real places. And if she wanted to, she could reach out her hand and touch history, the history of her people. Bethel where Abraham once was, and Jacob ... Ramah where, they said, Rachel's lamentations were heard when she rose from her tomb to weep for the children of Israel being carried off to Babylon ...

And now Jerusalem ... shapes and shadows in the dying sun. If only Yosef were here ... her heart was full of joy and laden with sorrow all at once.

'You'll lodge with us tonight,' she heard Richness saying to her as she stared, rapt, while the last sun bathed the Temple roof.

'Our friends will make you welcome, too,' Richness was assuring her.

'And you can have a really good rest,' Bar-Mitzvah boy was saying. 'And tomorrow I will ride with you on your journey as far as Rachel's Tomb.'

'But—' began Miriam.

'But no buts,' said Richness's husband.

'I don't even know your names.'

'Nor we yours,' the husband countered. 'My name is David. My wife's name is Zipporah. Our son is called David also.'

'My name is Miriam. I am the wife of Yosef.'

'Well, then, Miriam wife of Yosef,' said the husband, 'Let us make no delay. Our friends will be expecting us.'

He rode ahead with his wife. The boy rode with Miriam, guiding her through the labyrinth of streets, through squares and tree-lined avenues, past Herod's Palace, and the High Priest's house ... to what looked to Miriam like a palace, where their friends lived.

She couldn't take it all in, and was only vaguely aware of the warm welcome she was given, and the sumptuous meal they coaxed her to eat . . . *Yosef, Yosef,* she kept thinking to herself, *if only you were here with me, Yosef* . . . and she dreamed of him as she slept in luxury she had never known before.

And the morning came. And the boy, David, true to his word, rode with her as far as Rachel's Tomb.

When they'd stopped, Miriam thanked him. 'Not only for your kindness this morning,' she said, 'but for all your kindness on the journey from Nazareth.'

She had more to say. But he looked embarrassed, so she stopped.

'You know why it's called Rachel's Tomb?' he asked.

Miriam knew. But he had obviously rehearsed it all. She nodded. And listened.

'Jacob loved Rachel more than his own life. She died giving birth to her only child. She said to call the child Benoni, the son of my sorrow. But Jacob said, "No. Call him Benjamin, the son of my right hand." He became the father of the Tribe of Benjamin. Rachel was his mother. But she died and Jacob buried her here. That's why it's called Rachel's Tomb.'

'You're a clever lad, David,' Miriam told him. 'A generous lad. And you'll grow into a fine man.'

He smiled, an open, honest, manly smile.

They bade each other farewell.

And Miriam went on, with Bethlehem far over on her left, along the road to Juttah.

Miriam was in Juttah. And she was glad. It was the end of her long journey. At last.

She watched the sun folding itself away in the hills, and felt the cold creep in with the coming darkness. She felt no fear this time, though. The long journey in the scorching sun was over; the rough camps in the bleak, dark nights were gone. Tonight, she'd be among friends, and she'd sleep in a comfortable bed.

Suddenly she was tired. It was a tiredness she had struggled with and stifled all the journey long. She shook herself and rubbed her eyes. The dust of travelling was on her face.

She pulled her cloak, comforting, about her, and urged the donkey faster. She would be in Elisheba's house before the darkness.

Zecharias greeted her arrival, searched into her face, and smiled. Whether he knew her or not, Miriam could not be sure. But there was kindness and a look of welcome in the crinkled, bearded face.

She said 'Shalom' again, this time a little louder, for he seemed hard of hearing.

The old man mouthed 'Shalom alekum', but no sound was uttered from the shaping lips.

Miriam could not hide her surprise. Zecharias was dumb. She had not expected this. And she was sad. Involuntarily, in pity, she stretched her hands and touched him.

He gently took her hands, understanding the kindness that flowed through them, and lifted them to his mouth. Her fingertips barely settled on his lips.

Zecharias shook his head.

Miriam knew what he meant. He could not speak. Yet he was in no way sad about it.

He raised her hands to touch his ears, and nodded his head. *But he could hear.*

Zecharias released her hands and shuffled towards a table, beckoning her to follow. On a wax tablet he began to write.

Stooping over the table, in the fading light, Miriam watched and read, and learned how Zecharias the priest had become dumb.

I was in the Temple, the slow hand wrote, *serving the altar of incense. An angel of the Lord appeared. He was standing at the right side of the altar, where no man dare stand.*

Fear fell on me.

The angel said, 'Fear not, Zecharias. Thy prayer is heard. Thy wife Elisheba shall bear thee a son. And thou shalt call his name John.'

Zecharias rested for a while, and stood back to make sure Miriam could clearly see what was being written. And then he began to write again.

I said to the angel, 'I am an old man. My wife is advanced in her days.'

The angel answered me, 'I am Gabriel. I stand in the presence of God. And I am sent to speak, and show thee these glad tidings.'

There was no room left on the tablet. Zecharias paused. And then, as though each word he rubbed was Holy Writ, he slowly cleaned the tablet. And wrote again.

'And, behold, thou shalt be dumb, not able to speak until the day these things shall be performed. Because thou believest not my words.'

But it would be all right, he assured her, scratching excitedly with the stylo on the tablet, when his son was born. That was the word from God. And there was not long to wait now, for it was near to his wife's delivery.

Miriam wanted to tell him why she had come. But Zecharias was not waiting. He was leading her towards Elisheba's room. And as they went, at his shuffling pace, Miriam called out her greeting to her cousin.

The curtain at the door fell back, rustling behind them as they went through.

Elisheba was rising in welcome as they entered, her hands pressing, protecting across her stomach. She straightened herself, urging her hands to her sides, rubbing away the sudden pain that snatched at her. She shook her head, trying quickly to explain to herself the strange sensation that had overtaken her, trying to dismiss the pain inside her, hoping the excitement of meeting her cousin would not affect too much the child that kicked and leapt in her womb as though it would come to birth.

She sat slowly down again to ease herself, and smiled. But Miriam noticed the wince of agony the smile took time to smother. And when she spoke, her gentle voice was warm with welcome.

Miriam liked Elisheba immediately. And she was pouring out her story to her cousin whom she hardly knew, and could not remember ever having met before. Yet she felt there was a bond between them, and everything felt right. There was no awkwardness. There was nothing strange in what she was doing. It seemed the most natural thing in the world.

Zecharias was gone, and Miriam was aware that she had not noticed him going. She ended her story abruptly, embarrassed that since they'd met, she'd been talking non-stop, and had given her cousin no opportunity to say a word beyond her welcome.

She looked apologetically at Elisheba, and waited for her reaction.

It was quiet after the torrent of words. Only the complaining of the cicadas in the evening air jarred the silence of the room.

Elisheba breathed heavily, sounding tired. And Miriam was afraid she had offended the older woman by bringing her shame from Nazareth to her cousin's house in Juttah, the city of the priests.

Elisheba's pain eased away. The child no longer rollicked inside her, and she felt more comfortable. She looked long at Miriam, scanning the innocent face of this wisp of a girl, trying to make sense of her story.

Then suddenly she was speaking. Yet the words were not her own. They did not shape or form in her mind, nor was it her own voice that spoke them. Big, portentous words they were, the depth of which she could not fathom. It was as if she had been lifted from herself, and she uttered them as though a power outside herself used her as a mere instrument of speech.

'Blessed of God art thou among women, and blessed of God is the fruit of thy womb.'

The message issued from her, the speech came unthought. She chased words with her mind, measuring, searching to find a meaning for them, a reason.

Miriam listened, tense, nervous, sensing a familiar sound in the words.

'And whence is it to me that the mother of my Lord should come to me—'

Elisheba heard the words as though another spoke them. She paused, stunned.

The speech, so inexplicably begun, as inexplicably ended. Her mind was becoming her own again, and in returning to normality, the awareness of what had been happening to her slowly, slowly dawned.

She had, she realized, been in a state of ecstasy. For a fleeting moment of her life, she had been a prophetess. She a prophetess . . . It explained so much. And it frightened her. A prophetess, indeed. And the recipient of her prophetic word was none other than this woman, her cousin, whose experiences, for all she herself had learned in the months gone by of God's ways with Zecharias, she had been prepared to treat as a young girl's fantasy.

Elisheba trembled. And then, as fast as she could move, she rushed towards Miriam, apologizing, explaining. 'It was the oncoming ecstasy that made the child leap in my womb.'

Miriam listened gently, kindly, with no hint of having been embarrassed by her cousin's behaviour.

Elisheba could not help warming to her for her generosity.

'It began as soon as I heard the sound of your salutation,' she said.

The two women looked long at each other, neither of them sure what it all meant, or how it would end. And in the silence they knew there was nothing either of them could or needed to say.

Elisheba was the first to move. She saw the dust and grime of travelling clouding her cousin's face, cloaking her clothes. She clasped Miriam in her arms to complete the welcome, still not sure in her mind what kind of person it was she welcomed, yet feeling, somehow, that in those speeding moments of prophecy, they were both part of some great happening.

'And happy . . . to be envied . . . is she who believed,' she encouraged Miriam, 'for there shall be a performance of those things that were told her of the Lord.' And she led her away to wash, and make herself comfortable after the long journey.

Miriam said nothing. There was nothing to say. Elisheba's words still sounded in her ears. And as they impressed themselves deeply and more deeply in her mind, her dream in that lonely night came back to her, and she heard echoes of the angel's message, 'Blessed art thou among women—'

A week after Miriam arrived, Elisheba's child was born.

Miriam sat by her cousin as she struggled to bring the child to birth. Mopping the beads of perspiration from the furrowed brow. Smiling looks of comfort to the questing eyes. Touching drops of water to parched lips. Patting strength into cheeks paled and worn with pain, joining in the midwives' gutsy encouragement. And a little frightened by it all. Apprehensive. In four or five months from now she'd be facing all this herself.

She watched relief mix with joy in Elisheba's eyes when the pain and peril were past, the ordeal ended. And pride and pleasure colouring the wan, worn face when the child cried, and the midwives announced it was a boy.

Miriam kissed her cousin, and went to call Zecharias to see his son. She brought him back to Elisheba, her mind's eye seeing, as they walked, the slow hand of Zecharias writing, 'Thy wife Elisheba shall bear thee a son.'

Eight days later, Elisheba's cousins and the neighbours gathered for the circumcision and the naming of the child.

They said 'Amen' to the prayers, and stood in reverent silence till the boy was circumcised.

Then came the naming.

Almost with one voice, Elisheba's cousins spoke. They named him 'Zecharias', clapping and shouting with delight, congratulating the priest on producing a son in his old age.

'Not so,' rose Elisheba's voice. There was strength and determination and command in the sound. 'Not so.'

A shocked silence. Disbelief. The neighbours were surprised, Elisheba's cousins apalled.

Elisheba spoke quietly, 'He shall be called John.'

The house erupted. The solemn reverence that began the day's proceedings gone. The bright joviality that once named the child dulled, dimmed and disappeared.

'You can't call him John,' declared a cousin above the storm the other cousins created.

'What's wrong with Zecharias for a name? It's his father's name—' another noisily advised.

'There's nobody in the entire family called John—'

Was this what her mother would describe as a family row, Miriam wondered. While the neighbours watched, a row in the old priest's house . . . They now had gossip that would last them a week.

'Zecharias,' pleaded the oldest cousin present, 'tell your wife she cannot call your son John.'

Zecharias was helpless. Unable to speak, he could only gesture in reply, shaping with his hands, mouthing unsounding words.

'He wants a tablet to write on,' Elisheba offered.

'Get him a tablet, someone,' the cousins instructed one another. But not one of them moved.

Miriam went and brought back a tablet and stylus.

The cousins were quiet as Zecharias settled the tablet on his lap and gripped the stylus strongly to write.

'The father will choose his son's name,' the oldest cousin announced confidently, putting Elisheba in her place.

They waited. And the neighbours waited, discreetly. Though one or two nosed to spy what Zecharias was writing.

The eldest cousin took the tablet Zecharias stretched out to him.

He read it. And paled. And he was hardly heard when he whispered in disbelief, 'His name is John.'

Not a word was said. They marvelled all.

Zecharias stood up. And spoke. 'Blessed be the Lord God of Israel,' he proclaimed as he made towards Elisheba who was nursing her child. 'For He hath visited and redeemed His people.'

'Amen,' the houseful murmured. And said no more as Zecharias took his son from Elisheba's arms.

'And you, my child,' he soothed, cradling his son in his arms, 'you shall be called the prophet of the Highest.' He smoothed a gentle hand across the forehead, and tucked the swaddling clothes more snugly. 'You shall go before the face of the Lord to prepare his ways.'

Nobody said anything. They celebrated, but even the celebrations were quieter than they should have been.

Juttah seemed so very, very far away. And Miriam's being there, separated from him, made Yosef feel the distance immeasurably far.

No news, no word of how she fared, aggravated his sense of loneliness and separation.

The new moon had twice waxed and waned since Miriam's departure, and she had not come back. So, he decided, she must have been made welcome in the priest's house. And, of course, she was faring all right, he told himself over and over again. But whatever conviction there might have been in his arguments, there was little lasting comfort.

He had the dog for company, and he was grateful for that. The scavenger that had begun this association as a grateful beggar, content to lie waiting in the cool shadow outside, had, since Miriam's departure, insinuated himself inside and, by now, had laid claim to a corner where he could lie undisturbed, yet still keep watch on all that went on in the house.

He lay there now, his eyes half open, watching his master, the tail lying idle, but ready to wag delight at the slightest sign of interest from Yosef.

Yosef was glad he was there. It was a sound of breathing in a desolate house.

He chipped again at the stone block he was carving. He looked closer, and saw he'd almost missed the pattern he had marked. There was not sufficient light in the lamp, now, to see the line clearly enough for safety.

'It'd be stupid to go on now,' he commented to the dog. 'It'd do more harm than good in these conditions.'

He looked up when the light flickered in the soft breeze through the window.

A moth spiralled round the lamp, dancing, and then plunged its way towards the flame, singed in its rapture, and was nothing.

'The night cometh when no man can work,' he advised the dog. He laid the chisel and mallet carefully on the floor beside the block, and decided reluctantly to go off to bed.

It was a formality. Night-time was the worst time. By day

he could occupy himself, and distract his mind from the thoughts and fears and recollections that clamoured for attention. At night, there was no distraction. His body was tired and craved for rest. His will, weak from constantly mustering courage in the too-long day, shuffled off, exhausted, in the darkness, making way for sleep that dallied long in coming.

He lay tossing and turning, his mind the playground of cavorting thought that came unbidden and unwelcome. Faces, voices and events crowded him, jostling, jumbling in the confusion of tiredness . . . the hubbub in the Sabbath synagogue that stagnated to silence when he entered . . . the urging kindness of Barzillai who tried to coax him to leave the house he'd sweated to build, and live at his home till Miriam would return . . . the clustering gossips that huddled closer as he passed, preening the cacky feathers of their newly grown morality . . . and Shebna's hardness. It saddened Yosef that he had offended a man who was so long a friend. But, in his own way, he understood it. As he tried to understand the snide asides of workmates that gave new meanings to each workday act, envying what they imagined was his prowess in lechery, mocking when they reckoned it was stupidity . . .

And Naomi and old Azariah who set themselves to play father and mother to him . . . did he eat and wash and get his rest . . . They forced him, for nine Sabbaths, now, to eat at their home after synagogue. They treated him as an honoured guest, a son returned from a far country . . . And Yosef knew by now the oft repeated pattern of Azariah's conversation. He talked of weather, goats and recalcitrant sheep. Crops and grapes and Naomi's cooking. And, at the end of it all, as though his thought had strayed, wondered how the old donkey was, and had it managed the long journey with young Miriam to Juttah. The old man had parted with a friend . . . and in the drowsiness that now began to dull his mind and bring a little solace, Yosef found himself wishing that Miriam would return, if only that they might encourage Azariah to take back the donkey, as a gift from them.

Outside the night birds called. The dog, deep in sleep, shifted in the warm straw.

But Yosef didn't hear.

The day began to shred the darkness of the night.

And Yosef slept.

Miriam liked Juttah. It was quiet. Here nobody knew about her. Nobody bothered. To them she was just another married woman following the old custom of getting away for a little rest and quiet during her pregnancy. She was lucky, they told her, to have a husband who'd let her get away.

And she liked Elisheba. Elisheba was generous. The woman she once hardly knew had become a friend. And having just been delivered of a child herself made Elisheba understanding and sympathetic. And there was comfort in their womanly chatter that made the weeks pass quickly.

Yet, sometimes, she was afraid. Yosef's voice sounding in her head, repeating and repeating again the Prophet's words he'd read that Sabbath in the synagogue in Nazareth.

Down the long, scorching miles the words stretched, their tentacles reaching through the long-gone moments of dead days she wished had never happened. It was then the fear would take her. Creeping, quiet, slow, seducing fear. Pulsating. Her head tightening, her mind misting. Fear that bulged her heart till her body was full, gnawing in her throat till she thought she would suffocate. Paralysing, so that she could not raise herself to run to find a refuge. And all she could do was sit and wait till the terror was past.

She was sitting so, suffering, when Elisheba called her.

The sun was setting, the lamps were lit in the house, and it was time for the evening prayers.

Miriam heard the voice, and felt embarrassed lest her cousin find her in such a state, for it would be a slight on their kindness and concerned hospitality. Yet she could not move to respond.

Elisheba called again. But there was nothing Miriam could do but wait till the fear had inflicted its havoc and slipped her from its clutches, as a wolf, satiated, drops a lamb from its maw.

'Miriam.' Elisheba's voice sounded gentle as she came into the room.

Miriam forced a smile, trying to hide her conflict. Elisheba came towards her, stretching out her hand, to lead her to the big room where Zecharias waited to join the family prayers.

'A wife forsaken, Miriam, and grieved in spirit,' quipped Elisheba. And she said it like a catch-phrase, a line that aptly suited the sight she saw, but to which she attached no depth of meaning.

Miriam caught the sound – a wife forsaken . . . and the fear came back again . . . forsaken and grieved . . . the children of the desolate . . . the words torrenting through her head like a river tormented in its winter flood – I have forsaken thee . . . in wrath I hid my face . . . afflicted . . . tossed with tempest and not comforted . . .

Somewhere, outside herself, she saw the proffered hand, and took it. Through the lashing agony of her mind, she heard the faint, comforting voice repeating her name . . . Miriam, Miraim . . . soothing, soothing . . . and it came nearer . . . soft and strong and bringing peace . . . and she felt about her a new warmth.

Elisheba nursed her cousin, bearing the pain of the vice-tight grip in which Miriam held her hand, speaking her name, though even as she said it, the sound was smothered by the murmur of the poor girl's rambling talk, not sure whether just to sympathize and hope that speaking peace would prove medicine enough, or to slap her face and shock her back to sensibility.

She raised her hand, poising it to strike, but found she had not the heart, and let her hand fall back again, resting it again on Miriam's shoulder.

'Miriam,' she said again. This time with more command than comfort in the tone. 'Miriam.'

The face looked up, bewildered for a fraction. Till the tears gushed forth, bathing the fright from the eyes, drenching a touch of life into the fear-roughed cheeks.

'Elisheba,' she lisped, and pulled the hand she held, rubbing it against her face, washing it with tears.

Elisheba cuddled Miriam to her, and then, with her free hand, found a corner of her shawl and began to mop away the tears.

The sobbing stopped. Miriam stood up, still holding Elisheba's hand, and began to move towards the room where Zecharias waited.

'You're very sad, Miriam,' offered Elisheba as they walked. It was a trite statement in the circumstances, but she could think of no other way to come near the young woman to help her.

'It will pass,' said Miriam.

'But I have noticed it before, though never so bad as this—'

They halted, and Miriam turned to face her cousin. 'When I am alone it happens,' she said. 'Not always, though. On odd occasions, when I least expect it. The lesson Yosef read in the synagogue at home comes back to mind. And frightens me. It happened just now. I was recovering when you called me for the evening prayers. I tried to hide the sadness when you came.'

'I noticed,' interrupted Elisheba, trying to ease the intensity that was growing into Miriam's explanation.

'But then your greeting brought it flooding back again.'

'It was a quip, Miriam. There was no harm in it, dear child. It is a Scripture. It's so often read in the synagogue. It came unwittingly to mind when I saw you so forlorn. I said it only to raise you from your doldrums.'

'I know,' Miriam assured her. 'I saw no harm in it, and took it for a kindness. But it's the scripture Yosef read. "More are the children of the desolate than the children of the married woman, saith the Lord . . . for the Lord hath called thee as a wife forsaken and grieved in spirit . . . In a little wrath I hid my face from thee . . . O thou afflicted, tossed with tempest, and not comforted."'

Her voice was cold, flat, impersonal, jerking from phrase to phrase, as though jumping in her mind, escaping from one to do battle with the next, fearing that each encounter might overwhelm her.

Elisheba listened, feeling the grip tighten on her hand again, willing Miriam to go through the piece.

But Miriam had stopped. She said no more.

'But go on, Miriam,' Elisheba ordered. 'There is more to say. You have left out too much. And if you apply one part to your predicament, then you must also apply the rest. That's what Zecharias would advise.'

She paused, waiting for Miriam's reaction.

Miriam waited, ready to listen. And Elisheba finished the Scripture that Miriam had begun.

'For the mountains may depart, and the hills be removed, but my kindness shall not depart from thee, neither shall my covenant of peace be removed, saith the Lord that hath compassion on thee . . . Be thou far from oppression, for thou shalt not fear . . . and every tongue that shall rise against thee shalt thou condemn. This is the heritage of the servants of the Lord, and their due reward from me, saith the Lord.'

That was enough for now, Elisheba decided.

The tension eased from Miriam, and there was no fear, now, in her eyes. The two women finished their walk to the other room.

Zecharias, his prayer shawl dressed carefully on his shoulders, was already praying.

The days that followed were easier for Miriam.

Elisheba was wise, choosing her time, imparting her instruction little by little.

Miriam loved her for her wisdom, waiting for her every word, as gently, slowly, the priest's wife took the younger woman, like a disciple, through the Prophet's message, shaping, wondering, suggesting, here feeling after, there probing, till the piece had new dimensions.

And while she could not always share the dazzling vision of the Prophet, as Elisheba interpreted him, yet it was no longer frightening for her. The threat had gone from it.

And as the weeks went on, Miriam could call the words deliberately to mind, dwelling on them, newly measuring them, feeling a new illumination dawning in the once grim shadows of her mind. And sometimes she could even dare to hope.

But she grew homesick. It was her first time away from home. It was too long. And the novelty soon palled. The days grew too long. And Juttah, the sultry little town, became a broody place. She was lonely for her own people. And her loneliness gave her too much time to think. Sorrow fretted her recollections, and brought to mind the palling shadows that had darkened her wedding day.

In innocence, once, she had imagined so much, and had painted the picture so often, so brilliantly. The garden filled with happy people. The young men supporting the canopy for the ceremony. Herself adorned with jewels, and beautiful. The joyous roar of the people, 'Blessed is he that cometh', as Yosef would appear to conduct her from her father's keeping.

But the reality had been so different. The hovering shadows of suspicion had filtered into the minds of the handful who watched. Every formal act was agony. And joy chilled on their lips like the taste of death.

She could still see the pain her parents felt and tried so hard to hide in mouthing the customary benedictions at the end of the ceremony.

For her there'd been no parade through the streets of Nazareth, no avenues lined with delighted, loving neighbours, no well-wishers to strew the road from the wedding to her new home with money and sweetmeats and flowers. And no feasting. For all the preparation, there'd been no stomach to savour it.

They were married. It was sufficient. It was all they could ask for.

There was too much sadness in her thoughts. And the time came when Elisheba, for all her kindness, sympathy and understanding, could no longer console her.

She must go home again. She missed Yosef till the pain for him became too much to bear.

She must go home again. And even the fear of what might face her there could not dissuade her from going back to Nazareth.

CHAPTER SEVEN

It was clear to Antipater that Marcellus had wasted no time in responding to his request.

He was grateful. And feigned surprise when Herod told him he had received a letter from Marcellus. 'Marcellus . . .?' he exclaimed. 'But what matter could be so great and grave that Marcellus should burden the King?'

'Great and grave, my son,' said Herod.

Now, Antipater was genuinely surprised. And yet, he thought he heard a touch of humour in the voice. He hoped he was right, for the King had his own ways of dealing with great and grave matters.

'Grave for me, your father. For I am about to lose you, my son—' And he paused, enjoying to himself what the statement could imply. But then went on, 'For a while. Great for you, if I grant what Marcellus asks.'

'What is the request Marcellus makes, my King, my father?'

'A simple thing, really. He asks me to allow you to visit your friends in Rome for a while.'

'But, Father—'

'I believe you should go, my son.'

'You are a sick man, my father. I cannot just up and go to Rome, not knowing how you would fare in my absence.'

'The King believes you should go. The King directs you to go.'

Antipater bowed, reluctantly but obediently accepting the King's command.

'Will the King send his son Archelaus, also? Marcellus is his friend, too?'

'Archelaus,' Herod stormed. 'Do not even think of him in my presence. My comfort is that he stays far away from me—'

'I am sorry, Father,' breathed Antipater, pretending surprise that the friends of his youth in Rome should still remember him.

But the King was glad for him, for all his son's reluctance to leave Jerusalem and home. It would be good, the King advised him, to spend some time again in Rome. The contacts he would make at the Emperor's court would stand him in good stead in the years to come.

Besides which, Herod explained, there was a piece of work to be done in Rome which he would entrust only to his son. He was dispatching Sylleus the Arabian to be tried by Augustus Caesar for the murder of Fabatus, one of Caesar's commissaries in Jerusalem.

Antipater could only smile to himself. The King was scheming. He was softening Caesar for something.

There was no need to send Sylleus to Rome for trial. The King already had excuse and cause enough to kill the man. Leaving aside the Fabatus affair, Sylleus was already under sentence for the massacre of the leading men among the Arabians in Petra.

But none of that, Antipater knew, would move Herod. What hurt and wounded Herod deeply, though, was Sylleus's bribing Corinthus, one of Herod's own bodyguard, to kill the King.

Already Sylleus was languishing in gaol for that, waiting for Herod to signal the time and manner of his death. That his father was prepared to forgo that pleasure could mean only that he was manoeuvring for some favour.

Antipater looked questioningly at the King. But said nothing.

'It will please Augustus Caesar,' his father advised him.

Of course, thought Antipater. But wondered why. Herod pleased nobody just for the pleasure of it.

There would be the usual royal presents for the Emperor, Herod told his son. And ample funds for himself to cover his expenses in Rome.

And he would carry two letters to the emperor. One would be the usual formal note commending his son to Caesar. The second would contain a copy of the King's will ... with the request that Caesar grant him his wish to appoint Antipater to be his successor.

Antipater bowed low and silently in gratitude, his mind bursting with the thought that, at last, he was only one step from the throne. And before he left his sick father, he would have completed his scheme to take that step as soon as possible.

The journey to Rome, he decided, could not have been more advantageously timed.

The preparations for the journey were quickly made. With more than time for Antipater to draw his uncle Pheroras into the plan to murder the King during his absence in Rome.

Pheroras, in fact, presented no difficulties. Indeed, he seemed pleased to have been asked. 'Commissioned by the future King,' was how he put it. 'And honoured to have been commissioned.'

The plot laid, and even the poison provided, Antipater, attended by his freeman Bathyllus, set sail for Rome. With far more than he expected. He was a happy man. Things were working out well. Pheroras would remove the King.

And the ship he now sailed in was taking him far beyond suspicion. It would not be long before he was returned again. But this time, as by Herod's will decreed, he would be king.

It was the donkey Azariah noticed. It was his old donkey back – the donkey he had given to Miriam months ago. But he dismissed the thought that went through his mind before it became serious. It was impossible, he decided. His eyes were playing tricks with him, and he couldn't focus them enough to add more detail to the silhouette against the slanting sun. Yet the gait was familiar, and the droop of the head. And the pace that seemed a succession between going just another step and stopping altogether, was too character-istic for him to want to doubt much longer.

Delighted, he was on the point of calling out, but bit it back. A sudden shout from him would startle the animal, and there was no telling what might happen, then, to young Miriam riding it. And then he looked at Miriam, her face in shadow, her body moving to the slow rhythm of the ambling donkey, digging her feet, as though out of habit, every now and then, into the donkey's ribs.

He hardly knew what pleased him most, seeing Miriam return to be with Yosef, or knowing that the donkey was back again, even though it was no longer his.

It was all too good to be true. And Azariah was beside himself with excitement, battling to stop himself rushing forward. 'Better not to,' he advised himself. 'There'd be an accident. Better get away altogether.' And he turned abruptly, and went home again, bursting to tell Naomi the news.

Naomi was as excited as himself. She ran to him, hugging and kissing him when he told her. There was a string of questions: 'Did you talk to Miriam? . . . Does she look well? . . . What about Yosef? . . .' But she gave him no time to answer, and whatever he grunted in reply, she didn't hear in her pandemonium of pleasure.

And then she realized she'd forgotten Sarah. Sarah had come to buy olives, and now she stood, manhandling the full sack in her great fat arms, urgent to be away. This was a bit of news, indeed . . .

Naomi turned to apologize, but Sarah cut her off. 'There's no need, Naomi. I'm off now, anyway.'

And she was gone, hasting straight to her cronies at the well.

The house was empty when Miriam arrived. She'd expected that, she reminded herself, for Yosef would be away working on one of Herod's building enterprises. Yet she felt disappointed. It was a kind of anti-climax. All the road along, she'd looked forward to being home again. And for all she'd tried to prepare herself for Yosef's not being there to greet her, it was quite a different matter to stand, lonely, enduring the experience.

Miriam wept. All the emotions flooded over her together: elation, disappointment, joy, sadness, delight, fright, all at once in one great, confusing, petrifying, overwhelming conglomeration.

She stooped to stifle the sobs in her shawl, whispering with each stroke to dry the tears, 'Yosef, Yosef', as if sounding the name would bring him quickly home again.

She was aware of the room all round her. Neat and clean and orderly. Everything in its proper place, as though nothing had been disturbed since the day she'd left.

Only the far corner looked dishevelled. The sun through the window lit it up. A heap of straw, thrown down and flattened, loose straws, broken, split and jutting out, and spare grains scattered. Cared for it was, but it looked untidy, unkempt in such a well-kept house. It was too small for a man to sleep on. And, in any case, she couldn't imagine Yosef doing that, and being so slovenly afterwards. Some animal, perhaps that Yosef had – yet she could not recollect seeing any animal about as she'd ridden home.

And then she remembered the donkey, still waiting to be unharnessed. She didn't relish the prospect of the job, but the poor beast had served her well on the journey, and ought not to be left much longer unattended.

Quickly she poured some water from the jar by the door into the basin beside it, dipped her face, sucked in some water to freshen her mouth, then scooped in her hands and splashed her face.

The splashing made a lovely sound, and the coolness was a pleasure she could have dallied to enjoy, but the braying donkey outside reminded her there was work to be done.

She raised her head from the basin, swilling the water from her face, and noticed, from the corner of her eye, the shadow fall across the floor.

Flashing round, exhilarated, nervous, bubbling, she cried out, 'Yosef, you're home—' but the words died on her lips.

It was not Yosef.

Naomi stood awkwardly in the doorway, holding in front of her a laden tray, its contents daintily draped with a linen cloth.

Miriam saw the kind face smiling a welcome, yet apologizing at the same time for causing such a bitter disappointment. 'Oh, it's you, Naomi,' she said. 'Please come in.'

'You are welcome home, Miriam,' said Naomi, crossing the room, and making her way up the three steps to the upper floor, beckoning Miriam to follow.

'Azariah saw you coming along the road,' she continued, and then the sentence hung in mid-air while she set down the tray on the table, and took off the linen cover.

Miriam saw the food. A loaf, fresh baked and buttered. A

bowl of olives, goat's cheese, cucumber cut in glistening chunks, lettuce, crinkly, green and luscious. And a jug of wine that danced and sparkled at the brim.

Miriam felt hungry, painfully aware that it was some time since she'd eaten, and she was willing Naomi to invite her to sit down to the meal.

'He didn't call you,' Naomi went on, picking up her speech as though there'd been no pause, 'for fear his shout would frighten the donkey—'

'The donkey!' exclaimed Miriam. 'I forgot all about it. Forgive me, Naomi, I must go and unharness—'

Naomi was startled, but quickly recovered. 'Come, child, sit down and eat,' she commanded.

Miriam sat down.

And then, comfortingly, Naomi added, 'Azariah's come to look after it for you. It's my guess he'll have it unsaddled already. And by now he'll be watering it, and talking to it like a long-lost brother.'

Miriam paused in her eating and tried to thank Naomi.

Naomi waved the thanks away. 'Dear Miriam, it's the best thing that's happened to Azariah. You may not believe it, but the silly man has fretted about that wretched animal since you went off to Juttah.'

She turned away, went to the shelf and took down five cups. Deliberately, as if she were naming them while she took them.

Miriam watched. And counted. And wondered.

'Yosef's not used these since the day they were put there,' mused Naomi aloud, after a squinting inspection. 'They'll need to be washed,' she announced, already on her way to the water jar.

Miriam watched this old woman, amazed at the sprightliness that seemed to possess her. The Naomi she had left in Nazareth three months ago had taken on a new lease of life.

'But why five cups?' Miriam ventured, while Naomi completed wiping them.

'One for you. One for me. One for Azariah,' replied Naomi, as if she were instructing a child. 'And one for each of your parents – if Azariah hasn't got so tied up with the donkey that he's forgotten to go and tell them you're back.'

'And what about Yosef? He should be home soon.'

The old woman did not reply immediately.

Miriam noticed the pause. It was too long, she thought. And when, eventually, she spoke, Miriam heard the hesitancy in Naomi's voice. She was struggling with herself, a woman who couldn't tell a lie, but didn't want to tell the truth.

'We can never be sure of Yosef, these days,' she said.

Miriam watched as Naomi made her way back to the table with the cups. She tried to catch her eye, but Naomi deliberately did not look.

She filled two cups, pushed one towards Miriam, and sat down with one herself, still avoiding Miriam's searching stare. 'Drink up,' encouraged Naomi, 'and you'll feel refreshed.'

'Is something wrong, Naomi?' blurted Miriam. She tried to say it easily, casually, but it came out crisp, sharp, abrupt.

And Naomi sensed the tension trying to lose itself in the words. She was sorry for Miriam. Sorry, also, for herself. And she wished Azariah would come in, for he was so much better in this kind of situation.

She held the cup to her lips. But had no heart for drinking. And down, down in the cup she saw the wine sparkle and smile, and make a mock of her in her predicament. She put the cup away in disgust, banging it on the table, washing the still-mocking wine up the sides, where it slithered, leering, back to hide and wait in the shadowy confines she did not probe or penetrate.

'It's hard in Nazareth for Yosef,' she began, turning a

gentle face to Miriam. 'He's a lonely man, and they hate too much.'

'They still talk?' questioned Miriam, trying to lighten for herself, and Yosef if possible, the picture conjured in her mind by Naomi's words.

'They hate,' repeated Naomi, deepening the darkness. And then, with a kind of forlornness in her voice, as though the very hopelessness itself made the words difficult to shape, she said, 'But it's early days, and maybe things will change in time.'

'Poor Yosef.'

'We hoped things might have changed before you'd returned. But then we reckoned you'd be away for at least six months.'

'I missed Yosef.' It was almost an apology, as though in coming back to her husband she'd done something wrong.

Naomi sensed it, and realized that in trying to soften the blow, she was actually making matters worse.

'They were kind to me in Juttah. But I could stay no longer. I wanted to be home.'

'I understand, Miriam. And I only wish everything was right to make you happy being home.'

Naomi was delaying. All along Miriam sensed it. She was feeling for a way, hoping she could tell her bad news naturally.

'Tell me, Naomi,' she said.

'Yosef is gone away.'

The blow had fallen.

Naomi rose and moved nearer to Miriam to give her strength.

'He's gone away—' said Miriam, her voice whispering from the far shocked distance. 'When will he come back?'

Naomi sat down.

'It might have been better for you had you stayed with your cousin in Juttah, Miriam.'

Miriam looked up, and was about to speak, but Naomi stopped her.

'Just let me finish what I want to tell you, and then you'll understand. It's been difficult for Yosef in Nazareth since you went away. And it got harder as the months went by. So he took to going off to work in other places, coming home only every now and then. Two weeks ago he went away again—'

Miriam was listening. Feeling she was beginning to understand. 'Which means he could be back any day now,' she interrupted, eagerly, not minding too much the prospect of the few days' wait.

'Which means', checked Naomi 'that unfortunately it could be quite some time before he comes back to Nazareth.'

Miriam slumped back, disconsolate.

'It's because of the new tax-roll the Romans have announced.'

Miriam nodded. She'd heard talk about it in the caravan on the journey home. And while Naomi went on expanding about Quirinius the Roman Governor, and the decree sent forth from Caesar Augustus in Rome, and the need for every male Jew to attend the town of his birth for registration, Miriam knew exactly what the end of the speech would be.

'So,' she began, but found herself speaking the same words at the same time as her adviser, 'Yosef will have to go to Bethlehem.'

They laughed a little. A strained, hysterical sound that had no hilarity in it. And then were quiet, while Naomi wondered how to continue, and Miriam tried to muster courage to face the day she knew must come, when she'd be on her own again in Nazareth. Yosef would be a long time going to Bethlehem, and a long time coming back.

'Many of the men are gone already,' mused Naomi aloud. And her voice reverberated in the canyon of silence. 'I honestly think some of them are pleased, y'know. It's an excuse to get away from their wives for a while.'

Miriam feinted a smile.

'Isaac is gone, of course. He went off almost as soon as the decree was made public. Rushed off as if Jerusalem's future depended on his presence there', all the while eyeing Miriam, trying to ease into the news she had still to tell. But Miriam wasn't listening. She could see that. The girl made no effort to hide the fact. She was far away, consumed with her own thoughts.

Slowly she turned her head. She took in Miriam's face, and the far-off loneliness in the eyes that were too tired of waiting to behold the man she loved, the countenance worn and saddened with too-long neglected longing.

'And Yosef, I'm afraid, is gone, too,' she choked out.

Silence. And the sound of two women breathing.

'Yosef is gone,' whispered Miriam. The sound was soft, the melancholy voice of sadness when the heart is full and has no more room for sorrow. 'Yosef is gone.'

'He went two weeks ago to Nain, where he had some work to do,' said Naomi, matter-of-factly, hoping her mocked-up attitude would ease the situation a little. 'He reckoned if he got quickly finished there, he might come back. But if the job took longer than a week, he said, he'd go on from Nain to his father's home in Bethlehem.'

'I might have seen him, had I waited,' Miriam contemplated aloud.

'Aye,' said Naomi, knowing herself the irony of the whole thing. 'That was his thought, too. His first plan was not to rush off, anyway. But then he saw it as a chance to visit you in Juttah.'

'I ought not to have been so urgent to come home,' reacted Miriam, and reprimand tinged the regret.

'We need the air,' Naomi advised briskly.

She took Miriam by the hand and led her towards the door.

The sun was bright and danced at them from the sky, and they shielded their eyes till they had grown accustomed to the light.

Naomi looked, but saw no sign of Azariah. 'And he's taken the donkey with him, wherever he's gone,' she said.

And Miriam understood. And smiled a little.

Sarah ran and walked, scurried and scuffed along the broken pathways, cutting corners, dodging rubbish heaps, ducking low-slung arches, sweating, puffing, struggling through stifling, narrow streets. The bag of olives grew heavier with each heaving step, and she'd have been glad to drop the lot and sit down and rest. Sweat streamed from every pore in her body, and washed, torturingly down her face. But she had no hand free to wipe it away, nor clear its mounting torrent from her eyes. And her excitement wouldn't let her stop. She had too much to tell, and already her mind had raced ahead of her, reaching the well and wallowing in the pleasure of telling them the gossip bit by bit. And she could see their faces as she told them . . .

The emptying streets reminded her, every now and then, that she was in danger of missing her opportunity. Everyone was going home to eat, and then to sleep the afternoon away. The women would soon be gone from the well – if they'd not gone already.

The realization lent new urgency to her mission, but, sadly, gave no impetus to her tiring limbs. And she tried to forge ahead, as though for spite, punishing them in anger.

The length of the street, now, separated her from the square. And she could see the speck of glinting brightness through the line of arches that sturdily kept a passageway along this downward sloping shaft of darkness.

In next to no time, she decided, she'd be at the well, and slackened her pace a little.

There was a quietness everywhere, and a sense of suffocation. And Sarah felt it. The sunlight ran tentatively down the walls and died, stifled in the tangled shadows and the smothering darkness of a thousand corners. A breeze, slight, uneasy, nervous, whimpered along the rough surface of the alleyway, as though even the day's burning heat fretted for air in this suffocation.

She saw stalls, their awnings gawping, listless, the cloth in bales heaped up, forlorn, neglected, their gaiety gone from their colours. And bells and brass that hung, lacklustre. And tinkling trinkets, now bereft of all their joy, like melancholy, festooning so many beleaguered citadels.

Sarah walked quietly through, the dragging rhythm of her pace broken only at the steps that took her road down through the tenser blackness of each stony arch.

Over there a trader had made a space among his pots and pans, and now he was sprawled, snoring, his paunchy body rising and falling in its heaving, sleeping satisfaction. And there a woman, with a tray of bangles on her lap, crouched on a stool, cuddling herself to sleep.

A door gaped open to the street, choking to darkness the little light that trembled at its threshold. And by the well-worn step, a beggar lay, his head lost in the close-gathered frailty of his body, a grasping hand clutching his beggar's dish, his outer cloak tucked tight, sculpting the skinny outlines of his bony knees.

Sarah shivered a little, aware of the quietness all around her. She cuddled the bag of olives, not sure whether it was for warmth or confidence.

The silence was suddenly pierced with sound: 'Sarah.'

Sarah was startled, hearing her name reverberating along the walls and through the stony buttresses of the arches. 'Sarah.'

She looked away from the beggar at the doorstep, down the short length that still separated her from the square beyond, searching for the place from which the call came again. 'Sarah.' Frightened at hearing a voice in this valley of silence, relieved that somebody was alive in this noonday tomb, that there was a friend who knew her by her name.

And then she saw the woman coming towards her up the slope. And was annoyed.

It was only Rachel. And she didn't want her to be the first to be told the news. And, besides, Rachel would ask a host of well-meaning questions about Miriam, and even if she wanted to answer them, it would only delay her. And then, most assuredly, she'd miss the others at the well.

Sarah paced her way smartly now. She noticed how slowly Rachel walked, dragging herself along, trying her best to look alert. There'd be no stopping, though, Sarah decided. She was already planning how she'd cut Rachel off. And her head flicked like a cockscomb in confirmation.

'Sarah,' Rachel called again.

But Sarah remained silent, stepping out, making it too obvious that she was in a hurry, staring unswervingly ahead, yet keeping slow-moving Rachel in the corner of her eye, and noting how the girl, every so often, stretched out her arm, supporting herself along the wall.

It was a pity, she thought, that the street was not so much wider. But she kept on the far side from Rachel, making it clear that she had no intention of stepping across the narrow gap that divided them, as she drew level.

'Sarah,' greeted Rachel, preparing to stop. There was pleading in the speaking.

'You're early out,' retorted Sarah, smothering the solicitations in the sound she heard, hardening her gaze against the look of need in the poor face she saw.

It was a quip, Rachel reckoned, and was mustering a smile, till she glimpsed the hardness in the face that glanced past her, and was gone. Now Rachel understood Sarah's prancing and cockscombing down the street.

'And what ails you?' she cried after Sarah, turning round to make sure her voice reached the hurrying figure. 'Don't think you'll escape the noonday demons. They caught you a long time ago—'

The effort was too much. She had turned too quickly. She stumbled, but managed to save herself from falling, and propped herself against a shaky stall to rest.

Sarah belted on, the strain of Rachel's venom reaching after her.

She was at the square now, and she could see the knot of women gathering to leave the well. She was torn, not knowing what to do. She was sorry for Rachel, feeling she ought to have stopped. And she needn't have been so bitter. She hesitated in her haste, wondering if she ought to go back to Rachel. The poor girl looked as though she needed help.

Sarah stopped, turned, and almost began to retrace her steps. But her eye caught the group across the square setting off for home.

'Miriam's home again,' she shouted back along the hill of the street to Rachel, and felt her guilt and her responsibility lessen a little.

Rachel heard it.

The group across the square heard it, too. They paused momentarily to take it in, but hardly acknowledged the worn, tired, sweating, load-carrying Sarah who had announced the news. Instead, they moved steadily on their way, discussing the gossip among themselves.

They were deeply involved in it as Sarah joined them, and paid scant attention when she arrived, out of breath.

She joined herself to the group. Abigail was holding forth about the rights and wrongs of Miriam's coming back.

Indeed, she was only amazed that Miriam had the nerve to show her face at all in Nazareth.

Sarah felt a bit out of place. She wondered why she'd made the effort after all. She'd have been better off, she reflected, had she stopped and talked to Rachel.

Rachel was dead.

The beggarman slouched in the doorway found her when the sun had cooled somewhat, and he had awakened before the street had come to life again.

Waking so early pleased him. It was an opportunity to help himself to what he wanted from the unprotected stalls. And he was about his business when he came across Rachel. She was slumped against the wall. Her frail hands that had so often reached in kindness to him in times past now stretched, pleading to him for help when her poor parched mouth could not move to ask.

He gathered his tattered skirts about him, put away his begging bowl, and hoisted Rachel in his arms, and set out, carrying her carefully to Asa's house, where he knew she would be cared for.

But she died before he had reached the house. And Asa wept when the beggarman brought her in.

The grasping mourners howled and wailed, and Asa paid them well. They embalmed her, scenting her in death with the perfume and fragrance that had delighted her in life, wrapping the frailty of her frame in the most expensive linen Asa could afford.

There was no pain any more in the face they let him see now, before they masked its beauty with the grave-cloth. The closed lids looked as though the eyes might still waken from unmolested sleep. The deep-gouged lines were gone, and the face was young again. The skin shone clear, and nowhere now did any blemish mar its fragile loveliness.

Death seemed a little kinder to her than her life had been. The lips, paler now, still shaped in their familiar friendliness, looked as though about to speak.

Asa looked long, then bent and tenderly, gently, for the first and last time in his life, kissed them. And he turned, weeping, away.

He sat by the doorway of his little shop, hearing the soft keening of the mourning, moaning women round the corpse. He wept alone, his cloak wrapped tightly round him, shoulders hunched, arms hugged round his knees, his head deep in his lap, stifling the tearing, rending sighs.

In the closing day, when the sun had cooled, he walked by the bier. Forlorn, solitary, with none to mourn with him.

The carriers undertook their slow, relentless journey to the grave. There were no stops along the way. No comfort calls – 'Comfort ye, comfort ye, ye dear ones. Lift up your souls, lift up your souls' – to ease his ache. None to cry out the call that Asa himself had made so many times at funerals, 'Come unto me all ye who are of sad and troubled heart, and take part in the sorrow of your neighbours.' None cried. And none passed by to hear.

He tried to chant the psalm at the graveside, 'The heavens declare the glory of God—' choking on every uttered syllable. And the circuit seven times round the bier on which the white-linen-shrouded Rachel lay, was like seven years unremitting desolation.

And when they laid her in the grave, he tried to pray and say a blessing for her.

Then, searching through his tears, he picked his way from the house of death that the Rabbis proclaimed was the gate of life. He wanted to believe it would be so for poor, dear Rachel, the wayward offspring of the long-dead wayward woman who should have been his wife.

*

Miriam dozed, encouraging herself to sleep. On a mat spread out in a cool corner of the upper floor. She had finished the meal Naomi had brought, tidied the dishes away, and replaced the wine cups on their appointed shelf, searched out the mats where Yosef had them neatly stored, and laid herself down to rest. And now she was trying, but sleep would not come easily.

Azariah had not come back, wherever he'd got himself to. And whether or not he'd gone to tell her parents she was home again, she'd have to wait till siesta time was ended to find out.

Naomi was gone. She had waited long enough for Azariah to return, but when he didn't come, she had decided she'd get off home before the sun became too hot for being outside.

A chicken scratched in the window arch. Through sleepy eyes, Miriam watched its silhouetted antics, wondering where it found its energy in such stultifying heat. A wind started up outside in the burning day, but it came to nothing, leaving no more than a shimmer of dust where the sun lit polished wood.

Miriam snuggled into the palliasse. She felt good, secure. For all her being alone in the house, she felt a glowing sense of safety. She was home again, in the place where her child would be born. And it was not hard to stave off the threatening sense of loneliness from Yosef's being absent. He would be back again, and then they'd settle down to being a family.

Her mind painted happy pictures on the tired lids of her closed eyes. She'd be a busy mother: baking, cooking, and buying in the market place. And washing and drawing water at the well: hearing and joining in the banter and gossip with Martha, Leah and Sarah and Rebecca . . . Naomi's warning brimmed over from their half-forgotten conversation, '*They hate, Miriam, they hate—*' But before she had time to feel the fright the recollection conjured in her mind, Miriam was sound asleep.

Outside, the sun frenzied with heat, searing, parching, scorching. And then relented, giving the day a little time to cool before the night came on.

It was darkening when Miriam wakened sluggishly, as though she had been drugged, aware of unfamiliar noises in an unfamiliar place.

She tried to rouse herself, listening again for the sniffing sounds that had awakened her. A cold, wet smear across her cheek, and the *sniff-sniff* snorting in her ear.

Miriam was up, alert.

It was a dog, and she wondered whether to be alarmed or relieved. The flailing tail beat a lunatic rhythm at the end of its wriggling body, twisting, turning, advancing and withdrawing like a ritual dancer.

Miriam noticed the sheen on its coat, and its well-fed appearance. But where had the beast come from?

A shadow swam in the jaded light at the open door. And she knew the voice that called her name.

'Miriam.'

She was down the steps, across the floor, and already at the door when he entered.

It was Yosef.

Miriam was speechless, standing, staring. Afraid to believe.

Yosef propped his stick against the doorpost, let fall the bed roll strapped across his back, loosened the cloak from about his shoulders, and stretched out his arms towards Miriam, holding her face in his hands.

'Miriam.'

And they stood, silent. Staring. Loving. In long, tender, wordless looks.

Miriam felt the trembling strength in his hands upon her cheeks, and she touched them there, cherishing them to her.

'Yosef,' she whispered.

'Miriam.'

'You're back, Yosef.'

'Aye,' he said, and there was a touch of mock solemnity in the way he said it. 'Of course I'm back.'

They both laughed out loud, while Yosef turned her and put his arms around her shoulders, steering her towards the wine store.

'Pour your husband a drink before your parents come,' he directed, feigning severity, pushing her gently on her way, and sitting himself down, pounding his fist on the table. 'And be quick, wife.'

Miriam turned and curtsied. 'My lord and master,' she offered with pretended subservience. And then skipped lightly away to fetch the drink.

She poured the wine, and watched him slake his thirst with long swallows. And she felt proud, delighted, exhilarated. Yosef was home. Calling himself her husband. Treating her as his wife. And suddenly it were as though they had never been separated, and life had had no inexplicable twists and turns.

Yosef emptied his cup and, smiling, let it clatter on the table.

Mirriam poured, deliberately shaking her hand in mock fear of a tyrannical husband.

Yosef took the hand. 'Sit down, Miriam.' And he still gripped her hand when she sat.

'I missed you—' they both said together.

They laughed at themselves speaking the same thoughts, and then sat, silent, relishing each other's presence, neither of them making any move to speak again.

Miriam felt the comforting pressure of his hand, holding hers, and, every now and then, the thumb stroking the back of her hand, soothing strength, easing away the memories of the fretful separation.

There was dust on his face and hair from travelling, but she hadn't the heart to disturb him or to disrupt the bliss of the moment by preparing the basin for him to wash. Yet, as she watched him there, she thought the tiredness in his face was more than travel weariness. There was suffering there, and hurt in the eyes that said he'd borne too much, and lines that were hacked by sorrow and were not lost in the boyish smiles that creased his face when he glanced at her now and again.

Poor Yosef. Perhaps Naomi had not told all the story, after all.

'I thought you were not coming home yet, Yosef,' said Miriam, her voice sounding loud in the peaceful quiet. 'Naomi said you'd planned to go on to Bethlehem.'

'So I had. I thought I'd go there when I'd finished in Nain. I'd planned to register for the taxing, and then go on to Juttah to be with you.'

'And what made you change your mind?'

'I don't know. Somehow it didn't seem the right thing to do. So, instead of going to Bethlehem, I came back here.'

'We might have passed each other on the road.'

'Aye,' commented Yosef, weighing the consequences. 'But I didn't know you were back till I met your parents and Salome coming here.' He let go her hand, and stood up quickly. 'I'd better wash before they arrive. They'll be here any minute, I guess. They were kind enough to let me come on alone.'

They moved quickly. But Yosef was only barely ready when the entrance of the three – Anna, Joachim and Salome – announced the bedlam that was still sounding later in the pitch-dark watches of the night.

By then it didn't take much to persuade Joachim that it would be better if his family were to sleep the night's few remaining hours at Yosef's house.

*

Herod pushed his physicians away. The day had not properly dawned, and already they were manhandling him, while calling it care.

'It is not my body that's sick, today,' he growled at them. 'My mind is sad. My heart is heavy.'

They bowed their way backwards from his couch and stood, like chastened street dogs, in a cluster by the wall.

The King fell back on his cushions. Heavy-hearted. Sad. It was the loneliness, he told himself. He was sad because he was lonely. And he was lonely because he missed his son. He was lonely for Antipater. And suddenly he was sorry he had so eagerly agreed to Marcellus' request to send him to Rome.

It was only now that Antipater was gone that he realized how much he had grown to depend on him. How much he enjoyed his company. There was nobody else in the whole court that could take Antipater's place in his father's heart. There was nobody like him . . .

The King might have been content to brood on the qualities of his incomparable son had he been left undisturbed. His chamberlain, however, entered to announce that the King's brother, Pheroras, was in the palace, and had asked permission to visit the King.

It was too much for Herod. This man, who ignored the King's commands and spurned his good advice, this man presumed to visit him . . .

The failure of his plan to be rid of Pheroras's wife Jochebed still hurt Herod. He had had her like a fish in a net, and he'd let her go. Her escape still rankled in his mind. And Pheroras, his brother, for all the King's wheedling, bullying and coaxing, would not divorce the wretched woman. But this man still came and went in the palace, enjoying all the privileges and pleasures of the court.

Was the same brother calling now to taunt him with news

that his slut of a wife had at last given birth to her expected Messiah?

Herod had had enough. He would take no more. A wave of the hand signalled the chamberlain to admit Pheroras.

The greeting was cold. The meeting brief.

Herod wasted no words. The alternatives were clear. If Pheroras wished to continue in brotherly friendship with the King, if he wished to continue to enjoy the benefits, privileges and pleasures of the court, then he must divorce his wife. The alternative was permanent exile in his own Tetrarchy. He would not for any cause or reason, or on any pretext, cross over the frontiers of his own dominion. And never again would he or his wife or any of his offspring darken the palace door, or see the King's face again.

There was no argument.

Pheroras needed no time to consider the choice. He would go into exile in Perea, his Tetrarchy on the far side of the River Jordan.

The King dismissed him with disgust.

Pheroras bowed. And spoke as he bowed. 'And I swear this oath, my King and brother, that I will not come again to this place until the King is dead.'

But Herod wasn't listening. He had slumped back on his cushions. Sick. Sad. Lonely. The son he loved was far away in Rome. The brother he loved was lost to him for ever.

It was a comfortable voyage, Antipater reckoned. Even when all around him were succumbing, he had managed not to be seasick.

Whether he should be proud of that as an achievement, or just consider himself lucky, he couldn't be sure. But he wasn't sorry it was all over, now, and they had, at last, reached Puteoli. It was good to be near land again. And to be able to think of eating food that wasn't fish, for a change, or pickled till it was almost pure salt, or threatened a plague of worms.

He was the first to go ashore when the sailors had secured the ship, and laid down the planks.

Bathyllus, his servant, had enough to occupy him, seeing to the baggage and organizing its transport. It would be some time before everything was ready for the journey to Rome. In the meantime, Antipater would enjoy a walk around the city.

It was good to have the firm earth under his feet. It felt a bit strange at first. But it didn't take him long to find his feet, and soon he was stepping out steadily and briskly as though he'd never been near sailing ships or seas.

All round him, as he walked, the products of the world were set out on the doorstep of the Empire. In tidy piles, in great heaps, stacked high, or strewn on the ground. In warehouses, little booths, in guarded pens secured from thieving hands. Papyrus from the Nile. Gold from Dalmatia. Tin from Cassiterides near Britain. Glass from Phoenicia. Silks from Seres far off in the East. Cotton and spices from India. Marble from Greece.

Only in Tyre and Sidon had he ever seen such a variety of produce and merchandise. But never in such quantities. And men from every land under heaven sweated and toiled, coming and going from the ships, still adding pile on pile to the great stores.

The port itself resounded with the babble of foreign languages of toiling sailors and bargaining merchants.

Puteoli gave the impression of being a clutter of a place. It wasn't the port itself, nor the paraphernalia that goes with every port, the merchandise, the booths and shops and eating houses, the constant toing and froing of sailors, merchants, travellers, hawkers. Antipater understood all that and appreciated it.

There was no order, no system. Nothing seemed to be in its proper place. Workshops and warehouses smothered workmen's dwellings, with hardly space enough between them for a man to stretch his arms. Merchants' mansions sat incongruously in the confusion. And where there was no longer room to build at ground level, great *insulae* had been reared, dwarfing and overshadowing all and everything around them, and surely choking the people who lived in them.

He had seen *insulae* before. Years ago, when he was a boy in Rome. Five, six and seven floors built one upon another. Oblong-shaped, round a huge courtyard where the pervading atmosphere was noise and stench. Rows and rows of windows that never closed in summer and never opened in winter. And always, everywhere, children, scavenging dogs and flies.

As a boy, it had frightened him. Now, as he looked, it appalled him. No decent ventilation in summer. No heat in the winter. Little or nothing in the way of a water supply. And no sanitation.

Great port as it was, with the world and its merchants coming and going in its waters, Puteoli was no Caesarea. And it certainly would not come anywhere near his father's standards of what a city should be. The mind that could conceive and build a city like Caesarea or Jericho or Tiberias, Antipater reflected, could not but be upset and offended . . . sickened indeed, by the confusion and clutter of Puteoli.

A merchant passed him and turned into an alleyway on the far side of the street. A Phoenician, by his appearance, who stood out in the crowd.

Two servants followed behind him. They had difficulty keeping up as they manhandled their master's baggage past the chatting huddles and through the jostling crowds.

The merchant walked purposefully, as though he knew precisely where he was going.

Antipater was curious and, without seriously thinking about it, he was following the merchant.

The alleyway was a narrow space between a warehouse that stored fish, by the smell of things, and a potter's shop. Bowls and pots and jars stood neatly stacked outside the shop. And in the half-dark inside, the potter dipped and rubbed and pressed, oblivious to the hubbub from the patrons of the wine tavern further down the alley.

Antipater ignored the pleas of the beggar huddled against the side wall of the warehouse. He bawled at the two scavenging dogs that came sniffing at him, sending them scuttling down the alley in front of him.

He kept the two servants in view. And was almost alongside them when they came into the open space at the end of the alleyway.

Antipater wasn't surprised. It was to be expected in Puteoli. In the mdist of smells and work and merchandise, an open space and a villa.

He could see the house through the gates in the high walls that gave it privacy and locked out the noise.

For a while he stood admiring it. Till he got the smell of food from the eating house on the corner of the alley. He was impressed by the place. It was clean and cared for. The proprietor had an air of grandness about him, and, without saying so, made it clear that he could distinguish one customer from another, and could recognize royalty when he saw it, even when it walked incognito.

He ate well. Melon that was gentle and refreshing to the palate. Meat balls with lettuce and leaks. Apples and pears. And wine that surprised him. It was good wine. The best Falernian wine, the proprietor assured him. And he left after his meal, still smiling to himself at the owner's gesticulating assurances, 'Falernum . . . immortale.'

By the time he had finished his tour of the city and was back at the ship, his servant, Bathyllus, had everything ready for the journey. A *cisium* and driver that would carry him to Rome, and a wagon for the baggage. But Bathyllus, being the kind of servant he was, had not only organized the transport, but had the baggage already loaded on to the great, cumbersome wagon, and the driver made fully aware of where he was going in Rome.

The driver matched his wagon. A heavy, lumbering man. He grunted his acknowledgement when Antipater addressed him. And gave all the impression of being pleased at the prospect of a journey to Rome.

Antipater smiled as he inspected the wagon and the two horses that would draw it in tandem. Deep in the baggage, Bathyllus had already arranged a place for himself where he could travel comfortably. Bathyllus stood sheepishly by as he examined the spot.

Beside the wagon, the *cisium* Bathyllus had arranged for his master's transport looked frail and vulnerable.

'A wickerwork chariot,' Antipater thought to himself. And both horse and driver complemented it. The horse had an Arab look about it, and would not disgrace itself in a chariot race. And it would have plenty of encouragement from its alert and athletic young charioteer of a driver.

Antipater climbed in, and settled back on the furs and rugs that would later protect him from the cold as they travelled through the night.

He gave the signal to move.

Eager to start, the drivers simultaneously cracked their whips and the run along the Appian Way to Rome began.

With no undue effort, the lightweight *cisium* quickly outran the wagon. The drivers shouted and waved their farewells, promising to meet in Rome, and Antipater and his driver were out ahead, making their way alone.

They stopped every now and then to walk and stretch their legs. The Appian Way was obviously familiar stuff to this young charioteer. He knew the best places to eat and drink. And, certainly, Antipater had no reason to fault his judgement.

Towards evening, Antipater wondered aloud where they would rest for the night. The driver had ideas about that, too, and named several places. They were very high standard, he assured him, clean and well kept. And there was everything for a man's comfort.

That, of course, was if the intention was to stop somewhere for the night rather than to continue right on to Rome.

The idea hadn't crossed Antipater's mind. But it seemed a good one. And the driver seemed not only keen enough, but capable enough.

They'd travel on, Antipater decided.

A touch on the reins brought the horse to a walk, while Antipator wrapped himself warmly in the furs that had been his cushions through the day. And then the horse was trotting again. The *cisium* swayed gently along the road, and Antipater was soon asleep.

Nazareth heated and cooled in the rising and setting sun, but nothing got better. A few days home, and Miriam realized that Nazareth had not changed one little bit. She was no sooner back than the gossipmongers began again where they had left off three months earlier.

But they were aggressive now, belligerent, defiant. It was no longer just the ordinary, understandable crudeness of ignorant, hard-working women. Not just the natural, homespun prurience of earthy women with limited experience and not much imagination. Not any more. The early mockery had got out of hand. The first skirmishes of hate had become cruelty now. Persecution. Every word and look and comment was moulded, calculated, spiked and barbed to inflict the utmost hurt and pain.

And they succeeded.

Old Martha, for all her wisdom, and the authority of all her years, could no longer restrain them. The jibes and quips and scoffs of early days had grown beyond control, bitter and rancid, souring the lives of those who fanned the calumny, marring the hours of day and night for Miriam. The first brushes of scorn had become a full-scale war that neither side knew how to end.

Rachel was gone. And she was buried before they even informed Miriam she was dead. She had no friend among them any more. Had she admitted all that they accused her of, she wondered, would they have let the matter rest? Would they tolerate her, as they had tolerated poor Rachel. But she had denied their accusations, and they detested her.

Naomi was right: they *hated*. But even Naomi, Miriam felt, could not fully appreciate the venom in their hate. To Miriam it seemed as though the whole place had become a snake pit of spite. And she was frightened.

She avoided the town, and all the places where she knew the women went. She went no longer to the well, but depended on Yosef to fetch the water in the night, when the streets were empty and the women all gone home. Her farthest journey in the daytime was to Naomi's house. And, even then, she travelled cautiously to avoid the women that spied on her even there, and their long, loud ridiculing shouts of '*maggidala*', harlot.

Yosef was bitter. It was hard not to be in this gaudy town straddling the crossroads of the world, where soldiers leched, and travellers, merchants and townsfolk contributed variations in vice. Yet he waited and hoped and wished that things would change, that time might throw up another wonder for the women to gawp at, another scandal to titillate their minds and saturate the venom of their poisonous tongues.

But passing time brought them no relief. They were not wanted. There was no place for them in Nazareth.

*

Perea, so far as Pheroras was concerned, was a stretch of land that God had made between the desert and the Dead Sea, and then had promptly forgotten.

Even Herod had forgotten it. There was a day when Herod had entertained the greats of the Empire and the land in his newly built fortress at Machaerus. But those days were long gone. He'd no interest in that place now, and hardly even remembered it existed except when he sentenced a troublemaker to languish in its underground dungeons.

Bethany-beyond-Jordan, where Pheroras and his family lived, and from where he administered the sand and date palms of his Tetrarchy, was a little brighter. But compared with Jerusalem, it was dead. And he felt sometimes as if he presided over a perpetual funeral that lacked the dignity of a corpse.

Yet, there was a serenity about the place. The women, though they talked and yapped, had lost their gossiping intensity and their snarl. There was no intrigue now, or certainly none that he was aware of. Jochebed and himself enjoyed peace, and he was almost grateful to his brother. It seemed then as if the years ahead would come and go with nothing to disturb the even tenor of their way.

He couldn't know, however, that he had so little time left to enjoy it all.

His exile had no sooner begun than the embassy from Jerusalem arrived. The King was dying, and summoned his brother to attend upon him in Jerusalem.

Herod's dying was nothing new to Pheroras. He 'died' regularly. Pheroras knew that Herod sometimes used it as a ploy, and that it was not beyond him now, even with his own brother. It was a snare, Pheroras decided, a trick to get him and his family back to Jerusalem. If not for one reason, then for another – and none of them happy.

As Pheroras searched for a reason, it dawned on him that

the King had obviously discovered Antipater's scheme to have him murder the King while his son was in Rome.

And Pheroras cursed himself as a fool for having imagined Herod would not find out. Herod stayed alive by being always a step ahead of those who intrigued against him.

Pheroras recalled the almost forgotten days when Antipater had beguiled him into the poison plot that by now he had put completely from his mind. At that time Antipater had explained that the King had paid him handsomely to have no truck or contact with Pheroras. He would be no more than a fool, then, who could forget that the King would keep careful track of every movement Antipater made.

He was a fool, and Pheroras twice cursed the lethargy caused by country living that allowed him to become so careless. But then he dismissed the idea. He knew in his heart and soul that Herod, no matter who warned him, would not believe Pheroras capable of killing him, for all the plots he might be said to be party to. Pheroras was loyal to his brother, and Herod knew it. And, in a perverse kind of way, Pheroras had a deep love for his brother, and Herod knew that too.

It was not, then, for anything to do with Antipater, that the King summoned him to Jerusalem, Pheroras decided. It crossed his mind that maybe this time the King's plea was genuine.

But Pheroras wasn't going back to Jerusalem. He was just as obstinate as his brother. And if Herod's sense of outrage had forced him into exile, his own sense of outrage would keep him there. There was no going back until the King was dead.

And the messengers from Jerusalem could report that message to the King.

And, besides, he could not leave his wife, and certainly would not encourage her to travel when the time was so near for the birth of their child. Pheroras reckoned he knew, now, the reason for Herod's attempt to inveigle him back to Jerusalem. It was Jochebed, and Herod's fear of the prophecy that the son of her body would become the Messiah of Israel.

The messengers departed reluctantly. And Pheroras appreciated their reluctance, their fear of returning to Herod and the royal court, having failed in their mission.

They had hardly left before Jochebed's child was delivered. A boy – as the Pharisees' prophecy had foretold, and everybody confidently expected.

There was excitement and delight throughout the household, but Pheroras thought he felt an air of disappointment tinge the atmosphere, as though somehow a hope had died, and great expectations had come to nothing.

The midwives said nothing, though they had worked hard. Every move in their preparations made it clear that they were making ready for the birth of someone more significant even than royalty. They saw themselves as the handmaidens of history, the midwives of the nation's new birth.

Yet there were no portents at the birth. The heavens gave no signal to draw earth's attention to the moment. Jochebed sweated and shouted and heaved, and cried out in pain and confusion and joy and fear, like every other mother they had waited on. And the child, when he appeared, was like every other child. And they smacked him as they'd smacked the rest, to make him gasp and show that there was breath in him.

They washed him in salt, swaddled him in rich linen cloth, and placed him tenderly in his mother's arms. And waited for the nation's noise, thronging to greet the arrival of Israel's promised Messiah.

But the nation was quiet in the night, and only the chatter of cicadas seeped into the silence as Jochebed lay nursing her newborn son.

The midwives finished their work with the air of women jilted on their wedding day. Pheroras thanked them, and sat by his wife, watching her touch, with tender, hesitating, tentative caresses, the little face that glowed from its new-made womb of scented linen.

And when she turned her head to look at him, Pheroras saw the questions, too, in Jochebed's face, and in her eyes the hurt that the men who, only months ago, had loudly prophesied she'd bear Israel's Messiah, were not here now to celebrate his birth.

She'd been used, Pheroras realized. They'd both been used by unscrupulous men.

He was sorry for Jochebed, and that things had not turned out as they had been foretold. But, somewhere deep down, he felt relieved: glad that everything was, in fact, so very ordinary. The child was their son and nobody's Messiah. He felt sure that Herod would not take kindly to the thought of rivalry from a Messiah – especially one born from Jochebed's womb.

But he kept his thoughts to himself and said nothing. The smile crinkling his face told her that his only concern was that the child and she herself were safe and well. And Jochebed, when she was up and about again, would put all the upset behind her, and they could get back to the peace and quiet of their country ways.

What Herod thought of his refusal to come to Jerusalem or how he reacted to the birth of Jochebed's son, Pheroras never knew. He was, however, relieved that there were no immediate repercussions.

Then the King recovered from his bout of sickness.

By the time the news of his recovery had reached Bethany-beyond-Jordan, Pheroras himself had fallen sick: a sudden illness for which the physicians had no explanation, and for which they could find no remedy.

It was a shock to those in Jerusalem when the King set off

to visit his brother. He went quietly: no pomp, no royal trimmings. No entourage beyond the few physicians who bravely insisted they be allowed to attend on him.

And he appeared in Pheroras's palace unheralded, unannounced, as though he were no more than a neighbour visiting a friend.

Jochebed was frightened. She tried to hide her fear, her burning hate, as she clapped for servants to attend on the King. But Herod raised a weak hand, signifying that he wanted no formality. He had come merely to see his sick brother.

And Jochebed watched him shuffle, supported by two of his physicians, towards the room where her husband was dying. What vengeance had this man who played God with people's lives now sneaked in to wreak, she wondered, following the three men to her husband's bedside. The King himself was clearly dying, so could he not let another man die in peace?

'Pheroras . . . my brother,' the King lisped, as he reached down a scrawny, pock-marked hand. 'You must not die—'

Pheroras opened his eyes – a slow, laboured, painful opening – and looked at the King. 'My brother—' he mouthed, moving his hand through a small arc on the coverlet.

The King stooped. The two hands touched. The King wept.

Jochebed watched, till Pheroras's eyes closed again, and the King turned. She made to move, but Herod stopped her. And, as the physicians held him steady on his feet, he put out his arms to clasp her hands in his.

There were tears washing down Herod's face, and Jochebed saw them. She felt the strength of his comfort as he wept with her, sorrowing that she would be so soon a widow. And then he told his physicians it was time to leave. He would not hear of Jochebed accompanying him to the gate. No ceremony. No formality. He would go as he came. She must stay with her husband.

Jochebed turned back to sit at the edge of her husband's bed, taking the frail hand that inched towards her.

The hand pulled her forward, the eyes stared, searching, and she bent to hear the faint whispering.

'My wife . . . I was wrong about my brother's disposition towards me . . . I have hated him who is so affectionate to me . . .'

He paused. Jochebed pressed his hand.

'I have contrived to kill him who is broken-hearted before I am even dead.'

The head slumped, lolling on the pillow; the hand in hers went limp. But Jochebed felt there was more her husband wanted to say. And she waited, soothing love into the poor hand she held.

'Antipater beguiled me into agreeing to murder my brother—' Jochebed hardly heard the murmured confession, nor the jumble of words that followed. 'Antiphilus', he seemed to be saying, 'brought it from Egypt. Theudion brought it to me—'

'Theudion brought what, husband?' she whispered. 'What did Theudion bring?'

She waited long before he spoke again, and waited more as he struggled to shape the word. 'Poison,' he said, and repeated, 'Poison to destroy the King.'

Jochebed felt the hand pull away from hers, and it slowly lifted a finger pointing beyond the bed.

'Fetch it, wife . . . from the cupboard. Destroy it in the fire—'

Jochebed hesitated.

'Destroy it now . . . in my sight . . . that I may not be liable to the Avenger in the invisible world.'

He said no more, but lay waiting, his eyes wide open.

And they followed Jochebed as she went, searching the

cupboards towards which he pointed, till she found the phial.

'In the fire,' murmured Pheroras.

Jochebed opened the phial and began pouring its contents into the brazier that burned in the centre of the room. She stopped, suddenly, while there was still a little left. And found herself putting the stopper back in the phial. And wondered to herself why she had stopped. To keep some? For fear, maybe, of what Herod might still do to her when her husband was dead?

She hid the container away in her robes, and turned back to the bed.

'It's done, my husband—' But as she spoke, she already knew Pheroras was dead.

The messenger she sent to bring Herod the news reached Jerusalem not long after the King himself.

Herod wept openly.

In the city they claimed Herod had poisoned his brother. Herod ignored the lies, and took no action against those who spread them. He brought Pheroras back to Jerusalem for burial. He himself arranged the funeral and saw to it that in the place of honour were, among the mourning courtiers, Jochebed and her infant son.

And it would be wise and right, he told her, that she should make her home in his palace in Jerusalem.

CHAPTER EIGHT

Antipater took no time at all to settle in Rome. It was like coming home again. What had been familiar to him as a boy in the city all those years ago had hardly changed while he'd been away.

The things that entranced him as a lad still excited and enthralled him. The Tiber River proudly parading through the city, its route adorned with neatly laid out parks and ornate gardens along both its banks. Buildings still towered over him in the jumble of narrow streets and alleyways, cluttered and jammed with people and animals and traffic. And at the windows of the high-rise flats, they still grew flowers in pots, making the walls look as though they'd been planted with miniature gardens.

He loved it all. The noise, the smells, the grandeur. And the people. Hustling, shuffling, dreaming, scheming, sobbing, sighing, laughing, talking . . . endlessly talking.

This was Rome, and he relished it. Every minute of it.

Meeting the friends of his schooldays and his youth was just like old times. It was as though they'd never been separated.

Like himself, they were that much older now. But behind

the wear-and-tear, the wrinkles of maturity, they were still the same.

Publius had grown fat. Fatter. He had always been plump, Antipater recollected. And he still bore with patient joviality the banter Vitellus, Marcus and Marcellus heaped on him.

Suave, polished Marcus assured the company that Publius rarely took a bath, contenting himself with an occasional but not too frequent rub of scented oil.

'Like the Emperor himself,' defended Vitellus, mimicking Augustus Caesar's voice, pretending a limp in his left leg in imitation of the Emperor, and walking on his tiptoes to represent the thick-soled sandals Caesar wore to make himself look taller than he really was.

But Vitellus and the others became serious when Antipater asked Publius about his sister and his parents. Antipater expected Vitellus to mimic their old schoolmaster, Lucinius, who was also their mentor, disciplinarian, friend – *in loco parentis* as he used to put it himself. And he felt a strange sadness, a kind of loneliness, when Publius told him his father had died.

'Four months ago. Of old age. Nothing else.'

'And your sister and mother? Are they still in the old house?'

'They're not,' Publius told him. 'A month ago, my mother and my sister moved to live in Capri.'

'Doing something at the Emperor's villa,' put in Marcus to ease what might become too morose a conversation. 'But ask him about his sister,' he advised, 'the lovely Domitilla.'

'More beautiful than ever,' assured Vitellus, mincing in a circle round the group. 'You drooled over her when you were a growing lad, Antipater,' he reminded him. 'If you could see her now you'd run away with her.'

Practical, well-connected Marcellus put an end to the frivolities. Lodgings, so far as he was concerned, somewhere for Antipater to live, was the priority.

Marcellus would not countenance the idea of him finding lodgings. He would stay in Marcellus's own house. And they all laughed when Vitellus wondered if living in a house once occupied by the Emperor was beneath his Jewish dignity.

The house was near the Forum, and stood at the top of the Ringmakers' Stairs. And they were serious about Augustus Caesar once having lived in it. He had bought it from Calvus the orator. And lived there long enough after he had become Emperor. Until he'd bought Hortensius's house on the Palatine Hill, and made that a palace in a park preserved exclusively for the enjoyment of the Emperor and his family.

It was typical of its new owner Marcellus, Antipater thought, to live in a house fit for an Emperor.

On his first day in the city, the same Marcellus delivered to the Emperor's secretary the news of his arrival, and his father's letter.

Two days later, the Acta Diurna, posted up in the Forum, announced for all to read that Antipater, son of Herod, Tetrarch of Galilee, was visiting Rome. They were the quietest things Marcellus had arranged since his arrival. And it took him all his time to keep up the whirling social pace Marcellus and his friends set him.

But today he'd have to rest. There would be no drinking and philandering tonight. Tomorrow he would need all his wits about him. Caesar Augustus had summoned him to attend at his court.

Vitellus's mimicry of the Emperor did Antipater no good when he met Augustus face to face. The caricature was too deeply embeddded in his mind, and it was difficult to take the man seriously. It was hard enough not to burst out with the guffaws that were his first response to Vitellus's performance.

The limp was there. Not half so bad as Vitellus had exaggerated, but obvious, nevertheless. Antipater sympathized with the man. It was clear that he suffered from some complaint in the hip and thigh that made it painful and hard to move his left leg, disrupting an otherwise graceful gait. It was clear that Augustus tried his best to hide it.

But there was no hiding the deep, thick soles of the sandals. As Caesar walked, the skirt of his toga swirled high enough to reveal the secret of the Emperor's added inches.

Antipater wondered why he did it. It was hardly pride, for his appearance did not suggest that the Emperor was unduly proud or sensitive about the way he looked. Handsome, indeed. Remarkably handsome. But unkempt. His toga looked home-made. Its purple stripe was noncommittal, being neither narrow nor broad. It was hard to decide whether his yellowish hair was naturally inclined to be curly or was so because he cared little about how it looked.

As Augustus greeted him, Antipater noticed again the scent he had grown accustomed to from Publius. Vitellus was right: the Emperor did not bathe too often, but seemed more lavish in his use of scented oil than ever Publius was.

'You are welcome to our city,' the Emperor assured him.

'My Lord,' Antipater almost replied, but remembered Marcellus's warning in time. Augustus considered it almost an insult to be addressed in that way.

'Great Caesar,' he said, instead, with a deep obeisance.

'Your father writes affectionately of you—'

Antipater bowed his head.

'And would have you succeed him in Galilee.'

Antipater feigned surprise at the news. He was intrigued that Caesar wasted no time in small talk, but came quickly to the point.

Caesar moved towards a high stool. He took time to settle himself sedately, ordering the toga about his shoulders, arranging its skirt.

It was a deliberate gesture, Antipater felt; not the fussiness of a man who wanted merely to be comfortable. This was Augustus preparing to be imperial. He was setting the pose in which great Caesar was about to speak.

Antipater waited in the silence, feeling the awful distance that now separated Augustus Caesar and himself. He was impressed, over-awed. It was so simple a thing that Caesar had done. And yet, this simple ritual of sitting down had changed completely the tone of their meeting. The room became an awesome place, the stool the throne of Caesar's power.

And then, as though there had been no break in the conversation, Augustus spoke. 'Rome happily grants the request,' he said.

Antipater heard it. The sound of power. The voice of a man who owned the world, who knew that by raising a finger he could change the destiny of a kingdom. Any kingdom. Including his own father's.

He made a low bow, but said nothing, Caesar's 'Rome happily grants the request' sounding and resounding in his head. The measure of Augustus's simple statement, redolent with imperial majesty, made it too clear that Caesar was conferring a privilege on a vassal whose existence depended on the grace and favour of his overlord.

His father had begged well, Antipater decided. And felt grateful. His future with Caesar, at least, was secure – whenever that future would begin.

And while Caesar wished his father well again, and long years yet to reign as Tetrarch, Antipater realized he had not yet heard from Pheroras and whether or not the poison plot had been successful.

Caesar interrupted his thoughts. 'Go now,' the Emperor was saying. 'And we invite you to return this evening to dine with us. Tiberius and Drusus are home again, and you will meet my daughter Julia.'

*

Antipater was struggling with the toga Marcellus insisted he should wear.

'It's not really a toga,' Marcellus explained. 'It's called a synthesis. You're not a Roman, so Augustus would not permit you to wear a full toga.'

'I'm glad to hear that,' murmured Antipater, still manoeuvring his way through the muslin skirt folds of the synthesis to settle the tunic top about his shoulders.

'You'll be glad of it as the evening wears on. The atmosphere can be stiflingly warm.'

'I couldn't be warmer than I am now,' Antipater assured him wearily through the layer of muslin.

Marcus arrived. And laughed at Antipater's struggles.

'Are you trying to smother the poor Jew, Marcellus?' he quipped, pouring wine for the two men and himself.

'I understand it's a small party,' he announced.

'Intimate,' joked Marcellus.

'Indeed,' replied Marcus. 'Julia will certainly be there.' And he laughed, leaving all kinds of hints in the air.

'Julia is beautiful,' he advised Antipater, whose task of dressing for the dinner was almost completed. 'Marvellously beautiful.'

'But that's not surprising,' Marcellus put in. 'Look at her handsome father. And her mother, Scribonia, was still a beautiful woman when Augustus divorced her.'

Antipater's struggled ended. He was out of the mêlée of cloth and settling the synthesis with one hand, with a cup of wine in the other, when Publius arrived.

It was obvious to all that he had been to the baths. He was smelling not scented so much as thoroughly clean. Nobody made any comment. It was enough that Publius had such respect for the Emperor that he washed decently before attending dinner with him.

'We were telling Antipater how beautiful Julia is,' said Marcus as he poured wine for the new arrival.

Publius nodded his head in thanks. Then took a deep drink before he spoke. 'She is, of course,' he agreed. 'Beautiful.' And then added ominously, 'But she is also dangerous. No man is safe from her—'

'So be warned, Antipater,' put in Marcus.

Antipater laughed.

'Laugh not, friend,' said Publius sternly. 'Sex and Julia are synonymous.'

'She can't be so bad,' countered Antipater, with sufficient questioning in his tone to ask for further enlightenment.

Publius made to reply, but changed his mind. Instead, he took another draught. The others waited. He wiped his hand across his mouth, and then spoke. 'Put it this way, Antipater. Voracious is a mild way of describing Julia's sexual appetite.'

'What does her husband say?' wondered Antipater.

'Poor Agrippa. What can he say? He's ancient compared with Julia, and he's abroad the best part of the time.'

'What about her father, then? Surely he has something to say.'

'Would you believe the Emperor doesn't know?' joined in Marcellus.

'He's the only man in Rome who doesn't,' said Publius.

'Maybe he doesn't want to know,' put in Marcus. 'Or maybe he's too busy with his own womanizing to pay any attention to his daughter's goings-on.'

'But even if he did know, would it make any difference?' wondered Publius in reply. 'She seems to have been born to chase men.'

'An instinct,' said Marcus, 'which, no doubt, she inherited from her well-practised father.'

'And she quotes the poet Ovid in support,' added Publius. 'According to him, there's no seriousness in anything but the sexual chase.'

'We needn't start on Ovid,' interrupted Marcellus,

bringing the discussion to an end. 'It's time to be on our way.'

But Publius wasn't finished. 'A word of warning, Antipater,' he said. 'From someone who's had his own problems warding off Julia's advances. You'll be the only stranger there tonight. A new man for Julia. A new conquest—'

'Out,' shouted Marcellus. 'Everybody out. Not only will we all be late, you'll put the poor man off his food.'

His guests were already well into the meal when Caesar arrived.

The room rustled as the eight diners made to rise from their couches round the three tables set out in a U-shape.

It was a formality, Antipater felt, a ritual. Nobody except himself had any serious intention of standing.

Augustus responded with a similar appearance of indulging in a ritual, by signalling them not to move. They were welcome, he told them. The food and wine, he hoped, were entirely to their liking. Then he settled himself in the centre of the couch facing the table that formed the base of the U, with his wife, Livia Drusilla, on his left.

Antipater reclined on the couch to Caesar's right: the most honourable position for an honoured guest.

Her father's late appearance, Julia explained to Antipater, wasn't meant as a discourtesy. 'It's an old habit, and we're all used to it.'

Reclining at the table set at right-angles to Antipater's, she was at the most honourable place at that table. A measure, Antipater wondered, of how much Augustus cared for his daughter. Or maybe a deliberate gesture to give pleasure to his guest. Whatever the reason, Antipater was certainly enjoying Julia's company. And Caesar seemed happy enough to leave them to themselves.

There was no faulting his friends' opinion of her beauty. Everything about her was beautiful: the carefully braided hair capped with a diadem; the cheeks demurely blushed with pink, the full lips shaped deep red with lipstick. Precious stones sparkled in the jewellery adorning her neck and wrists and fingers.

'My father is not a great eater,' she was saying. 'Indeed, he's no drinker, either. He'll pick at the little that's put in front of him. And not long after the *commissatio*, or drinking session, has begun, he'll leave us.'

Antipater became aware of Publius watching him from the far end of the table on his left. He glanced his way and Publius frowned his advice for Antipater to take care. Antipater smiled back, but could see no good reason for Publius's concern. Indeed, he was prepared to doubt his friends' opinion of Julia's morality. Nothing she had said or done since the meal had begun even hinted at her being a seductress. Quite the opposite, she seemed demure, sophisticated, educated, cultured and cultivated.

'And then, he'll be off to Syracuse,' she continued, 'to work late into the night.'

'Syracuse!' exclaimed Antipater. 'Why Syracuse? It's hundreds of miles away.'

Julia laughed, easing herself on her couch. 'You fell for that, Antipater. Everybody does who doesn't know my father.'

'So, what about Syracuse, then? Is he *not* going?'

'Of course. He goes there every evening after dinner.'

Antipater waited, enjoying the look of her playing out her riddle.

'Syracuse,' she said eventually, 'is what he calls his study, his work room. It's at the top of the house. And he calls it so in honour of Archimedes . . . of Syracuse.'

Augustus raised a hand. The company fell silent. Servants appeared with wine, and set about filling the cups.

They had brought wine enough, Antipater reckoned, to

keep everybody drinking well into the night. The Emperor's cup, though, he noticed, was only half filled. And then topped up with water.

'We drink a toast,' Augustus announced. 'To our honoured guest. To Antipater, son of Herod, Tetrarch of Galilee.'

They drank, each of them emptying the cup at one draught. Even Julia, Antipater noticed. He raised his cup to her in acknowledgement.

Caesar bade them all goodnight. And left.

'For Syracuse,' joked Antipater to his neighbour.

'Of course,' she said, and lay back on the couch. 'And now we're left to our own devices. Whatever Caesar's honoured guest desires—'

Was there at last a hint of the seductress in her tone, Antipater wondered. And he noticed, as she moved, the circlets on her ankles, and her toenails painted red.

But he hadn't time to judge further before Publius, Marcus and Marcellus were at his side.

'Ask for your sandals,' Publius instructed him.

'But—' began Antipater.

'No buts. We're leaving now.' And he signalled the servant who had taken charge of their sandals at the beginning of the evening to fetch them right away.

'I've had no chance to talk to Tiberius and Drusus,' complained Antipater.

'Another time,' eased Marcellus. 'Publius is right: it's time to go.'

Julia pouted. 'Going so soon?'

'Seems so,' returned Antipater.

'Well, maybe we'll be luckier tomorrow,' she suggested. 'Perhaps I'll see you at the races.'

The four men left, walking in silence. Antipater was angry. They had treated him like a child.

They were almost at Marcellus's house when Marcus broke the silence. 'Consider yourself lucky,' he told Antipater. 'She almost had you in her clutches.'

'And there'll be no races tomorrow,' added Publius.

Antipater stared at Marcellus.

'He's right again, Antipater,' affirmed Marcellus. 'But don't fret about disappointing Julia. She'll be too busy touting at the Circus, like the seasoned harlot she is.'

Pheroras's funeral was over, the days of mourning past. Herod was sorry his brother was dead. But he was a sick man himself, with his own health to worry about. He had long ago lost interest in the gossip that he himself had murdered Pheroras. And he might quickly have put his brother's death from his mind, had not two of his freedmen encouraged him to dwell on it.

They sidled into the conversation after the physicians had left, and were tidying away the towels and basins and ointments the doctors had used to soothe the pain and swelling in the King's distorted body.

There was evidence enough, they assured him, to show that Pheroras had been murdered. They pleaded with the King to look into this untimely death, and avenge his brother's murder.

Herod was intrigued, and encouraged the men to talk. Their work could wait.

'The King will remember that his brother had been sick for some time—'

'Of course the King remembers,' interrupted his companion. 'Did not the King, in his love and concern, journey to Perea to visit—' and he trailed off, realizing he might have overstepped the mark in presuming to remember for the King.

Herod tried not to smile. 'Talk to me of the murder.'

There was a silence as each man waited for the other to

speak. A quick glance then between them, and the spokesman was decided.

'Well,' he began, 'the King's brother, during his sickness,
normally ate alone. And there were some foods he could not
touch at all. For all he enjoyed them in other circumstances,
during his illness he could not eat them, for they made his
sickness worse.'

'He was poisoned, then?' suggested Herod, and was sorry
he had interrupted, for the man looked disappointed at
being hastened in the story he so obviously enjoyed telling.

'Aah,' replied the spokesman. 'Came the evening when
the King's brother had supper with his wife.' He paused for
Herod to measure the import of this statement. 'Man and
wife dined together, and during the meal the King's brother
was given a potion concealed in some food he did not
normally eat. This time, though, he ate some and, sadly,
died soon after.'

'You think it was the potion that killed him?' offered
Herod.

'The potion,' declared the spokesman.

'Who administered the poison?'

The spokesman shrugged – and looked blank enough to
suggest that he knew, but would not dare to breathe the
name in the King's presence.

Herod noticed this reluctance. 'Was it my brother's wife?'
he demanded. 'Was it Jochebed?'

The spokesman winced noticeably, glanced at his companion, then turned back to the King. But still said nothing.

Herod interpreted the silence, and did not press the
enquiry. Instead he asked, 'Where did this poison come
from?'

'It was supposed to be a love potion,' advised the spokesman's companion. 'It was brought from Arabia by a woman.'

'This woman', the spokesman informed the King, 'was a
friend of one of Sylleus's mistresses. Pheroras's mother-in-law

and her daughter Naomi visited her. They persuaded her to sell them the potion, and brought it back to the palace the day before the King's brother had that supper with his wife.'

The story was ended. Herod enjoyed the telling of it. He might have been satisfied to leave it at that, had the content of the tale not been so serious.

He signalled the men to leave. They gathered the towels and basins and ointments in armfuls, and bowed their way awkwardly out of the chamber.

There were people to be punished, Herod decided. But before he knew whom to punish, and what punishment to inflict, he would need a deal more and harder evidence. He would begin his search with the obvious people.

The women's slaves were tortured. They admitted nothing. The degree of torture was increased. And while they still confessed nothing, one slave girl in her agonies cried out a prayer that God would send upon Antipater's mother the kind of agonies the King now inflicted on them.

Herod heard the prayer, and intensified the torturing.

The chamber that had, a little earlier, been a haven of peace where men strove to bring ease and comfort to the sick King, was now a screeching bedlam. Torturing soldiers cursed and shouted obscenities. Tortured women, degraded by their inquisitors, screamed and protested their innocence, pleading for mercy.

Herod sat unmoved, waiting, listening to the strangled words from the broken slave girls.

He thought he heard something new. Doris's slave had spoken, he thought. A raised hand stopped the punishment.

The girl tried to speak. 'Antipater', she said, 'hated you, his father, and wished you dead.' Her voice was weak and faltering, no louder than a whisper.

Two soldiers brought her closer to the King. Herod leaned forward, straining to hear every word, fearing she had left her confession too late, and that she might die before she had ended her revelation.

She told him nothing of the poison. All she spoke of was Antipater, his son. His son had complained to Doris, his mother, that the King had lived too long. He had accused the King of murdering his other sons, and it was out of fear that the King would kill him, too, that he had contrived his visit to Rome.

There was no more; the slave girl died as she spoke. The soldiers carried her body away, and beat the others out of the chamber.

Herod was only sorry that Antipater was so far away, in Rome, for now he was in a mood that could conjure exquisite punishment for the son he once imagined he could trust above all the others.

The torturing, however, was not ended. It was now the men's turn, and Herod enjoyed the irony that among the victims was a man who bore the same name as his son, Antipater – and was his son's Procurator.

He did not protest so much as the women before him, and Herod was grateful that he did not scream so much. It did not take long to encourage him to reveal that Antipater had prepared the poison, and had given it to Pheroras to administer to the King, while Antipater himself was in Rome, far removed from all suspicion.

Herod buried a swollen face in swollen hands, murmuring, in sobbing whispers, to himself. 'Son of my loins, Antipater . . . you know the throne is yours when I am gone. I have arranged it so. Would Caesar permit it, you would be reigning, now—'

There was a hush over the chamber. A pitying hush for the King, slumped, limp, crumpled, the poor flitters of an old man, pain-racked and dying.

Even the tortured victim no longer moaned from the

agony coursing through him, nor fidgeted at the blood still oozing from his lacerations. Tortured and torturer alike remained mute, as if enveloped in the King's lisping melancholy.

'You wish me dead, Antipater, but I would not fault you . . . I myself wish for death, for then I would be free from all this pain and sickness . . . sickness, Antipater, beyond physicians' knowledge . . . pain, my son, that my body cannot bear.'

The King was no longer aware of anybody else in the room. He spoke as though his son were there beside him, his tormented words trickling, like the sweat from his brow, through misshapen, pock-marked fingers.

'Wish me dead, my son, and I could think it was your love for me . . . but to plot to murder me . . . Antipater, I am your father who bred you and gave you life and riches and majesty and a place among the great men of the world . . . and for all that you would murder me . . . murder me, then, but not with poison . . . even a pig, my son, is not so low that a man would poison it.'

The King wept, his heaving, heart-rending sobs smothered in writhing hands, and his pleading voice whispering, whispering, repeatedly whispering, 'Antipater, my son. My son, Antipater.'

As suddenly as it began, it ended. The King sat up. A servant mopped his brow and face, cooled his hands in a basin, and wiped them dry again.

Herod surveyed his audience as though he had done no more than pause a while to compose his next question.

'But how did Jochebed come to have the poison?' he wanted to know.

The question took the tortured informant by surprise. He could not remember having mentioned Jochebed. He was confused. But hesitation meant the torturing would start again, so he talked.

'Antiphilus,' he began, 'one of Antipater's friends, brought the poison from Egypt. It was delivered to Pheroras by Theudion, the brother of Doris, Antipater's mother. Jochebed had it because Pheroras, her husband, had given it to her to keep safely—'

Herod had heard enough. It was time, he decided, to talk to Jochebed. He dismissed them all, and sent a chamberlain to fetch his brother's widow.

Jochebed sat on the covered terrace, shaded from the sun. Two nurses played with her baby son over by the pool. They picked flowers and made flower chains, or plucked the coloured petals and threw them in handfuls into the air. And she heard the lad's cries of delight as the petals fluttered back to earth again.

She felt a pang of sorrow that Pheroras was not there to enjoy it all. She shook her head, pushing away the sadness, searching for a memory that would ease her sense of awful loneliness. But she was lucky, she told herself, for her brother-in-law, since Pheroras's death, could not have been kinder. It was he who had insisted she should stay at the palace, and not go back to Perea.

Her thoughts were broken by the chamberlain's arrival. It surely wasn't time to eat, already. Instead, he brought a message that the King would see her. He would accompany her to the King's chamber.

Jochebed hesitated, but the chamberlain encouraged her. As they walked, she pondered on his quiet insistence, and felt herself shadowed by foreboding.

She was ushered into the King's presence, and was shocked. The King sat propped up, but he looked as though he had just come back from the dead. This must be the reason for her sense of foreboding: the King was dying.

She made obeisance, her 'Long live the King' sounding a hollow mockery. She put out her arms to comfort him.

Herod pushed her back. 'Where is the poison?' he demanded.

'Poison?' she repeated, dumbfounded.

'The poison my brother, your husband, had planned to kill me with,' snarled the King.

Foreboding's shadow darkened as the night, and Jochebed felt overwhelmed. This was the old Herod again. He had grown tired of showing kindness, and had decided to be rid of her.

'The poison,' growled Herod again. And Jochebed heard herself tell him that she had it safely hidden away. She might have been wiser to have denied all knowledge of any poison, but the admission was out before she could stop herself.

'They told me you had it,' confided Herod. 'And that you had it safely hidden.'

Jochebed nodded, relieved that she had not lied. At least, for the moment, she had escaped torture.

'Is it here in the palace?' enquired Herod. 'I would be grateful if you would let me see it.'

'I have it here in the palace, my King. And if you would permit me, I would go and fetch it.'

Herod approved, and Jochebed withdrew as hastily as she dared, still careful to observe the courtesies due to the King's majesty.

Once outside the chamber, she raced along the corridors to her rooms, her mind in turmoil, her whole body trembling with fear of the punishment Herod would assuredly inflict upon her.

Wildly she rummaged among the robes that had once been her husband's, scattering them as she went, till the floor around her was strewn with the remnants of royalty. And found the box.

Memories and fear and loneliness flooded in on her, the grief of her bereavement, the hopelessness of her plight, all drained her. And she stood, clutching the wretched box, staring, unseeing, at the window, not knowing where to turn or what to do . . . till suddenly there was no longer any floor beneath her, and she felt the air rush past, and saw the high bright sun cast shadows far below her . . . and felt a jarring pain rampaging through her. . . .

She heard the voice. Its sound was far off in the distance, and she could not make out what it said. It grew nearer, through, and clearer, and now she could hear.

'You must have fallen from the window,' it said.

It was the King's voice. She knew it too well to mistake it. She tried to turn her head to avoid the awful stench of him, but she could not move. Her eyes opened. The face of Herod stared down at her, his lips moving, the smell of his stinking breath suffocating her till she wanted to retch.

'You are safe now,' he was saying. Over and over again. 'You are safe now.'

She felt two women lift her up and prop her with cushions round her on the couch.

'You're quite all right,' one of them comforted her. 'There are no bones broken, but you'll be very sore for a while. The bruises are beginning to show. You were very lucky.'

Jochebed smiled back. The women were kind.

She looked around slowly, for her neck hurt, and it was not easy turning her head. It struck her as strange that she was back in the King's chamber. She was sure she could remember leaving it, and running down the marble corridors, and past the statues. And searching among clothes and finding a box, and pushing the box into her bodice for safety's sake . . . And there her recollection stopped. She could remember no more.

Herod sat patiently. He could afford to wait. Occasionally, as the women fussed around, making her comfortable, Jochebed glanced in his direction. He smiled reassurance.

'You are a lucky woman,' he told her, when he decided it was time to begin talking again. 'You know you might have killed yourself with a fall like that. And that would have been a pity. You have a son to rear. And still a lot to live for.'

Jochebed bowed her head shyly, embarrassed by the King's concern for her.

'You went to find something for me?'

Her hand went involuntarily to her bodice. The box was there. Inside it the phial of poison that Pheroras had instructed her to burn.

'I found it, my King,' she said, her hand still clutching the box beneath her robes.

'Then we have much to talk about,' he told her, easing himself forward on his couch with the confidentiality of a conspirator.

A servant moved to settle the cushions around him, but Herod waved him away.

'You may talk freely,' he assured her. 'I will depend on you to tell me everything – the whole truth. Do that, and you have nothing to fear.'

Jochebed looked as though she was about to speak. But she hesitated, and said nothing.

'Tell me all,' advised the King. 'Tell me the real truth. And, on my oath as King, I promise you, whatever your wrongdoing, you shall suffer no punishment whatsoever.'

Jochebed looked too satisfied, he thought. He had given too rash a promise, and made it too easy for her to escape.

'My King—' she began.

Herod raised his hand and stopped her. 'But, know this,' he warned her, 'if it transpires that you have not told me the truth, or if you conceal anything from me, then, by my oath, you *will* be punished.' And he took pleasure as he watched the fright cloud her eyes. 'I will have your body so torn by torments that there will be no part left of it to bury.'

Jochebed tried again to speak, but no words would come.

No thought would shape in her mind. Speechless, she searched the puffed and scabby features of this man who could so coldly outline his bestial brutality in almost dulcet tones.

She wished she could have died where she had fallen. And now she remembered that she had deliberately, impulsively thrown herself from that window. And this was why: this man who sat in front of her. This man who planned to murder her slowly and painfully, and relish every spasm of her agonies.

The King wanted the real truth. He would have it. And, before she died, he would know from her how all men hated him.

'The poison you talk about', she began, 'was brought from Egypt by Antiphilus. His brother is a physician in Alexandria, and could procure it easily. Antiphilus gave it to Theudion, who then delivered it to Pheroras your brother, my husband. To keep it safe, Pheroras committed it to me.'

She paused.

The King was looking blankly at her, as though he was not even listening.

She would make him listen.

'But why do I speak of these great secrets,' she called to the King, 'now that Pheroras is dead? To keep secrets hidden would only tend to spare Antipater who is all our destruction.'

Herod was listening now.

'The poison plan, from beginning to end, was arranged by Antipater, your son, to murder you, my King. Before he went to Rome, he cajoled my husband into agreeing to poison you. He beguiled you into thinking you yourself had arranged and ordered his journey to Rome. Antipater, your son, deceived you to your face. He planned and contrived the journey himself with the connivance of his friends in Rome. And he is there today for no more reason than to put him above all suspicion.'

Herod stared. And Jochebed thought she saw a shadow of sorrow in his face.

'Hear then, my King, and be yourself, with God himself who cannot be deceived, witnesses to the truth of what I am going to say.'

The King slumped forward, smothering his face in his hands.

'Antipater, my son,' the King was mumbling to himself. 'My son, Antipater.' There was crucifying sorrow in the tones. But sorrow tinged with venom, and the threat of vengeance.

Jochebed felt almost sorry for the King, and watched him, racked and heaving with grief, sucking at the air to give himself breath, mumbling, mumbling till the audience chamber was filled with the sound of his sorrow.

Yet this same man, she reminded herself, before the day was out would see her killed with inhuman tortures. Her body so torn that there'd be no part left to bury.

So be it, then. She too, could inflict torture. And her voice screeched out into the sorrow-sodden air. 'Antipater, your son, was not alone in wanting you dead. All men, my King, all men hate you. With such loathing hate that they would poison you a thousand times a day—'

Herod slowly raised his hand to call a halt.

Jochebed ignored him. 'And women, Herod. Women hate you. Your wife, O King, was privy to the poison plot. Your wife Mariamne, who shares your bed, and lies in the ghost's shadow of her namesake, the wife you murdered—'

'I will hear no more, Jochebed,' murmured the King. 'You have tortured me enough.'

But Jochebed hardly heard him, her own voice echoing round the room.

'And while his daughter plots your death, her High Priest

father, Simeon, prays God to curse you with the sorest
afflictions—'

She paused for breath. Or was it to relish the pain she saw
she was inflicting on the mumbling King in front of her? She
couldn't be sure.

She nursed the phial of poison in her hands. And then she
spoke again, softly, this time. 'This phial, my King, contains
the little that is left of the poison your son, Antipater,
delivered to my husband.'

Herod raised himself, and stretched out his hand for the
bottle. But Jochebed clutched it tightly, burying it in her
bosom.

'My husband, the King's brother, could not, would not
murder you. As he lay dying, he ordered me to destroy the
poison.'

Herod lifted his head. His eyes looked the condemnation
he was about to speak.

Jochebed prevented him. 'I destroyed it all. Save for this
little. That I kept for my own use, against my uncertain
future, and out of fear for what you might do to me.'

'You are too clever a vixen,' mocked Herod, 'even for a
woman.'

As he spoke, he shifted himself, signalling to a servant to
prop the cushions round him as he sat up.

'Write down my sentence, chamberlain,' he called.

The chamberlain moved, ready to write.

Jochebed moved, too. The King would not have her.
Whatever he had in mind, he would not accomplish . . . and
she had the phial unstopped and to her lips as she was
thinking how she would thwart the King.

'Stop her,' roared Herod. 'She shall not die.'

One of the women immediately lashed out at her, knocking the phial from her hand, sending it smashing its way
along the marble floor, the tiny tincture losing itself in the
air as the bottle fell.

Herod smiled. It was almost benign. And Jochebed could not understand it. She had failed. And now she waited to hear Herod pronounce the sentence.

'Write down my sentence, chamberlain,' he said again.

'God guide the King in his judgement,' mouthed the chamberlain.

'Simeon, the High Priest, my father-in-law, shall be removed forthwith. Strip him of his robes of office. His place shall be filled by Matthias, son of Theophilus of Jerusalem.'

He waited till the chamberlain bowed to show that he was finished.

'There is more,' the King advised him. 'Draw me up a bill of divorcement. I will divorce my wife—'

Jochebed waited, her whole body trembling, her shaking hands smearing the tears all over her face.

Herod was in no hurry, smiling to himself as the chamberlain noted the King's instructions. And Jochebed hated him for the pleasure he so obviously got in delaying the announcement of her punishment.

'And now my judgement in the case of my brother's widow,' and he looked round him, taking in every face of every silent attendant.

It was her turn now. She was about to learn what torture he had devised for her, so that she would die slowly, in the bitterest pain, and with the utmost indignity.

'I promised you', he began, 'that were I not satisfied with the truth of your confession, you would most surely die.'

He paused, and let the company grow tense in expectation.

'The word, if I remember, was that your body would be so torn that there would be no part left of it to bury.'

Jochebed could hardly see through her tear-filled eyes. But mocking her from across the floor were the smashed pieces of the poison bottle.

'I am satisfied,' Herod was saying. 'You have told the

truth. But I detest you for your maliciousness. You took too much pleasure in telling the truth. And told me more – too much more – than I expected.'

If only she had drunk the poison when she'd first found it . . .

'I gave you the King's word. You are free, therefore, to go.'

Jochebed was numb.

'You are free to go,' the King repeated. 'I am dismissing you. The examination is ended.'

Jochebed could not move.

'The company is dismissed,' announced the chamberlain, beckoning to the women to lead Jochebed out.

'Chamberlain,' called the King, as the women took Jochebed's hands, 'Wait here till the rest have gone. I will have you write a letter to my son, Antipater, requesting that he come back home.'

It was still early, but they were glad to be up. They could not sleep anyway and, now that they had decided to leave, it was as well to be gone quickly. The early start, Yosef suggested, was a good thing. They'd a long journey in front of them, and they could be well on their way before the sun got really unbearable.

The cold of the dawning day bit at his hands as he saddled the donkey, and tied on the panniers packed tight with what they had kept of their home. The rest they had either sold or given away. To Joachim and Anna, to Salome to fill a bottom drawer when she became betrothed, to Naomi, and to Azariah who would not take his donkey back. Barzillai had bought the house, and Yosef choked with gratitude as he recalled how Barzillai had handed him the payment. 'I'm buying it, Yosef,' he'd said, 'but it will be yours again if ever you return to Nazareth.' But Yosef, as he adjusted the pannier strap so as not to chafe the donkey on the journey, could not imagine anything that would ever bring him back to Nazareth. They were now going to Bethlehem, and were leaving Nazareth for ever.

Miriam waited. A light, rising breeze snarled cold at her, and she cuddled herself to stop the sudden shiver. She watched Yosef, glad that he had decided they should leave, though the going was not so easy as it seemed when first he had suggested it. Going meant leaving a lot behind: the family she loved, the few kind, staunch friends; the hills and sky of Galilee, the roads and fields and the familiar places that had shaped and coloured her growing up. And memories that crowded on her now – of laughter, life and loving people; mad moments and hours of unrelenting happiness.

But, whether he liked it or not, Yosef had to go to Bethlehem to comply with the Census Edict from Rome. She smiled to herself as she thought of how decisions in Rome, that far-off city she would never see, by people she would never know and who were not even aware that Yosef and she existed, could so easily be party to the reshaping of their lives. Rome said 'Go', and Yosef had to go. But she liked the firmness of his voice re-echoing in her mind as she watched him making ready. 'The law says I must go to Bethlehem, because it is my father's home and the place of my birth. But there is no law which says I cannot take my wife with me. And, law or no law, I shall not leave you here in Nazareth to suffer all alone the cruelty they would afflict on you.'

And for a while the surging recollection of those agonies smudged the gaiety of the conjured scenes of childhood and her growing years.

A small group gathered while she stood bemused. A chicken brushed against her skirts, and pecked at invisible morsels on the ground.

Yosef patted the donkey, and turned it, ready to move off. 'It's time to go, Miriam,' he called.

Salome hugged her. Anna wept. And kissed her, whispering, 'Daughter, daughter,' reluctant to let her go.

Joachim fought back the tears. But there was the sound of weeping in his voice when he mouthed his parting benediction that blessed them both, and the child she carried.

Azariah stood, stroking his beard to hide his quivering lips. Naomi bade farewell, and quickly turned to comfort Anna.

Yosef helped Miriam on to the donkey, waited for her to settle herself comfortably, then waved silently and tugged easily on the bridle.

The donkey nudged him, flicked an ear, and they were on the move.

A little way behind, biding his time to make sure he was welcome on this journey, followed the dog.

In Joachim's house they tried to eat, and Anna did her best to make Naomi and Azariah welcome. But it was hard work, for Miriam was on her mind. She had no enthusiasm, and wondered, as she picked at the food Salome had set in front of her, if she had been wise inviting Naomi and her husband back. Yet it was the least she could do; they had been so kind. Naomi had hesitated, but Azariah had jumped impulsively at the invitation, and suffered a long, reprimanding look from Naomi in consequence.

Anna now noticed, though, that whenever Naomi glanced at her husband across the food-laden table, there was the flicker of a smile in her eyes. And when Azariah looked up every now and then, from the ever-emptying, ever-filling platter, he beamed back at her with packed-out cheeks, his hands full and grease on his beard. He enjoyed his eating, and didn't speak. He was paying his hosts the highest compliment by the noises coming from his side of the table: crunching, gulping, and sucking at his fingers.

Salome kept him well supplied, and Anna was grateful for her flitting backwards and forwards. The movement gave a sense of liveliness, staying for a while the smothering pall of melancholy that threatened to overwhelm their house.

But there was no rousing Joachim. The food went stale on his plate. He paid little heed to the desultory talk around him. He sat morose, forlorn. Even Naomi's brave attempt at reassuring him that everything would be grand, did nothing to lift him. His daughter was gone. A stranger among people who were not her own people. To a town of strangers. And he tried to travel with her in his mind along the road. But his journeying ended a few miles from Nazareth, and faded, jaded memory could not pull back and recognize the sights and signs along the way he'd seen once as a boy of twelve coming and going with his parents to Jerusalem. Faces came back to him. And names – Amos, Benjamin, Reuben – but they were dead men now. And the games they'd played when they should have been asleep out of the high sun, when the caravan of pilgrims to the Passover had halted to rest both man and beast. He remembered the heat that gave him sunstroke. And the nights of petrifying cold. And his mind stretched out tender, searching arms: binding his travelling child to him, warming her against the creeping chill of the darkness.

He shivered involuntarily. It was cold in the morning air, he decided, and got up to bring more life into the fire, apologizing to his guests for allowing it to get so low.

Azariah watched him move, and was sorry for him. He was afraid for Joachim, who had suffered so much already, bearing quietly, uncomplaining, the scorn and ridicule the neighbours heaped so unpityingly upon him for the wrong they had decided Miriam had committed.

He looked at Naomi, willing her to speak, hoping she would say something that would unlock the prison gate of sadness that so bitterly held Joachim in thrall. But Naomi said nothing. And Azariah studied the bent, spent figure of his friend.

'Joachim, would you help me in the olive grove today?' he asked after a while. It was a stupid suggestion, but all that came readily to mind in the circumstances.

Naomi jerked her head. And Azariah waited for the rebuke by word or glance, but she encouraged him.

'And there's a ewe in lamb, and ready, Joachim,' Azariah continued, not paying too great respect for the accuracy of what he was saying. 'I think it'll be today.'

Naomi winked at Anna.

Joachim noticed it, and saw Azariah raise his eyebrows, acknowledging Naomi's acquiescence. Azariah, he knew, could manage well enough in his olive grove, and it was a long time since one of Azariah's ewes had produced a lamb. But they were trying to be kind, and Joachim was grateful.

'If you're going to help, then, we'll leave as soon as you've had a bite to eat,' suggested Azariah, injecting new urgency into the affairs of the new day.

Joachim smiled to himself, moved back to the table, and began to eat.

'I'll be glad to help you, Azariah,' he said, but kept his eyes on Salome as she replaced the cup of goat's milk in front of him.

Azariah waited as Joachim ate, suddenly realizing how hungry he was. And when he had finished, they both went out. The women sat. Nobody spoke.

In the broody silence, Salome began crooning a psalm. 'The Lord hear thee in the day of trouble,' she sang, but the effort was half-hearted, it had no spirit, and she gave up, trailing off the verse as if with no further interest in it.

Anna pushed the plate and cup away from her, slowly, unconsciously. Idly, her fingers traced the pattern in the now uncovered space.

Naomi sat, pitying. Wondering how to rouse her.

'It'll get no better,' murmured Anna to the space on the table, her voice sounding far away. 'It'll get no better,' she repeated, as though her tongue struggled to tease the ravelled turmoil in her head. Her finger etched the myriad confusion of the lines that ran from the ugly misshapen knot in the table top. 'It'll get no better.'

Naomi moved to put her arms round Anna, to console her – but stopped. 'Give it time,' she recommended. Then she gathered up some dishes to give reason to her having moved.

'Give it time,' responded Anna, not lifting her head, not ceasing the tracing movement of her hand upon the grain. 'There's been so much time—' She slowed her hand, circling it in, kneading her finger round and slowly round the botched outline of the knot. 'Go away, Miriam, they said. And give it time till they forget—'

Naomi heard the anger creep into her tone. She flicked her head, and Salome, taking the signal, collected the dishes within her reach and went out. Naomi moved nearer to the disconsolate Anna.

'There's been so much time, Naomi.' Her voice was angry, but the eyes that lifted up, searching into Naomi's face, were fearing eyes. 'It will take for ever, and they'll never forget.' And the promised anger had died. The rising emotion quenched itself, and the words lisped from her lips as though even her tongue were too tired to shape them. Broken, beaten, defeated, she fell forward into Naomi's bosom, and wept.

Naomi sat still, feeling helpless and useless, not knowing what to say, her arms around the sobbing, convulsing body of her friend, nursing her like a child, feeling the fist thump a spasmodic tattoo upon her chest.

Then the sobbing eased, and Anna wept no more. They sat, the comforting and the comforted, their huddled sub-

stance taking shadow in the warming morning sun that
seeped in to meet the melancholy in the room.

Anna stirred, and Naomi loosed her hold.

'Hadn't you better eat, Anna?' she suggested. 'You need
something substantial to start the day.'

'By and by,' Anna replied. 'I'll eat in a little while. But
first I ought to prepare something for the men. They'll be
hungry after their work.'

As she spoke, she got up. Naomi joined her as she busied
herself with the food for Joachim and Azariah.

She had wrapped Joachim's parcel, and was handing it to
Naomi to put it in the second basket, when she paused. 'Do
you think we ought to leave Nazareth?'

Naomi's mouth dropped, her hand holding the parcel in
mid-air. It wasn't a question, her mind told her, for there
was hardly a hint of question in Anna's voice. It was, rather,
a statement proffered for approval.

'Who?' asked Naomi, automatically, stupidly.

'Joachim, Salome and myself,' measured Anna.

Naomi heard the firmness and, while knowing the answer
she would get, still found herself asking, 'Why?'

Anna, her eyebrows raised in surprise, began to offer
reasons, but Naomi gave her no chance to get started.
Instead, she asked another question. 'Where would you go,
Anna?'

'To Capernaum, where I lived before Joachim married
me.'

'But you have nobody there now. You know nobody—'

Anna spread out her hands, and the gesture explained
everything. Anna's mind was made up.

'What does Joachim say about that?'

'I've done no more, as yet, than hint at the idea. I know
he loves Nazareth . . . but they've broken his heart as much
as mine.'

Naomi nodded agreement.

'But you know Joachim—' Anna cut short her reply as a scuffling sounded at the door. There was really no need for her to finish, anyway. Naomi knew that, however Joachim might feel, if Anna asked to leave Nazareth tomorrow, he'd pack their belongings and go.

A stunted lamb gambolled through the door, and it limped slightly as it frolicked.

'It's the storm lamb,' explained Anna, as thought Naomi would immediately understand. 'It's come for some bread and milk.' And she mixed the bits of bread left over with some milk, and set it down for the lamb.

Naomi watched Anna lavish tender care on the animal as it snuggled against her before tackling its food.

'It's going to be another scorching day,' said Naomi.

'Aye,' said Anna.

'We'd better get these baskets to the men, then.'

'Aye,' replied Anna. But her attention was now on the lamb.

And Naomi was pleased she had found this distraction.

Nazareth was noisy in the dawning day, and the city was already about its business. Merchants with their wares, soldiers, travellers, the pious, the debauched and the debauching, pilgrims, peasants and priests jostled in the city streets.

Yosef and Miriam pushed their way along, she ceaselessly scanning about, searching for old familiar sights, impressing long last images of them on her mind, fastening them in her memory. It seemed a sinful thing to be leaving for ever the city she was born in, and she felt like a thief sneaking away – like a marauding fox fleeing the sheepfold at the breaking of the day.

She confided her sense of guilt to Yosef.

He guessed how she felt, but reckoned that it would not

be wise to treat these feelings too seriously just now. Instead he joked gently with her, and told her to take care to cover up her face lest some passerby recognize her, call out her name, and brand her a criminal in the sight of the throbbing city.

She joked back, but hid her face, hunching up small on the donkey's back.

And they laughed with a strained merriment, knowing they pretended, yet encouraging each other.

And when he thought she brooded again, now and then as they came to a corner or paced their way through a narrow, bustling street, he would draw close and whisper to her to beware of Herod's spies. 'They're planted everywhere, lurking at corners, hiding in the guise of pedlars and beggars, bargaining behind the jangling stalls of beads and bells and bracelets.' And she'd laugh, and hide her face again. 'Or they'd even pass by looking no more sinister than a man leading a donkey that carried his wife great with child.'

And she enjoyed that, mocking him, 'Are you one of the King's spies, good sir?'

They pressed on through the city, the crowds lessening as they drew nearer to the countryside beyond. And as they made their way on to quieter roads, she listened as Yosef talked of Herod and the scandals of his household, and of the rumours that Herod's dynasty would come to an untimely end.

'It needs no prophecy, Yosef,' commented Miriam, 'if all the tales we hear of him are true. By the sound of things, he seems to spend his time killing off his own family.'

Yosef agreed. 'He doesn't leave himself with much.'

'He's not got rid of Archelaus, though,' said Miriam. 'There's one man who'll do Herod's house no good.'

'Aye,' commented Yosef. 'But they say the prophecy has frightened Herod. And he's lashed out with death and destruction in Jerusalem.'

'And who's this new prophet in Israel?' Miriam enquired. 'Who's announced the prophecy?'

'They say someone in Jerusalem started it off, proclaiming that "God hath resolved that the rule of Herod shall be ended, and his descendants shall not inherit it."'

'That sounds like something Shebna would say,' inter- jected Miriam.

'It wasn't any of Shebna's crowd,' Yosef advised her. 'It was someone from the Pharisee Association in Jerusalem. And it appears some members of the Sanhedrin were involved.'

'They took a risk—'

'They did, indeed. And some of them are dead now, for their pains. Herod conducted a purge among the Pharisees.'

'The King wastes no time.'

'He does not,' agreed Yosef, 'though I don't suppose he had much option. Especially when the people putting out this prophecy were the same people reported by his spies to be plotting to kill him.'

'But that's not new to Herod,' Miriam observed. 'He lives his life staving off plots to kill him. If it's not someone from outside, it's his chamberlain. And if it's not him, it's one of the King's own family.'

By now they were clear of the city, and they halted where the road began its long dip down towards the Jordan valley. Out in the hills and vales beyond, the fields rolled up and down, their colours patchworked like the cover on a well- tossed bed. The trees and walls and hedgerows were like a thick thread of green and grey and sandy-brown seaming it all together, patch to patch. Morning scents lilted, lazy in the heating day. A passing breeze fetched life into a nearby tree, bringing its rustling leaves to life. Two birds cavorted in the cloudless air, wheeling their unmolested flight towards Nazareth that now nestled far off, glistening and serene, as though no disquiet or vexation could ever be harboured in the sun-made splendour of its snow-white purity.

Miriam choked a little at the sight, thrusting away the mocking contradictions that welled up from her too-long tutored mind. And she wept softly.

Yosef cherished her. In Bethlehem, he assured her, everything would be all right. The house was small, but, as his wife, she would be made welcome there. And there she could have her child in peace.

But Miriam still wondered. And all the long journey south, in the hammering heat of the day, and during the cold, clawing nights, a fear of the future tortured her. She was afraid for the child in her womb: her child would suffer. And she knew that, for all his banter and assurances, Yosef himself was frightened.

Isaac was back in Nazareth, home from Jerusalem. He'd done his duty as a citizen. He'd obeyed Caesar's decree, and been to his birthplace to register in Caesar's Census of his Empire. Not that Rome would ever know that he had done what was required of him . . . but you could be sure they'd have their own way of finding out if he hadn't. Anyway, it was done now, and he could get back to living his life again. Back home with Deborah his wife. And back in his baker's shop.

The shop was now full and he was in his element, holding forth to the women, his audience hanging on his every word. Even Deborah was quiet, standing beside him, preening herself and basking in the reflected glory of her so-far-travelled husband, quite distracted from her job of making sure Isaac kept a careful watch on the bread baking in the oven.

There was so much he had to tell of. Sights and sounds and situations. The things he'd said and done. The people he'd met. Gossip from Rome, heard from the lips of Romans on the very stamping ground of Augustus Caesar's civil servants in Jerusalem. And fresh news of Herod's goings-on.

The risks and deprivations of the journeys both there and back. And Jerusalem itself, where there was more than just the Temple and its priests and pomp and sacrifice to occupy the minds of the population.

He could not tell it all at once, nor did he want to. There was a proper time for everything, and Isaac would decide when that time was. And until then it was all packed in his mind, like the loaves in the oven, stored, leavened, and shaping for the ripe moment to be retailed.

For now he revealed enough to whet their appetites. He held the flask aloft for all to see. Carefully, protectingly, his hairy hard-worked hands moulded themselves round the seasoned leather, as though he held the source of life itself.

'Healing water from Bethzatha,' he told them, saying the words like a prayer. 'The pool is by the Temple slaughterhouse in Jerusalem,' he added. 'From far and near they come, bringing the sick and dying to be dipped in its healing waters.'

While he talked, the stench and foulness of that place came back to him, the dereliction of the maimed, sick and suppurating bodies, the sad desolation in the faces crowded tight in misery. But he could not talk of that.

He paused, overcome. This involuntary recollection made him want to retch again, as he had retched when first he'd seen the degradation of it.

The women waited, silent, oblivious of Isaac's struggle within himself. He recovered from his nausea, aware of their eyes riveted on the bottle he held in his sweating hand. He squeezed the bottle.

'At certain times, they say, the waters at Bethzatha move, as though an angel of the Lord has stirred them. And, when they move, whoever is first into the water is healed of his diseases.'

'Did you see that happen, Isaac?' ventured Leah, at last

breaking the long hush, her whisper betokening the measure of her amazement.

'No,' said Isaac, his disappointment clearly showing in his face.

The soft rustle among his listeners told him they too were disappointed. They felt let down. But he would not let them go away dissatisfied. The murmuring died away as they watched him undo the thong securing the neck of the leather bottle. It took time, but they waited.

And then the thong was loose, and Isaac, the stubby fingers of his great strong hands moving gently, tenderly opened the neck.

They craned forward as the bottle tilted. Deborah pushed a plate under it, and slowly, slowly Isaac eased the precious thing till one drop fell . . . then two . . . then three – till round now upon the plate, the pygmy pool glistened in a shaft of light.

Isaac stood back. Proud. Nobody spoke.

He tied the thong secure again, and waited, pleased. He had satisfied them, and none could speak for bewilderment.

Leah moved, lifted her hand towards the plate as though to touch it. But drew back again.

Old Martha watched, wondering. Her eyes roamed over them all to see how the rest reacted. She fixed her gaze on Sarah, willing her to look round.

Sarah did look, and Martha nodded.

Sarah inched towards the plate, and paused. She looked again at Martha, who lowered her head in mute command. Sarah bent over the plate, blocking the shaft of sunlight from its contents, and stared at it long. Then she dipped her finger, examining it before raising it to her tongue. And then, gingerly, apprehensively, she touched the moistened finger to her tongue.

The room held its breath.

'It's water,' said Sarah, her voice soft, incredulous. 'It's water,' she repeated. 'It's only water . . . Here, take it and taste it!' she screamed, reaching out to snatch the plate. 'It's no different from what you get at the well.'

But Deborah whipped the plate beyond her reach. Confusion fought with disappointment, consternation vied with disillusion for pre-eminence in the bedlam that replaced the awe and reverence. Arms flung out, hands gesturing, eyes flashing, heads wagging, feet stamping, mouths moving, bellowing, roaring . . . But nothing clear – no word that the ear could hear.

Till Rebecca gathered herself together and forced out a deafening 'Stop.'

And in the sudden silence Isaac murmuring, 'Of course it's water. Of course it's water.'

By now they had recovered, and did not notice Isaac, still clutching the bottle, slip behind the curtain after Rebecca informed them, 'Miriam's gone away.'

'Which Miriam?' questioned Sarah.

'Joachim's Miriam.'

'Yosef's Miriam, you mean,' Martha corrected her.

'Whoever's Miriam,' Rebecca spat back. 'She's gone away.'

'When did she go?' asked Leah.

'Before the sun was up this morning. She went off with Yosef. I believe he's sold that house he spent so much time building, and they've gone off—'

'Come on,' advised Sarah. 'Let's go outside. It's too hot in here.'

And they responded like sheep to her shepherding. Only Leah stayed behind, remembering what she'd come for.

'Isaac,' she called.

Isaac came out of hiding, looking dejected.

'Bread,' she said.

He smiled. 'Sarah didn't like the water.' And he turned to the oven.

'No,' said Leah, watching him pull the batches out. 'And I won't like that bread,' she said, when she smelled the burning.

Jacob hugged Yosef. His son was home again. The old man could hardly believe it. They'd have a feast, his excited mind decided spontaneously. He'd kill a calf, and call his friends and neighbours to rejoice with him that his son was home again.

He stood back, holding Yosef at arm's length, admiring him, delighting in him, touching his face to be sure this was all real. Yosef! After the long, long years, Yosef was home. And he had brought a wife . . .

Then suddenly Jacob was distraught, searching to apologize to Miriam for having been so churlish and unwelcoming to her. His son had brought home a wife, and a doting father had forgotten to notice her.

He spoke her name, 'Miriam,' and the way he said it gave it almost a new meaning.

She took to him instantly, and wondered to herself if her liking him so easily was just because he looked like the husband whom she so dearly loved. He seemed just an older edition of Yosef: the same red hair, though flecked with grey, and the ruddy, weather-worn face, leaner maybe with the years. But the same eyes: shrewd, searching eyes that probed deep, yet able to look with sympathy; there was compassion in them. And Yosef's warm, generous character. A kind man, Miriam felt, who would rather himself be hurt than cause another harm.

She watched his hands reach, gesturing towards her: manly mason's hands, marked and worn with the toil of his trade. And the stoop of age could not diminish those broad, strong shoulders. Though when he walked, Miriam noticed, he moved slowly, deliberately, yet angry with the pace, as though a lively, energetic brain endured frustration in his slow-responding body.

And she smiled to herself at the unobtrusive way Yosef took his father's elbow, helping him along as they turned and went into the house.

But old Jacob would accept no help in preparing the lavish spread he laid in welcome for them. Tomorrow, maybe, she might assist, he told her. Today they were honoured guests. For she was Yosef's wife. And Yosef was his son.

And they sat and ate and drank and talked, and listened and laughed and joked and remembered and explained and planned and hoped.

For a long time.

And it was dark.

The rains began as soon as Miriam and Yosef had reached Bethlehem.

The house was small, as Yosef had warned. It suited Jacob's needs – an old man, alone – but the arrival of Yosef and herself meant everything was cramped. By day this was bad enough; the nights were harder. In this weather there was no sleeping on the roof. And when the animals were brought in for shelter it was a struggle to find a decent amount of room to enjoy a comfortable sleep. But it was somewhere to live.

The days passed. And Nazareth seemed a thousand years ago.

Friends kept coming, and relatives. To meet Yosef after the years of his being away from home. And to see the bride.

They came early. They stayed late. And they talked long. Everybody was kind, in an awkward kind of way. They strained to make everything seem ordinary, and tried not to gawp too much at this young woman who told the story of an angel making her with child. They were sorry for Yosef: he'd been landed, they reckoned. But they were proud that he'd cloaked this young woman's condition with the respectability of marriage. At least no shame would attach to the innocent child.

Though, maybe, Miriam thought, her imagination read too much into their looks and words and actions.

Still, it was a relief when the dry spell between the rains began. The countryside looked new again. The animals were out in the fields, and the men at work, sowing and ploughing.

And Miriam knew that by the time the rains had come again she'd have her baby. She had not much longer now to wait.

The moth still frenzied in its dance around the lamp, swooping and swirling. But then it swooped too near. The flame spluttered, momentarily brighter, and the moth was gone; its singed dying made no sound to disturb the stillness Herod had imposed upon the room.

The messenger waited. When he saw Herod turn to look at him, he began to repeat his news. But Herod dismissed him.

'Tell them, whoever they are, the only King the Jews will have in place of me is a son of mine.'

The messenger, frustrated, saluted and made his way back across the room.

'And tell them, too,' called Herod after him, 'that the King's latest sons are all daughters.'

Herod sat back, impressed by his jocularity. His health must be improving. And, when he thought about it, he felt he was so much better. The pain had eased a little, and his breathing was lighter. That was encouraging. And he cheered himself a bit more with the thought that a few more days of such progress, and he'd be fitter than he'd been for months.

Thus he convinced himself and, in his pleasure, he mustered strength enough to push himself from the chair, and walk to the window, where he leaned on the sill and looked out across the city.

Out to his left, the Temple roof gleamed in the moonlit night. Admiring it, Herod felt proud of the patient years he'd spent planning it, and seeing it rebuilt. Out below him spread the city square he'd laid, its avenue of trees making dancing shadows.

He was proud of Jerusalem and, no matter where he looked tonight, he could pick out tokens that made him proud. Monuments that would still adorn and beautify the place when he was dead and gone.

Out in the distant dark, specks of light in houses beckoned like glow-worms, and here and there the bright flare of torches marked the routes where men walked in the streets.

But what noisy people Jerusalemites were, he thought, becoming aware of the sounds reaching up from the boisterous city. Yet he enjoyed that, and felt sorry that he could not be down there rollicking amid it all, as in days gone by. Those days when he'd put off his royal attire and dress just like one of them, and roam his city's streets, quaffing cheap wine with the working men, swapping their stories, or listening to tales they told of the King's latest cavortings.

Sturdy days they were, Herod reflected, warming in nostalgia.

But not for long.

The messenger he had dismissed a little while ago was now replaced by Samuel, the captain who controlled Herod's network of spies, not only in Jerusalem but in all the major cities of the Kingdom.

The man took his job seriously, so Herod reckoned he had not come simply to bid him good evening. The King acknowledged the salute but detected a touch of insubordination in it, and decided the captain considered the messenger was dismissed too lightly. If this man could get away with it, he'd have the nerve to reprimand the King.

'You wish to speak, captain?'

'My Lord, I sent a messenger—'

Herod smiled. He had judged right. And, in his own way, this officer was going to inflict a reprimand.

'I sent a messenger a little while ago, but he returned to tell me you had dismissed him.'

'I did. I have grown tired of new kings—' Herod waved an arm, hoping the captain would be as easily dismissed as his messenger.

'My King, I would not send you a messenger on any light matter.'

The reprimand, indeed, thought Herod. The man had gone as far as he dare.

'You would not, of course,' he said. 'But when you appear yourself, it must be a matter of enormous urgency.'

'With great respect, it is, my lord.'

'And you are now going to tell me about it.'

The captain tensed to speak. 'Since early afternoon, my lord—'

But Herod could not resist the temptation to interrupt him, by way of retaliation for the officer's well-disguised rebuke. A reminder, too, as to who was supreme here, and even officers who thought so highly of themselves spoke only so long as the King gave them leave.

'Say no more. Support me to my couch.'

Showing no reaction, the captain helped Herod from the window, eased him on to his couch, and, under the King's instructions, placed cushions to support him.

'*Now* I will give you leave to speak.' Herod thought he

saw the faintest flicker of a smile in the soldier's eyes. And he admired him: a strong man. King and subject were now quits. Herod leaned back to listen.

'Early this afternoon, my lord, there was talk in the city of a group of men come seeking a newborn King of the Jews.'

'Jerusalem is full of chatter, as you know well. You also know that we've just got over that Pharisees nonsense. And I think we've managed to give Jochebed her comeuppance.'

'I know, my King. But when my messengers brought me word of these men's assiduous enquiries, I examined the matter myself. I met the visitors: twelve of them in a caravan of camels and horse. With costly gifts they say are presents for this new King.'

'You brought me the gifts, captain?' joked Herod. But he was leaning forward, listening intently.

'I learned from them, sir, that they had travelled from Sippar near the city of Babylon. They claimed to be descendants of the Jews taken captive to Babylon by King Nebuchadnezzar, and they are members of a school of astrology in Sippar. Somehow, they have tied their recent observations of the stars to an ancient Jewish prophecy and concluded that in Judah a new King of the Jews is already born, or is about to be born.'

'And they have spread this wild gossip,' reflected Herod, when the captain had finished, 'so now Jerusalem is full of speculation. Can you put your hand on these men, now?'

The captain could. Already he had a troop of his men pitch camp nearby to watch their movements in the night. He could bring them in at any time.

'When the day breaks will be soon enough,' advised the King. 'And summon the chief priests and scribes of the people to attend me here at that same time.'

'The chief priests will not be pleased,' ventured the captain. 'They'll be attending the morning sacrifice in the Temple.'

'The chief priests will make it their business to be pleased,' retorted the King. 'I appointed them, and they know what sacrifice there'll be if they rile me. So tell them to be here. And I know I can depend on you to be discreet in your handling of this matter.'

'None, sir, shall know of this save those whom the King commands shall attend.'

'See to it, then, captain.'

The man saluted, and was gone.

Herod sat contemplating this new threat to his power. He felt all of his sixty-seven years. After forty years of intrigue and managing to keep one step ahead of plot and counterplot, he was tired. The blood and corpses that littered the dark corners of his memory lit up in the wan light of recollection.

Was it all to end in nothing? Were the Pharisees going to be proved right, after all? Was his house and lineage to be now cut off?

Early morning, and Herod was up.

The captain had been thorough, and had fetched the Chaldees from their camping ground while it was yet dark. The priests and scribes were now being assembled in the audience chamber.

Herod had already laid his plans. He would meet the priests and scribes first, to search out what prophecy these Chaldees were talking about. Then he would interview the travellers themselves.

The captain eventually reported everyone assembled. When he was ready, Herod signalled the bearers to carry him in his chair to the audience chamber. He did not intend spending much time with the priests. He had little respect for them, as they were part of the Sanhedrin which he despised.

His question was plainly and quickly put. 'Where is Messiah to be born?'

The captain noticed the use of words. The 'King' these

travelling astrologers were seeking had become 'Messiah' in Herod's thinking.

The scribes knew the answer and their spokesman explained that the prophecy had been made some seven hundred years ago by the prophet Micah.

'*Where* is he to be born?' demanded Herod. He didn't want a long lecture.

'In Bethlehem of Judaea,' said the leader of the scribes. And then he spoke the text as though rehearsed twice each day all the days of his life. 'In Bethlehem of Judaea,' he repeated. 'For thus it is written by the prophet, "And thou, Bethlehem, in the land of Judah, art not least among the princes of Judah. Out of thee shall come a governor that shall rule my people Israel."'

Herod sat silent. Vaguely, seeming far away, he gestured that the audience was at an end.

The captain then dismissed the priests and scribes, who showed their surprise that the meeting had been so soon ended. But the captain stared blankly at them, with nothing more to say, and they left.

He waited for further instructions from the King, but Herod did not stir. The King was patently troubled – thinking deep, deep thoughts. And so he sat for what seemed time interminable. Until, at last, he announced that he would see the Chaldees.

As they approached, Herod watched them and measured them: especially the three who led them in. An old man with white hair and a sweeping beard. Beside him walked a younger, swarthy man in the prime of life. And next to him a beardless, ruddy youth. Behind them came the rest and altogether, Herod counted, there were twelve. He signalled them to speak.

The old man made a deep bow. 'Majesty,' he began, 'we have come seeking the newborn King of the Jews. We saw his star at its rising, and are come to pay him homage.'

Herod asked when they had seen this star.

The swarthy man set off explaining about the conjunction of the planets they had observed a year earlier – and it had happened again: Saturn and Jupiter in the constellation of Pisces.

Herod let him ramble on, though astrology was not his great interest, nor did he understand it. He left all that to his priests and necromancers.

But, as the Chaldees talked, even Herod understood that they were talking of the Jews' Messiah. And a multitude of questions poured from him, searching, probing. And all they said gave answer to the thoughts that had so possessed him since the priests had left earlier.

He quoted to them the words the priests and scribes had already told him, amazed as he spoke them that he knew them almost by heart. 'In Bethlehem of Judaea. For it is written, "Thou Bethlehem, in the land of Judah, art not least amongst the princes of Judah. Out of thee shall come a governor that shall rule my people."'

The Chaldees bowed in gratitude. The King was kind and gracious in his majesty.

'Go then to Bethlehem,' said Herod, 'and search for your child-king.'

As they began withdrawing, Herod gave instructions that they should be well entertained before they set out on their journey. And then, as something of an afterthought, Herod commanded them, 'Search diligently for the child. And, when you find him, bring the news back to me, and I will myself go and pay him homage.'

Herod still wondered, once the men had gone, at the words he'd spoken. Yet, having said them, they did not, on reflection, appear strange to him.

Tyrant and despot he might be but what he was, he was for Israel's good. If he were at peace with Rome, it was not because he loved Rome, but because that friendship preserved his nation's life. If the truth were known, he hated all things Roman. His ambition was to see his Jewish nation independent. Its ultimate achievement though, would mean driving out the Roman tyrant. He himself, he knew only too well, was not equipped to undertake the task. But this promised Messiah, Israel's deliverer, might do just that . . .

Herod hoped so. Sick, worn and old, knowing his reign could not last much longer . . . Could it be that God allowed him to preserve the nation for such a day? He could have no better successor than the Messiah.

And he, Herod, would be the first to pay him homage.

The night hung sullen in the sky. Stars picked pinpoints in the dark, dancing brazenly like hussies. It was cold, and father and son felt it. They paced up and down, trying not to make a noise for fear they'd drown the sound their ears waited for, straining to hear.

Jacob saw the soft light filtering beneath the door, and thought of the warmth and snugness on the other side, and felt a little sorry for himself at having to endure the discomfort of the cold outside.

But childbirth, he assured himself, was women's work. It was no place for a man, so it was right that he and Yosef should be left outside.

And suddenly he could not resist a snigger to himself. Here he was, an old man, his family reared and having left him, who had long ago put such tense, pacing waiting in the cold nights far behind him, now ousted from his own house and going through it all again. And for a child his son would claim he'd never even fathered.

Yosef heard the titter, and looked questionly at the old man. But Jacob, shaking his head, offered no explanation.

Lightning flashes in the hills beyond beckoned for their attention, and they stood and watched the storm frolic in the sky, streaming across the hills, joining heaven and earth in sudden, blazing brightness: now like noonday, now plunging dark, fitful and fretful in rumbling thunder, clapping, cantankerous.

Yosef wondered how long it would be before the storm turned their way and felt sorry for his father.

'It shouldn't be too much longer now,' he said.

'Let's hope not,' commented Jacob easily. 'But when did you see a storm so beautiful as that?'

And they pulled their cloaks even tighter, and continued their pacing back and forth outside the door. Waiting. Listening.

The tinkling of water sparingly poured. The tread of hurrying feet. A muffled whisper. Instruction, comfort, advice.

It was all she was aware of. And the awful pain.

It was painful to bring a child to birth. Her body heaved and sank and heaved again. The dread and terror of the past months pummelled her mind.

A faint light flickered near her face. A hand soothed her brow. The crucifying pain drained from her body. And she heard the whimper of a newborn child.

'A boy,' they told her.

'A boy,' they repeated, as though she had not heard them.

Her whole being thrilled, and she felt the strength surging back into her spent frame.

She hardly dared to look.

Her child.

She nestled the frailty to her bosom. And peeped nervously at the little face.

CHAPTER NINE

Jacob fretted backwards and forwards, stamping his feet every few paces, slapping his hands against his shoulders to warm himself against the cold night that threatened constantly to unleash upon them the storm that rampaged in the fields beyond.

Yosef stood, enveloped in his cloak, wishing his father could manage without so much noise. Occasionally he shushed the old man to be quiet. And Jacob responded. But as quickly forgot, as he felt himself getting colder. And he stamped his feet and swung his arms harder to bring back the warmth.

'Sssh,' signalled Yosef.

And the old man was quieter.

They listened. And faintly heard the cry.

'It's over,' said Jacob. And they sat down.

It seemed an endless time before the midwife, Ruth, came to tell them. And when she eventually came, she held the door ajar and waited to be sure that everything inside was right.

And all the while Jacob smelt the warm air filter through, enduring his deprivation through Ruth's sense of propriety, his torture aggravated by his urgency to see his newborn grandchild.

'Is it a boy?' he called through the chink of comfort.

But Ruth made no reply. She was busy making doubly sure that all was right and ready for the men to enter, and would make no move till Dinah gave the signal.

He turned to complain to Yosef, but stopped as the door swung open, and Ruth, removing her apron, drying her hands on it, stood back to let them in.

Jacob was in quickly, and made straight for the fire, warming himself while he cast respectful glances at Miriam lying on the mat nearby, glad she was well, and thanking God that she was safely delivered of her child.

'She's brought forth a son,' Ruth said as Yosef passed.

He heard it as though they were familiar words. The room felt warm and clean. And Yosef was grateful to the women for their thoroughness. The atmosphere in the little house witnessed to their kindness to his wife. The merry fire whose heat was drying the last damp patches on the well-washed floor. The birth cloths washed and waiting for tomorrow's sun. The last of the salt that washed the baby, put carefully by, ready to be stored again when the new day rose.

In the well-dressed bed, placed comfortably near the fire, lay Miriam, her bright eyes beaming, rejoicing, snuggling her child.

Yosef made no sound as he walked, and hardly knew the steps by which he came. He knelt by the mat spread out on the floor, and held the hand stretched out to greet him.

'Miriam,' he said. And then eased back the cloth to see the newborn child. And he blessed the lad.

He was still bent over the child when there was a knock at the door.

Ruth went to answer it, muttering loudly as she went, 'It's started. Neighbours, already! You'd think they'd have more sense at this hour of the night. Does nobody sleep in this town?'

But they were not neighbours, as she realized when she pulled open the door. Camels, and men with bearded faces. Total strangers. How many were there . . .? had they no common sense, calling at this hour?

'There's a child just been born,' she told them, as sweetly as her bad humour would allow, just in case they'd any ideas about expecting hospitality.

But they didn't understand a word she was saying. They just smiled in reply: the three faces she could barely make out in the glimmer of light through the doorway. They were obviously expecting to come in – as indeed were the rest of the group standing behind them, docilely waiting.

The three men she managed to see bowed gracefully, and stepped into the house. Ruth made no effort to stop them. Nor would she. She mightn't agree with it at the moment, but custom was custom. And the old habit of hospitality meant she must not refuse them – whoever they were.

Miriam watched as the men came in. Quietly they came, and deferentially.

Yosef was already standing to greet them. But they were hushed and reverent as they spoke, so that Miriam could not make out clearly what they said. Even Yosef, she noticed, was at a loss, gesturing every now and then, as they did themselves, creasing his brow as though finding it hard to understand them.

He listened as they explained again: about Israel's star that they had seen, and Israel's new King, and their journey from Babylon to be present at his birth.

And he tried to be patient with them. They were welcome, of course, in his house. But they were in the wrong place. Kings, as they must know themselves, were born in palaces.

It was no comfort to him when they assured him they had been to Herod's palace, and had been told by him to seek their King in Bethlehem.

For all they talked softly, and like wise and serious men, their conversation frightened Yosef. For what these men sought and thought they'd found, Herod himself could just as easily find . . .

When there seemed no more to say, the men opened their bags and brought out their gifts, placing them near the bed roll where Miriam and her infant lay.

Miriam watched them. Three came, three went, three came, three went, till she wondered how many there could be. And she counted them. There were twelve. Each man bowed – subserviently, Miriam thought. And then they all were gone, as quietly as they had come.

'Gifts for a King, Miriam,' exclaimed Yosef as he untied the leather bundles, calling out excitedly, trying to ease the tension the visitors' coming and going had created. 'There's gold . . .', pushing the contents of the parcels '. . . and frankincense . . .' nearer to Miriam. 'I tell you, wife, there's myrrh . . . They're gifts fit—'

'For a King,' interrupted Dinah. 'We know, Yosef. But your wife has had enough for today.' She stooped down, moving Yosef aside, tidying the thongs and leathers from off the bed. 'Clear everything neatly away, Yosef. Let Miriam sleep.'

As she spoke, her firm, experienced hands took the newborn babe, wrapped the swaddling clothes about him, and laid him in the manger.

'He'll be safe there, dear,' she assured Miriam, 'and warm. Now you try to get some sleep.' And turning, with the same tone of authority, to Yosef, 'If you'd any sense, you'd take a tip from your father, and get off to bed.'

Yosef took her advice.

Dinah herself unrolled a mat, and settled down in the far corner beside Ruth who, judging from her contented snores, was already fast asleep.

Miriam dozed, drowsy, dreamy. Visions and hopes for the future shaped in her mind: settled in Bethlehem, in its peace and farming plenty. Yosef working amongst his own people. Their family growing up in their own little home, near the great city of the faith of their fathers.

'He shall be great . . . and shall be called son of the Highest . . . and the Lord shall give him the throne—' The words of her dream long months ago stole into her reveries.

She looked towards her child in the straw-cage cradle on the wall, and it crossed her mind that this was a strange beginning to greatness.

But there was no chance to follow her surmisings. Suddenly bedlam filled the house. The animals, brought in for the night, scurried for the quieter corners. And the family, not long gone to bed after the ordeal of the birth and entertaining a group of foreigners, was up again, entertaining yet more strangers who had arrived to greet her newborn son.

Shepherds they were. And Miriam didn't take to them. The smell of their flocks was heavy in their sheepskin wraps. They talked like drunken men, and what they were saying frightened her. Shepherds were dangerous men; she knew all about them. 'Let no man make his son a shepherd for their craft is the craft of robbers,' was the old saying. And it was right. They were subverters. And they spread their subversion. She had heard of them and their wanderings to and fro from the pasturings, carrying messages between the rebel groups, and spreading tidings that passed in the nights from cave to cave along the bloody road from Jerusalem to Jericho, of the nationalists' latest forays against the government.

These men were too quick to brand her son as a future leader, a deliverer, a Messiah . . . and she was afraid.

Their Messiahs came and went, cheapjacks who panned the dregs for greatness, and made nationalism a cover for their lust. Her son was none of this.

The rest of the house laughed, and chided her for taking things too seriously. The shepherds were drunk, they reckoned. They were teasing her. The things they said were just the things men say when boys are born.

She searched out Yosef's face in the half-dark. His laugh was weak, and his smile hardly masked his worry. Miriam knew that she was right to be afraid.

The shepherds took long in their going. She could tell the direction of their journey as their fading clamour reached back along the night air.

But, even with them gone, the night gave her no peace. For in the spells of quietness, when no neighbours came, her thoughts filled and filled again with the jabberings and prophecies of the shepherds. She wondered what new sparks they'd fan in the back alleys of Jerusalem, and what plots they'd hatch in the hills with those who were urgent for insurrection.

Only the dawning day was quiet. Miriam watched the new light scatter the darkness, wide awake, tired, and frightened.

Antipater lounged on the patio, enjoying the sunshine and the sight of the sea, glistening in the distance.

He was in Cilicia. Not by choice, but because Marcellus had decided it would be good for him to have a break from the whirl and suffocation of Rome.

After three days in the sumptuously appointed villa, Antipater was happy to agree with him. There was an air of peace and ease about the place. Even the servants went about their business quietly.

He was content just to lie back, shaded by the blossoming trees, and enjoy the scents wafting on the gentlest breeze. Maybe he couldn't take this for ever, he told himself, but for the time being, at any rate, this was contentment. In this atmosphere, Jerusalem was forgotten: the intrigues and palace plots – all worlds away. His mother Doris, Salome, Pheroras – all in another life.

'A letter for you,' called Marcellus, coming through the gap in the shrubbery. 'And, judging from the seal, it's from your father.'

Antipater felt a twinge of disappointment. A letter from his father meant the King was not yet dead. What was Pheroras thinking about?

Marcellus dropped the letter on his chest. Antipater took hold of it as he sat up, and broke the seal. It was his father's seal, all right. And, as he unrolled the letter, he saw his father's signature: the tired scrawl of a sick man.

Marcellus made to leave as Antipater began to read. Without looking up, Antipater signalled him to stay.

'I'll tell you what it says when I've finished reading,' he said.

Marcellus settled himself on a couch shaded by a palm tree.

'I can't believe it,' Antipater muttered to himself. 'I've never known the man be so affectionate—' as he went on reading, 'It must be his sickness . . . The man must be dying.'

Then suddenly he laughed out loud, waving the letter in the air. 'Would you believe it? My mother is still causing trouble. He throws her out of the palace, and she's still at it . . . He'll kill her one of these days.'

Marcellus laughed in response, as Antipater went back to his reading.

'Pheroras is dead,' he called over after a while. 'My father's brother.'

'I'm sorry,' sympathized Marcellus.

Not half so sorry as I am, thought Antipater. The plan that so much rested on had come to nothing. He finished reading.

'He wants me to come home again,' he told Marcellus. 'He seems to have a presentiment that some harm may befall him, the longer I'm away.'

'Then you must go home.' Marcellus sat up on his couch, and turned to face Antipater. 'I'll be sorry to see you go. I think, though, if your father needs you—'

'There's too much affection in this letter, Marcellus. I just wonder if he's up to something.'

'But what? And what can he do? Augustus has already approved the succession.'

'I don't trust the man,' confided Antipater.

'Does he trust you?' wondered Marcellus.

A serving girl appeared quietly. The two men sat silent while she set down a basket of fruit, poured them two cups of wine, presenting one to Antipater first, the other to Marcellus.

Once she was gone Marcellus stood up. He took a deep sip before he spoke.

'I think you would be wise to go home, for all kinds of reasons. And certainly, if your father is dying, then you ought to be with him.'

Antipater nodded, but did not speak. His father dying didn't upset him. What suspicions his father might have, what mischief this unusual affection might be hiding was what really worried him.

'Anyone who likes', went on Marcellus, 'can fill your father's mind with all kinds of suspicions about you. And, because you're absent, there's nothing you can do about that.'

He finished his wine in one long draught, and filled his cup again, offering to top up Antipater's too.

'It's the same in any royal court, Antipater. Wherever there's power, position, or favours to be gained, greedy men will intrigue and plot, and toadies will crawl and stab men in the back. Your father's court is no different.'

Antipater agreed. He knew only too well what went on at court.

'So long as you're away from home,' Marcellus was saying, 'every enemy you have can take advantage of you.'

'True, true.' Antipater nodded.

'Your brother Archelaus,' mused Marcellus.

'My half-brother.'

'Brother, half-brother,' dismissed Marcellus. 'I remember Archelaus when we were all growing up in Rome. He spent most of his time envying you. Does he still resent you?'

'Maybe he does, maybe he doesn't,' Antipater replied. 'It's years since we've seen each other. D'you know, the longest time I ever spent with Archelaus was when we were boys here in Rome, in Lucinius's house. He spends his life in Samaria, pretending he's a King – and living like one. He's never at the court in Jerusalem. And I seriuosly doubt if he's there now.'

'Serious doubt is not certainty, Antipater,' Marcellus advised him. 'He's your father's son. And son enough to be able to cajole and coax a dying father enough to secure the Kingdom for himself.'

Antipater roared with laughter. 'Archelaus cajole my father?' he exclaimed, struggling to get up from the couch. 'They hate each other – as enemies hate. My father will not have him within a whisper's distance of him.' He was up from the couch, clapping a hand on his hip, trying not to spill wine from the cup in the other. 'If he could manage it, my father wouldn't give Archelaus the light of day. He certainly wouldn't give him the Kingdom.'

'So it's not Archelaus,' Marcellus interrupted. 'But your father's not a fool. If he wants you home, then there must be good reasons. And if you've enemies plotting against you, the only way to deal with them is to be there, and face them.'

He paused, expecting Antipater to respond, but the other man made no move.

The Chaldees could not make up their minds whether to be disappointed or not. They were not sure if what they had seen was what they had expected. The Deliverer of Israel born in so lowly circumstances? The Messianic Age had begun in a peasant's house?

But they allowed the old man, who had led them all the road to Bethlehem, to console them when he told them that these were the ways of the God of Israel. In Israel's history it was ever thus.

'Moses', the old man reminded them, 'was born a slave, and nurtured in a wicker basket by the water's edge. And the Patriarch Joseph kept sheep. Saul who was chosen of God to set the Kingdom up, ruled under a tree. In its time, Israel has known prophets who have been no more than goatherds and dressers of fig trees. And great David himself was taken to be King from tending his father's flocks.'

When they looked about Jerusalem, they were a little more confident. Here was a city to be proud of. And they felt that, for all his lowly start, when he had come of age, their 'Deliverer' would be monarch in a city of whose splendour he need not be ashamed.

Herod, they decided, had been a good forerunner to Israel's Messiah. And they admired his handiwork. The palace he had built, rising in magnificence and solid majesty along the south-west wall. The airy avenue that swept its triumphant, tree-lined way to the vast square, through noble houses, to the Hippodrome.

They travelled through the city awed, lost in admiration. Everything they saw matched, and often surpassed the best they knew in Babylon. But outstripping all for grandeur, majesty and beauty was the Temple that spanned time, and brought them close to their own forebears. Here, they felt, they stood in history. They could touch the very stones their distant forefathers had laid, with hands brutalized by slavery, when they returned from their captivity in Babylon. And what those home-come exiles had laboured to produce, Herod had enhanced.

The Chaldees were proud of Herod.

And yet, for all their pride and gratitude, they had an uneasy feeling about coming back to tell the King how and where they had found Messiah.

It was the atmosphere in the city itself, perhaps. They felt it in the Valley of the Cheesemakers, with its crowded, bustling streets, as they moved among the wool dealers and the clothes bazaars. It was difficult to pinpoint, to put into words. It felt as though the citizens were in bonds, afraid to speak their minds except behind their hands.

For all the multitude of priests that thronged the place, the city seemed to be overwhelmed by evil.

Herod was everywhere. His buildings towered over everything: his house, the castles he had built reared themselves higher than King David's wall. His eagle, a standing insult to devout Jewry, glittered in the Temple . . .

They talked about it round their camp fire in the night. And wondered if their uneasiness, now, was what they'd had an inkling of when they had first been brought to Herod's palace. The secrecy had concerned them then: it worried them now. And, on reflection, they decided, where another monarch might have judged a newborn King a threat, Herod had seemed too helpful and too keen.

They slept the night with their fears. But when one of them wakened in the morning, and told them of his warning in a dream, they knew what course of action they would take.

They would not go back to Herod.

They left Jerusalem, and set off towards Babylon, on a different route from that by which they had come.

Yosef was proud, but did his best not to show it. He was a modest man, and Miriam noticed how he blushed at the ribaldry of the men who congratulated him on the birth of a son.

The weather was warmer. And the break in the rains brightened things a bit. The tension in the house eased. They were obviously glad the birth was over, and seemed surprised the child was normal. The comings and goings of the neighbours had more or less stopped, and the household routine was beginning to get back on an even keel. Even the overcrowding didn't seem so bad any more. The new baby had everybody's attention.

The child's circumcision when he was eight days old was their first real occasion for a celebration. For all its solemnity, the rite was also something of a joyous event. Miriam and Yosef saw it as a chance to thank everybody for their kindness and generosity at the birth.

Jacob was pleased when the friends and neighbours gathered. He could not remember when he last played host to such a crowd. Though, when he saw them milling round, he reckoned everyone in Bethlehem must have come, but he was not surprised. After all, he told himself, the lad was Yosef's firstborn. And he was proud of Yosef.

And the gathered friends were proud of Yosef. They took pleasure in Yosef's having brought his wife to his own native town for the child to be born there. It was good, they reckoned, murmuring their approval to each other, that a descendant of David the Ephratite should be so proud of his descent that he would honour his son with being born in David's city.

The blur of conversation suddenly died. Only the scrape

on the hard floor broke the quiet as a chair was put in position. It was the Chair of Elijah, forerunner of the Messiah, patron of the rite of circumcision, and unseen participant in the ceremony for which they were gathered.

Solemnity and excitement tingled the atmosphere. All eyes watched. The child was brought in and laid on Elijah's chair. They waited till Yosef, the Mohel and the Sandak took their places.

There was no sound till Yosef spoke.

'Blessed be God,' he began, 'who hath sanctified us by this commandment, and commanded us to enter our sons into the Covenant of Abraham.'

His prayer marked the beginning of the ceremony.

The Sandak moved and took the boy, holding him in his lap, while the Mohel stooped and quickly, cleanly made the cut.

And the ceremony was ended.

But there was no stir in the assembly, nor any sign of moving till Yosef spoke again.

'His name shall be called Jesus,' he announced.

It was a good name, they all noisily agreed. An honourable name, they said, turning now to eat and drink and call to mind the great men of Israel, the saviours of the nation who had borne the name.

Miriam was tired when it was all over, and the last guests were gone, and Ruth and Dinah had tidied the house again, and advised her to take some rest.

'And get some strength,' they told her. 'In a few weeks' time you'll be presenting your infant in the Temple in Jerusalem.'

Miriam was looking forward to that. Three times, already, she had been through the city, but had not really seen it. There'd been no time, nor, indeed, any inclination to stay and look around.

But this time, Yosef promised her, this time, they'd be in no hurry.

She fell asleep still listening as Yosef conjured pictures for her of the Temple courts, and the vine tracery that adorned its gates, the pool of Bethzatha, and the olive groves stretched out on Olivet . . .

Herod lost interest in everything. His sickness worsened until what was once a recurring fever now became a constant fire whose burning never ceased, aggravating the intolerable itching all over his body. His intestines were a mass of pain, as though worms incessantly burrowed. The swelling round his belly and his feet was grotesque. And the King stank. From the putrefaction of his genitals and the loathsome stench of his breath.

He hovered between the wish to die and the obstinate will to live just long enough to see his son Antipater punished.

Officials came and went on royal business, but were peremptorily dismissed. They went away again, relieved to be out of the room whose air no incense could ever sweeten.

Only the doctors were concerned. But felt useless. They knew his disease. They had seen it often enough, and had known it could afflict whole communities, and wipe out half their children. Recognizing it, however, brought them no nearer to a cure.

They compounded medicines, and obediently Herod swallowed all their nauseating concoctions. And, with the docility of a lamb, suffered their manhandling when they larded ointment all over him in their attempts to soothe his aching, misshapen body.

Some hazarded the view that the King's disease might have been contracted from bad water in which he had bathed.

Would good water cure him, then? It was worth a try.

Their patient was willing to try anything. So far as he was concerned, if it did not cure him, the treatment might hasten the death that was infinitely preferable to the unremitting and degrading torture he was enduring.

Would the King graciously agree to going to Calirrhoe where the asphaltic waters were said to have curative properties?

The King would agree to anything. Graciously or otherwise. And he winced a smile at his little joke.

Little time was wasted. The King, his physicians and a host of servants moved across Jordan to Calirrhoe on the east side of the Dead Sea.

Herod, buoyed with the new hope of a recovery, allowed himself to be bathed and bathed again in the curative waters. And, when his physicians directed it, almost gluttonously swallowed large doses of the water. And found it sweet to drink.

But it had no effect. Though they stayed weeks at Calirrhoe, the King showed not the slightest sign of improvement.

At least the resort was more comfortable to bear than the confines of the city, and the suffocating stench of Herod's bedchamber. Nobody was in a hurry to advise the King to return, so they stayed.

The physicians nursed their sense of having failed again, worrying to find a way to destroy the mites that they guessed had got in through the King's skin, and were the cause of his loathsome affliction.

If they could find something that could penetrate the pores as easily as the mites had done – perhaps that would bring about a cure.

They were serious when they considered that the cure might be found in bathing the King in warm oil. They knew the danger, of course. But they knew, too, that left as he was the King would die anyway.

Whether it was hope or resignation that shaped Herod's decision, they could not be sure. But when they proposed the idea to him, he accepted readily.

A vat, big enough to take Herod's bloated body comfortably, was filled with oil.

The servants who lit the fires beneath it and watched it heat, reckoned the doctors mad. But none dared comment.

When the physicians considered the oil was ready, they gave directions, and supervised as the King was lowered into it.

Herod screamed, cursing and roaring with the pain, blinded, blistering with the heat.

They pulled him out, scalding themselves, and laid him on the ground, furiously rubbing the blotched, red body with rags and robes and anything that would remove the sizzling oil. All the while the King screamed in agony.

Then stopped. And lay, lifeless, still as death.

The servants erupted, their earlier frustration bursting bounds, rampaging against the doctors for their stupidity, accusing them of using their outrageous cure as a means to kill the King.

The physicians were helpless. They had no defence. They could offer nothing that would pacify their accusers, or mollify their threats of vengeance.

But Herod stirred.

And as suddenly the atmosphere changed. Quietly the servants dressed the King. Gently. Like a newborn child.

Miriam stood, silent. Yosef was nearby. All round them, in the courtyard of the Temple, pilgrims, citizens and strangers massed. But Miriam felt alone, nursing her infant son, watching, intent. Towards the Pinnacle of the Temple, the great rock that reared sheer from the Valley of the Kedron, supporting the south-east corner of the court.

High up upon the rock stood the lonely priest, searching the east, across the Kedron darkness, to spy the day's first gleaming sheening the crown of Olivet.

'The sun is shining,' called the priest. And waited till the cry came back from his companions far below him in the court.

'Is the sky lit up to Hebron?'

The priest looked out again, lingering on the sight of Olivet, freckled with pilgrim tents, moving sleepily to life with the early-riser up to greet the dawn. Then he looked to the far-off reaches of the land, spread north and west, his arms flung wide as though he would embrace it all.

'It is lit up,' he cried. 'And lit as far as Hebron.' Taking a last look, he descended from the rock to join his brother priests and return with them to wait in Temple silence till the day's first sacrifice and the silver trumpet sounded throughout Jerusalem to Olivet itself.

The Dawn Ceremony was over.

The priests gone, the watchers moved. Women, their children in their arms, who had come to the Temple for their Purification after childbirth, made their way, chattering, to the Court of the Women.

Miriam and Yosef went with them. But once through the outer gate, Yosef left her, to wait for her under the porticoes that ran along the east wall.

It was an awesome place. Miriam was overwhelmed with it all, hardly seeing what she looked at, aware only of the splendour rising in steps to the crowning glory of the Sanctuary, its towering, gilded walls dazzling back the brightness of the morning sun.

No sound now, but the mumble as women offered thanksgiving for their safe delivery, and prayed for their children, hoping their prayers would rise with the morning's incense, and be heard by God.

A trumpet sounding gave warning that the sacrifice of the morning had been offered, and signalled the time for morning prayer.

And then the great Nicanor Gate was opened. Looking beyond the crescent steps supporting it, Miriam could see the Great Altar, and the golden doors of the Holy Place, topped by its golden vines from which hung grapes in clusters taller than a man.

A Levite accepted the two doves she presented as her Purification offering, and took it to the Court of the Priests where it was burned on the altar of the morning sacrifice.

A priest returned, and with the blood of her sacrifice, he sprinkled Miriam, pronouncing her ritually clean. Her forty days were ended. Now she could return to worshipping in the congregation.

Her first task now was, with her husband, to redeem her son.

The Law of Moses required that a firstborn son be presented to God, and consecrated to God's service, like Samuel in the ancient days. The Law, however, allowed that parents, if they wished, might be absolved from this obligation, and 'redeem' their sons, by paying five sanctuary shekels instead.

Yosef joined Miriam by the steps, and took the infant in his arms. A priest came, and stood before them.

'My wife, who is an Israelite,' began Yosef, 'has borne as her firstborn, a male child which now I give to you, as God's representative.'

'Which would you rather do?' enquired the priest. 'Give up your firstborn, who is the first son of his mother, to Jehovah, or redeem him for five shekels, after the shekel of the Sanctuary?'

'This is my firstborn,' replied Yosef. 'Here, take unto thee the five shekels due for his redemption.'

He stretched out his hand, still speaking as he offered the redemption price. 'Blessed art thou, O Lord our God, King of the universe, who hast sanctified us with thy commandments, and commanded us to perform the redemption of a son. Blessed art thou, O Lord our God, King of the universe, who hast maintained us, and preserved us to enjoy this season.'

The priest took the money in his right hand, and passed it round the infant's head. Then laid his left hand on his brow.

'This money is instead of this child. May this child be brought to life, to the Law, and to the fear of heaven. And as he has been brought to be ransomed, so may he enter into the Law, and good deeds.'

The ceremony was near its end.

Yosef and Miriam bowed their heads as the priest laid both his hands upon their infant's head, and pronounced his benediction.

'God make thee as Ephraim and Manesseh. The Lord bless thee and preserve thee. The Lord lift up his countenance upon thee, and give thee peace. Length of days and peace be gathered unto thee. And God keep thee from all evil, and save thy soul.'

Their son's redemption was complete.

Miriam and Yosef turned to leave, making their way through those who still waited to redeem their firstborn sons.

An old man stopped them as they walked.

'The lad's name?' he enquired of Yosef, the voice, soft with age, barely audible.

'Jesus,' replied Yosef, taking in the well-trimmed beard, and the robes round the body that the years had shrunk, making the robes too loose, too large for the frame that carried them.

'Jesus, you say,' whispered the old man. 'Joshua – it means salvation,' as his aged arms stretched out.

And Yosef, unthinking, let him take the child.

As he cuddled the infant, the old man spoke. 'Now let thy servant, Lord, depart in peace, according to thy word. For mine eyes have seen thy salvation—'

And Miriam heard the modulated, well-tongued Hebrew, '*joshuatika ra'u 'enai*' and wondered at the old man's punning on her son's name.

She wanted to ask him what he meant. But, as though he already knew her intention, he leaned towards her.

'Your child', he told her, 'is set for the fall of many in Israel, for many will reject him. But also for the rising of many who will believe on him, and live. He is sent as a sign which shall be spoken against, and will meet reproach and contradiction, which will reveal the thoughts of many hearts—'

Miriam did not understand. Nor did Yosef, when she looked questioningly towards him.

Only the old man still spoke. 'Indeed, a sword shall pierce thine own soul also—'

A widow woman, passing as he spoke, caught the old man's words, looked at the infant in his arms, and began to echo his speech to those parents still waiting for their sons' redemption.

They brought Herod back from Calirrhoe to the palace in Jerusalem. Not one jot improved.

He lay, propped up in bed, surrounded by his palace staff.

He beckoned to a servant who brought him another dish of fruit. This time the King took an apple, and slowly, straining, pared it with a knife, while two other servants fanned incense round him to fumigate the room.

'What news of the Chaldees since I've been away?' asked Herod through his noisy, messy munching.

'Chaldees, my King?' enquired the chamberlain, not sure what Herod meant.

'Chaldees . . . from Babylon—' roared Herod.

The chamberlain was slow to recollect.

Herod cursed his stupidity.

'They came from Babylon seeking the Messiah,' he shouted. 'I sent them to Bethlehem. And when they'd found him, they were to bring me word—'

'They have not come.'

'Not come!' screamed the King, throwing the knife and the half-pared apple at his chamberlain. 'They have not come—' convulsing all through his body. 'But I sent them more than forty days ago—' And each word was pushed through lips that could not control the retching.

And still Herod screamed. Demented. Pulling at each hand to steady it.

His doctors grabbed him, trying to restrain him. His madness gave him strength, and he slung them away, and still roared, vomiting each word he uttered.

'The Chaldees mock me. But I will be revenged.'

Then he quietened. The retching and the screaming stopped. Only his body shook, but the convulsions eased.

'Kill every boy in Bethlehem that is not yet weaned from his mother's breast.'

When nobody in the chamber moved, Herod commanded them, 'Do it now.'

Jerusalem was a haze in Miriam's memory. Everything was confused. Faces, houses, priests, people, shops, sights and sounds. All jumbled together. Overwhelmed by the one thing that kept coming back. The old man and woman, dwarfed by the grandeur of the Temple. And their soft-spoken words: 'This child is set for the rising and falling of many . . . a sign that shall be spoken against. Yea, a sword shall pierce thine own soul also.'

The words frightened her then, and they frightened her now each time the frail, aged voice re-echoed in her mind.

The task of shaping a new life in Bethlehem did nothing to distract her thoughts or lessen the sense of foreboding, the premonitions that steadily, stealthily took possession of her.

Jacob, her father-in-law, wondered if she thought too much, and placed too much value on an old man's emotion.

Yosef listened when she confided her fears, but could make no comment. He went about each day's work, helping his father in the fields, planning a house to build in Bethlehem.

But then, it happened. Yosef was up in the middle of the night, making ready to get out of Bethlehem before the morning light.

Miriam wakened to the hubbub of Jacob reasoning with Yosef. And Yosef arguing back.

'It's natural to dream like that,' his father was saying. 'It's no more than your waking fears following you into sleep.'

'But the dream was too clear, Father. As though God himself stood in front of me.'

Jacob made to speak, but Yosef went on. 'The warning is too strong, I dare not ignore it. "Take the young child and his mother" was the warning, Father, "and flee into Egypt—"'

Miriam was listening.

'Herod will seek the young child to destroy him.'

Jacob threw up his hands, dismissing Yosef's dream as fantasy. 'Herod', he explained to him, 'doesn't even know the young child exists.'

But while the two men argued, Miriam herself made ready. And wrapped her child warm against the cold air of the night's journeying.

CHAPTER TEN

Jacob wondered aloud about Yosef's snap decision to go to Egypt, his remarks addressed to nobody in particular.

He confided to the bed rolls, as he gathered them up, that he wasn't sure it was a sign of wisdom in a man to go galavanting off to a place he knew nothing about on the basis of a dream.

'And with an infant who has only grown accustomed to his mother's breast,' he explained to the pannier bags he laid out, ready, for Miriam to fill.

Yosef listened and heard. But made no comment. There was no malice, no vindictiveness in his father's chuntering. It was no more, Yosef knew, than the habit of an old man who'd lived too long on his own.

Yosef nodded, now and then, to Miriam, hoping she'd understand, and not be drawn to interrupt.

'And at this hour of the night,' the old man remarked to the donkey that kept fidgeting while he tried to saddle it for Miriam and the child. 'You ought still to be in your stall,' he sympathized. 'We all ought to be in bed. If they must go chasing off, they'd be better for the journey after a good night's rest.'

Yosef agreed. And told himself his father was right. Of course, he was right. Maybe all the asides were no more than his way of preparing for the new loneliness that faced him when they were gone. But he was right.

Any other time, Josef would readily have acquiesced. But not now. The voice in the dream was too commanding, the presentiment too strong: 'Get up. Take the child and his mother. And flee to Egypt—'

He wished, for the love he bore his father, that he could have explained it all. But what he could not explain to himself he could hardly begin to make plain to his father.

He turned to speak to Jacob. But his father was already beside him.

'You're ready, now, Yosef,' he whispered. 'Make no delay.'

He rubbed a hand across his face, and took Yosef in his arms. 'The Lord watch over you,' he murmured. 'And take no account of my mad chatterings tonight.'

It was a quick embrace. Jacob turned and led Miriam out.

'God bless you, Miriam, my daughter,' he said, helping her to mount the donkey. 'And God bless the lad.'

Miriam saw the tears in his eyes. And watched till he became a tiny figure as they rode away.

They took the mountain road, over the western slopes, towards Gaza, till they joined the 'Way of the Philistines', that ran along the coast.

It took them three days to reach the River Rhinocolura, the River of Egypt.

They crossed the riverbed, dry now, waiting for the rains. And on the south bank of the river, they felt safe for the first time since they left Bethlehem. Now they were beyond the reach of the Tetrarch and his threats.

Miriam was glad of the long rest which Yosef reckoned they needed and deserved. And she thought it right to spare a little of their water for Yosef to wash and soothe his feet, cut and scarred, and caked with the dirt of walking the roads.

When they moved off again, the journey was easier, the pace less hectic, and there was time to dawdle sometimes and talk.

They talked of home, her parents, of poor Rachel, and Naomi and Azariah, laughing sometimes at the pomposity of Isaac in his baker's shop. She crooned to her child of an evening, and watched the sun setting over the sea, while Yosef tended the donkey, and tethered him for the night.

They encouraged themselves that, if they must leave their homeland for their child's safety, then Egypt was not the worst place in which to be exiled.

Egypt was flooded with Jews, Yosef reminded her.

'Since the days of Moses, when they were all slaves,' quipped Miriam, making Yosef laugh out loud.

But the Jews in Egypt, now, he assured her, were prosperous. They had their own temple. Their scholars had even translated the Hebrew Scriptures into Greek. And Jews were among the most successful traders in the country.

They came to the sea port of Pelusium. Here they bore south, travelling still along the 'Way of the Philistines', heading for Heliopolis.

'They say it was in Heliopolis that Moses was reared by Pharaoh's daughter,' Miriam advised her husband, 'as a prince of Pharaoh's house.'

Yosef nodded. 'And became a general in Pharaoh's army, and fought his wars for him.'

'And knew exactly what he was doing when he led the Israelites to break out of Egypt,' observed Miriam.

'Did his mother realize all that would happen when he was snatched from her by the riverside, and taken off to Egypt?'

'I wonder—' said Miriam. And there was a faraway sound in her voice.

When they could see the city in the far distance, Yosef reckoned it would take them not much more than two days' journeying.

'How long will we be, Yosef?' asked Miriam. 'Will we ever go back to Bethlehem?'

He didn't know. All that he knew, though he didn't understand it, was his dream that told him to escape to Egypt.

'And stay there till I come to you again,' said Miriam, finishing the command he'd said he'd been given in his dream.

'And we've no idea at all, Miriam, when that will be.'

'Aye,' she agreed.

But, for all the strangeness and uncertainty, as they got nearer to Heliopolis, Miriam's sense of hope and confidence and security seemed to grow.

She knew that, for as long as they lived there, they would never be poor. Her child would never go hungry. The gold the Chaldees had brought, now safely carried in a pannier bag, would guarantee that.

And Yosef would have no difficulty getting work at his trade. Hadn't he told her how Jewish tradesmen in Egypt had formed themselves into guilds—coppersmiths, goldsmiths, silversmiths, weavers, needlemakers, nailmakers – who supported strangers of their trade till they were properly settled? Yosef could depend on the members of his own craft, the stonemasons.

'The masons look after their own,' he told her. 'We'll be among good friends.'

Flowers grew around the infants' graves, a morning's walk from Bethlehem. Bethlehem's heart still ached. Sorrow tinged the town's talk. Its mothers still lamented the tragedy Herod's mad cruelty had inflicted on them.

Herod, however, had altogether forgotten his act of

butchery. Though, had he the conscience or the physical strength to remember, it is unlikely that he would have had the time. His mind, in the moments when it was not delirious, was occupied with other matters.

Antipater, his son, was back from Rome.

The King was entertaining Quintillius Varus, the newly appointed President of Syria. It was the briefest of visits, Varus explained. He was on his way to Antioch to take up his appointment.

Herod understood. He would be grateful, though, were Varus to agree to act as judge in his son's trial.

'Of course,' Varus agreed. 'But I must be on my way to Antioch the day after tomorrow.'

'The trial', Herod assured him, 'will begin and end tomorrow.'

Antipater entered as the two men talked. Bold, proud, and dressed in purple.

Herod noted his pretensions to kingship, and watched the purpose in his pace as he approached to salute. And he felt frightened, vulnerable.

'Even this,' he burst out, stretching his arms to protect himself, 'Even this is an indication of a parricide.' He turned his head away as he spoke. 'Trying to get me in his arms when he is under such heinous accusations.'

Antipater stopped, taken aback. It was not the reception he had expected.

'Vile wretch,' roared the King, the sound bellowing round the room, 'May God confound you.'

Antipater knew, now, he had made a grave mistake. He ought never to have come home. He ought to have trusted his instincts back in Rome. The lavish affection in the letter was a trick. His father had not changed.

He watched his father fight for breath, wrapping his arms around himself as he struggled to speak.

'Do not touch me,' he was shouting. 'Do not come near

me till you have cleared yourself of the crimes that are charged against you.'

The King paused, and turned, looking beyond Antipater. His voice was soft when he spoke. Cold.

'I have appointed a court to try you,' he said. 'It will meet tomorrow. Varus here will be the judge.'

Varus bowed his head in acknowledgement.

Antipater withdrew, stunned, speechless.

The court was assembled and ready to start the trial when Antipater was called in.

He felt his blood run cold when he saw the crowd. The King's friends, his own friends, his servants. And when he looked at them he wondered what tortures they had endured, what they had revealed. He saw Salome, his sister, and searched for his mother, Doris, but could not see her. Till he looked again, and found her, degraded, among her domestic servants. They, too, had been tortured.

He could not take in all the faces, massed as they were. His vision blurred till he could no longer see them clearly.

He made his way through the crowd to take his place before the King. He bowed. A deep obeisance.

A hand touched his elbow, encouraging him to sit. He turned his head, and looked into the face of Nicolaus of Damascus. His father's only true friend and confidant. And the prosecutor.

Antipater sat. There was no doubt his father was in earnest. And the outcome he intended was made too clear by having Nicolaus prosecute. He was condemned already.

Quintillius Varus called the court to order. Antipater felt the tension, the hate in the hush.

The assembly waited for Herod.

Their waiting gave Antipater his opportunity. He fell on his face, prostrating himself at Herod's feet.

'Father,' he called out, 'I beseech you, do not condemn

me beforehand. Let your ears be unbiased, and hear my defence. If you will give me leave, I will demonstrate that I am innocent.'

'Stop,' roared Herod. 'Hold your peace,' kicking at the body prostrate at his feet.

And then, as softly, spoke to Varus: 'I cannot but think that you, Varus, and every other upright judge, will determine that Antipater is a vile wretch.' He paused. And then, with something of a smile in his voice, 'I am also afraid that you will judge me also worthy of all sorts of calamity for begetting such children.'

Varus smiled back. 'Perish the thought.'

'This profligate wild beast,' explained Herod, 'when he was young, I appointed him as my successor. And he made use of what abundance I had given him against myself. I seemed to him to live too long. He could not wait so long for me to die, but would be a King by parricide.'

The King paused. A servant mopped his face, and swilled his hands in a bowl of water. He was drying his hands, with the King urgent to go on again.

'This parricide presumes to speak for himself and, by his cunning tricks, hopes to obscure the truth. Be on your guard, Varus. I know this wild beast. I foresee how plausibly he will talk. I already hear his counterfeit lamentation—'

Antipater made to rise to interrupt.

Herod, despite the pain shooting through him, stormed towards Antipater, standing over him as a hunter stands over his prey.

'This was he,' he proclaimed, pointing a hand the length of Antipater's prostrate form, 'This was he who came to my very bed, and searched, lest anyone should lay snares for me. This was he who took care of my sleep,' his voice rising in a long crescendo, 'This was my protector, the guardian of my body—'

His voice dropped, so that the court could hardly hear. Varus leaned forward to pick up the words.

'I can hardly believe I am still alive. Yet, Varus, I am resolved that no one who thirsts after my blood shall escape punishment, although the evidence should extend itself to all my sons.'

Herod wept.

Antipater heard the sobbing, and looked up. He could see Nicolaus rising, at the King's signal, to present evidence against him.

'My father,' Antipater called out. 'You yourself have made my apology for me. How can I be a parricide, whom you declare was always your guardian?'

He felt the assembly listening.

'You call my filial affection lies and hypocrisy—' As he spoke he knelt, reaching into his cloak as he moved. 'Rome is a witness to my filial affection. So is Caesar, the ruler of the habitable earth. Caesar oftentimes called me Philopater, a lover of his father—' He pulled out a packet from his cloak. 'Take these letters Caesar has sent. These are more to be believed than the calumnies raised here. These are my apology.'

Varus directed an officer to collect the letters.

There was a hubbub through the assembly. Antipater waited to let them all digest his speech. The court, he felt, was moving to his side.

'If I be a parricide,' he said, measured, slow. Making sure that every person present, and Varus in particular, should hear and understand each word. 'If I am to be condemned, I beg you not to believe those who have been tortured. If I am a parricide, let fire torment me. Let the rack march through my bowels. Ignore the lamentations this polluted body can make . . . If I am a parricide, I ought not to die without torture.'

He stopped, fell to the ground and, prostrate before the King, convulsed with weeping and lamentation.

The court was moved, and Varus with them. Some wept. Only Herod ignored Antipater, treating his protestation of innocence as no more than the performance of an actor.

The hearing might have ended there, and Varus might have ruled, but Nicolaus rose. The prosecution, he pointed out, had been interrupted by Antipater. It still had to complete its case.

Nicolaus was neat, efficient. And bitter.

He settled his papers while he explained that he could only stand amazed at Antipater's wickedness. 'Although this man has had benefits bestowed on him by his father, enough to tame his reason,' he told them, 'yet this man could be no more tamed than the most envenomed serpents. Even those creatures', he declared, 'admit to some mitigation, and will not bite their benefactors. But this Antipater—'

He no longer addressed the assembly, but turned to Antipater, directing every damning word at the defendant himself.

'You would kill your father. And devised such a sort of uncommon parricide as the world never yet saw. You laid your treacherous design against your father. And did it while he loved you, and was your benefactor.'

He paused to allow his words to register with the court. And then, with the quietness of a physician advising the sick, 'You have a mind more cruel than a serpent.'

The soft tones did not last. Stooping down to be near the ear of the man he now considered his opponent, he roared, 'And from that mind you sent out poison. Against an old man.'

His rage was not abated as he continued, 'You allege that those who were tortured told lies, that those who are the deliverers of your father must not be considered as having told the truth. But,' and Nicolaus whispered his calculated, honeyed sarcasm, 'but your own tortures may be esteemed the discoverers of the truth.'

He stopped. Antipater made no move. Nicolaus turned away from him, and bent over his desk while he gathered his documents into a neater pile. His voice had lost its anger.

'Will you not, Varus, deliver the King of the injuries of his kindred? Will you not destroy this wicked wild beast who appears to be the bloodiest butcher of them all?'

He was nearly finished. He had noticed earlier on that Varus was prepared to be swayed by Antipater's appeal. There must be no fear of it happening again. He was here for his friend Herod's sake. To see Antipater condemned to die. Varus, therefore, must be left in no doubt about his duty.

'You are aware, Varus,' he began, 'that parricide is a general injury both to nature and to common life.'

He had Varus's full attention.

'The intention of parricide', explained Nicolaus, 'is not inferior to its preparation. And he who does not punish it is injurious to nature itself.'

He bowed to the judge, and sat down.

'Has Antipater any defence to make?' asked Varus.

Antipater lay long in silence. 'God is my witness that I am innocent,' was all he said.

Varus ordered that he be imprisoned, in chains, to await Caesar's advice as to his sentence.

The court rose.

Next day, as he had planned, Varus left Jerusalem to take up residence in Antioch.

Caesar Augustus received Herod's ambassadors.

He congratulated them on pursuing their King's business with such proficiency. He appreciated the urgency of the matter, he told them. He would make no delay in reaching a decision. They would, of course, understand that he must, first of all, make a careful study of the report of Antipater's trial.

The two men were grateful to Caesar.

He motioned to a servant to pour wine for his guests. Another brought lavishly laden fruit dishes, set them down, and then ordered the couches for the ambassadors to sit.

Caesar was already reading Quintillius Varus's report.

He liked Varus's style. Clipped, crisp, precise, economic. No word wasted. The plain language of a soldier. The style of the fine officer he was. He would make an efficient President in Syria.

He found it hard to believe Antipater could be tried for treachery. He had had no cause to judge him a deceitful man all the time he was here in Rome. And that not all that long ago. Indeed, he called him 'Philopater'. Once. By mistake, if he remembered clearly. In any case, it sounded somewhat more congenial than 'Anti-pater'.

Maybe, though, it was Herod's old problem all over again. Wanting to be rid of a son he'd grown tired of . . . But how could a man want to destroy his own flesh and blood, the fruit of his own loins? Not even the wild beasts in the fields did that. Better to be Herod's pig than Herod's son – but he was musing when he should be reading. He went back to the report.

Whatever the Tetrarch's motives, it was clear that Varus was on Herod's side. And Varus was nobody's fool.

But the prosecution! Caesar read it again. What a man was Nicolaus of Damascus! He minced no words. And was not mealy-mouthed in the charges he brought. Parricide! There were not many who would dare accuse a King's son of parricide, and make no bones about the verdict he expected from the judge.

Antipater, he reckoned, would need the mind of a sage

and the eloquence of a god to defend himself against such an onslaught.

He read Varus's question. 'Has Antipater any defence to make?'

'Ahaaa!' exclaimed Caesar. 'The reprobate's old standby.'

Startled by the outburst, both ambassadors looked over to the Emperor. They were glad, in fact, of the break in the long silence.

'It is a curious thing, gentlemen,' the Emperor addressed them. 'The man who has no virtue lives his life as if no god exists. He works according to his own inclinations, as if he believed the gods were unconcerned in human affairs. But let something go wrong, let him be in danger of being punished for his crimes, then he will try to overthrow all the evidence against him by appealing to the gods.'

He turned back to Varus's conclusion.

'The court', he read, 'judges Antipater guilty of the charges made against him.'

'Nothing less,' agreed Augustus.

'The court humbly waits on Caesar to pronounce sentence.'

'Ah, no, Varus!' said Caesar, and realized in time that the ambassadors were present. But he talked in his mind. Herod knows what the appropriate sentence is. What sentence he wants. But I will not play butcher for a Jew in Jerusalem. If he wants his son killed, he must do it himself.

'I have made my decision, gentlemen,' said he to the ambassadors. 'By tomorrow when you leave, my secretary will have prepared my letter to your King, with my seal upon it.'

The two men bowed, expecting that this was the end of the audience.

'You are, however, his ambassadors. I will speak to you, therefore, as into the ear of the King.'

They waited.

'By Caesar's word, Antipater, the Tetrarch's son, is condemned to die. Yet, if the Tetrarch, his father, has a mind to banish him, Caesar permits him so to do.'

They moved the King to Jericho.

Salome, his sister, had instigated the move. Herod was grateful, and told his sister so.

'I love it most of all the cities I have built,' he told her, stretching a shaking hand across his bed towards her to show his thanks.

She knew, and touched his hand to reassure him, as his servants bolstered him as best they could to ease the coughing spasm and make his breathing easier.

He waved the servants away, and beckoned Salome nearer. 'The number of my days is short,' he said, holding his chest to give some steadiness to his speech.

Salome said nothing. She watched and pitied this poor, broken man gulping the air.

'I want to meet my principal men.'

Salome didn't understand. 'Principal men?'

Herod was agitated. Did she not know it was agony to speak? And he had to fight to shape words to give her the explanation he hadn't thought would be necessary.

'The Seven Good Men of the Town,' with annoyance in the feeble voice. 'The men who care for the welfare of the people in their town.'

She could see neither purpose nor meaning in his wish. 'Of course, my brother,' she said, humouring him.

Herod eased himself up. 'The principal men of every town and village throughout my Kingdom', he said, commanding Salome as though he were issuing a decree, 'will attend on their King here in Jericho.'

'But my King, my brother,' Salome interrupted, 'you are too sick for audiences. Would you not rather wait till you are recovered? Besides, there would be too many even for the palace here.'

Herod stopped her. 'Salome,' he said, and he was barely audible, 'I am dying . . . Before I die . . . There is a reason . . . They will assemble in the Hippodrome.'

'The Hippodrome—' she reacted. But stopped the rushing reprimand she was about to administer. Her brother, maybe, but her King also. And the King brooked no contradiction. But her mind was picturing the madness an assembly in the Hippodrome conjured. Chariot-racing, horses, gladiators, raucous crowds . . . And the King, as in old times, rubbing shoulders and rollicking with them all. It would kill him. But, he was dying, anyway . . . her thoughts trailed away.

Herod smiled at her, as though he had guessed what she was thinking.

'In the Hippodrome, Salome. The King commands it.'

The King had spoken. She was silent, and looked long at him, wondering if she should gainsay him. She could not dare, and could not help admiring her brother who, even as he lay dying, still thought about his people.

The principal men were not impressed. Had they the courage, they would ignore the King's command.

'And die—' Jonathan advised his colleagues in his house in Bethlehem.

'It would need every council,' offered Joshua, the leader of the group, 'in every town and village of the kingdom to refuse.'

'To have blood washing through every street in the Kingdom,' Jonathan retorted. 'Have you forgotten Bethlehem a few years back? Innocent children they were—'

'The King is dying,' Joshua replied.

'He was dying when he massacred the infants,' Jonathan lashed back.

'And if we disobey his order, there'll be another massacre in Bethlehem,' Caleb advised his brethren.

'It could be different now, Jonathan,' soothed Joshua. 'It could be that the King has in mind to do his people some good.'

'Like do away with the tax they've been paying for years for Jericho.'

'We won't know,' interjected Caleb, 'if we don't go,' pleased with himself for his observation. He reckoned they'd have to go whether they liked it or not.

'If he's all that well intentioned,' commented Jonathan, 'why has he chosen Jericho? He knows we detest his city as a place of abomination. And look at his command! We will assemble at the Hippodrome—'

'Sin and abomination and degradation and every work of evil,' put in Caleb. 'The man has calculated how best to offend and insult us. But be sure of this, brethren, if we don't go, we are dead.'

'Caleb is right, my brothers,' said Joshua, hoping it put an end to the argument.

They all, reluctantly, agreed.

'And who knows,' he added, as they made ready for the journey, 'it could be that by the time we reach the Hippodrome, Herod will be dead.'

They made no delay in setting out. All along their twenty miles to Jericho, they were joined by countless more making their way to obey the King's command.

Salome and her husband stood, with the silent attendants, by the King's bed.

Alexas moved to comfort his wife, whispering gently that he thought the King was dead.

Salome watched. Sad, pitying, numbed. For a while. Till her mind began to race with tormented thoughts. The succession . . . Her brother had died without changing his will. With no word, yet, from Caesar, Antipater would be King. Poor, broken Herod. How sadly he must have died if he had thought of his wretched son . . .

The King shifted, opened his eyes, and smiled when he recognized his visitors.

Salome's hands flashed to her mouth, involuntarily, stifling what would, otherwise, have been a scream. She felt her husband's hand touch her. It was not the time for hysterics, it said. We made a bitter mistake. Your brother is alive. He is still the King.

'The King's command has been obeyed,' Salome told him. 'His wish has been fulfilled,' hoping that the whim that once possessed his mind had, now, by the passing days and his own nearness to death, been blotted out.

The servants had to recover quickly from their shock. Herod waited till they had lifted him, placed cushions all around him, scattered incense, and propped him comfortably in his bed.

The King was generous in his appreciation of their work. His face wore a smile of satisfaction as he spoke, his eyes burrowing into Salome. 'I know well enough,' he began, 'that the Jews will keep festival upon my death.'

Salome was sorry for him, and tried to reassure him otherwise. 'Even now, my King, they are gathered in the Hippodrome, from every corner of your Kingdom, in obedience to your command, and out of love for you, and deep sorrow for you in your sickness.'

Herod ignored her. 'However,' he went on, 'it is in my power to be mourned when I am dead. And to have a splendid funeral. But—'

The King paused. Salome listened.

'It all depends on you, Salome, my sister, and whether or not you will be subservient to my commands.'

The words came slurred and slowly. Salome had to listen closely to make out what the King was saying.

'Take care of those who are assembled in the Hippodrome. Feast them well. And make sure that everything they
need and want is lavishly supplied. They must not think ill
of their King's hospitality.'

Salome nodded enthusiastically. She would feel no hard-
ship being subservient if this was what the King intended.
She smiled warmly at her brother. And would have told him
how readily she could comply with his wishes, but Herod
raised his hand.

He had more to say. 'Take care also, my sister, to send
soldiers to encompass those men who are now in
custody—'

She heard 'custody', and suddenly could no longer understand her brother. 'Custody,' she mumbled. 'But why?'

Herod continued as though she had not spoken. Every
word he spoke was clear and strong and measured. 'And slay
them immediately upon my death.'

A smile wreathed his face. There was a lightness, a new
clarity in his speech, as though his condition were improving
and his sickness ended.

'Then,' he declared, 'all Judaea, and every family of them,
will weep when I am dead, whether they like it or not.'

Salome tried to shout, but no sound came. She choked.
Her brother was mad. And she wished him dead.

Her husband took her by the arm, and they left the
bedchamber.

Herod could not tell whether it was night or day. The
windows were shuttered to block out the tormenting sun.
What little light there was came from the tallow lamps that
smoked, and added suffocation to the bedchamber already
reeking with his own stench that even incense could no
longer camouflage.

He had no strength, now, to sit up, even with the cushions

like a wall around him. His attendants held him constantly
so that he could breathe.

Pain, unrelenting pain, urged, like a serpent's venom,
through his body. The very hair of his head pained him.

Fever burned him. And an itch, an incessant itch, scraping
like thorns in every pore. The itch itself, with nothing more
to torture him, would drive him mad.

A spasm of convulsions racked him, pounding, shaking,
tossing, till his attendants could control or hold him no
more. He fell back on the bed, smothering, unable to
breathe, until they manhandled him and got him sitting up
again.

O God, if they would let him be. And let him die . . .

He heard himself, through his convulsive cough, calling
for food and more food to satisfy his voracious appetite. A
new affliction, as though his torments already were not
enough.

He took an apple from the dish of fruit they brought.

His shaking eased. Cushions bolstered round him would
be enough, he told his attendants. They needed rest, and he
would be alone.

He held the apple in his hands, wondering how they
could be so misshapen. He had no knife to pare the apple.

'A knife,' he called.

A servant brought one, and waited till the King dismissed
him.

Herod stared. His hands. The apple. The knife . . . the knife
. . . the knife . . . and there was no one near enough to stop
him. Up went his right hand . . . up, slowly up, as high as the
pain allowed . . . and down . . . 'aaaah'. . . smashing down
towards his breast, his heart. He would soon be dead . . .

His cousin, Achiabus, heard the King's roar, and raced to
the bed, grabbing Herod's hand, crying out for help to stop
the King killing himself.

The knife clattered to the floor.

Bitter, angry, frustrated at his dismal failure, the King wept, and cursed Achiabus for his interference.

His attendants were all round him again, holding the King, the body that swelled and pained and stank and itched and burned and ached to be filled with food.

'My King,' intruded the voice. Formally, officiously, as though nothing were amiss.

Herod looked up. Through the tears still in his puffed eyes, he recognized his visitor.

'Chamberlain,' he said.

'My King, the Chief Gaoler begs an audience.'

'The Chief Gaoler!' exclaimed Herod. 'Would he gaol me for having tried to kill the King?'

The chamberlain acknowledged the King's quip, and smiled obediently.

'The Gaoler brings word about your son, Antipater.'

'Is he dead?'

'He has not said, my lord. He would speak only with the King.'

Herod nodded. The chamberlain called out. And the Chief Gaoler came in.

'God save the King,' said the Gaoler, introducing himself.

'God is not at all kind to the King, Gaoler.'

'State your business quickly, and be gone,' the chamberlain advised him. 'The King, as you can see, is sick.'

'Your son, my King, by your own command, is in my charge, and bound in chains in prison.'

'And so he shall stay, Gaoler, so he shall stay. Till Caesar says he will die.'

'My King. Your sickness has concerned us all, my lord. And . . . may the King live for ever . . .'

'A man could die for wishing such torment on his King,' commented Herod drily. 'But get to my son. That's why you're here.'

'I will be brief, my King.'

'Or short-lived if you don't soon state your business.'

'Your son heard rumours that the King was dead. Yesterday, he pledged large sums of money and great honours to the gaolers if they would break his chains and loose him from prison.'

'And—?'

'I chained him even more securely. And am come now to tell you, my King.'

'Antipater will die,' bellowed Herod, his whole frame bursting with sound and anger. 'Caesar or no Caesar, Antipater will die. Get you six men, Gaoler, and torture him to death. And be careful that he is dead before the sun sets today.'

The Chief Gaoler left.

As Herod watched him go, he felt the man would relish obeying the King's command. Before the day was out.

'Archelaus will be King,' Herod proclaimed when the Gaoler had gone.

Five days later, Herod himself was dead.

Archelaus was a light sleeper. He wakened easily to the muffled commotion at the door of his bedchamber. His chamberlain, doing his best not to raise his voice, was explaining that he dare not wake his master at so early an hour.

The discussion at the door was obviously going to continue. Archelaus reckoned he would get no more sleep. 'What is it, chamberlain?' he called.

'A messenger from Jerusalem, my lord. He says he brings an urgent message.' And then, as if to defend his having wakened his master, he added, 'For you alone.'

Archelaus eased himself up slowly, turned himself, pulling his night clothes around him, and sat on the side of his couch.

'We will hear the urgent business, chamberlain.'

Three men were ushered in. Two of them were soldiers, escorting the messenger. The soldiers' presence signified the importance of the news he carried. Smart men, but still covered with the dust of travelling. Their slightly unkempt appearance meant they had wasted no time on their thirty-mile journey. And no time at all in making themselves presentable for this audition.

'I bring a letter, my Lord Archelaus,' the messenger began, 'from Ptolemy, the Keeper of the King's Seal.'

He handed the thin roll of parchment to the chamberlain, who then approached and bowed, and handed it to Archelaus.

Archelaus recognized Ptolemy's handwriting on the roll. He knew it well. He saw it often enough, for Ptolemy kept him well informed and advised about the goings-on, secret and otherwise, at his father's court. But always at a decent time in the day. Never in the middle of the night.

Archelaus was surprised when he broke the seal and opened out the roll. He expected to have to wade through Ptolemy's usual flowery, long-winded way of telling things. Instead, this was a short note – well, short by Ptolemy's standards.

Antipater, the King's son, the note stated, was dead. Executed by the King's own command. 'And, by the King's express command, you, my gracious lord, are named as your father's illustrious successor.'

Archelaus was pleased with the news – with both pieces of news. But it might have waited, he felt. It surely wasn't necessary to get him out of bed to tell him. Ptolemy must know he wouldn't grieve over his half-brother. And being named as Herod's successor was no guarantee he'd ever sit on Herod's throne – as Antipater had clearly proved . . .

But, but . . . He was reading the rest. Ptolemy was strongly urging him to come to Jerusalem.

Archelaus read it again. Slowly and intently. 'The King, your father, is dying. He has but little time left. The infamy of Antipater whom he loved has broken his heart, the physicians say.'

Archelaus smiled wryly at the thought that struck him. He who would be King was dead. And the King who denied him the pleasures of the palace was now making space for Archelaus on the throne. Ptolemy's advice was sound, he told himself. He would make no delay in getting to Jerusalem.

'Dismiss the messenger, chamberlain,' he announced, rolling the letter carefully. 'Instruct the Captain of the Guard to prepare a chariot and troop. I'm travelling to Jerusalem.'

The chamberlain beckoned the messenger and soldiers to leave.

'And send my servants here to prepare me for the journey.'

The chamberlain bowed his way out.

'And, chamberlain,' shouted Archelaus, as the man reached the door, 'send in some food.'

The servants came. The food was brought.

And when Archelaus had eaten and was dressed, the Captain of the Guard appeared to announce that his chariot and the troop were ready. And, with what could be mistaken for the panoply of a King, Archelaus and his guards set out on their fast journey to Jerusalem.

He could bear the dust they were kicking up with the speed of their travelling. And every now and then Archelaus smiled to himself as he recalled Ptolemy's signature on the note: '*Ptolemy, Keeper of the King's seal, and Keeper of the King's will, who, by God's divine favour, will proclaim my gracious lord's succession to the throne.*' A wordy and a pompous man, but useful.

Salome watched her brother die. She found it hard to be sorry for him in his slow, torturing, degraded agony. There was too much about him to remember. Thirty-seven years too much. Too much cruelty. Too many murders. Too much spilt blood. Too many deaths. And every memory caused her pain. And hate.

The King's physicians pronounced him dead. The attendants who had nursed the King so long covered his face, their task now ended.

There were no tears, Salome noticed. No deep lamentations. Not even from the chamberlain who had been, for so long, so close a companion and adviser to the King.

'The principal men imprisoned in the Hippodrome,' she said quietly to the chamberlain. 'Send word to the Garrison Commander that the King has changed his mind.'

The chamberlain seemed about to ask a question.

Salome prevented him. 'Instruct the Commander that he will immediately release all those he holds in custody in the Hippodrome. And he will take care to send them safely to their own homes.'

The chamberlain did not speak. There was a look of admiring gratitude in his face. He made no delay, but was gone gladly to deliver the instruction.

Salome had enough to occupy her while she gave the chamberlain time to release the men in custody. In any case, she dared not pass the news to the Garrison Commander till those at court had been informed of the King's death. And before them all, the new King must be advised of his succession.

She could send no messenger, however exalted his rank, on such a mission. She must undertake that task herself, for all she so thoroughly despised Archelaus. He was unfit to be a King. 'But then,' she reminded herself, 'what son of Herod was fit to be King?'

She sent a captain of the Palace Guard to Ptolemy who held the King's Seal and was Keeper of the King's Will.

Ptolemy would address the people, read Herod's will, and proclaim the succession. He would enjoy that, she decided. He was as pompous and as proud as Herod made him. Ptolemy, she judged, would lose nothing of his power. He was close friend to Archelaus. He could, in fact, expect even more favour now than ever he enjoyed from Herod.

Jochebed was in Salome's mind. She sent an embassy immediately to Jochebed, in isolation, now, in Perea since the days of Herod's poison trial.

Salome pitied Jochebed who still believed she had borne the son that might yet be proclaimed Messiah. And convinced herself that Herod had so often spared her life because he dared not kill the Messiah's mother.

Jochebed might not come near the funeral, but Salome knew she would be glad to hear of Herod's death. An exile she might have to remain for the rest of her life but, from now on, she could live without constant dread. There was no need for Salome to undertake her journey to Archelaus. He was already in Jerusalem – already looking like a King.

The Amphitheatre was a cauldron of sound billowing its bedlam in deafening clouds into the springtime sky, blanketing the people, raucous, gaudy, boisterous, massed tier by teeming tier.

As though it were a holiday, Salome thought.

Up from the arena reached the roaring and screeching and clanking of war as chariots and horses and war's machinery settled in their appointed place. And soldiers marched and countermarched, in their troops and bands to the commands of their centurions and their mustermen, ordering themselves to acclaim their King.

'The gladiators, now, are all we need,' Salome thought to herself. 'And then it would really be a festival.' And in the smothering clamour, she heard the whispering in her mind. Her brother's voice, hoarse with the sound of sickness, 'The Jews will make festival on my death.'

Even his son made festival.

Salome watched him. Purple-robed, with every accoutrement of royalty but the crown. Already in the King's seat, preening. Like Caesar himself preparing to receive the plaudits of the people. And all round him in the King's enclosure, pressing him on every side, the sycophants, the cronies. Fawning, toadying. Not for love of him, but for the favours he could bestow. And painted, braided, brazen women vying with each other for his attention.

'Poor Herod,' breathed Salome. 'How right he was.' And, for a moment, she was sorry for him.

The blare of blasting trumpets brought silence for the start.

Archelaus hardly acknowledged her bow when she stood to read Herod's letter to the soldiers. Herod, she told them, thanked them for the good men they were.

The soldiers cheered.

He blessed them for their fidelity . . .

The soldiers cheered again.

And Salome knew they meant it. And Herod meant it. He loved his soldiers, their roughness, and bravery and bawdiness and ruggedness.

'And your good will towards me—' shouted Salome over the noise, but they cheered whether or not they'd heard what she'd said. She waited till they were quietened before she spoke again.

Only the neighing horses broke the quiet as she read the dead King's hope that they would afford the same fidelity and good will to the son he had named King.

And again the roar went up from the soldiers, their centurions and their mustermen.

'They cheer today,' Salome thought as she bowed again

to Archelaus. 'But what will it be tomorrow, when they have taken your measure as their King?'

She had not sat down before Ptolemy was up, reading Herod's will.

A cluster here and there in the crowd paid some attention; the rest seemed bent on making holiday. There was nothing in Herod's will that could be of benefit to them.

Ptolemy read. It was a formality that must be fulfilled. Whether they listened or not was a matter of indifference to him.

He told them how happily Herod their King had died.

Salome thought she heard the sound of mockery and disbelief as the people mumble-mumbled back. There was derision almost in the chattering that countered Ptolemy's attempt at comforting them in their loss of their King.

Not even Archelaus paid too close attention, Salome noticed. Though, maybe she saw him pause when a hidden voice called out what comfort it would be to see Herod's prisoners released. 'And our taxes lightened,' called another, with clapping approval from the mob around him.

But did the pompous, puffed-up Ptolemy hear, she wondered. Perhaps he did, for he brought his homily to an untimely and untidy end.

Then raised his arms aloft, calling all the crowd to acclaim their King.

The people responded. They acclaimed their King. It was their duty. Shouting, clapping, roaring, stamping, pounding, banging – more for the relief they got in making the noise than from any great enthusiasm for their King.

The King rose, spreading his arms to embrace his people.

'He thinks he's Caesar!' Salome told herself. 'Caesar receives the plaudits of his people.' And then she smiled as the question crossed her mind. 'But Caesar has not yet approved the succession. Supposing the Emperor declares he cannot be the King!'

The King had had enough. Tomorrow would be a gruell-ing, busy day, and tonight he must feast and entertain his friends.

He signalled an end to the proceedings. The trumpets blared. The people roared their last hurrahs. Archelaus turned and left the royal enclosure. His court followed, their robes lilting as they moved. The enclosure fluttered purple and gold and white, green, blue and yellow.

Salome watched Doris tag herself to the tail end of the group. And pitied her. Bent with grief. Not for the King who was her husband once, but for her dead son. And heartbroken that the man acclaimed the King was not Antipater.

Archelaus watched the faint streaks of sun lighting the dawning day. He had been awakened by the wailing women who had begun their keening for his dead father.

He listened to the lamentation that pulsed through the palace, and thought of it sifting its sound into the bedcham-bers of last night's revellers who, not all that long ago, had gone to sleep.

If the wailing women had not wakened them, he was sure that the clattering of the servants, now up and noisily busy about their chores, would make sleep impossible.

But they would need to be up, anyway. His order – his first order as King, he reflected – to Ptolemy had been that just as soon as everything was ready and in order, they would set out on the funeral procession to the Herodium where his father had commanded he would be buried.

The din that assailed him through the window told him Ptolemy was diligently about his task.

Not only did he hear, but now he could see some of his father's bodyguard positioning the bier of gold the dead King would be carried on.

Its gold gleamed. The precious stones set in it glinted, sparkled in the sun.

'The simplicity of brutal soldiery,' he thought as he watched them. As though it did not glisten enough, when they had set it down, and mopped their brows, they rubbed it with their hands to polish it.

Good men they were, he decided, who so obviously cared for their King. No wonder his father had thought so highly of them, and revelled in their company, and talked of them as Augustus's most generous gift to him. Four hundred of them, when Cleopatra died. The King's Bodyguard . . . they're mine . . . I am the King . . . And he realized he was talking to himself.

On every road that led to the palace, as far as the eye could see, soldiers were forming up, their spearheads glinting, their uniforms making great splurges of colour against the sand-grey ground. Beyond them, the crowds of slaves and freedmen, carrying the spices for his father's body in the tomb. They already had their incense burning, for he could see the blue wisps cloud above them as they stood in waiting, chattering groups.

And off over there, as he looked around, the Corps of Thracian Bowmen. Aloof almost, proud. Dressed for war, mounted on their no less proud Arab chargers.

The German Regiment was there, as he had bidden Ptolemy. And the Regiment of Gauls. Between them all, his father's four favourite regiments.

As he surveyed the scene spread out beneath, and far beyond the palace, Archelaus was pleased. His father would be buried like an Emperor.

He clapped his hands as he turned from the window.

Two servant boys appeared, carrying the purple robe between them, and helped him to dress. They were bowing their way out when Ptolemy entered. Archelaus dismissed the boys abruptly. There was no need for them to dally, but turn round and be gone.

Ptolemy was careful to remember that the man he faced now was the King. He bowed. 'My King,' he said.

Archelaus nodded permission to speak. And reckoned to himself that he could grow comfortably accustomed to this kind of subservience.

'All things are now ready.'

The King was pleased.

'If the King would be gracious enough . . . The family is now assembled in the banqueting hall, ready to join the procession.'

The King acknowledged the arrangement.

'The Garrison Commander offers his loyal and respectful compliments, and wishes to advise the King that the centurions already bear the dead King's couch. And await the King's convenience.'

It was a long speech, Archelaus thought. But then, Ptolemy liked that kind of thing. He was pleased that their friendship had not encouraged Ptolemy to take liberties with the formality royalty required.

'Advise the family', instructed the King, 'that we approach. They should now take their places alongside and behind the bier.'

Ptolemy bowed and left.

The Garrison Commander with four centurions from the King's Bodyguard, met the King as he came from the bedchamber.

They saluted, then escorted him through the long passage to where the centurions were bearing aloft the couch with the body of the dead King.

Archelaus took it all in quickly as the Commander gave the order to move. The couch in royal purple. His father's body draped with a purple pall. On his head a crown and diadem. In his right hand a sceptre.

Archelaus shielded his eyes when they came out into the glaring sun.

Ptolemy was right. He had done his work well. All things were, indeed, ready. But Archelaus could not take in the vast crowd that would make up the procession. What was a manageable sight when he looked from the high-up window was now overwhelming.

The centurion escort led him to his chariot. When he had taken his seat, and been settled comfortably, the procession began its days' long journey through the desert of Judaea to his father's burial place.

The death of Herod, the King of the Jews, took its place in the gossip rounds of Heliopolis. It filled vacuums in tavern chatter, lent a new excitement to conversations at the feasts, and gave know-alls a wonder to be sure about.

Rumour added spice to the chat, with one rumour outdoing the other. He committed suicide, they said. Ah no! I'm told he tried, but someone stopped him. Another knew for certain he'd been murdered by his son. Which made a change, a gossip felt, for a King who seemed to take pleasure in killing his offspring and relations.

One thing the rumours and the gossip were agreed on was the manner of his death. He died like a dog.

Every Jew in Heliopolis believed it, and thought it right. God could not be in heaven and allow a man like Herod to have a calm and peaceful death.

Sabbaths, when they ate together and entertained each other after synagogue, were serious times.

Those who had exiled themselves because of Herod's rule, wondered if it would be safe, now, to risk going back to the land of their religion and their birth.

There was a sense of homesickness among her friends, Miriam felt. Egypt, of course, had been good to them, they said. They'd prospered. And, if need be, they'd be content enough to end their days in Egypt. But to be at home . . .

Miriam agreed. It was how she felt herself. She and Yosef had prospered with the years, and watched their son growing up secure and safe. But, like her friends, she fretted sometimes for home. And now, with Herod's death, and his threat dead with him, the fret turned into longing.

She noticed, though, how noncommittal Yosef was. As talky and as gossipy as the next, but never making his own mind clearly known. And that was unusual for her husband, she thought. A man who had a mind and opinions of his own, good grounds to support them, and no fear in expressing them.

Yet, as the weeks went by, she noticed sometimes that he talked of Bethlehem. How lovely the land would be looking now, in the springtime there. And the sowing and the ploughing, and bringing the early lambs to birth.

He dawdled, she thought, in his recollections. There were times when his eyes were sad for home.

'Be thou there,' he'd say resignedly, 'until I bring thee word.'

But for all the resignation, and, perhaps, impatience, too, as Miriam listened, she heard the sound of hope.

She was right.

And delighted when the day came, and Yosef was up with brighter eyes and a new liveliness in his step.

'I dreamed a dream,' he told her. 'And we're going home.'

'To Bethlehem?' she wondered.

'To Bethlehem,' he said.

They knew the road. They'd travelled it before. But how different everything looked now. There was no haste, no danger, now. They could stop and rest when they wanted to, and talk to travelling strangers on the way. Even the desert did not seem so harsh, and when they began to climb into Judaea's hills, they felt they were nearly home.

They would stay the night in Gaza, then go across the hills that led them down to Bethlehem.

The inn was not too crowded.

Miriam's first concern was to see her boy was fed. The innkeeper was generous to him.

Yosef was smiling. A far-off, ruminating smile. And nearly spoke. But there was no need. Miriam knew his thoughts. How different everything was the last time we were here.

The innkeeper kept an eye on them, and when he saw the lad was satisfied, he set down a meal in front of them.

Had they travelled far? Had they far to go?

They told him they were on their way to Bethlehem.

'Bethlehem?' exclaimed the innkeeper. 'You must be mad,' he told them, and added quickly lest he should offend them, 'Unless, of course, you have to go there.'

Yosef looked at Miriam and then at the man.

'Don't you know what's happened since Herod died?'

'Archelaus now reigns in his place,' answered Yosef.

'Indeed,' said the innkeeper. 'And in no time at all, the same Archelaus has massacred three thousand people. And at Passover emptied Jerusalem of every pilgrim, and would not let them celebrate the Feast.'

Yosef and Miriam listened.

'Herod was bad. But this man's a thousand times worse. All Judaea is in chaos. Nobody's safe.'

He filled out more wine, and left them to their meal.

They hardly ate, and for a long time sat in silence.

Till Yosef spoke. 'I wonder, Miriam, is it wise to go to Bethlehem?'

'But where, then, Yosef? That was to be our home.'

'But we had a home once in Nazareth. And we could have one there again.'

'Nazareth. You think Nazareth would be safe?'

'Safer, Miriam, than anywhere in Judaea. We'd be safe and secure from Archelaus. He has no jurisdiction in Galilee.'

Miriam agreed. It seemed right.

She cuddled her son into a bed roll. And was not long out of bed herself.

But she found it hard to go to sleep. Her body was too tired. Her face still stung from the dust and burning sun of the journey. The innkeeper's voice still sounded in her head. And Yosef's plan. All mixed up, crowding, pounding, confounding . . . Archelaus and Naomi and her father and Herod and Shebna and Rachel and Salome and Elisheba and Egypt and Barzillai and Heliopolis and Azariah and her mother and the synagogue . . . Till the whirling stopped and there was a quietness, a stillness where words gathered and shaped themselves together, without her thinking, as a prayer, a prayer of praise and thanks.

And they poured in, flooding her mind.

My soul extols the virtues of the Lord, my spirit exults in God my Saviour. He has looked kindly on the affliction of His servant.

From now on, all generations shall call me blessed, for He has done great things for me. And holy is His name.

His mercy is on those who fear Him.

He has ruled with His arm, scattered the haughty in their illusions, toppled the powerful from their seats. And exalted the despised.

The hungry He has satisfied with good things, and sent the opulent, impoverished, away.

He has helped His servant, a virtuous woman, remembering the mercy He promised to Abraham and his seed for ever . . .

The words faded.

The breeze rustled the starlit darkness. The rhythmic melancholy of sleep lay on the air like the dew of sound.

Miriam pulled the blanket closer around her.

'Tomorrow—' she thought.

But she was asleep before the thought had properly formed.